Too Gentlemanly
An Elizabeth and Mr. Darcy Story

by Timothy Underwood

Copy edit done by DJ Hendrickson

D1527501

Acknowledgements

I would like to thank my beta readers Betty Jo, Steeleo, and Brooke who read the manuscript and provided extremely valuable feedback on it. I also want to thank my editor DJ Hendrickson. Their help was valuable, important, and made this a better novel. I am deeply grateful for the time they spent reading and for telling me what they thought.

Chapter One

Pemberley, November 1811

Georgiana's eyes were red. Her tears had come and gone many times and left a salty residue on her cheeks. "Please, please. Don't make me marry him, don't make me marry anybody. I beg you — anything, please, anything but that. I don't want—"

"Georgie—" Colonel Fitzwilliam snapped harshly, "you ought to have considered *that* before you let your father's beloved pleb get a child on you. Mr. Carteret will accept Wickham's child. You shall marry him, and marry him fast."

Georgiana knelt on the rug and embraced Darcy's trousers as she broke into fresh sobs and begged again not to be made to marry. She trembled, and her posture hid the small bulge in his sister's body which grew more prominent day by day.

This was his fault. Darcy could not let Georgiana suffer for his failing. But what to do? He wanted to rip at his hair. Darcy took her hand and softly pulled Georgiana up to stand again. He saw his cousin's annoyance at how softly he treated the girl, but Colonel Fitzwilliam had not been the one stupid enough to trust Wickham's cousin Mrs. Younge with stewardship of Georgiana. The woman had always lived on Darcy's land and appeared of good character, but he should have *known*.

Never again. He must *never* again fail to ensure Georgiana's happiness.

But *how*?

Until today he had assumed Georgiana wanted her reputation restored and protected by marriage to a respectable man. It had not been easy to find a trustworthy man who would accept a fifteen-year-old bride pregnant with another man's child.

Mr. Carteret had four healthy sons, the youngest of whom would enter Oxford in a year, from a previous marriage and his estate earned a little more than a thousand a year. He would have been a barely allowable match for Miss Darcy, the debutante with thirty thousand pounds. Miss Darcy, the ruined and shamed girl, had different expectations. Darcy distantly knew Mr. Carteret, who was the much older brother of a friend at Oxford. They had been acquainted almost a decade and Darcy had little fear of him mistreating his sister.

Reason said he should make Georgiana marry him, now that Colonel Fitzwilliam had convinced Carteret to accept his sister.

"Stop crying. You will marry. You will be happier than you deserve, and you will no longer be *our* problem." Colonel Fitzwilliam wrinkled his nose and flapped his hands as if wafting the air coming from Georgiana away from him. "You gain far better than you deserve."

Darcy pressed his hand over his eyes. He could not look easily on her pain. "Georgie, what do you want? What do you expect if you do not marry Carteret?"

"Don't—" Fitzwilliam's face screwed up savagely. "By God, don't let her tears make you an idiot. She needs to marry."

Georgiana's pale blue eyes were wide and shot with red. Darcy ignored his cousin and brushed the tears off her face with his fingers. "Georgie, we will not force you — Fitzwilliam, we will not — but what hope do you have for the future if you do not marry?"

"I'm scared — he was so unkind after we...and it hurt, I never expected it to hurt so much — Fitzwilliam, I am so scared. Don't make me face another man like that. He only wants my fortune as well. Maybe...maybe some far-off estate, and...and I would live there alone forever and never bother anyone again."

Colonel Fitzwilliam rolled his eyes and sneered. "You are a child living out fantastical notions."

Fitzwilliam was right. Just as they had proven incapable of caring for her, Georgiana had proven incapable of caring for herself. But she had once chosen wisely.

When Georgiana and Wickham arrived in Scotland two days ahead of Darcy's pursuit, Georgiana had thrown herself at the knees of the vicar Wickham found to do the ceremony and begged all of the witnesses to keep her away from Mr. Wickham until her brother arrived.

Darcy hoped at first the damage from her elopement would be modest. Georgiana was gaunt and cried for weeks. She did not play her music anymore — though due to his anger at her, Darcy may not have permitted it during the first weeks. During those simpler days, he alternated between rage at his sister and a fiercer, deeper and truer rage at himself. He had decided they would go to Matlock so Georgiana could stay with her aunt and uncle for a few weeks, and be lectured about her bad behavior by a person who felt less guilt than he did.

Then Georgiana's courses came late.

Now the situation was pregnant.

Darcy sneered in amused disgust at his pun. Georgiana had said nothing, so he had not thought her to be violated. Until Colonel Fitzwilliam returned from the continent with his regiment and a harsh new look in his eyes, Darcy's prickly and proud efforts to find a husband for his sister had borne no fruit.

And now she did not want one.

"Georgie" — Colonel Fitzwilliam sneered again — "it surprises me not one damned bit—"

"In front of a lady?" Darcy cut his cousin off.

"Weeell…" Colonel Fitzwilliam dragged the word out. He curved his mouth into a hard smirk. "She abandoned such designation." He patted Georgiana's shoulder, and though usually affectionate, Georgiana flinched away. "An illegitimate child! *Lady* is not the word customarily used."

"I know I am no lady — but don't make me marry. *Please.*" Georgiana looked at Colonel Fitzwilliam's stony face."

"It surprises me not a *damn* that Wicky proved a bad lover. No woman ever accused *me* of such. A man can act with his tongue and fingers to make the act ecstatic for the woman. I will give Mr. Carteret advice on how to properly please a woman — with so many children from his first marriage, I doubt he needs it — we shall write into the marriage settlement that he must use that advice to enjoy the income from your fortune."

Georgiana's eyes and mouth popped wide. Darcy exclaimed, "Do not speak so crudely in front of my sister."

"God's sake! No longer a child, and she wishes to not be a gentlewoman." Fitzwilliam grabbed a decanter from the card table. He poured himself a stiff tumbler of brandy and swallowed it in a fast jerky motion. His hands trembled the way Darcy had seen several times since he'd returned from his long sojourn in the Peninsula. "You damn fools with your home disputes. I found a blasted husband for her, and now you plan to waste my effort out of a stupid desire to let a *child* have her way."

That was the core of the matter, was it not? Georgiana *was* still a child.

Darcy said firmly, "No, Georgiana, you need not marry Mr. Carteret. I will make no further effort to convince you, and the entire effort was mistaken from the first. As our cousin has repeated, you are yet a child, and a child is not fit for the duties of marriage."

Darcy's eyes fell to the bulge in his sister's belly. A child was not fit to raise a child either. But she would have him to help her and care for her.

He would make her happy.

"Damn, Darcy! Damn. You are determined." Colonel Fitzwilliam spat. He poured brandy into the thick-bottomed cup again. "My God, people are dying out there." Fitzwilliam waved his hand vaguely in all directions. He drank the amber liquor in a single swallow. "Enjoy your way. Choices, Georgie, Choices. Respectable society will ostracize you, no woman of fashion will speak to you, and that stain will settle on your brother and my family. I cannot care. I'll be killed when I return to the continent, and I am damned tired of wasting what time I have in England on you. Darcy won't make you marry, and I can find other disreputable woman whose company I will enjoy enormously more. Goodbye, to both of you, and I am damned sure you'll enjoy the adieu."

Colonel Fitzwilliam slammed the crystal tumbler so hard it cracked. He frowned at it for a long time. He took the bottle and drank a long swig.

"Richard, do not leave like this— you are not well. You have been like this since you arrived. I have been absorbed in my own worries, and—"

"Damn you, Darcy. I wasted two weeks of the time I have before they throw me back into that furnace finding your slutlike sister a husband, and you could not be...be...deuced to use my effort. Damn you."

The door slammed as the officer left the room. Darcy sat down and pressed his long fingers against his forehead. He should pursue his cousin. He already missed Colonel Fitzwilliam. But he felt too sick to argue or beg with him — and he was right. Darcy was throwing away the respectability of them all, and of his ancient name, for his sister.

Georgiana looked between him and the door as she continued to cry.

Deep in his soul Darcy *knew* he had made the right choice. Georgiana was his ward. She depended upon him. It was his duty to care for her, no matter what.

And he loved her.

Chapter Two

November 1816, Hertfordshire

Little Anne crawled up onto one of the seats of the carriage, and sat on both of her knees while pressing her face up tight against the window to look out. Darcy smiled at the blonde girl, and he kept a hand on her shoulder to steady his niece if the carriage jolted.

"And what do you call that?"

Georgiana pointed out the window to the steeple of a country church. The little girl screwed her face up into an adorable pout, and she turned to Darcy and blinked her eyes adorably and asked with a child's lisp, "Please, Uncle Will? A hint."

Darcy laughed. "No, sweet, you must learn to remember words on your own."

The little girl settled herself on Darcy's lap and stared out the window with a frown.

Georgiana smiled at them, "It begins with a 's'."

Eventually they prompted the girl into saying steeple, and a new target was chosen.

As Georgiana played with her daughter, Darcy lost himself in a reverie. The road was rural, but decently maintained. Darcy believed they had just passed through Meryton, the market town closest to Bingley's estate. There should only be another twenty minutes until they saw his friend again and could rest from the long road.

He hoped Georgiana would be happy here.

This was the first time she would be the guest of another family since Anne was born. Until Mrs. Bingley visited Pemberley with her husband this summer, Georgiana had not been part of a friendly conversation with another gentlewoman for four years.

It had surprised Darcy that Bingley took his wife into such a harbor of vice as Pemberley had become. He openly allowed an unmarried mother to stay resident. Jane Bingley was such a sweet woman that Darcy understood immediately. Her angelic nature was such that nobody could think ill of *her*. Mrs. Bingley and Georgiana immediately took to each other, and Georgiana, who Darcy realized then had been gasping for female conversation, soaked up all of the attention the other woman gave her during the Bingleys' weeks of residence at Pemberley.

Bingley a few months later extended an invitation for Georgiana and Darcy – and of course darling little Anne — to repay their visit and join them at Netherfield. Mrs. Bingley had written the letter of invitation in her neat feminine hand, promising in Bingley's words deuced fine hunting and excellent opponents at billiards when the weather did not allow them to ride or shoot, while for herself Mrs. Bingley wrote Georgiana would be very welcome, and likely to make friends.

Georgiana had been so lonely, with no other woman to speak to.

A soft drizzle fell from the sky when the carriage turned up the drive to Bingley's house. The driveway was bordered on both sides by lush evergreen Italian cypresses, and then the carriageway opened up to show a handsome red brick building of two stories and near hundred feet on a side. Heavy white marble columns framed the portico on which Mr. Bingley and his wife stood protected from the rain with several servants.

As soon as a footman opened the door, Darcy stepped out and turned around so Anne might exit by jumping to him. She delightedly shrieked as she jumped. The girl had been wonderful, but she was worn down a little by the two days of constant travel, and she would be happy to be able to run around on solid ground again. Darcy easily caught her and twirled Anne around before he softly lowered her to the ground. Anne laughed and ran to the blonde angelic Mrs. Bingley, who greeted the little girl with a friendly smile.

Georgiana exited the carriage more slowly, carefully stepping on the little platform and holding the footman's hand. Darcy was not able to help her out as Bingley had immediately seized his hand, and shook it vigorously.

"You look fine! All three of you. Deuced fine. Mud on road? Of course not — quite good time. Quite good. Delighted! Deuced good to see you."

Bingley threw his arm out and gestured expansively at his estate, "Welcome to Netherfield. Welcome! Fine building, don't you say?"

The crowd hurriedly entered the house, as the early winter air had a sharp bite. The entry hall was tiled with black and white marble diamonds. A large brass chandelier hung from the ceiling, and the rows of tall mullioned windows illuminated the twelve-foot-tall paintings hung about the walls. The woodcarvings in the ceiling were exquisite.

Bingley grinned at Darcy. "No Pemberley, but she is home."

"You did well for yourself."

"Ha! Darcy, you know not the half of it." Bingley put an arm around his blushing wife. "The estate came with a woman."

Mrs. Bingley giggled, somehow elegantly, and smiled up at her husband. "I was *not* in the lease articles."

"To the nursery. To settle Anne — eager to see Bennet again?"

Anne smiled and nodded. She was not nearly so lonely as Georgiana since she was friends with the children of the servants and tenants, but she had managed well with Bingley's son who was a year younger than her. Darcy far preferred his niece making playmates of persons gentle born, like herself.

The cavalcade proceeded upstairs, surrounded by the Bingleys' servants. The nursery door was opened, and the sleeping Bennet was woken up, crying. But he remembered Anne, and they were cleaned off and left to play under the supervision of both nurses.

Darcy and Georgiana were led to their spacious rooms, and they washed off the dust from the lengthy journey. When they entered the drawing room to rejoin their hosts, Bingley stood and happily waved his hands around in large circles. "At home! At home! Darcy, Georgie, consider Netherfield home. And down, down. Sit down."

The drawing room was well appointed with thick rugs, a few vases full of flowers acquired from a conservatory despite the season, and thick stuffed sofas. A large piano with the Broadwood maker's mark stood in the corner, and there was a large angled desk for drawing in another. It was fashionably and elegantly decorated, displaying excellent taste and a preference for durability and comfort over catching the height of fashion. The room snugly fit Darcy's understanding of Mrs. Bingley's character. A portrait of Mr. and Mrs. Bingley with their son clasped in Mrs. Bingley's arms rose above the grey marble fireplace, and the couches and chairs all used a uniform yellow and blue color scheme.

Bingley repeated several times, as Darcy glanced around the room, "I'm deuced glad to see you again. Deuced glad. It was far too long. Far too long." Without allowing any silence to grow, he exclaimed, "Tomorrow! An assembly is to be held tomorrow, you both must come. It will be an excellent chance to meet the neighborhood. I'm deuced glad to see you! Jane's family — you shall meet them there—"

"Bingley, I am not certain..."

"It is no lack of concern," Mrs. Bingley spoke, "Lizzy, Mama and Papa had thought to call today, but Lizzy thought you might not wish to deal with a crowd of new people after two days of travel. Rest, tea, a fine bath, and the company of dear friends, she said. Tomorrow we will prepare for the assembly ball — Lizzy and Mama as well — Papa never attends assemblies — a three miles trip between Longbourn and here, so *most* convenient if we meet at the ball. Georgie, I am *so* eager for you to meet Lizzy — you also, Mr. Darcy."

Unease blossomed in Darcy's stomach. It was a poor idea to try attending an assembly. Georgiana's color and expression said she felt the same. A girl with her history attending an assembly would be bold indeed. Such would show disrespect to the community. "I do not think an assembly is a good idea."

"Ridiculous!" Bingley slammed his hand against his arm rest. He spoke in a bluff voice, as though no other interpretation was possible. "A friendly neighborhood. Why, I had not been here two weeks before it was as though I had known everyone half my life. Such friends. Not two weeks! I told everyone — Jane too — Georgie Darcy is the sweetest girl in the United Kingdom. Upon my honor, France too."

Darcy saw in the tilt of Georgiana's face a little hope. She was wondering if she *could* attend a ball. Every girl liked balls, even the shyest, and his failure to protect her had deprived his sister of that chance. Darcy desperately wished she could enjoy the life a woman of her birth and position ought to be able to.

Bingley gripped his wife's hand and said, "Janie, you told other ladies — at those no-men present calls and garden parties and nonesuch — you told how admirable a girl Georgie is?"

"Lizzy is eager to meet you. Despite" — Jane blushed and looked away — "you are a good girl. No kind Christian creature could think it improper if you attended an assembly. No! I am unable to imagine such. I have lived in this neighborhood my entire life. I know everyone most intimately — everyone. You only lived with poor Mr. Wickham" — Darcy harrumphed at him being described as "poor", dying at Waterloo had been much too good for the man — "a bare handful of days — you acknowledge your fault and it has been some years. We possess Christian charity *here*."

Showing the killer instinct which Bingley only possessed when press ganging his friends into society, Bingley sensed Georgiana's weakness. "Pray do, do promise you will come, Georgie! You'll enjoy the dance so much. Aha! I see your eyes. That smile. A ball catches your fancy. Do promise to come — I will have a terror of the time dragging Darcy without you. If he does not come we...we might as well all stay home. That would be melancholy — your brother stands so tall and he cuts a terrifying figure on nights when he has nothing to do."

Georgiana laughed, nervously.

She looked at Darcy, her eyes attempting to see what his opinion was.

Darcy frowned. Bingley sounded so sure... "We" — Darcy gestured between Georgiana and himself — "we flee self-deception. Georgiana is a fallen woman; she will be seen by your neighborhood, by *any* neighborhood, as such. It is exceedingly improbable that—"

"You always worry — remember *that* time at Cambridge! I was right then!"

"Which time at Cambridge?" Darcy smiled thinly, too worried for his sister to be amused.

Bingley gesticulated wildly. "You know when, we—" His face reddened, and he coughed, and he looked between the women. "It went very well indeed."

Darcy looked at Bingley as though he had no memory of the particular evening involving too much strong drink, two goats, three university dons, the nudity of a mutual friend, and a grand view of the sun rising over the university town while sitting on the slippery roof tiles of a tall building. "Could you add specifics? I am unsure *what* event you refer to — that is all I have to say about *that time*. It ended well, in the end."

"I know my neighbors. By my word, friendliest persons in all England."

Darcy rubbed his chin. Georgiana's blue eyes were downcast. She awkwardly smoothed out the sleeve of her dress again and again.

She wanted to go. She would receive some rudeness. But it likely would go no further than refused introductions. Bingley was the largest landowner in the region and his father-in-law was, from what Darcy understood, the second.

Georgiana would like to watch the ball, even if she could not participate in it. And she would at least be able to dance with himself and Bingley. Every opportunity to enjoy a season and the entertainments young girls fantasize about had been cruelly held distant from her. Every woman, Darcy had been made to understand, thought a ball was a wonderful thing.

"Well, if you are sure it shall not cause a scandal." Darcy sighed, fearing this was an error. "We shall attend tomorrow."

Georgiana's worried smile at Darcy's pronouncement was almost painful.

Mrs. Bingley clapped her hands. "Now you need something perfect to wear, Georgie."

Chapter Three

Elizabeth Bennet whistled as she completed her morning walk. Fine brisk day, without the real cold of winter, yet having something of stark beauty. She walked through the little shrubbery behind the front entrance of Longbourn and up to a backdoor which opened into her father's study. She quickly opened and shut the door. A cold gust of wind followed her, shifting the papers upon Papa's desk.

"Pray, shut that door, dear." Papa shivered theatrically and smiled her. "The air bites shrewdly; it is very cold."

Elizabeth laughed at the line from Hamlet. "It is a nipping and an eager air?"

"What hour now?"

"I think it lacks of twelve — by most of the day — you are the one with the clock in your room."

"Come sit here." Papa gestured at her chair. "You were supposed to let me say 'No, it is struck.'"

"The clock struck twelve? Indeed I heard it not... uhhh... the season wherein the spirit walks."

"You have forgotten your Shakespeare." Papa laughed good naturedly. "But sit here. Help me with these figures — I made some mistake adding the accounts."

Elizabeth laid a friendly kiss on her father's forehead right beneath the wool cap he wore for warmth. She laughed when he recoiled.

"Your lips are frozen, Lizzy. You may love winter walks, but I prefer to be warm."

Papa then pulled her head down so he could kiss her cheek.

Elizabeth settled into the brown leather chair which always sat next to her father's chair for her use, and she pulled in front of her the account book he'd been looking through, and the paper to the side where he'd attempted to add up the entries for the last month in pencil.

Papa looked at her with the pleased smile he always had when they were together. His eyes were bright and alert, and his dark grey sideburns bristled several inches out from the sides of his face.

He wore a thick red cap that had been tipped back by Elizabeth exposing the front of his bald area. His hands were encased in a pair of gray wool half gloves that left his fingers free to easily manipulate the quill, but kept his hands somewhat warm.

While the air in the room was hot in comparison to the freezing outdoors, Papa had kept his room chilled so far this winter. It was a small economy to save on coal that he had adopted when the crash following the end of the war reduced their rents substantially only a few months after the fund Mr. Bennet had set aside for his daughter's dowries had been depleted by Kitty's marriage. There still was a substantial amount set aside for Elizabeth, which Mr. Bennet intended to grow once more, but it was insufficient to be really comfortable upon.

"You completely missed this purchase of feedstock for the horses — and the purchase of the new grey to replace Molly when she died. Also, when you added up the income, you incorrectly added the value of Mr. Green's rent." Elizabeth took a bite of a juicy apple from a bowl Mr. Bennet kept on his desk, so he would not need to interrupt his studies by calling for a servant if he grew hungry before dinner. "There. Correct now."

Papa grinned at her, pulling the account book back towards himself. "What would I do without you?"

"Hire a steward."

As Papa looked at the figures himself again, muttering quietly as his finger jumped from number to number, Elizabeth looked back out the window again. Today was beautiful, gray, overcast; the bare sticks of trees looked sharp in the pale sunlight, and the background of clouds promised rain or flurries of snow. In places little dustings of snow from yesterday's surprisingly early winter snow remained unmelted.

Elizabeth never complained about the weather. There was so much beauty in it.

And she was returned to her favorite place in the world: Papa's study while Papa was also there.

"Very, good. Very good." Papa now wrote the final sums into the big account book, and blotted the ink before closing the accounts. "Your walk? Did you call upon anyone?"

"I speak too often on the delights of leafless trees and cold air for you to wish to listen to me enthuse about *that*." Elizabeth frowned, rather displeased by what she had learned. "The Lucases told me the committee which manages the assemblies, you know — Lady Lucas, Mama, Mrs. Long, Mrs. Goulding — they absolutely will not allow Jane's female guest to be admitted to the rooms tonight. Sir Lucas had set off a bare quarter of an hour before I called to inform Bingley, Jane and the Darcys."

"Poor girl. To be given the cut direct by the whole of the neighborhood at the first expedient date after her arrival." Mr. Bennet raised his eyebrows. "Mrs. Bennet told me nothing of the matter—"

"Mama will be *quite* displeased to find the other ladies dared such a thing in her absence."

Papa smiled. "Her nerves will be disordered for some time — they have been present much less of late, since Mary and Kitty both married last year — perhaps it is time for a return visit."

Elizabeth and her father shared a smirk. Neither held much sympathy for her mother's damaged consequence.

"It was kind," said Elizabeth, "insofar as kindness can be attributed to such an occasion, *her* daughter hosts Mr. Bingley's friend and his scandalous sister. My mother could not be an uninterested party in pursuing the duty of the committee to maintain propriety and protect the moral standards of the neighborhood."

Mr. Bennet laughed. "Standards? Propriety, defense of the community. A brave stand against the moral degeneration of this late age? That makes it sound disinterested and...effortful."

"A woman who has become a *Matron* need not cease to be *Missish*. And young ladies! Think of those girls, such as Maria, or I — I am not yet old enough a maid for my eyes to survive sight of a fallen woman without smudge."

Elizabeth finished her apple and tossed the core into the undecorated waste bin next to Papa's big writing desk. The apples were stored in Longbourn's cellar, and because of how cold the year had been, it would be at least several months before they lost their juiciness and flavor.

"My dear" — Papa patted her hand and smirked — "you are not old at all. You may trust the word of a man who *is*."

Elizabeth knew perfectly well she was not an old maid. She appeared more beautiful than ever in the mirror. But she possessed no desire for men and their controlling ways — most men, her father was perfectly indulgent. Elizabeth Bennet had neither need nor want for marrying. And at four and twenty she now possessed too much cleverness and wisdom to ever feel the sort of insane passion Lydia or Jane's Miss Darcy had felt for Wickham.

"I am old enough in this matter," said she. "A woman of twenty and four could not be polluted by conversation with a shy, reclusive girl of twenty. Miss Darcy is barely past being a child."

"You, my dear, are more likely to pollute her with *your* opinions than the reverse."

"Jane enthused about Miss Darcy: sweet girl, modest, shy, unassuming, repentant, accomplished, intelligent, elegant, etc, etc — the child likewise. And then they send a delegation to inform her immediate upon her arrival she is not welcome. For a single mistake, made many years in the past."

"She has a child." Her father held his hands open with a wry expression, as though to say *he did not make the rules*. "A product of an illicit connection she openly lives with. The young woman cannot *expect* to be freely received by respectable company."

"Unkind," Elizabeth replied. Papa also had some sympathy for poor Georgiana Darcy, but Papa relished clever arguments, especially when Elizabeth brought him to admit he was wrong. "If she should expect to be excluded, there is no need to send out a messenger to inform her of that exclusion."

Papa's eyes had his combative gleam. He removed his spectacles and leaned towards Elizabeth. "Jane did not expect such, and she knows the neighborhood—"

"Pray! Use not our *Jane* as the exemplar of what a person *ought* to know — she *never* imagines ill!"

"Your sister is merely one instance of the principle: Oft persons recognize not the obvious. Kinder for a single person — a violently inoffensive one, such as Sir William — to be sent to ensure she *does* understand. Thus she can avoid the deeper embarrassment of being cut by an entire community at once."

"A certain slight to avoid chance of an even worse insult? Were *I* in such a situation, the insult to my good sense would be as great an annoyance as anything else."

"You mean greater than everything else." Mr. Bennet grinned. "You have a great sensitivity to any slight against your cleverness."

Elizabeth laughed. "No — I do not approve of how society treats Miss Darcy. Her sin is no different than Lydia's: an action undertaken under promise of marriage. And with the same man."

"*Mrs. Wickham* married her seducer."

"Perhaps she should not have. You never visited her. Lydia was miserable and she nearly died with the babe. *Our* wellbeing required them to marry, but Lydia only benefited from his early demise."

Mr. Bennet grimaced. "*I* am delighted Wickham had himself shot before he was in service long enough for my son-in-law to be obligated to pay for more than his captaincy. If only I could recover the three thousand I settled upon Lydia. The girl shouldn't have the stuffing to flit to London when she prefers."

"You *have* changed. The problem occurred because you wished her elsewhere."

"I proved to be a poor father. I know." He shuffled the papers in front of him into something a little like order.

"You might like Lydia today — she is hardly the same girl she was four years ago."

"Deuced young, a fool, and too happy in the company of gentlemen for *my* comfort. I don't trust her discretion."

Elizabeth pinched her lips together and nodded. Lydia was *very* fond of the company of men. Her younger sister had explained to Elizabeth, when she visited her at Newcastle, everything she *now* knew about how to please and be pleased by a man without risk of pregnancy.

"I do wish," Papa added, "I could receive the money again — for your sake. You *are* like to marry — but no certainty *there*."

"And leave you? Nonsense. In fairness — Lydia has as great need of independence as I ever will."

"Lydia can marry again, if she must — you are unsuited for ordinary marriage. I always saw. From when you first crawled about after me, you would study my books with me before you could properly walk."

"I know." Elizabeth had always felt special, more tightly attached to her father than to anyone else. Her affection was reciprocated and she was treated unfairly by both her parents. When Mr. Bennet came to the conclusion he would have no sons after Lydia's birth, he decided money must be saved, not to ensure the future of his daughters and wife, but almost solely for *her* interest. Near five hundred pounds were cut from the estate's annual expenses, and while Mr. Bennet sold his hunter and the pack of foxhounds, most *feeling* of deprivation came from her mother.

Mr. Bennet had never been much of a sportsman. Mrs. Bennet wished an extra pair of footman, to dress Jane in new expensive and fashionable gowns each season, and to have the most impressive delicacies on her table when she entertained.

Mrs. Bennet, correctly, blamed Elizabeth for this diminution of her consequence and, she claimed, her happiness. Mrs. Bennet scolded Elizabeth for turning her father against her, begged her to convince her father to let them spend money more freely, and railed against Elizabeth for thinking she was better than her sisters.

At that age Elizabeth fully shared her father's every opinion. So Mrs. Bennet's conviction that Elizabeth was wrong for thinking herself better than her sisters only fed a belief she was in fact better.

Elizabeth had been rather spoilt as a child.

Likely she still was.

"If I had ever realized I would have to pay out such a large sum to see Lydia married..." Papa sighed. "It seemed at the time a cheap and convenient means for her to find some pleasure. You were right, and I have long since admitted it."

Wickham had agreed to marry Lydia in exchange for Mr. Bingley and Mr. Bennet providing him one thousand pounds apiece, to cover his immediate debts. Mr. Bingley undertook to purchase a commission for Wickham each time he become eligible to purchase a higher rank, and Mr. Bennet settled an additional three thousand upon Lydia, and fifty pounds income as her share of Mrs. Bennet's fortune.

Fortunately, when Wickham's captaincy was purchased he transferred to a regiment which would a year later be posted to defend the Hougoumont farmhouse during Waterloo.

"Lydia has not abused what independence she has." Elizabeth kicked her foot deeper under the desk, wriggling into her chair.

Mr. Bennet shrugged.

Papa wished a different topic of conversation, so Elizabeth returned to the earlier one. "The difference in how Miss Darcy and Lydia are treated is fashion not morality."

Mr. Bennet tapped his finger on the dark wood of his desk. He nodded decidedly. "Allowing such a woman to participate fully in a community would provide a bad exemplar for younger ladies, such as yourself. They say it themselves. Neither morality, nor fashion, but practical reason drives the unfortunate creature's exclusion."

Papa winked and Elizabeth giggled. "This commits you to the claim that Mrs. Wickham provides a good example."

"Aha! I see what you mean to do — my disapproval of *that* married woman is well known to you."

"Unkind! Your own daughter!"

"I confess my former mistake; Lydia *is* a fine example for the women of *other* families. She shows the importance of marrying for love and affection and adolescent whim."

Elizabeth opened a compartment in the desk to take out her dainty stationery so she could write a letter to Mary, who was the wife of the vicar who lived thirty miles from Longbourn in Essex. She began to sharpen the nib of her pen. "I can have nothing further to say. Except if the purpose is to prevent imprudence, the presence of a girl who will preach against such behavior is likely to be more salutary than *Lydia's* advice."

"How *does* Lydia advise her unmarried sisters? I have always wondered since the first time you mentioned such advice."

Elizabeth flushed. "An indelicate subject. Enough on *her*."

"Defeat admitted. My victory, again."

Elizabeth rolled her eyes at her father's crowing. She dipped the quill into the ink and began to scratch out her letter.

Mr. Bennet stood and browsed the bookshelves. As he pulled down Cicero's letters, he asked, "Pray, give your opinion, your true opinion. Do you wish to befriend Miss Darcy?"

"I know not, not yet." Elizabeth glanced up and returned her eyes to her work. "Jane likes her very much. I ought to need no further recommendation."

"But we all know Jane only sees the good."

"Miss Darcy is a darling shy and sweet creature, I am sure. But the imprudence! Imprudence demonstrated by all involved. Especially in how her brother left the young Miss unguarded. The bare facts of the story leave me prejudiced against the participants."

"Her brother ought have made her marry Wickham or another?"

"Goodness! No!"

Mr. Bennet smirked, showing he'd known Elizabeth would reply with such horror.

"Such a permanent solution as *marriage*! And to a man she did not love? That should never be considered as a solution to anything, not even an equally permanent scandal and an illegitimate babe. Perhaps marriage would have benefited the child, but Miss Darcy's daughter has privilege enough. That superficial appearance of legitimacy cannot be a requirement for her happiness."

"You were enthused by Pemberley's grounds when you visited them before Lydia's misadventure with my ill mourned son-in-law."

"The delight of the well-designed grounds perhaps reflects only upon Mr. Darcy's designing ancestors—"

"Or perhaps," Papa smirkingly interrupted Elizabeth, "poor guardians make good gardens."

Elizabeth rolled her eyes. "Not even a pun."

Mr. Bennet looked unpleasantly smug nevertheless.

"Mr. Peake spoke highly of Mr. Darcy," Elizabeth added, "and Mr. Darcy's affection for his sister is clear from how he kept her and her daughter with him — their presence at the house at all times meant we could not tour the house, but only the grounds."

"Oh, yes, Gardiner acquired Peake during your Northern trip."

"We did not go past the midlands."

Papa waved his hands as though that was a triviality. "How did Gardiner meet Peake again, I never had the story quite straight."

"At Darcy's estate itself — he was an under steward at Pemberley, and because he was Mrs. Gardiner's cousin, he gave us our tour of the estate, and then he called at our lodging in Lambton, and Mr. Gardiner convinced him to leave his position and join Mr. Gardiner's firm."

"Piece of good fortune for us all to match the ill fortune of Lydia's misbehavior. Gardiner says that without Peake's help he would have gone under within the last two years."

"Mr. Gardiner told me as much."

"A balance of expectations and stories — you plan to see Miss Darcy with your own eyes, and then make a judgement?"

Elizabeth smiled impishly. "Given my advanced age, I have no need to fear what harm may come to my reputation when it is known I consort with such women."

Rather than laughing Papa sighed and pulled off his wiry spectacles. "Lizzy. You are only twenty and four — not an old maid, not on the shelf. Had your goal been to marry expeditiously, you would have good reason to be shamed for having reached such an *advanced age* unmarried, but your goal never was to snag the first eligible bachelor."

Elizabeth laughed, made uncomfortable by Papa's serious tone. He could not intend to suggest, like Mama often did, that it was time for her to marry. "Since my goal never was to entrap any bachelor, eligible or otherwise, I can socialize with a scandalous woman without worrying what Mr. Several Thousand a Year thinks."

"Your *age* is not where your freedom derives from." Mr. Bennet paused, Elizabeth looked at him. He had an expression of wishing to say something, but uncharacteristically lacking words. "Do dismiss all thought of marriage."

Papa hurriedly added, "There is no gentleman who could interest you in this neighborhood, but widen your circle of acquaintance, maybe in London—"

"You wish me to leave you alone to face Mama's nerves? Never. You would be lonely without me." Elizabeth rubbed her hand harshly over the edge of their desk. She remembered Lydia, swollen with child, complaining about marital duties. Jane and Bingley's bland friendliness. Despite her cleverness and sensibility, Mrs. Gardiner always deferred to her husband.

"Lizzy, I shall not live forever." Mr. Bennet's voice made Elizabeth look at her father, almost unwillingly. He was no more than five years past fifty and a healthy, if not vigorous, man. But in the lines and gray hair, time was slowly catching him. "Understand what you truly want. You do not need to marry. Were I to die tomorrow, there is already sufficient in the funds for you to be almost comfortable, but...someday I shall not be here, and I fear, my dear girl, you will be lonely as well."

"Most husbands I have seen would hardly make a good companion."

"Find a gentleman who is unique, as you are unique. I ask you only to be open to fortune's bringings. This is your happiness which concerns me."

Elizabeth's heart glowed with tenderness towards her father when he showed his deep concern for her wellbeing. She did not want a husband to come between their closeness. If Papa had his way, he would do nothing but spend endless hours with his books, but affection for her had led him to work to make the most of the estate and to control his wife enough to allow economies to be found.

They had always, for as long as Elizabeth could remember, been bound close. She'd spent nearly as much time in this room with her father as she had asleep.

"Papa—" Elizabeth held her father's arm and kissed him on the forehead. "I am not made for unhappiness — or loneliness — you know I am not. You are healthy and will live another twenty years. At least! And when you do die, many, many years from now, I shall cry a long time, and then I will find some other spinster old maid who is quite clever and who loves to laugh as much as I do, and we shall combine our resources and be very happy together. You have my oath: I love you too much to ever allow myself to be really unhappy."

"My dear daughter." Papa kissed her on the cheek. "I only worry for you — that you will miss forms of happiness. Do not close yourself."

Chapter Four

A certain enthusiasm towards the assembly grew in Darcy over the course of his first evening at Bingley's manor. Georgiana had no clothing suitable for such an evening out, not having expected any such opportunity to occur. She and Jane planned how to alter a dress to make it look suitable, and both ladies and their maids spent hours in embroidery and stitching. Anne was allowed into the drawing room with Bennet and she clapped her hands and enthusiastically watched her mother and Mrs. Jane.

The next morning Sir William Lucas called to return unhappiness to them all. "The committee — we're beholden to each family of the neighborhood. You must understand, you must — young ladies there. Young girls, just come out. Please understand."

Sweat glistened in small beads on Sir William Lucas's bald head, and he absolutely refused to meet the eyes of either Mr. Bingley or Mr. Darcy. His eyes lit for a second on Georgiana, sitting next to Mrs. Bingley on a blue and yellow sofa with a floral pattern. He flinched away from Georgiana's white, calm face. "Not London! We are not London — or Derbyshire where you have such great houses and scandals. Miss Darcy's delicate situation — her...well... This is quite... You know. Moral standards must be maintained! Propriety! You cannot blame me. Or the committee—"

"Do not expect me to approve of you." Darcy sneered. "My sister had a child out of wedlock, and we have not done the fashionable thing and found some way to hide the whole event. So your little, small country assembly will not allow her attend a ball, because you have raised your daughters so poorly that you are convinced imprudence is catching. You have had your say. Be gone."

Darcy waved his hand dismissively, and turned and walked towards the divan Georgiana sat upon. Sir William sputtered and attempted to reply. Bingley winced at Darcy's curt dismissal of his neighbor from Bingley's house, and then clapped his hand on Sir William's shoulder and talked in a quiet voice trying to convince Sir William to go back and change Lady Lucas's mind.

This was a mistake. This whole trip had been a mistake.

Darcy silently gripped Georgiana's hand, once Bingley and Sir William left the room toward the hall. After a few minutes Bingley returned.

"Well, I never! I had no idea—" Bingley hemmed, hawed and stamped his feet. "I have more than half a mind to never attend an assembly myself again. Certainly we shall all stay home. I understand Sir William — a kind man — he should not—" Bingley finished with an angry snort. He stamped his foot again.

Darcy eyed his friend with a little disgust. He *told* Bingley — but Bingley insisted. Bingley insisted the neighborhood would not care. Then Bingley and his wife gave Georgiana hope. Now she was fighting tears. Darcy saw her sadness in the strained set of her mouth and the tightness around her eyes.

Bingley held his hands up defensively. "Really no idea. We'll not attend anything to which you are not invited. Not while you are guests here. Tomorrow we'll hire musicians. We shall have a ball here — I won't invite any of the neighborhood — they'll learn how angry I am."

"No." Georgiana spoke with a teary catch in her tone. "You must go. Do not offend your neighbors on my account. I deserve my treatment, I know it. I don't expect other people to — you and Jane should go to the assembly. Jane, you looked forward to it very much. You too, Fitzwilliam. You would be bored with just me and Anne here. And it would be terribly rude to Bingley to not go with him."

"Now, Georgie, you are our guest. Awful hosts if—"

"Don't...don't ruin your enjoyments on my behalf."

Georgiana was near tears, and Darcy sat next to her and put his arm around her.

Georgiana slid closer into Darcy's embrace. "Please, Fitzwilliam, you give up your own pleasures for me so often. You don't plan to go for me, but...I'll be terribly unhappy unless you go to the ball."

Darcy sighed. He did not even wish to go to the ball except for Georgie's sake, but he had never been able to refuse his sister when she had those tears in her eyes.

Chapter Five

The Netherfield party arrived late to the Meryton Assembly rooms. Elizabeth was already dancing when Bingley and Jane introduced Mr. Darcy to Mrs. Bennet. So, without introduction Elizabeth watched from the edge of her eyes his progress round the edges of the room.

He sneered magnificently.

Mr. Darcy had a tall noble figure, with thick handsome sideburns and piercing eyes. He turned about the room with an expression that shifted from bored, to a curled lip showing disgust, and then back to bored. He avoided all opportunities to converse, and when he settled in a seat for a few minutes, and Mrs. Long tried to speak to him — no doubt hoping to settle the last of her nieces upon such a rich gentleman, even if his sister was a fallen woman — Mr. Darcy had nothing of her conversation. Instead of replying he showed that haughty curled lip and drew his bed head back, as though recoiling from a smelly gift left by a dog.

Elizabeth saw his eyes dart about the room and when he saw that Mr. Bingley was otherwise occupied, he stood and walked away without replying to Mrs. Long.

The rudeness was delightful. She had never quite seen its like.

Everyone, of course, knew everything there was to know about the rich friend of Bingley's. But, while the room was predisposed to think well of any friend of Bingley — even one with an illegitimate niece — Mr. Darcy finely disappointed every such hope to like him.

Elizabeth danced almost every set, and she paid all the attention to her partners they deserved, and she had a fine party. The ball lacked the spice of novelty such events held when younger, but a fast dance with a handsome young gentleman — or even with a not so handsome, not so young gentleman, if fate was unkind — was a pleasure which never lost its luster.

Once Elizabeth would have been confused by the friendship between Darcy and Bingley given the obvious dissimilarity in their characters. However she had known her brother-in-law long enough to discover that he could easily form an affection towards a large rock and decide it was a dear friend. More amazing yet, his friendliness would drag out of the rock a reciprocal feeling.

Were they Papists, after his death Bingley would be declared the patron saint of good-natured amiability.

Still, if Mr. Darcy was determined to despise the neighborhood, why had he come to the assembly? He was a philanthropist, Elizabeth decided after some consideration, for he had done the neighborhood a good turn. He had given them an excellent subject of conversation, and a man — even better a handsome man — to look upon with dislike.

Everyone loved to have a villain nearby to hate.

Near the middle of the evening Elizabeth found herself obliged to sit out a dance due to a temporary lack of partners. As Elizabeth always had a partner for the far greater part of her evening, such was an event she took philosophically. And Elizabeth was always a vigorous dancer, so her legs were sore. She enjoyed the tall spectacle of Mr. Darcy walking his tall self about the room.

He came near to her, only a bare ten feet away. He examined the large portrait of the King hanging on the wall, well lit by a pair of silver candleholders set into the wall on either side of it.

Mr. Darcy sneered.

Elizabeth bit her lip with a delighted smile.

Bingley walked up to Darcy and clapped his taller friend on the back. "Darcy, dear man — make *some* effort to enjoy yourself. My friends are here. They shall think quite ill of you, if you make no conversation."

Darcy replied with a rich baritone — he had a very good voice, one he could project, one which would be a pleasure to listen to in conversation, or if he read from a book.

The words were less pleasant.

"I am not present to make friends. I see little to like here."

"Nonsense. *Of course* you are here to make friends."

Darcy sneered. Bingley grinned happily back.

"My word, you never used to be half so ill tempered." Bingley clapped his hands together in delight. "You need a dance. With a pretty lady!" Bingley waved to Elizabeth. "Lizzy, here. Come here — Darcy wishes to dance with you. You've not been yet introduced I believe—"

Elizabeth walked up with a bright smile; she expected to be amused whether he agreed to dance with her or not.

"I assure you — what my mood lacks will not be cured by being forced to endure a desperate spinster's simpering company for half hour."

To her surprise Elizabeth felt a little twinge of rejection at Mr. Darcy's words, but the absurdity set her to laughing nonetheless. "My goodness! Bingley, your friend seems quite uncivilized — I thought the wilds of Derbyshire had been tamed many a year ago, yet here he is: a barbarian from times before Rome come to join us."

Bingley looked at his friend openmouthed, shocked that he would say that to his sister-in-law, while Mr. Darcy's cheeks turned an embarrassed shade of red, and he seemed caught between the inclination to sneer heartily at her, and the awareness he had gone too far and must apologize.

Once Elizabeth's laugh finished, she was still terribly amused by Mr. Darcy's twisted expression, and she said with a bright smile, "Mr. Darcy, you broke my brother's politeness, so I must introduce myself to you as he is too busy thinking you behaved shockingly."

Elizabeth curtsied. "Elizabeth Bennet, at your service. And let me forestall the apology you think you should make. For it was in fact quite insightful of you to recognize that I am a desperate, simpering spinster. I cannot stand my own company either. Half an hour dancing with you would be quite as miserable for me as it would be for you. Alas — I cannot escape my own company so easily."

"Miss Bennet, I am very—"

"You need not say it! I may deserve great pity for always bearing my own company, but I am a proud woman, and I do not wish to know that I am pitied."

"That was not—"

"Say nothing!" Elizabeth patted Darcy on the arm. It was a muscular and well-shaped arm. No reason not to enjoy his person along with his personality. "You need not say it. You need not. But I thank you very much for the thought."

Mr. Darcy opened his mouth again, but Elizabeth quickly curtsied and walked away, intentionally putting a little bit of extra sway into her hips.

===

Darcy felt thunderstruck. He'd become angrier and angrier over the course of the evening, and something of the past years of little cuts against himself and Georgiana had destroyed his old patience.

He should be disgusted with himself for what he said. But as he watched the backside of Elizabeth Bennet, wrapped in a fine yellow silk dress, walking away, the only thing Fitzwilliam Darcy could think was that Miss Bennet was a damned fine woman.

Darcy half whistled.

"Ah-ah, Darcy." Bingley grunted to get his attention, though Darcy did not look away from Elizabeth until she started enthusiastically speaking to another gentleman. Bingley said, "Lizzy — she never simpers."

"I can see." He looked back at the woman with her laughing eyes.

"Go — apologize to her in fact, else Jane will be annoyed with you."

Darcy looked sideways at his friend. He had only spent a total of five weeks in Mrs. Bingley's company, but she had *never* been annoyed in that time. Darcy took a deep breath and consciously set off towards where Miss Bennet stood.

But as he did, Darcy thought, *Why should I be required to apologize*? Miss Bennet was twenty-four; quite old to be unmarried. Mrs. Bingley had talked up her sister a great deal — every time he poked his head out of Pemberley, he was thronged by poor woman who hoped that if they convinced him they would overlook the stain on his sister's character, he might give them the joy of an income which was ten thousand a year, and likely more.

Gentlemanly etiquette required one apologize for truth.

He was yet a gentleman.

Before Darcy managed to work his way around the room, Miss Bennet had been led to the dance floor. She waited across from her new partner for the music to start. Darcy settled into a chair with the plan to approach her for a proper apology — which he must do for Bingley's sake — as soon as the set ended. The chair was an old wooden thing that was three inches too short for his height and creaked under his weight.

The air was laden with the scent of sweat and spilled wine. The strings of the light Scottish reel grated after several hours of listening to similar music.

Darcy hated balls.

Miss Bennet was a graceful dancer. Darcy watched her with a heavy frown, determined to see fault, despite his initial impression of her attractiveness. He had excellent eyesight, and he could see that she smiled readily, with rosy blooming cheeks and dark flashing eyes. She had a light, easy step and she danced both with greater energy and elegance than her partner. The yellow dress fit her perfectly, showing off the neat curves of her figure while not being at all immodest.

Damn. There was nothing of the old maid in her appearance to despise. He might look for fault, but could find none, besides a few failures of perfect symmetry in her face.

She was twenty-four. In a few years that — exceptional — beauty would desert her. She must be desperate to find a husband. But he could not imagine Miss Bennet ever acting like the young misses desperate for his attention, who oriented all their behavior towards attempting to please and impress.

She never simpers.

When the next set ended Darcy leapt from his cramped chair to approach Miss Bennet. He felt distantly annoyed by his own eagerness to speak to the young lady and how hopeful he felt that she would yet have a set free tonight to dance with him, when he asked as part of his apology.

"Miss Bennet—" Darcy spoke as he stepped up next to her and the gentleman she spoke to, but he stumbled to a halt when she looked him directly in the eyes. Her eyes were really delightful.

She smiled at him cherubically when he did not speak. "Mr. Darcy."

He stiffened himself to look more solemn and made a modest bow. "Miss Bennet, I am most sincerely apologetic for my faux pas, and I beg you to forgive me."

"Does he look sincerely apologetic?" Miss Bennet turned to her companion. "That is a very disapproving expression."

The young man shrugged and held his hands open. "I have not been introduced to the gentleman, so I hardly would dare venture an opinion — he *does* look disapproving."

"Of course!" Miss Bennet slammed her hands together with enthusiasm. "Mr. Lucas, this is Mr. Fitzwilliam Darcy of a giant house with a delightful park in Derbyshire. Mr. Darcy, Mr. John Lucas of Lucas Lodge a mere half mile from here."

Darcy frowned. "Is your father Sir William? Who called upon us this morning?"

"Do not judge Mr. Lucas by *him*," Miss Bennet replied. "He is the less inoffensive son of his inoffensive father."

Sir William *had* offended Mr. Darcy. But the two gentlemen bowed to each other and said what was appropriate. Miss Bennet's reference to Pemberley reminded him that Mrs. Bingley had said her sister had visited Pemberley some years ago. An event he vaguely recalled, not because he met the party, but because his under steward of the time, a promising young man of about twenty named Peake, had been a cousin of the Bennet's aunt, and had been convinced to leave service with him and join the firm of their uncle.

Since she'd seen Pemberley, of *course* she was desperate to capture him. No woman could ignore the charm of such an estate.

Once the introductions were complete Miss Bennet asked again, "Now that you have been introduced to Mr. Darcy, you have no reason to hide your true opinion — do you think Mr. Darcy looks sincerely apologetic?"

Mr. Lucas smiled. *"You* are the one who prides herself on excellent judgment of character."

Darcy frowned. "I assure you, I know I ought not have said that. It was a thoughtless and unconsidered statement."

"Pray tell" — Mr. Lucas had a very interested expression — "I fear I am missing the most significant element of the conversation, what statement does Mr. Darcy feel a need to apologize for?"

"He only turned into words what every gentleman must think upon meeting me for the first time — why, look at that woman, she must be thirty and five. A spinster and desperate for a husband. I do believe she will attempt to flatter and ingratiate herself with every gentlemen."

Mr. Lucas laughed. "Are you blind? Our Lizzy doesn't look a day over thirty."

Miss Bennet laughed and pushed Mr. Lucas's arm, and though Darcy thought she looked pretty as she laughed, he felt more than a little offended that she laughed at him. "I have apologized. You are still quite attractive, Miss Bennet, and nobody would think you look like an old maid *yet*, and I'm certain your advancing age has not made you desperate. You still have a few years."

That had not come out precisely right.

Mr. Lucas's mouth fell open, and Miss Bennet's eyes snapped to him. Her lips shaped a delighted smile. "I knew you would be worth knowing! A man who says what he thinks always. But I worry for you; my age is not near so advanced as *yours*. Are you desperate for a wife? For if this is how you choose to flirt, you are likely to remain desperate for some time."

"I can marry near any woman I choose whenever I desire her, my fortune ensures that, and it shall not diminish with age." Darcy's mouth twisted with a little annoyance. "Even were I quite old, I would never become desperate for a wife. You, naturally, ought to understand that your charms are of a more limited duration."

"Pardon me—" Mr. Lucas spoke as Miss Bennet drew herself up with flashing eyes, "do you attempt to apologize, or explain why your statement was true in the first place?"

"My apology was refused."

"I daresay," Miss Bennet spoke, "there are many stupid women. You shall always be able to marry one of them. But never a clever one. However, stupid men like stupid women. So, you have nothing to fear."

"Ah — you are wrong, for in my experience, clever women like money more than the rest."

Miss Bennet arched one eyebrow and gave him a skeptical look. "You have met a clever woman? I fear you may have been deceived."

"You are spinsterish in your personality. Insulting those happier women who have found a husband."

Darcy saw in Mr. Lucas's expression that he had again stepped over some line. However he didn't care. He felt again every annoyance of the entirety of the ball, and he imagined Georgiana lonely at home, playing with Anne and wishing that she *once* could be allowed, for only a few hours, to act as every other girl. And this lady had the temerity to insult him and refuse his apologies. His normal politeness was gone, and he had this desire to find some insult which would stick and make her flinch.

"That would be an excellent analysis of my character," she spat, "*if I wished to marry*. You, sir, are an exemplar of why I do not."

"You truly possess the mind of a spinster. Astonishing. Shouting to everyone that it is your own choice not to marry. Not only is that a lie to protect your dignity, but also a stratagem born of desperation; you hope gentlemen will slacken their vigilance near you if you claim to have no interest in them. And then once they have wandered too close, like a bear trap you will clamp upon them."

"Does it astonish you *so much* to imagine a woman might not have any interest in you?"

Darcy shrugged easily and said in a mild tone, "It does. I do find it unbelievable."

Miss Bennet looked skyward, her pretty eyelashes fluttering up, and bringing Darcy's eye to the clear thin line of her eyebrows. "Heavens!" She said, "You are the perfect gentleman. Vain, overconfident, and with the most horrid beliefs about women."

"Vain? I do not have vanity — I confess that I am proud. But where there is real superiority of character, pride will be under good regulation. You though, you are a bitter old maid, snapping at everyone about you, and disliking other women, and making a pretense of disliking men."

"Under good regulation? I assure you, Mr. Darcy, this conversation proves you are not under good regulation."

The moment snapped into clarity, and Darcy flushed feeling more embarrassed than he ever could recall. Had he just spent the past minutes insulting a young lady? He had seldom been in polite company since Anne's birth, but his good breeding should not have deserted him.

It was no excuse, but there was something incredibly provoking about Elizabeth Bennet.

Seeing that her words had struck him, Miss Bennet gave him a triumphant grin and said, "I, of course, accept your apology, Mr. Darcy." She turned to a gentleman who had approached them as they spoke. "Mr. Goulding, I believe my next dance is yours?"

For the second time that evening Darcy watched the sway of Elizabeth's yellow clad hips as she walked away and he thought to himself, *that is a damned fine woman*. The thought was joined with an absolute certainty that he was an idiot.

        ===

A few hours after midnight the clatter of the returning carriage and the doors being opened by his wife and Lizzy woke Mr. Bennet from his nap. When Lizzy burst into the drawing room and kissed his cheek, he could see from her delighted air that *she* had enjoyed the assembly.

"How was your evening, dears?"

Following his usual practice, Mr. Bennet avoided the crush at the assembly hall and spent the night with a book in a comfortable chair next to the piled fire in the drawing room.

"Oh! That horrible man!" Mrs. Bennet shouted. "That man may be Mr. Bingley's friend, but Mr. Darcy is the most odious disagreeable man I have ever had the misfortune to be introduced to."

Mr. Bennet raised his eyebrows and shared a smirk with Elizabeth. "The very most disagreeable? How remarkable."

Elizabeth plopped herself inelegantly onto a sofa and said with a laugh, "On the contrary, I found him most insightful."

Mrs. Bennet cried out again, "Heavens! Awful, what he said about *our* Lizzy! Bingley and Lizzy tried to hide it from me, but Mrs. Long overheard! She — the scheming woman rejoiced in the knowledge, I dare say — rushed to tell me. He called our Lizzy a spinster. A *spinster*. Our Lizzy! She is very old now — I've always said she is very old — she must be losing her beauty at a rapid pace for her to be remarked on so harshly."

Elizabeth rolled her eyes.

Seeing that Elizabeth was uninjured by whatever had been said, Mr. Bennet placed his book to the side and reached over to pat Elizabeth on the arm. "Now, dear, that hardly shows any great insight on his part. For though, contrary to your mother's claim, your beauty is undiminished, he must have heard from Jane or Bingley that you are twenty and four. An age where some might begin to consider you, ah, what is the term — on the shelf."

Elizabeth laughed. "No — identifying me as a spinster showed merely an ordinary level of observation, though to say it as I walked up to join him and Bingley required an *extraordinary* level of frankness. The insight came from realizing that I am both desperate and simpering from a single glance."

"Simpering you say? Great insight into your character. You do seek to ingratiate yourself with all you meet. I shall exert myself to make a better acquaintance with such a Pericles."

"You must! You must! Papa, you shall find him delightful. He was of course ordered by Bingley to apologize, but when he did...it was wonderful! While he *apologized,* he made it clear he yet stood by his view that *of course* I was desperate to marry him, *and* he added he could not believe that a woman would *not* wish to marry such a man as him."

"You liked him very much indeed."

"Such arrogance, such conviction of every woman's admiration — that cannot help but appeal." Elizabeth laughed and yawned. "I am to bed now."

Chapter Six

Fitzwilliam Darcy calmly pasted the creamy butter from Bingley's pantry onto his roll. "Mrs. Bingley, I shall properly apologize. I behaved in a wrong and uncustomary manner to your sister last night, and I shall make it right."

Jane Bingley daintily wiped a crumb from her lips and smiled sweetly at him. "The behavior was unlike you."

"My word! I'll wager a guess! Darcy likes our Lizzy." Bingley grinned like a mischievous child who had stolen a cookie and elbowed Darcy's ribs.

Darcy glared back at his friend. Bingley's chair scraped against the wooden floor as he pulled himself a half foot further away from Darcy, but he did not cease grinning impishly.

Jane tilted her head and looked at her husband.

Darcy's mind painted a vivid portrait of him intimately close to Elizabeth Bennet, with her flashing eyes, laughing red lips, and yellow clad hips. *The deuce.* "You shall not push your sister upon me — even if she has nothing of the spinster's look about her."

"Nothing of the spinster about her *yet*." Bingley laughed. "I have never been so entertained as when Mr. Lucas reported your attempt to apologize. *Now* I grasp why you never married."

"I offended Miss Bennet but that deals no fatal injury to my chances if I wish to pursue her."

There was a pause. Bingley put down the piece of ham he'd begun to lift with his fork and simply looked at Darcy. Delightedly smiling.

"I do *not*," Darcy added, in an annoyed voice.

Damnation. There was nothing impressive about her. She had been rude to him, but she was a damned fine woman. If only her image would leave him alone.

It would be deuced uncomfortable if he was filled with lust for the hoyden when the Bennet family called on Netherfield in a half hour. "I confess, she is an impressive woman, and I desire to remove the insult I uncharacteristically uttered."

"Impressive woman? Do I hear the parson's mousetrap snapping shut? Is marriage nigh?" Bingley grinned with that irrepressible boyishness again and backed a bit further away, and pulled his silver plate piled with sausage and berry tarts with him.

Little Anne piped up from where she sat at the breakfast table on a chair with a big cushion so she could sit tall next to Georgiana. "Uncle Will will marry someone pretty, pretty, pretty." She grinned childishly at Darcy and waved her pastry about, causing crumbs to fly over the dinner room.

"Not after your introduction." Bingley added, "She'll refuse you; she's had her share of suitors. Maybe if you brag more about Pemberley..."

Georgiana grabbed Anne's hand and firmly took the lemon pastry away from her and put it on the table. "Don't wave your hands about so when you eat." She kissed her daughter on the cheek and said, "Fitzwilliam, this story is most unlike you — I wish we were not meeting anyone. They all judge me, and I put you in an ill mood."

It was like a kick in the stomach. He hated that Georgiana knew of his misbehavior because of Bingley's thrilled amusement at how he'd mistreated Miss Bennet. And Georgiana was right about *why* he'd been in a poor mood, but she should never blame herself for it.

"Georgie..." Darcy put a hand on his sister's shoulder. Their parents had never been physically demonstrative of affection, but he'd learned during the months of her pregnancy that fraternal touches could help to comfort Georgiana, so he made himself embrace her regularly. It was pleasant for him as well.

His sister's smile was brittle.

Jane exclaimed, "Lizzy will not hold a grudge! And she will adore you too, my dear Georgie!"

Bingley leaned forward and patted Darcy's arm. He whispered in a loud voice, "Don't be sanguine — Lizzy *can* hold grudges."

"Charles!" Jane poked her husband, who brightly poked her back.

A half hour later the children had been sent up to the nursery and the adults waited near the crackling fire for the Bennets to arrive and be ushered in. It was a particularly cold day, so they had decided not to wait outside for their guests, but to have everyone brought inside quickly so no unnecessary time would be spent in the freezing temperatures.

Darcy looked through the frost gathered on the windows. Darcy watched his sister with concern. She was always nervous when meeting new people. She sat stiffly on the yellow sofa in her blue dress, with a sort of trembling visible in the way her hair shook. But she noticed Darcy looking at her, and calmed and smiled at him. The drawing room had a pleasant smell from the burning pine wood and the few red and yellow flowers brought from the small hothouse Jane maintained.

He had failed his sister in many ways, but Darcy had made the right decision when she begged not to be made to marry. He could have protected his own reputation by selling his sister's person, future, and fortune to a barely known man. It would have made him miserable.

Darcy had been happy these past years.

Georgiana and Anne kept the house full of laughter and sweetness. His habits had always been such that he did not enjoy parties and large gatherings overmuch, and the excuse that the neighborhood refused to acknowledge Georgiana had left him happily able to avoid such clumpings. He maintained an extensive correspondence with his friends; he hunted and fenced with his neighbors; and the three of them had traveled extensively on the continent after the peace came.

A clattering of carriage wheels sounded outside. Through the window Darcy saw the Bennets' brightly colored carriage roll to a stop. Two horses pulled the chaise, one black with white markings on the face and the other a bay horse.

Bingley had told Darcy once that his father-in-law preferred to avoid expenses that merely served to enhance his consequence, instead putting the money towards a fund for his daughters' dowries. Darcy approved of such thrift. If Bennet's estate had been unentailed, the matter would have been different though.

Mr. Bennet left the carriage first. He wore a tall top hat and a tightly fitted grey coat whose tail flapped behind him. He first helped his wife out, a fine looking middle-aged woman whose coloring was similar to Jane's, and then *her*.

Elizabeth Bennet looked as fetching in the distance in a heavy bundled coat as she had yesterday in the ballroom when a low-cut dress displayed her feminine attributes. Where did the fascination with watching her come from? It was the sway of the dress.

Something about the sway. She wore a pretty yellow bonnet with a lace fringe which hid her hair, except a few black curls which fell around the edges of her face.

As if drawn by his gaze, Miss Bennet looked up at him. Their eyes met and there was a spark in his chest, and Darcy looked away, feeling disconcerted at having been caught staring.

He walked back to his armchair. His stomach was unsettled, and there was an odd awareness of where he placed his hands. Where should they go? He would *not* show any interest in this woman. He would *not* let anyone, even a dear friend, push a woman upon him.

Besides, she would dislike him after their argument the previous day. Darcy clung to that thought to calm his nerves.

The door opened and they all stood up. Bingley waved Mr. Bennet forward. "Bennet, my friend, Mr. Darcy of Pemberley; his sister Georgiana."

Darcy shook hands with Mr. Bennet. He was a bald man with sparkling eyes and a sardonic grin. "An exquisite and abnormal pleasure, Mr. Darcy. Sleep was denied me for many hours last night by tales of your sayings. There were even weepings and tears."

"I beg you to allow me to apologize to you, and your family for my—"

"None of that." Mr. Bennet waved his hand. "Not to *me*. You captured Lizzy's character perfectly. Without hearing her say a word — the usual manner with which a man judges a woman's mind."

"Papa." Miss Bennet elbowed her father. "I confess to being provoking last night."

She was provoking now. Darcy could not keep from looking at her. Such eyes. Such a face. There was a mole to the side of her nose, and her fine lips twisted in a delightful smile, and her dress was pulled in with a ribbon beneath the bosom that showed off her form.

After waiting for him to say more, Miss Bennet turned to Georgiana. "It delights me to meet *you*. I swear I shall not judge you by your brother's discerning opinions upon my person and character. I shall judge you by Jane's opinion of your character — high as the clouds."

Georgiana shook her blond hair, and blushingly stammered out a reply. That had been the time when he should have apologized to Miss Bennet again.

"Come—" Miss Bennet drew her arm through Georgiana's elbow. "Over there. We'll sit on the sofa and properly acquaint ourselves. Leave men to manly nonsense."

She walked away from him, again. Her hips clad in a dark pink dress made as compelling a sway this morning as they had the previous night.

Darcy realized he was staring at a young lady's rear directly in front of her father, so he jerked his eyes away and said to Mr. Bennet, "I do not deserve such condescension, but I pray you will not judge me solely upon my words last night."

"I'd expected a different sort of man than you appeared to be last night."

"I was utterly dissimilar to myself."

"Alas disappointment! If you behave in the mode of yesterday every day, *I* would derive great amusement."

Darcy had been told that Mr. Bennet had a teasing, sardonic manner. "I would by no means curtail your pleasures. But I do not make a practice of insulting young gentlewomen."

"Young? We know your *real* opinion. At my daughter's age, her looks are a tender subject."

Darcy's face stiffened into an authoritative mask. He knew he was being made fun of. He deserved some punishment, but he *despised* that his own actions had turned him into an object of fun.

Mr. Bennet looked like a happy cat playing with a mouse. "Say *something*. What weepings and wailings I endured last night!"

Darcy glanced at Miss Bennet, who faced them, but all her focus was on Georgiana as she spoke quietly to his sister, who nodded as Miss Bennet spoke. Darcy did not believe she'd cried at all. He looked back at Mr. Bennet. "I ought never have allowed my ill temper to lead me to say such things to your daughter. I made an effort to apologize to her last night. I earnestly hope she was not very hurt."

Mr. Bennet tilted his head. He yet gave the impression of a cat — but now the cat was curious. "A superb gentlemanly mask over your emotions. I cannot perceive if you feel terribly guilty or are secretly laughing."

Such a question deserved no reply.

"Lizzy told me your apology — you explained she ought take no offense, as you are deeply attractive to women due to your substantial wealth and oversized pile in Derbyshire, and that you know she must be desperate for a husband since her charms will not last long. Incorrect. I assure you, my Lizzy shall always be charming."

"Don't be like that." Bingley clapped his hands. "Darcy tried to apologize."

"But did he *sincerely* wish to apologize?"

Bingley grinned. "Darcy, were you sincerely apologetic?"

Darcy had *not* been sincere then. He was not entirely sincere now. Miss Bennet probably *was* desperate for a husband at her age. He looked at the women again. Her white hands were waving about. Georgiana nodded eagerly as Miss Bennet spoke. There she was, trying to befriend Georgiana, no doubt to impress him.

"Well?" Mr. Bennet's catlike smile was back.

"I...it was entirely my fault that I failed to apologize properly."

Mr. Bennet raised his eyebrows, making a pretense of being dissatisfied by Darcy's half apology. However, Mr. Bennet radiated amusement. Ill-tempered irritation rose again, and Darcy took an extra second before speaking to rein it in, so he would speak evenly. "I was wrong to call Miss Bennet a spinster where she could hear. And I was impolitic when I defended myself, instead of admitting that I simply should not have said what I said. I can admit wrongdoing, and I will say nothing further on the subject."

"Only should not have been said — you yet believe her old, mercenary, and desperate."

Darcy despised this sort of expectation of polite dishonesty. He did not *know* if Miss Bennet was desperate for a husband, but his was not an unreasonable guess.

"Far more delightful than the usual run of rich, arrogant gentlemen." Mr. Bennet grinned and rubbed his hands together with unalloyed amusement. "Lizzy noted *that* aright."

"Now, Bennet," Bingley looked uncomfortable, "Darcy apologized. This was sincere. No need for your teasing manner towards him."

Both men looked at the youngest of the three.

"I forget — my son despises disputes." Mr. Bennet extended his hand to Darcy. "Then, for my part, the apology is accepted. Pray, forgive my treatment of you. Elizabeth is a most beloved daughter."

"I do sincerely hope she was not injured."

Mr. Bennet smiled, less harshly. "Lizzy found nothing but amusement in what you said; thus no harm done."

Darcy glanced at the women again. Miss Bennet was looking at him and their eyes met. She frankly looked at him with that mischievous twist to her lips and her dancing dark eyes. Darcy felt himself begin to flush and he turned away. He did not like being an object of amusement to her.

"Pray tell," Mr. Bennet asked, "how do you stave off the horrors of boredom and the Byronic ennui which affect all cursed with any sense and born to too much wealth — besides bringing middle-aged ladies to tears."

"Your daughter is not middle aged."

Mr. Bennet glanced at the ladies. He did so quickly and lowered his voice, smirking slyly. "You brought my *wife* to tears with your aspersion on Lizzy's looks."

"I said nothing against your daughter's appearance." Mr. Bennet raised his eyebrows. Darcy quickly added, "She is an exceptionally attractive woman."

"Who is excessively attractive?" Miss Bennet's bell-like voice interrupted them.

Darcy flushed and looked down. *Keep a grip upon yourself.*

Bingley laughingly said, "You, my dear sister — he admires you, but still has the schoolroom belief that pulling a girl's hair is the best way to show his admiration."

"I do not!"

They all looked at him. Darcy realized he was becoming unsettled again by her presence and losing his usual firm control of himself. He'd secluded himself for so long, and avoided women. He was simply not used to being near a woman who attracted him.

"I shall assume that he meant he is not attracted to me, for it is clear he *does* think pulling a girl's hair will attract her." Miss Bennet laughed. "Had any of my vanity survived the previous night, it would be crushed by *this*. I have *never* had a man so sharply reject me *twice*. But I fortunately only have pride, not vanity."

"Miss Bennet, I beg you to allow me to apologize to you once more. What I said the previous day absolutely should not have been said."

"None of *that*! You still believe I am desperate for a husband. I empathize with your distaste of women, such as me, and every single other single lady, who have set their caps for you. I despise such polite niceties. You are an original and I quite prefer your open misogyny to polite nothings."

"I must apologize, for I did not speak to you in a gentlemanly manner."

"Fah! Gentlemanly manner— the most gentlemanly speaking man I ever saw was the worst."

"You see," Mr. Bennet said, "my Lizzy is herself an 'original'. If you wish to court her, insulting *her* will go far better than pretty nothings."

"I do not wish to court her!"

Miss Bennet looked at him frankly with her intense eyes. He flushed again, but this time refused to look away. The connection between their eyes roiled in his stomach. Their gazes lingered. Something changed in her eyes, and it was she who looked down with a reddening face. Darcy wanted to explain himself to her, to take back the expression of disinterest and to say something pretty to her.

Singular.

"Pray, tell true." Miss Bennet sucked her crimson lip under her white teeth. "Is it because you believe us all mercenary that you have not married?" Her lower lip was moist from where her tongue had touched it.

Darcy could not gather himself to speak.

Bingley laughed. "He despises the company of women — you know my sister Caroline, 'twas quite the joke the way she would chase him from room to room, and Darcy too polite to say he did not wish her company. But she *was* mercenary."

"Unkind! Unkind to say that of your sister! And in front of an avowed misogynist!" Miss Bennet giggled. "The horror is I cannot defend her from the insult in good conscience."

"I am not a misogynist."

"But you despise the company of women?"

Miss Bennet's challenging gaze was back. Darcy could not think when her eyes were turned on him. "No!" There was a pause. He thought Miss Bennet was suppressing another giggle. Darcy added, "My affection for my sister has led me to spend enormous time in her company."

"Perhaps your love for your own blood overcomes your general distaste for the fair sex? Can you name any other woman who you have spent a great deal of time in the presence of."

"My mother; my Aunt, Lady Catherine; and—"

"Lady Catherine? Of Rosings Park? If *she* were who I had to judge the gentler sex by, I would be a misogynist too. Not that I mean to insult your distinguished aunt to your face. But I just did, without intent."

"I am not a misogynist."

"Is there any woman who you have spent much time with who was not your near relative?"

Caroline Bingley had been the closest to such a woman. He had hated her.

"Aha!"

"That does not mean I hate women, I enjoy their company, much as any man."

Her gaze was now frankly skeptical.

Mr. Bennet said in an amused tone, "One can enjoy the presence of women without thinking well of them."

"I—" Darcy paused. "Miss Bennet, given the nature of this conversation, I hope it does not insult you if I turn the question around. Pray tell, why have *you* never married."

"Mr. Darcy, an indelicate inquest! Your celebrated frankness returns!"

"Perchance you suffer from misandry?"

"Darcy — I do not know what you two are about," Bingley exclaimed, "but Lizzy is in the best of health! No sickness ever about her."

Everyone looked at him. Bingley pulled at his cravat and looked down. "Misandry is not an illness?"

Miss Bennet smiled, flashing her white teeth. "Your friend wished to know if I hate the male sex."

"Of course!" Bingley laughed good humoredly. "No surprise you both know words I don't."

Bingley's self-effacing expression made everyone laugh, and broke the tension of the argument. They all smiled at each other.

Darcy recollected a discussion perhaps five or six years previous where he could almost swear he remembered Bingley using *misandry*. It would be very like Bingley to make fun of himself to break up what he saw as a too aggressive dispute.

Miss Bennet extended her hand out to Darcy. He took her warm, delicate hand and shook it with a grip that lingered a little long before he let go.

She said, "I accept your apology, Mr. Darcy — though in part because your sister begged me to. She believes the entire matter was her fault, which I take as an extraordinary notion, but she is as sweet a girl as Jane claimed, and I could not deny her earnest request."

"My sister is the dearest woman in the world. My affection for her is unbounded, and I am pleased you like her." There was a cast in his tone which reflected his slight skepticism. Likely Miss Bennet wished to enthrall him, and she must know that Georgiana's affections were the surest way to his own.

"Your affection is returned." Miss Bennet replied, "She has an appalling adoration of your opinions. You have turned her into quite the idolater."

Bingley said, "I thought you had declared truce?"

"I have." Miss Bennet laughed. "But Mr. Darcy must confess his sister looks up too much to him."

Mr. Bennet said, "Lizzy, what it *seems* a man must admit to is oft a different matter entire from what he *will* admit to. Let us test the question: Darcy, does your sister look up too much to you?"

"No." Darcy did not like to discuss his sister and he suspected they were questioning her character, and referring to how she had been seduced by Wickham. He stood stiffer and taller. She had been young, and he had failed to guard her.

He never would fail that way again. He would always be present with her to guide her and ensure Georgiana knew what to do.

"No offense! No offense!" Miss Bennet laughed. "I begin to read you. There is that stiffening in your posture. I do not know what you are thinking, but I mean no aspersion upon your sister. She *is* a fine young lady. But she ought to have more independence of mind at her age. She is sensible and she should not refer every time she is asked for her opinion on a matter of fashion, or politics, or books, or whether we shall call upon each other tomorrow, to *your* opinions."

Darcy tilted his head. "Is that all you meant?"

Miss Bennet and her father shared a long glance. Mr. Bennet twisted his mouth in a wry manner and Miss Bennet nodded. Darcy felt an odd envy for how she and her father seemed able to communicate without words.

He oddly wished to converse with her in that intimate manner.

Miss Bennet said, "I assure you, there was no hidden reference to the origin of your niece. I do not judge women of twenty for the actions of their fifteen-year-old selves."

"My gratitude."

"You are a prickly sort." Miss Bennet laughed, throwing her head back and displaying the line of her white neck. "But you have earned your ill temper honestly. Yet seeking a hidden motive in everything said to you will lead you into much error."

Darcy looked closely at Miss Bennet. She met his gaze frankly again. Perhaps she was *not* trying to seduce him. "I possibly am vain. What I said last night about only having pride...perhaps I was wrong."

Miss Bennet clapped. "The examined life is the only one worth living."

Darcy grimaced at her display of enthusiasm for his admission of wrongness, and her reference to Socrates. Too great learning in a woman led to mannish and immoral behavior, but it was also alluring. Like everything about the deuced woman. "I am no misogynist. The fair sex can be tender and honest. Harsh experience has shaded my attitudes, but I know not every woman is motivated solely by mercenary considerations."

"My word!" She clapped her hand over her mouth, dramatically. "You are no longer convinced that my sole goal is to entrap you into marriage. I did not *mean* to imply you should stop thinking that."

Darcy raised his eyebrows at that. Was she flirting with him?

"Thinking every woman desires silver and the pretty things it can buy — which I do, most everyone does — that is not the entirety of misogyny. I see nothing to dislike in your sister, but I suspect you believe it is *good* that she thinks too highly of your opinion."

"She does not think too highly of my opinion, if her high regard is deserved by me."

Miss Bennet had an open expression that invited him to say more. It also kept her eyes prettily on her face.

"She needs guardianship and protection. Her judgement can be led astray easily. But so long as she trusts me to know what is best for her, Georgiana will be safe from further errors."

"You still judge her by the actions of the fifteen year old."

"No! I judge her as I would if such an event not happened."

"Your sister is twenty. Far too old to be swaddled as a child."

"Women always need protection and guidance. No matter what their age."

Miss Bennet grinned again, in a manner that almost was a snarl. Her eyes were dancing again, but with anger instead of amusement. "Protected and guided, no matter how old? Must we be?"

"My intent is not to offend you."

"That, Mr. Darcy, is a terrible beginning to any speech which will be taken without offense. How much guidance do *I* need from my guardian gentlemen?"

Some impulse Darcy did not understand took control of his mouth, as he wanted to see how her eyes would look if she became authentically annoyed. "Woman can make household decisions, but in matters of great moment the female incapacities will appear. I cannot look with approval on the modern fashion for romantic and passionate marriages. It is well for a man who can control his passions to choose a partner in life for himself, but once a woman's affections are engaged her reason will always lose."

Miss Bennet glared at him. Anger *did* give her eyes an extra beautiful richness. Mr. Bennet hid his laughter with an unbelievable cough.

"You see," Darcy added, magnanimously, "you were correct that my speech would give offense."

"You blundering *gentleman*. Yes! Yes I suffer from misandry — *this* is why. This is your sober and *reasoned* opinion. That women cannot reason because our emotions and passions are too strong. This is why I have not married."

"History proves woman cannot manage their passions. Those who preach female education and reason the furthest are those most prone to losing control of themselves."

"Gentlemen always maintain themselves in good regulation." Elizabeth sneered at him.

Darcy flushed at the reference to his words the previous night. He did not think he was well regulated now either. There was something about Miss Bennet that made him behave differently.

"Men are alike with women." Miss Bennet added, "You and I are the same sort of being."

"Women are tender and sweet and vulnerable. Some fiends choose to abuse a woman's soft, affectionate nature, but gentlemen seek to protect those women who are precious to them. I am one who acts as a true gentleman — I try, at least."

"You *are* a misogynist."

"I adore my sister; I think highly of many women."

"You think ill of us all. You have said we are all weak and unable to reason."

"Surely you know *many* examples of women who cannot reason when their affections are engaged. *Your* sister Lydia, I understand, is as much an example of this frailty as my own sister."

Miss Bennet rolled her eyes and sneered. "And you pretend to be able to reason? You speak for women, but I could speak for men equally well."

"I understand you. You can bring up an example of a man's foolishness for every foolishness I have seen committed by a woman. A clever reply."

Miss Bennet rolled her eyes, clearly unimpressed by his admission that she had a point.

"You are learned."

"I will *not* be flattered by *that*."

"But despite your reason, when a great passion takes you, you will be unable to pick prudently, and it will be the responsibility of your father" — Darcy nodded towards Mr. Bennet who inclined his head with twinkling eyes — "to protect you and ensure you make a wise choice. And if he cannot, then your brother." Darcy gestured to Bingley.

"Nay! Do *not* bring *me* into your spat!" Bingley had been looking between the two of them. He glanced towards the window and coughed. "The sun! How bright it is! A perfect day for shooting! Much warmer than before. Darcy, I promised fine game. Mr. Bennet, with us!"

Miss Bennet sneered and curtsied. "I see we have strained my brother's patience with our argument too far. Good day."

She curtsied, barely, and walked where her mother and Jane talked with Georgiana.

Chapter Seven

It was determined during the course of the Bennets' visit to the abode of the Bingley family that the women of Netherfield Hall, Jane, Georgiana and little Anne would the following morning return the call upon the ladies of Longbourn, escorted by the sweetest young gentleman in the world, a young man with what Elizabeth considered the unfortunate name of Bennet Bingley.

The father of Bennet, Charles Bingley, had switched from his joking conviction in Darcy's attraction to Elizabeth to a desire to keep the two apart, and he insisted the gentlemen go shooting. To Elizabeth's mild surprise, her father agreed to participate a second time in two days in the high and difficult art of murdering birds from afar with a long rifle.

"That Darcy of yours. A delight—" Mr. Bennet chortled as he bundled up in his long brown overcoat. "The way you struck back at him. Mr. Darcy is an acquaintance well worth seeking, if only so I can find an opportunity to study you both in a room when our excessively amiable Bingley will not break the fight up just as it becomes heated."

"I do hope, Papa, I shall not show an excess of antagonism towards him."

"Not *that*! It would be quite a bore if you do not."

"He did apologize, almost sweetly. A fine-looking man. A very fine-looking man." Elizabeth smirked. She had been unsettled by their childish staring contest — that was all it had been when they looked challengingly into each other's eyes until she flushed and looked down. A childish staring contest. "Perhaps I ought to flirt with him instead."

"Good god! No! That would drive him away. You've seen how skittish he is. If he is this paranoid of the motives of a woman who teases him mercilessly, think how he would see a woman who makes a show of liking him — nay, you'll not land this elephant with honey."

Elizabeth rudely snorted.

"His appearance caught your notice." Mr. Bennet smirked. "Be strong, my darling. Be strong! He railed against all women. Strike back; find some claim that will bite him — for the honor of the fair sex!"

"Papa, we shall not fight merely for your amusement."

"Ha! I wish you to fight merely for *your* amusement." Papa squeezed the last button of his jacket closed. "I ought to lose a stone or so. This coat does not fit as it did when I had it made."

"You might have the stomach let out."

"Admit defeat? Not yet."

He held out his cheek and Elizabeth kissed Papa's bristly sideburns. "Revel in the violent death of birds."

"I shall revel in the conversation of your favored antagonist."

Mr. Bennet went out the front door and closed the door quickly behind him, a breeze of cold air shivering in behind him. He leaped onto the back of his horse with a surprising spryness for a gentleman who had from a young age preferred study and books to more sportly sports.

Elizabeth watched her father through the drawing room window. She loved her father; when he was gone she picked up a book to read while she waited.

It was no great duration of time until the Netherfield party rolled up the road, ensconced in their large fine carriage, and pulled by two pairs of matched bays and with a resplendently dressed coachman with a jaunty cap seated neatly in the driver's seat.

Mrs. Bennet smiled out the window contentedly, eager for Bennet and his small friend to arrive. Besides Jane, Mary had a child, but as she was settled some twenty miles distant, Mrs. Bennet could not dote upon that granddaughter the way she doted upon her beloved Bennet. Kitty's most recent letter announced she was expecting, and the babe had quickened. The pile of Bennet descendants was to increase.

Elizabeth and Mrs. Bennet bustled to the front door. Mrs. Bennet opened the door wide, letting in a draft and preempting Mrs. Hill's role as the housekeeper. "In! In! Out of the cold! The children could catch cold."

"Grandmama! Grandmama!" Bennet rushed up to Mrs. Bennet and widely hugged her.

"See—" Bennet pointed at Anne. "My friend! With me! Wheeee!"

Mrs. Bennet knelt to kiss Anne's cheek. The girl shrank away, and then giggled when Mrs. Bennet tickled her. "Sweet children. In, in — do not catch a cold!"

Elizabeth examined Georgiana Darcy, trying to trace how this shy, quiet and proper girl could be related to the frank and arrogant man Mr. Darcy was. Both were tall, they had a similar cast of features, and they preferred not to speak in groups of people.

When they were scuttled into the drawing room, the children attacked the toys Mrs. Bennet kept in a chest for Bennet.

"Many of these toys are from when we were girls." Elizabeth smiled at Georgiana. "The doll was brought down in hopes of entertaining Anne."

"Oh!" The young woman clapped and knelt on the Persian rug to pick the moderately beaten wooden girl up and stroke the horsehair head. "Sweet creature — *my* girlhood dolls are kept about my rooms. I hope this is not too dear an object, Anne can be rough. I assure you she *is* the sweetest natured and never means to—"

"A pet! A sweetling!" Mrs. Bennet exclaimed. "I know children. I raised so many! You need not defend your Anne, I am smitten with her."

Georgiana blushed and looked down. "Thank you, Ma'am."

"None of that formality. No, no, no! I adore you as much as your daughter — if only the neighborhood had not been so foolish as to refuse to admit you to the assembly." Mrs. Bennet growled. "We shall make a success of you, and prove them all wrong."

"No, I assure you," Georgiana shook her head vigorously, "I am content. I do not desire to be forced upon anyone who—"

"Nonsense! You are a young girl. You want your share of party and entertainment. You have been horribly, horribly abused by your brother keeping you from such things."

"Fitzwilliam is a perfect brother. He has done what he could. I do not deserve to participate in society."

"Deserve! Of course you deserve. Sweet thing. You are Jane's friend! Society will recognize you! My consequence will *not* be spurned — Jane, you and Bingley must hold a great dinner. Invite everyone. Everyone except Lady Lucas — I have cut her the past week for convincing the committee to ban Georgiana."

"They just did what they thought was right..." Georgiana quietly spoke to her hands. "Fitzwilliam would not like it if we made a pest of me to your neighbors."

"Mr. Darcy!" Mrs. Bennet growled. "I would never say anything against a friend of Bingley's, every friend of my son is a friend of mine, but I shall despise him forever for saying my Lizzy looks old."

"That is *not* what he said," Elizabeth replied for Georgiana's sake.

"Please don't," Georgiana whispered. "Fitzwilliam is very good — it was all my fault, and—"

The drawing room was opened, and a young cat who belonged to Elizabeth stalked proudly towards Elizabeth, with his back high.

Anne shouted, "Kitten!" and ran towards the startled animal. Poor little Mr. Hume fled in the opposite direction, with skittering paws, and hid under the black piano.

Both Bennet and Anne giggled and clapped their hands and then chased off towards the poor creature, circling around the piano, but unable to get under the tight spaces that the cat could fit into.

"Such adorable children!" Mrs. Bennet squealed. "Circle round, Bennet, round to the other side of the piano."

Bennet followed his grandmother's advice and reached close enough to grab the cat's waving tail, but the alarmed animal wriggled away and reaching the open floor took off and hid under the couch beneath Elizabeth.

The two children bounded over, laughing and giggling. Elizabeth placed a hand on each of them. "You've startled poor Mr. Hume."

"Sorry, Aunt Lizzy." Bennet smiled cherubically up at her, calming down.

Anne then bobbled her own little curtsey and smiled brilliantly. In her smile and expression there was a similarity to the late, charming Captain Wickham.

Elizabeth held up a finger. "Perhaps I can coax Mr. Hume out — then you might pet his fur. Softly."

She got off the sofa and looked under. The cat's wide eyes looked back at her, framed by adorable striped fur. Elizabeth softly made a *ch ch ch* sound with her tongue and held out her hand. The cat sniffed Elizabeth and, no longer scared by loud squealing from the two children, Hume stuck first his little pink nose out from under the couch, and then in a flowing movement he jumped into Elizabeth's arms.

She picked him up and settled the little creature on her lap. He rolled over so his tummy could be rubbed. Elizabeth nodded to the children.

Bennet nudged Anne so she could go first, and with wide eyes the little girl softly placed her hand on the cat's belly. Hume purred loudly, and Bennet came around the other side of Elizabeth to scratch him behind his ears.

Georgiana smiled. "What a pretty animal. How old?"

"Not yet a year."

Anne exclaimed, "Kitty!" again, and her excess of enthusiasm led Mr. Hume to rouse himself and walk in a dignified manner away along the couch. Bennet picked the cat up and got batted with a paw, but the boy giggled and held onto the cat.

"Not too rough," Jane warned.

Bennet looked at his mother, and the cat escaped once more and ran to the other side of the room. Rather than hiding, Hume stopped in the middle of the floor and looked back at them. Elizabeth suspected her cat had decided he was comfortable and wanted to be chased.

The two children squealed and obliged him by running at the small animal. Mr. Hume waited until they were a few feet away to skitter in a different direction.

"Your brother," Mrs. Bennet spoke to Georgiana, "could have no objection to you meeting the respectable people of the neighborhood. *Some* still respect the name of Bennet. A grand party for you at Longbourn, and another, even grander yet, at Netherfield. Bingley can hold a proper ball — our rooms are hardly big enough for a half dozen couples."

Georgiana's eyes widened.

Jane added, "Your brother wishes you less lonely and more social — meeting all our *true* friends in a private setting would be the best way."

Goodness, the poor woman was trembling. Elizabeth leaned forward and touched Jane's shoulder, as the children ran across the room once more, chasing Mr. Hume to a new hiding spot. "Miss Darcy, you do not *want* to meet a vast room of strangers. A small group instead. Two couples perhaps; particular friends. John Lucas and his wife. And Mr. and Mrs. Goulding. Old and particular friends of Jane and I."

"You think?" Georgiana's shoulders and trembling relaxed. "I...I might like that."

What had Jane been *thinking* to plan to take this poor girl to an assembly? Poor Georgie would have been too terrified to do more than stand in the most isolated corner and hope nobody saw her.

Mrs. Bennet sniffed. "Lady Lucas led the campaign against Miss Darcy. Her children will do nothing for us, *even* though we are such old friends. It is like when Charlotte stole Mr. Collins."

Elizabeth rolled her eyes. "She was well welcome to him. Lucas is one of my oldest friends, he will come if I beg him, and his wife is a kind woman everyone loves."

"Do not *beg* anyone..." Georgiana nervously wiped her hands on the sleeve of her dress. "After what I have done...they have the right to avoid me."

"Lord! What ridiculous notion!" Mrs. Bennet narrowed her eyes and chopped the air eagerly. "All hypocrites, every one. *Every one* of them."

"No...not after how I acted."

"How *you* acted? Heavens! A *little* imprudent, but I dare say every woman in the neighborhood anticipated their vows as you did."

"What!" Both Jane and Elizabeth sputtered together, staring at each other and then their mother wide eyed.

Mrs. Bennet sat up higher on the sofa and said with an air of dignity, "You did not believe it an accident that Jane was born eight months after our wedding?"

The sisters looked at each other. Elizabeth asked Jane in a hesitating voice, "Did you and Bingley ever..."

"No, never!" Jane replied in a shocked voice. "Of course I did not!"

Mrs. Bennet sniffed. "The worse for you and Bingley. Elizabeth, you should have given them more space during all of those walks — you were a quite poor chaperone. Entirely different from *my* sister."

Elizabeth looked wide-eyed at her mother.

"Lizzy was a perfect chaperone!" Jane exclaimed.

"Surely not..." Georgiana looked around at all three of them. "I cannot believe any *good* woman would—"

"Believe it!" Mrs. Bennet spoke firmly. "I did, Lady Lucas *certainly* did. I remember her, they were much poorer then, and I was still a girl, but she was *showing* with Charlotte's bump on the day the marriage was solemnized. Sir William had not been too eager *then* for her, so they waited till the babe quickened to start the banns." Mrs. Bennet laughed disgustedly. "*Now* she hurts a perfectly sweet girl to gain position over me by harming *my daughter's* guest."

Elizabeth could not repress helpless, horrified giggles at the story and the very unwanted information about Jane's conception.

Jane laughed with her, followed by Georgiana and Mrs. Bennet.

The children gathered around the adults, begging to be told what was so funny.

Jane picked Bennet up and swung him around. "An adult matter — quite boring."

Mrs. Bennet beamed adoringly at the children. "You must be hungry after all that running! Lemon tart? Do you want? Come with me to the kitchen."

Elizabeth smiled to herself; it was not *wise* to feed children sugary treats so early in the morning, but they both happily clapped at the promise. Jane went with Mrs. Bennet, but Georgiana hung back, and from her expression Elizabeth saw she wished to say something to her alone. Mr. Hume hopped onto Elizabeth's lap. Georgiana folded her hands together and looked to the side, demurely sitting in a graceful curve on the sofa.

Elizabeth smiled encouragingly. "The two of us, we shall be good friends."

"You could see I frightened, when your mother suggested a large group."

"Shyness is no reason for shame."

Georgiana smiled and ducked her head. "I cannot even correct servants when they are wrong for fear of giving offense."

Elizabeth laughed, and slowly petted the lightly purring cat on her lap. "Good servants can be dreadfully hard to correct."

Georgiana smiled, but she then gripped her hands tightly together and twisted them around.

"Out with it. Out. What is on your mind?" Elizabeth smiled comfortingly.

"You quarreled with my brother again — Bingley said."

"Ah."

"Please, I wish us to be dear friends as well — Fitzwilliam is so good. Do not smile with that doubting manner. He is!"

Elizabeth replied in a philosophical tone. "What is goodness?"

"My fault put you at odds. He was in an ill mood after Sir William banned my attendance. *I* insisted he attend the assembly nevertheless and..."

"You need not defend your brother. His behavior and opinions are his own."

"He was so angry I'd been refused entry. I do not even desire to go to a ball. Not much. I would only like to watch one once, and dance a set with Fitzwilliam — pray, think kindly of him..."

"I blame him no longer for the night of the ball. Yesterday, he irked me with no excuse of ill temper."

Georgiana blinked at her.

Elizabeth buried her hands in her cat's dashing fur. Mr. Darcy had infuriated her. "I do not approve of his attitudes towards our fair gender."

"How can you not! Fitzwilliam is the best, kindest, and noblest gentleman in the world. He will do anything for me — I was ruined, and he did not throw me off, he allowed me and Anne to live with him, he has given up so much, and the shamefulness of our presence has kept him from marrying—"

"Him! *Wish* to marry?"

"—he is always so kind, so willing to spend time entertaining me, he always gives up his own pleasures for my sake...he is the *best*."

"He, like you, deeply dislikes oversized social gatherings, and he suffers the profoundest annoyance in the presence of too many women. He is convinced we are only desperate to catch a wealthy husband — this is not a matter of conjecture — he told me direct."

"But—"

"You shall not succeed. You worship your brother, but he is a man, and he has shown his feet of clay to me. You shall not convince me he is angel, spirit, or Grecian hero."

Georgiana sighed. "He is the best of men. You misjudge him."

"He holds you in close affection, and he has supported and cared for you for many years — *your* affection is natural. I freely admit he has virtues."

"Then why do you dislike and argue with him?"

"My dear Georgiana — this is a misapprehension. That two persons argue with each other does not signify that they dislike each other."

"But you *do* dislike Fitzwilliam."

"I am undecided. There is much for a sensible woman to dislike."

"You *will* like him eventually, if you are undecided."

Mr. Hume reached his soft paw up to bat Elizabeth's face, bringing the scent of his clean-licked fur to her. She shrugged. Maybe Georgiana was right. Maybe she already liked Mr. Darcy, despite his deficiencies. A very handsome man.

"You will come to see how he is sweet and loving. The treatment society gives me has made him cynical."

"I doubt very much he *ever* had friendliness for women outside intimate circles. Your brother is a clever and well-read man, and he absorbed the foolishness male writers attribute to women. And a man who combines such a fine person with such a fine estate must have been pursued avidly by women since he has been in society. The genesis and genius of his distrust."

"I was not able to control my passions."

"A child without her guardian. *And* you detached yourself from Wickham before he gained your fortune."

"I deserve no credit. You misunderstand. I learned Wickham's character, and that I would be miserable with him, and that he loved nothing but my wealth. His mistake was only not to continue the charade until we had been tied by marriage."

"I *do* admire you. And today you are no unguarded child. You are a woman, full of sense and sensibility."

"What do you mean?"

"Your brother said you could never make a good choice for yourself, not because your past makes him mistrust you, but because you are a woman. He said directly I would be as incompetent as you had been if I formed a passionate attachment."

"Fitzwilliam said *that*? About you?"

"He did. But I promise, I shall strive to see his better features — many virtues are in your brother. I demand in exchange that *you* look in yourself and see the virtues and sense *you* possess. Learn to trust yourself in matters of importance."

"I could never go against my brother's wishes."

"One day *you* will wish to marry. And when that day comes, *you* must choose your own happiness, not him."

"I never will marry! Absurd to imagine."

With a loud bustle the door to the drawing room was burst in, and the two children ran in, jumping up and down, made energetic by the treats stuffed into them. Mrs. Bennet and Jane followed them in.

Anne ran towards them, alarming Mr. Hume, who meowed and jumped up to run once more under a sofa.

Instead of chasing Hume, Anne childishly leaped onto Georgiana's lap. The mother opened her arms and held her close. "Tasty! It was! The pastry! Bennet says his Grandmama *always* has treats. She told me that I am a perfectly dressed young lady. Grandmama Bennet is such a nice woman. I wish I had a Grandmama."

Georgiana kissed the girl's forehead.

The little girl turned to Elizabeth, "Your mama is so nice!"

Elizabeth giggled. "Might I hold her?"

Georgiana pushed Anne to crawl into Elizabeth's lap, while Elizabeth held open her arms. The child made a fragrant, warm weight.

"You like my mother?" Elizabeth asked.

"She gave me *so* many tarts." Anne held up three fingers, one of which had a smidge of jam left on it. "Mrs. Bingley is nice too!"

"Everyone adores Mrs. Bingley."

Elizabeth cuddled the little girl while she and Georgiana played silly little games with her.

Then a knock and the door opened again.

Anne jumped off Elizabeth's lap. "Uncle Will!"

Mr. Darcy swept her up into his arms in a single effortless movement, sitting the girl high in his arms and listening with a smile while she happily babbled.

Lord! He made a handsome figure. Elizabeth's insides twinged at seeing him appear so fatherly. Her breath caught.

The attractiveness of a man was usually increased when he showed care for a child. But this was more intense than ever. Elizabeth helplessly watched Mr. Darcy's innocent smile as he nodded at his niece. His was lit by the window, making every strong angle and firm contour of his remarkable face jump out at her eyes.

Anne pointed towards Elizabeth. Her winsome voice lisped, "My new friend! Miss Lizzy! Come meet her. She is so nice!"

Mr. Darcy looked at Elizabeth, and an embarrassed flush crept up Elizabeth's neck at being caught leering at the gentleman.

She looked down and quickly back towards him. He still looked at her, but from his expression she had no sense of what he was thinking.

Anne pulled at the lapel of Mr. Darcy's coat and begged him to go meet Miss Lizzy. He walked towards her, easily and securely holding the child in one arm.

Almost helplessly, Elizabeth rose to greet the approaching man.

He stuck out his free hand to her. "Miss Bennet. I am pleased to see you."

Elizabeth quirked her mouth mischievously as she shook his hand. "Even though I have defeated you in honorable verbal combat twice."

"Once only, madam." He smiled back at her. It made his face glow.

She'd once encountered in a terrible novel for young women obsessed with marriage the phrase *He was unfairly handsome*. An absurd notion, she had thought then.

Fitzwilliam Darcy was *unfairly handsome*.

"I believe I gained victory twice." Elizabeth had a bubbly smile.

"Nay, you had scored against me in our second match, but while bloodied, I was yet undefeated when Mr. Bingley divided the combatants."

"I am surprised he allowed you freedom to seek out a third match."

"I resorted to stratagem. Georgie, are you well? I worried about you."

That was why she could resist Mr. Darcy. What did he imagine was to happen to his sister in their house?

Darcy's care for his niece was sweet. That for his sister was cloying.

Georgiana glanced at Elizabeth as she smiled. "Very well. We played and talked. I do like Miss Bennet."

"You do?" Darcy smiled at Elizabeth. "Then I must thank you again."

"She has promised to think more nicely of you."

Elizabeth bit her lip and then smiled very widely. "That was not *precisely* what I promised — you made a promise of your own!"

"Oh." Georgiana blushed and looked down. "You did say you would look for Fitzwilliam's better features."

Elizabeth looked at the gentleman. Goodness, that grin was a *very* superior feature. And he was almost a foot taller than herself. And such well-muscled arms. And those deep eyes when he looked at her.

"And what, Miss Bennet, are my better features?"

"Your tall figure." Elizabeth clapped a hand over her mouth and giggled as both Georgiana and Darcy looked at her. Anne squirmed to be set down by Darcy.

"This is why I must remain clear on what your *failings* are." Elizabeth shook her head. "Else you will place me at quite a disadvantage."

Was his face a little red? Or was that disapproval of her accidental forwardness?

Darcy said, "I would not wish you at a disadvantage."

"You would."

He intently studied her and said in a low, vibrating voice. "Perhaps I would need you at a disadvantage, if I were to best you."

No wonder Wickham had turned out so charming, with this as his competition. Despite his rudeness and every other failing, she was fluttering. "You hope for us to engage more often?"

"And for me to win." His voice was soft.

"Then, you will need every advantage."

"I know."

"You do not reason much better than the usual, for an educated man."

"And you reason exceptionally well, for a learned woman."

"I detect the scorn in *that*. You do not approve of too much learning in a woman."

"Here you defeat me once more. I always considered learned women to lose some part of their feminine grace and charm — Miss Bennet, you possess every feminine charm."

Elizabeth's face flushed at the way he said that. She would soon be at a terrible disadvantage. To be able to look away from his magnetic eyes she gestured to the couch and they all sat.

"I will not let you gain my good graces through flattery." Elizabeth sternly wagged a finger in front of Darcy's face.

"I do not expect to be in your good graces — no matter how I might wish to be."

"A man who does not believe in learning in a woman — I am the most learned woman of my acquaintance, I must take that as scorn against me personally."

There was a soft smirk on Darcy's face. "It does strike against you."

"Fitzwilliam," Georgiana said in a cautious voice, evidently a little confused by the conversation. "You must not... Miss Bennet, he does not mean he disapproves of learning. He has always encouraged me to study, and to do anything I might to improve myself."

"Oho! What knowings are admissible to the tender, weak, and easily influenced mind of a female creature."

Darcy began, "We both admit men are not always paragons of reason and virtue—"

"I freely admit *that*."

He smirked at her. There was a long pause as he tilted his head and studied her. Elizabeth felt something in the air between them, something that ignored the presence of his relatively young sister sitting between them. "Surely you acknowledge women do not have the same spark in their souls as a man. A very clever man will always be *more* than a very clever woman — the great poets, scientists, philosophers, statesmen — they are never women."

Elizabeth growled. Infuriating man. To flirt with her and *then* make such a stupid argument. "Women are not given opportunity to grow and display our talents! You know that means nothing. We are expected to live dull lives of useless dullness and — Your premise is false. False! The Greeks agreed that Sappho was amongst the greatest of their poets."

"One name." His eyes were light. There was some spark in them. "Besides, she threw herself off a cliff over the love of a ferryman."

"Spurious story, invention of those men who despise female poets because their fragile pride cannot survive if men are not superior in all areas."

"Suicide and immorality. Her, Wollstonecraft, other women with too much learning. You will not convince me it is well for your sex."

"Wollstonecraft: the first refuge of every gentleman with a desire to mock female learning."

"She wrote proper education could overcome the passions, and then was driven entirely by her passions to two attempts at suicide and an illegitimate child. She had need of a firm hand from a gentleman who cared for her interests." Darcy smirked. "You cannot accuse me of speaking of that which I have not studied — I read *The Rights of Women*."

"Bravo!" Elizabeth rolled her eyes. "Wollstonecraft's advice to reject passion seems to be of a piece with your attitudes. Not of mine. You learned too well from her philosophy. A wise person will find a union of passion and reason."

"Women cannot."

"Men can? One day you too will find yourself victim of such imprudent passion, and with nothing but your reason to defend you, and your reason will fail."

"When we talk in possibilities, anything is possible. But in actualities women are more easily driven by their passions than men."

"I oppose to you Shakespeare. Othello, Macbeth, Romeo, and Bottom the rude mechanical — *men* driven into error by their passions."

"Bottom? The one turned into an ass?" Darcy quirked his mouth. "Unfair. Shakespeare is no historian."

"Then I offer you that low creature beloved by history: The common politician. If all the great statesmen and philosophers are men, so are all petty politicians, dishonest lawyers, and gentlemen wastrels."

"Fitzwilliam," Georgiana asked, "are you *attempting* to provoke Miss Bennet?"

Darcy's mask broke and he blushed and looked down and rubbed his sleeve. He opened his mouth and closed it.

When he looked up, Elizabeth met his eyes steadily and in a twisting sensation that caused butterflies to flutter upwards from her stomach into her chest and throat, she realized he *was* intentionally provoking her. He admired her, but had not learned that annoying a woman did not lead to her heart.

Or could it?

A *very* handsome man.

"Oh!" Georgiana exclaimed and blushed. Darcy and Elizabeth blushed as well.

Anne poked Georgiana, wanting more attention. Hoping to look maternal Elizabeth stretched out her arms in offer, and the girl let Elizabeth sit her on her lap. "What do you really think, Mr. Darcy? Are you convinced my mind is inferior to yours? Plato supports that notion, but we shall never be real friends if that is your considered belief."

"No, no — not like in the Republic." He glanced at Georgiana and said in a lecturer's voice, "Plato had the notion that men and women were alike in all important respects, except women were at all points inferior. A woman could do anything a man could do, but not as well. He was wrong. A woman is a different sort of being than man, not an inferior variant of a man. Miss Bennet, you cannot believe men and women are the same. That we have the same pattern work of strengths and virtues."

"No..." Elizabeth frowned thoughtfully and rocked Anne back and forth. "You claimed a clever man will always be more clever. That offends me. *That* is not where man's superiority lies."

"Where then is a man superior?"

Elizabeth laughed. "No, no, no! I will not reply to that."

"You hope to deny male and female difference?"

"In mental points only — the physical differences are obvious; I celebrate *them*!" She boldly let her eyes admire his person. With a smile she looked back up to meet Mr. Darcy's eyes. "Do you not celebrate them as well?"

He blushed, like a school boy. Darcy glanced at his sister. "Is *that* your considered belief? Males and females possess no differences in the mind."

"Are not differences in the body enough? They explain other matters." She wanted to leer at him again.

Darcy said nothing, He just looked at her, deep into her eyes. Her stomach was flipping again.

He broke the gaze and looked at the fire with high color. "Nay, nay...some great men have been deficient in the body, but not the mind — Homer, Milton, the blind poets. The difference between man and woman is not a matter of the body alone."

"Sappho — and Wollstonecraft. A greater thinker than *Burke*."

"You dislike Burke?"

Georgiana laughed. "*Now* I understand why Bingley separated you two." She took Anne from Elizabeth's arms. "Fitzwilliam, whether Miss Bennet or you are right about which sex is the cleverest, she is as learned and clever as *you*."

Darcy blinked as his sister walked away. "Miss Bennet, what did you say to my sister?"

"Perhaps you two have not spoken often about the intrinsic inferiority of my sex? For my part, I think anything that makes her begin to see you more as a mere human is salutary."

"I beg you to leave my sister to my management."

"I shall treat her as any *adult* woman of my acquaintance."

Darcy grimaced. Handsomely. It was unfortunate: He did *everything* handsomely.

"You worried she was lonely. Now you worry when she has friends."

"She is my sister. In my care. And I love her — I shall always worry, no matter what." The mischievous glint returned to his eyes. "I expected her friends to have the nature of Mrs. Bingley."

Elizabeth swooned and fluttered her eyelashes. "I am one of *those* women! Not safe for impressionable young girls? You *do* know how to flatter a woman."

He smiled, also handsomely. "And you claimed flattery could not move you. You *like* being said dangerous."

"I have never been called that before." Elizabeth grinned unabashedly. He did know how to flatter a woman. "I beg you not to hide your sister from my influence."

"You are too good hearted to intend her real harm."

"I am good hearted? Am I also an angel?"

"An imp."

Elizabeth laughed. She placed her hand on his well-muscled arm. "Mr. Darcy, we shall be friends."

He grinned back at her. "You like my manner of flattery."

"No one flatters me like you do."

"None of the hordes of gentlemen circling round you?"

"At mine age, spinster already, how many gentlemen do you think there might be?" Elizabeth dramatically touched her breast, and then she laughed buoyantly. They both knew they were flirting with each other. Her whole body was oriented towards Darcy, and he faced her.

"You have as many admirers as you wish." Darcy paused for a beat and grinned boyishly again, showing that he knew how arrogant what he would say was, but that he said it for the fun. "We are very much alike in *that*."

Elizabeth laughed. "Your pile draws every rational or passionate woman — I refer to your hair, not your home or your rents."

He shrugged, roguishly smiling, and pulled at his locks. "Deuced fine head of hair."

"I empathize with your difficulty in fending off admirers — I *do* have many."

Darcy laughed. "Miss Bennet, I declare, we shall be good friends."

Chapter Eight

The following afternoon Darcy found himself in the midst of yet another shooting expedition arranged by Bingley. Oddly his friend had not improved his aim despite his enthusiasm for the sport. Once again Mr. Bennet was part of the party, and Darcy found himself coming to like the sarcastic wit of the older gentleman.

During the course of their shooting, Mr. Bennet said, "My daughter declares you declared yourself amiable antagonists."

"We certainly declared no truce," Darcy replied as he pushed the ball down the long gullet of his hunting rifle. "That would not entertain. And she has too ill an opinion of my opinions."

"What are your *real* opinions? Can women never be so clever as men?"

"My rejoinder shall please neither Miss Bennet, nor, it is my sad suspicion, you. Your daughter holds that it is a matter of circumstance. Women experience different modes of education than men, so they develop their faculties in a different manner. This determines the differences in accomplishment between the sexes — I confess, the ring of plausibility is present."

"You do not believe it?"

"No." Darcy shook his head.

Bingley called out, "Take a break from your argument, they are about to flush the covey!"

Both gentlemen lifted their fowling pieces to their shoulders. They waited alertly, and with a squawking flap the birds burst over the treetops, seeking a safe height.

With a near simultaneous crack three guns went off and two birds fell squawking from the sky.

"The deuce!" Bingley exclaimed, as Darcy and Mr. Bennet released their dogs to retrieve the catch.

Mr. Bennet said in an even voice to his son-in-law, "You forgot, again, to account for the wind. Too impatient."

"I understand Darcy." Bingley replied, "The man does everything deuced well. But at your age and with all the time you spend with books, you ought not be able to beat my catch so easily."

"My eyesight is kept in good practice by the books." Mr. Bennet looked at Darcy. "Why are you yet convinced men are superior in the mind, despite the example of my daughter?"

"Different, *not* superior."

"Ah, men are only superior in the ways which are important, while women have superiority in those which are not important."

"Miss Bennet became almost vicious after I suggested men have greater cleverness."

"Any aspersion on her sharpness and cleverness will land you more grief than one upon her age and fading looks — if your goal is to court her, you have done a fine job so far."

Darcy grimaced. Was Mr. Bennet mocking him for how he'd insulted Elizabeth, mocking the idea that he might admire her, or simply mocking him — or maybe Mr. Bennet, in his sardonic manner, told the truth, and he thought that the verbal sparring he had with Elizabeth excited and exhilarated her as much as it did him.

"Your opinion considering Lizzy's cleverness." Mr. Bennet tapped the butt of his rifle against the ground. "Give it. What says your frank and original mind?"

"You wish to know because I am courting your daughter?"

Bingley laughed. "A joke, Darcy. I was joking. The two of you would make a horrid couple. Mr. Bennet sees that. So much argument — it would exhaust a spirit."

The dogs returned carrying the dead birds in their muzzles, and Darcy took his bloodied bird from his hunting hound. He opened the string of the bag, deposited the dead pheasant, and tied it up once more. Darcy wiped his gloves off on the cloth provided for that purpose by the gamekeeper and calmly reloaded his gun.

"I question," Mr. Bennet said, "every gentleman who shows such understanding of my daughter's character."

"A claim about the cleverness of females deals in generalities Your daughter is a particular... I may attack *female* cleverness without saying anything against *her*."

"Slippery, slippery. But clever — Elizabeth will not accept such slipperiness."

"The idea that men and women have the same potential endowments in mental pursuits *feels* entirely wrong to me. I confess I have no *proof* beyond the general experience everyone has of the world, which different persons interpret in different manners. It would be a most peculiar matter if the Lord created man and woman so different in all other respects, woman so well adapted to being man's helpmeet and support in body and appearance, if she was not also formed to be his helpmeet in her mind."

"A religious fanatic's reply, then."

"Nay." Darcy shrugged. "I attend church; I believe. But I am no enthusiast."

"I do not believe."

"And Miss Bennet? She named her cat after that Scottish atheist."

"Do not assess her opinions in this off mine. She believes, at least a little — Hume is worthy of admiration by all."

"I appreciate the philosopher's arguments, even if I am unconvinced by his irreligion. His history of England is unparalleled."

"Deuced good story."

The guns were reloaded, and the gentlemen waited for the gamekeeper to flush the next covey, leaning on their tall rifles. The cold wind rustled through the bushes.

Bingley filled the quiet. "Bennet, will you join the fox hunt this year?"

The older gentleman shook his head. "I've no taste for the sport anymore. Young man's game."

"You are enjoying this shooting so much."

Darcy did not wait for him to reply to Bingley and asked Mr. Bennet, "Your philosophy regarding women and men? Do you share your daughter's radicalism?"

""Lizzy is cleverer than I." Mr. Bennet shrugged. He made little circles in the dirt with the boxwood stock of his rifle while looking at the trees. "And I have a high regard for my own cleverness. So my general experience of life is entirely different from yours."

There was the crashing sound, and the next covey was sent up. Darcy sighted his rifle carefully, and he hit his bird once more. It was deuced fine shooting on Bingley's estate. There wasn't as much space as in Derbyshire, but more than enough birds for their group.

Mr. Bennet checked his rifle carefully to ensure it had in fact fired with the other guns.

Darcy thought the older man was annoyed that this time he had missed while Bingley struck his bird. "I clearly heard three shots."

"Yes. I am satisfied it *is* unloaded." Mr. Bennet pointed his rifle at Darcy. He said in a surprisingly intimidating manner, "Be warned, my daughter will *always* expect to have her will indulged."

"I..." Darcy stared down the gleaming dark metal barrel of the unloaded — he *had* heard three shots — rifle. "I agree, she is very willful."

"*I* raised her that way." Mr. Bennet punctuated his statement by thrusting the rifle forward.

"Bennet—" Bingley was half torn between laughter and concern. "Darcy *isn't* courting Elizabeth. Our man here would never want to argue with his wife. He likes command too much. He knows Lizzy is willful."

"He likes my Lizzy. I watched your eyes the day past." Mr Bennet waved the gun around, its muzzle making small circles, moving between Darcy's chest and his stomach. "You admired her person to an excess."

"I had realized it was impolitic to stare at a woman in such a manner whilst her father stood next to me. *This* is an extravagant reply to my stare."

"Now you claim I should care less than I do for my daughter's welfare? Those are the words of a scoundrel."

"I do not — merely that you should not threaten him with a gun, every time a man looks on her with...ah...matters are *not* serious."

"You do not know if you will become serious — do not decide speedily, I am not worried about you 'hurting her', and I feel no requirement to defend her honor. Lizzy can protect her own heart, and you are an honorable man."

Darcy looked at the rifle. It *was* unloaded. "If I am an honorable man, why—"

"The deuce!" Mr. Bennet wildly waved the gun and pointed it at Darcy's face. "Women do not exist for us. They have their own ideas about matters. If you cannot accept that you have no business marrying, and if you do not *desire* a willful wife, content yourself with unguarded leers at my girl."

"You take this matter too seriously," Darcy replied, unsure whether this was no more than a joke from the odd gentleman.

"By waving an unloaded gun, which you have *seen* discharged, at your chest?"

"That does *not*, to my surprise, entirely undercut the menace of an angry father threatening the unwanted suitor. I confess ignorance of your purpose."

Mr. Bennet laughed and set down the gun. He waved their worried attendant forward to help him begin to reload his gun. "I said my piece."

Darcy shrugged and finished reloading his own gun.

Chapter Nine

Elizabeth set out after breakfast on a bright, November day to visit the Lucases, specifically John Lucas and his wife, so that she could invite them to dine at the same table as Georgiana Darcy.

The past day had been full of cloudy prognostications of doom for her purpose. Mrs. Bennet talked once Georgiana and Jane left at thudding length about those scheming Lucases, the condescension she had shown to Lady Lucas, and the way England had fallen into decline in these latter days.

Mrs. Bennet had never entirely forgiven Lady Lucas for Charlotte's deeply lamented marriage to Mr. Collins, and this latest provocation heaped great addition onto existing complaints. Elizabeth received *some* of the opprobrium heaped upon Lady Lucas; after all, the woman would never have *dared* such a thing if her daughter was not to inherit Longbourn.

Elizabeth had always known Mrs. Bennet held some confusion about the details of the entail, but to forget that it was Mr. Collins, not Charlotte, who was the inheritor, struck her as a worsening of the misapprehension. Though the laws of England did make a man and his wife one person.

Who was the man?

Mrs. Bennet predicted Elizabeth would suffer a ghastly failure when she asked Mr. Lucas to attend their party. Why would John Lucas, a dutiful child, undercut Lady Lucas's desperate, doomed leap for social superiority over the Bennets and Bingleys?

There might be something to her mother's mistrust of her dearest friend. Elizabeth nonetheless thought *her* friendship with Lucas and his wife would overcome family loyalty.

"Hullo! Hullo!" Elizabeth smiled broadly as the housekeeper shooed her into the low-ceilinged drawing room. She was not sure if it was fortunate that Lady Lucas was absent, but Maria sat embroidering with Mr. Lucas's wife and the gentleman himself.

"Good day! Good day!" Lucas stood enthusiastically, and with rustic sophistication took Elizabeth's hand and kissed it. "My dear Eliza, as always you brighten our day."

Elizabeth smiled back and pressed her hand to her face. "Goodness you make me blush."

Lucas's wife Felicia said, "'Tis true. Even if my husband speaks as a coxcomb."

"I confess, I am here to brighten the day," Elizabeth replied as she sat. "First, what news."

"All of Johnny's teeth have arrived!" Felicia laughed. "I can sleep at last now that he is not gnawing and crying every day."

"Sweet boy!" Elizabeth laughed with a feeling of relief — teething was a frequent cause of convulsions, digestive dysfunctions, and sometimes the untimely death of children. The wait for teeth to erupt always worried those who loved the child. "Bring this paragon forth, so all may admire his magnificent jaws and teeth."

John Lucas rolled his eyes. "Do not talk of my son like a horse to be sold at auction."

"I do not — such a grand beast would never be sold."

Felicia laughed. "For my part, you can freely call the boy a grand beast. Though I love him dear."

As she spoke the maid brought the giggling toddler into the room.

"I believed you would want to see him," Felicia said. "I called for Johnny as soon as I realized who our visitor was."

The child crawled in Elizabeth's lap and cooed and touched her face. "Luzzy!"

"Wholly correct! Luzzy!" Elizabeth giggled. "How many teeth do you have?"

The child held up his chubby fingers as he counted out all of the teeth, before losing track half way through. He then proudly opened his mouth so Elizabeth could examine for herself. "Teeth!"

Adorable. If only she had her own child to cuddle, kiss and play with.

That was a new thought. What strange quirk of the female animal gave her *now* this desire for her own little child to climb about her, and to beg for her attention, and to wholly depend on her.

Lucas pulled his chair closer to Elizabeth's. "What errand brought you?"

Elizabeth felt a slight nervousness before asking the question. She would feel terrible if she could not introduce Georgiana to these friends. Worse, a refusal would occasion a substantial degree of awkwardness.

Lucas would accept her invitation. They had been friends forever. Not so close as her and Charlotte before Charlotte's marriage, but close. Lucas even had a *tendre* for her when they were both younger.

"I have an invitation to dine at Longbourn. But only for two of you" — Elizabeth gestured to Lucas and Felicia, then waggled her finger at Maria — "No disappointment! You are too impressionable in your maidenly state to survive contact with Georgiana Darcy."

Lucas and Felicia looked at each other. Lucas asked, "You wish Miss Darcy to be introduced to the neighborhood in a *circumscribed* manner?"

"Circumscribed! A fine word. We hope the circle shall widen — never fear, Maria, your maidenliness will protect you from contamination."

"Who else? The Gouldings?"

"And perhaps an extra man so it will be a set of matching couples. All of an age with us. If a success, Bingley shall throw a *private* and *exclusive* ball for her to be showcased to the best — that is the least Missish — of the neighborhood. You would not wish to miss it."

"Oooh! A ball!" Maria exclaimed, clapping her hands. "What would I wear?"

"You would not be invited."

"But—"

"Remember, your maidenly delicacy!"

Maria stuck her tongue out, showing that she'd been acquainted with Elizabeth since before she could walk. "I want to meet Miss Darcy. She cannot be so *indelicate* in her speech as *our* Mrs. Wickham. And no one stops me from talking to Lydia."

"Yes, Maria," John Lucas said, "but Lydia was a married woman — you should know nothing else about the matter."

"Oh Lydia *told* me everything about *the* matter."

Elizabeth raised her eyebrows and asked in a slightly breathless voice. "What matter, pray tell?"

"You know *the* matter." Maria blinked a little helplessly, plainly having not expected to be questioned on *the matter*.

"I know nothing of the sort. Which matter?"

"Ummm, when two—" Maria blushed and looked at her brother and his wife before looking down. "The matter."

Elizabeth seriously nodded.

Maria said accusingly, "You are teasing me."

"She always is," Lucas replied for Elizabeth. "*I* shall talk to Father about reducing the circle of your acquaintances."

"It is a matter too late," Elizabeth replied, giggling internally at using the word *matter*. "Ignorance of *the* matter cannot be regained."

"I want to go to the ball! There are never enough balls. The neighborhood is too small. I wish I'd had a season in London!"

"Do not worry." Lucas patted Maria on the shoulder. "I shall tell you every detail."

"Faith! You never remember anything." Maria crossed her arms with a huff. "I want to go."

"If it cheers you," Elizabeth said, "Mrs. Bennet hopes to keep your *mother* away, due to her horrid efforts to elevate her consequence above her natural consequence."

"Lady Lucas *was* pleased that she was listened to, and that the committee agreed it was a kindness to exclude *your* mother from the decision." Felicia wryly shaped her lips. "But it was entirely done in kindness."

"She *was* being kind." Lucas pushed his wife's arm. "You and Lizzy always seek hidden motives. It was *right* to ban her. No matter how good of a girl she is, a standard of decency must be maintained. I am my parent's child that far. This is Hertfordshire, not London where anyone might do as they please."

"Not in the London *I've* visited!" Elizabeth replied with a quick laugh.

Lucas rolled his eyes, but there was also that squire's mulishness about him.

Elizabeth suppressed the desire to argue that Georgiana should have been permitted to attend the assembly. It was wrong, of course, what Georgiana had done, but not such a terrible sin. Elizabeth recalled what Mama said about Lady Lucas being advanced with Charlotte when she married. "I will not argue with you, but even if she cannot be expected to be treated as an ordinary young Miss of twenty, even if you think she should be kept away from girls such as Maria—"

"Our *Lydia* is the one who should be removed from contact, as proven by our conversation here. If you believe there is no harm in Miss Darcy, I trust you. So long as such contact is limited and private — not intimacy or showing particular attention to Miss Darcy, I would not hesitate to allow Maria to meet the young lady."

With that Elizabeth knew she had her old friend. "You mean you do not think she must be kept from all the impressionable young women?"

"It is the men I worry for," Lucas replied solemnly. "She might make a great impression on the bachelors with her loose ways."

"And her thirty thousand."

"A yet greater impression with that."

"Will you then enter the den of iniquity our angelic Jane has transformed Longbourn into?" Elizabeth grinned.

"You seriously wish our presence?" Felicia asked.

"I do — I confirm Jane's report — no one ever trusts *her* when she describes a person as good, because she *is* Jane — nothing except sweetness and excess of shyness in Miss Darcy. The opposite of her brother; though the family connection can be traced."

"Is this to flirt with Mr. Darcy?" Lucas replied quickly, smirking.

He laughed at the way Elizabeth's mouth fell open. "Ha! Our Lizzy, at last. You want to impress him! Grown so desperate in your spinsterish years as to—"

"Mr. Lucas, to claim a woman — a spinster—"

"Darcy claimed you were a spinster."

"To claim a *respectable* old maid would actively seek to impress a gentleman."

"Fie! I saw how taken you were with him. I see through you!"

"Never."

"Oh yes! You were taken by him. Deuced tall fellow." Lucas held his hand up high above his head to demonstrate.

"I did not deny *that* — just your ability to see through me. I hide depths."

Felicia inserted, "She does."

All of them laughed. Lucas and Felicia looked at each other, and she nodded. Lucas said, "Lizzy, I dare say we'll be attending your dinner."

"Oh! I wish I could meet Miss Darcy," Maria exclaimed.

Mr. Lucas elbowed his sister. "Running to perdition with Lydia? Not today."

Chapter Ten

When Elizabeth returned home from her visit with the Lucases, she softly walked around the garden to the back entrance so that she might avoid her mother's questions about the meeting. Elizabeth was in a fine mood, and she had no desire to hear Mrs. Bennet's pique about Lady Lucas once more. She entered through the unlatched heavy green back door that led to Papa's study room.

A bluster of cold air came with her, rattling Papa's sheets of paper, and making him draw his unfashionable, but comfortable, brown woolen dressing gown tightly about himself.

"Fine walk?" Papa asked such a question most times too.

"Success!" Elizabeth almost bounced as she pulled off her lambskin gloves and coat and hung them on the rack next to the door. Papa would prefer if Elizabeth always used the front entrance, to avoid adding the cold to his room, but he did not begrudge her the opportunity to avoid questioning by Mama.

Elizabeth walked to the piped stove to stir up the fire and add a few new coals, letting her nose and cheeks warm from the cold. The weather had turned poor enough that Papa had begun having a fire always lit in his favorite room.

Papa picked his book up again and said as he thumbed through the pages, "John Lucas allows his bride to meet such a scandalous woman as Georgiana Darcy? I hope he knows what he is about."

"They have been married near four years now. Hardly newlyweds." Elizabeth enjoyed the flurry of sparks that flew towards her face like fireflies after she put the new coals onto the fire. She closed the door and held her hands close to the hot metal.

"Ahhh. Married long enough that he *hopes* she will be corrupted."

"By mine and Jane's Georgie?" Elizabeth laughed. "Disappointment waits him."

Elizabeth went to her chair and pulled her stationery out to place on the worn surface of her father's walnut desk. She had several letters to compose for her circle of friends. Most significantly she owed Charlotte and her Aunt Gardiner reports upon Mr. and Miss Darcy.

Elizabeth first scratched out a few paragraphs to Charlotte. She *had* met Lady Catherine's nephew who broke Anne's tender heart, Mr. Darcy, and his sister who *never* was spoken of, except in hushed tones (for Lady Catherine). Elizabeth added her impressions of Georgiana, and then a laughing sketch of the first night at the assembly when she met Mr. Darcy.

Halfway through the letter Elizabeth laid down her pen and nibbled on the back of her spiky feather. The memories were vivid. Arguing with Darcy, his handsome smile, the amusement that he managed to turn into anger, and then back into amusement. The sense she'd beaten him *that time* in their little verbal combat. Then other meetings.

He made her angry — actually angry.

But he was so handsome. So, *so* handsome.

Those smooth firm lips, the length of sideburns, the angular shape of his chin. The way his coat fell around his hips. The long tapering line of his legs. The shape of his fingers. Elizabeth shook herself. She needed to finish the letter to Charlotte.

Elizabeth did, and then she began a letter to Mrs. Gardiner. First she asked for news — was it true Mr. Gardiner had made Mr. Peake a full partner after only five years in his employ? What were the details of *this* news? Then Elizabeth wrote about meeting *the* Mr. Darcy of Pemberley. And her mind wandered.

Of course it wandered to Mr. Darcy. Elizabeth stared outside at the rattling branches of the oak tree, the withered hedges, waiting the return of a warm season to blossom into greenery once more. The bushes more like grey piles of sticks than plants. So beautiful. But her land's beauty gave her a dissatisfied ache: she had seen these hedges and this winter many times before.

There was some new desire in her being. Some sprig of verdure, and it ached for *more*. For different.

Elizabeth pushed that nameless sensation away, confused. Her mind settled on Mr. Darcy, and his tall, lean form. Little Anne leaping into his arms. He would make a fine father one day — hopefully to a son, since with his attitudes he should be given no control over a *girl*.

Georgiana turned out well, though quiet...

"Tuppence for your thoughts, my dear."

Elizabeth startled at her father's words. She blushed, realizing it had been some minutes and the fire had burned much lower since the last time she had moved.

"My mind was wandering."

"From whence to where?"

Elizabeth looked at the banked fire again. Red coals glowed in the grate. The air was lightly chilled, but Elizabeth was warm. She had been thinking of Mr. Darcy. As a parent. She blushed and shook her head. "No, I intend such knowledge to remain *private*."

"It must have been a serious matter to distract you from a *letter*."

"I *have* written industriously."

"Not a line for at least twenty minutes; if you *are* working, you do so much like the hare in the tale, industrially resting so you might outrun the tortoise in the end."

"No! It has not been near that long since I stopped writing."

Papa pointed to the tall old pendulum clock he kept next to one of the book cases in a corner of the room. Its brass arm hypnotically swung back and forth. "I timed you. Twenty minutes."

Elizabeth glanced at the black painted box of the clock. The hour was surprisingly late.

"What bothers you, Lizzy?"

"I am...concerned how our introduction of Georgiana shall go."

Papa raised his eyebrows and peered at her over his eyeglasses. "Really?"

Elizabeth blushed at her small dishonesty. Papa knew she had something else bothering her. "My friends will accept her." Elizabeth said confidently, "Everyone knows many people do...such things."

"Do they?"

"They do."

"But what concern were you really worrying upon?"

"Mama told me a story about Jane and your marriage that surprised me. Is it true?"

Mr. Bennet opened his mouth. He closed it and blushed. "No new subjects till we have exhausted the first. We were examining the matter that bothers *you*."

"I like Georgiana. Expecting manners to change so that a woman in her situation would be accepted at any assembly is absurd — such will never happen — but she deserves chances to dance, and dress well, and flirt with the young men. I will see to it that she has that opportunity!"

"But what were you *really* thinking on?"

Elizabeth sighed and scooted her chair closer to Papa. She could not hide from him. She took his hand and rubbed it.

"Is it *so* horrible?" He smiled warmly at her.

"Oh, Papa, I have become *bored*. That is horrible to you, since you are perfect."

"Bored! You?"

"Every week I do the same thing, and I have only realized it now. I walk the same winding paths, then read a book — usually of a sort I have read many times before — I meet the same persons. All tiresome! I wish a change."

"At your age! But you are so old. Most who have reached *your* age wish to live in unvaried retirement."

Elizabeth rolled her eyes.

"London? With the happiest will in the world I will give you the money for a good visit. There is no lack of variety *there*."

"London? In this season, with the fog? No! Besides the sort of people to be met in London! In the country one is bored by the sameness of people, but in Town one is horrified by the variety. And the constant balls and routs — I have tired of balls. I could never have *imagined* as a girl *that* could occur. But other than seeing Georgiana do well, I anticipate no pleasure for myself at the ball Jane is planning."

And dancing with Mr. Darcy, a low voice in her head sounded.

Mr. Bennet laughed. "Not even *balls*!"

"Oh, be still. I am an old enough old maid to value sleep over dancing till the light brightens the horizon whilst I am in the arms of a stumbling young man."

"Do all your young men stumble? Perhaps your problem has been *them*?"

Elizabeth laughed.

"To crave a difference after a period of some years is no strangeness." Mr. Bennet pulled off his spectacles and paused, looking at her intently. "You could visit one of your sisters; we could travel about, you and I. Explore some place you long to visit."

"You would do that for me?" Elizabeth smiled brightly. She added glowingly, "But I know you hate to travel, and I would not do that to you. My strange longing would not be satisfied."

"Have you thought of marriage?"

"Marriage?"

"I shall lose you one day, Lizzy, and I shall miss you exceedingly, but I will also be very happy, and—"

"Ridiculous! You will never lose me because I am too particular and strange in my ways. I would only take a husband who has all of your goodness, and who I can confide in as I do you."

"Pray, find a husband not *exactly* like your Papa. But you must choose carefully—"

"I'll not choose at all. No, I thank you kindly. I have never felt anything which would lead me to make such a wild choice."

"Not even that Mr. Darcy who you send those sharp glances at every time you meet?"

"Mr. Darcy!"

Papa smiled at her expression, but he titled his head in a demand she say more.

"You mean I send sharp retorts at him."

"With the glances."

"He is completely wrong. Completely — I would be ridiculous if I married such a man. With his decided opinions on women, and—"

Papa smirked at her, clearly enjoying the passion she was working herself into. His expression also doubted her pretense of disinterest.

"I may like to look at him — I confess that — I may like to flirt with him, but know the difference between a *small* infatuation and love. What I feel for *him* is not love."

"One may lead to another."

"Ha! He would be quite resistant to my charms, even if I wished to catch him."

"I considered his arguments with you a form of determined courtship."

Elizabeth laughed. "No, no, no. And I would be as poor a match for him as he for I. He wants a woman quite the opposite of me. Sweet; tender; easily ordered. A woman who argued with him at every turn would never do for *that* man."

"You have thought about what woman would do for Mr. Darcy then."

Elizabeth blushed. "I determined that she was my opposite in every point."

"If Mr. Darcy desired a woman who always made the pretense of sweetness and obedience, he would have been wriggling in the Parson's mousetrap many years past."

"Yes," Elizabeth replied sourly. She hated the idea of Darcy being married to anyone but her.

That was not good.

Her feelings were moving beyond simple admiration for his form and frankness into a real attraction.

Elizabeth was a reasonable creature, and she would not permit herself to fall for a man such as Mr. Darcy. No, she would not.

"It would have made his happiness, had he married such a woman." Elizabeth said, "Alas, his happiness is nothing to me."

"As a fellow human being, a kind person would care for his happiness, while an infatuated woman would make pretense of caring not at all."

This deserved same particular gesture of disdain. Elizabeth reached her arm over and moved the collection of essays Papa had been reading to the opposite side of the desk from him. Then for emphasis she softly placed it on the ground.

"Lizzy," Papa replied with a mild mournful tone.

"I confessed already a *small* infatuation. No need to tease me further."

He shrugged and smiled.

"I am too wise to be trapped."

"Lizzy, I beg you not to depend upon your *wisdom*. You have never been in love, and—"

"Not *this*. I hear enough of how a woman in the grip of a passion cannot reason from *him*."

"Reason always thinks itself reasonable, while it justifies the hidden reasons of the heart."

Elizabeth picked up the book and handed it back to her father.

"At least, Lizzy," he waited to speak until she looked at him, "I beg you to be in no hurry to know either your own or his heart. Do not make any enduring decision in haste."

"I promise."

Papa's expression relaxed. He smiled at her. "Back then to books and letters. If you want to travel from Longbourn, anywhere, tell me — funds and my presence are on call."

"That is the sweetest." Elizabeth patted her father's arm. "You will always be my dearest man."

"Will I?" He had placed his spectacles back on, and he now tilted them down his nose, and smirked at her.

"Always."

Chapter Eleven

With the meal past, Darcy was decidedly surprised how *well* the dinner at Longbourn with Georgiana had gone. Mrs. Lucas and Mrs. Goulding immediately took to Georgiana, and while Mr. Lucas insisted on winking and teasing Darcy about the day that they had met and how he had insulted Miss Bennet, Mr. Lucas was an intelligent man who rather reminded him in some ways of Bingley without the shine of sophistication that the time he spent in the city gave Bingley.

Georgiana was happy. That was what mattered.

Elizabeth sat next to Darcy at dinner, teasing him regularly, but she had real friendliness in her manner for the first time. *He* felt more friendliness as well. Even if the plan to make Georgiana the center of a ball held by Bingley before Christmas did not succeed, he had never seen Georgiana like this, chattering with new social acquaintances.

The men did not remain gathered in the dining room for long, and Mr. Bennet led them back to the drawing room after less than half of an hour.

Soon as he entered the drawing room, Mr. Lucas looked about and clapped. "A dance, a dance! We must have a dance! You do not mind, Mr. Darcy? There is no entertainment which crowns civilized society better than a dance."

"I *can* enjoy a private dance," Mr. Darcy smirked, "though the art also is practiced widely amongst the uncivilized."

Mr. Lucas laughed good heartedly. "I conceived you to be no great friend of the art when you resisted the temptation presented by all our local beauties, *even* the elderly ones, at the assembly."

"Mr. Lucas learnt his philosophy about dance from his father." Elizabeth tapped both Darcy and Mr. Lucas on the shoulders. "I forsee a problem — we did not hire musicians. Who must sit out so they can play?"

"Lord!" Mrs. Bennet said, "I wish I had learned, so I could indulge you. I am far too old *now* to dance. Lizzy, you did learn. You ought to display."

"Mama! You are yet young enough. And me play?" Elizabeth laughed, her lips entrancingly wide. "Not with any skill. But I sit if demanded."

"Lizzy *can* play well," Jane said to Georgiana and Darcy.

"I doubt it not," Darcy replied. Rather than looking at Elizabeth, Darcy looked at Georgiana. She had ceased to play after Wickham seduced her. He missed his sister's playing, but he had never begged her to resume, because the first time he suggested her playing, she had become unhappy and made her disinterest clear.

"Mrs. Goulding will happily play the first reels." Mr. Goulding said, "There is only room for a pattern of four couples, I shall turn the pages; we will happily watch you all turn about."

"Then I shall need to dance." Georgiana tugged at the sleeve of Darcy's dinner coat and half whispered. "I do not know... I do not wish the Gouldings to need to lose the pleasure. Perhaps, I should..."

"Pray, is something amiss?" Elizabeth looked at his sister. "Georgie, do you wish something other than dancing? The party is for you, and if you would rather cards or conversation—"

"Oh! No! I wish to see you all dance."

"*That* would hardly make me a good host, if I permitted you to sacrifice your *own* pleasure. Besides Frances must sit out to play the piano."

Georgiana stared at the pattern of twined flowers and leaves in the rug.

Elizabeth added, "We need you for the pattern. It shall be cards otherwise."

"I cannot dance in such a group! I never have."

Mrs. Goulding smiled kindly at her. "You must, for it shall be a great disappointment to us all if you do not."

Elizabeth looked at Darcy. He somehow understood what she wished him to do, and he felt an odd annoyance. He'd hoped to ask *Elizabeth* for a dance. But if they continued for a few sets, he would get his opportunity.

"Miss Darcy" — He formally bowed to his sister — "Pray, I beg you, it would be my deep delight if I might have this first dance tonight from you."

She giggled. "It would be an honor, fair gentleman." She smiled a little more confidently. "Though I *have* danced with you before so it shall not be such an adventure."

"Never in company."

Georgiana rose, and took Darcy's hand.

The other couples arranged themselves into matched pairs, while Mr. Bennet and Mrs. Bennet sat benignantly on the chairs that had been cleared to the side, and Mrs. Goulding seated herself with a graceful gesture upon the piano's dark black varnished bench, with her husband next to her, smiling, and arranging the white sheets of music. With a flex of her wrists she started a pretty rollicking Irish air.

Despite his concern for Georgiana, Darcy could not stop looking at Elizabeth. Her rich, healthy brown hair bounced in time to her athletic steps. There was such gracefulness in her movements.

When the set was done Georgiana laughed and smiled. "That was a delight."

She immediately sat down, losing the opportunity for any of the other gentlemen to ask to switch with her.

Seeing that this only left three couples which was not enough for the pattern, Mr. Bennet pulled Mrs. Bennet to her feet from where they had sat and watched the first set. "You shall not escape the dance, my dear."

"Oh, Mr. Bennet! At my age!"

"You are yet a fine-looking woman, and I have not forgotten *entirely* how."

Darcy had not marked Mr. Bennet as the sort of man to push himself and his wife to dance. But this definitely freed him from a need to partner with Georgiana for the second dance.

He bowed to Elizabeth and asked her hand. Mr. Smith who had danced with Elizabeth during the first set also sat down. He was a man whose wife was away for a long visit to her declining mother's bedside, and who had been invited to make up a full set of couples. Elizabeth took Darcy's hand. Mr. Bingley and Mr. Lucas switched wives for the set.

Darcy and Elizabeth stood, with his hand in hers, only their gloves betwixt their hands. Darcy felt giddy and odd, like a lad who had conjured the courage to ask a girl he'd been fascinated by for the month past for her favor.

Mrs. Goulding began a melodious English tune. They danced the cotillion. At last he was dancing with Elizabeth.

He was lost. Her hands, the spinning, the way they looked at each other. There was none of the comparative privacy of a large ball in this small pattern, and Mr. and Mrs. Bennet were among the couples. Darcy was not sure what to say.

"Come, Mr. Darcy, we must have some conversation." Elizabeth grinned at him, her face lit up by the blazing candles.

"I agree, and merely delayed to speak as I sought about in my mind for a phrase to begin with that would go down into posterity with the eclat of a proverb."

"You did! I have in the past sought to construct an unforgettable statement as well — no need to worry! *One* phrase spoken by you shall be heard by posterity. I shall repeat the tale of your apology to me til we are both old and grey."

Darcy coughed.

Mrs. Bennet said, "I heard you, Lizzy. Do not run on with everyone as you do with Mr. Bennet."

"Ah, but Mr. Darcy, he knows I am *old*."

Everyone laughed at her.

Mrs. Goulding called out, "Laughter? No!" She began a jig which had them jumping from side to side until everyone collapsed breathlessly. Mr. Bennet had to retire several minutes before the other gentlemen with a laugh about his age, but Mrs. Bennet paced them til the end.

Darcy was surprised by that.

Everyone sat on the sofas that had been pushed to the edge of the room to open space for the dancers.

What did Elizabeth mean by her reference to his rudeness at that ball? Did it mean she was yet offended, or did she mean to refer to a shared past, and an intention of a shared future — for if she expected to have nothing to do with him when she was old and grey, there would be no reason to repeat the embarrassing story.

Elizabeth smiled at him when she noticed his regard.

"Miss Bennet, did you ever create a proverb?"

"What?"

"You said you would attempt to find some statement that would be remembered forever — did you succeed?"

Mr. Bennet laughed. "She said things *I* will recall always."

"Oh?" Darcy leaned towards Mr. Bennet. "I would be delighted to hear such stories."

"No embarrassing stories. No!"

"What about when you stole a Christmas pudding?"

Elizabeth buried her face in her hands and shook her head. "I cannot convince you to withhold the story?"

"Are you so pusillanimous as to fear it?"

Mr. Lucas laughed. "I can speak it if Mr. Bennet will not — I have heard the story told several times."

Elizabeth groaned. "And if Mr. Darcy has no interest in the tale and would prefer a different topic of conversation?"

"I assure you," Mr. Darcy said, "I am quite ready, nay eager, to listen to any embarrassing tale about Miss Bennet."

He winked at her and Elizabeth laughed.

Mr. Bennet said, "This was when — oh fourteen. Lizzy had been reading Plato, and a few days before Christmas she had a desperate craving for one of the puddings and could not wait—"

Mrs. Bennet said, "Our Christmas puddings are of the finest quality. Everyone in the neighborhood agrees. The Bennets have made the finest Christmas puddings for generations."

"Which is *why* Lizzy stole one from the pantry." Mr. Bennet continued, "I expected to punish her, as she knew they were not to be touched till Christmas Day. But Lizzy sat in a corner of the house, with a completely empty plate, not even the crumbs left—"

"Unfair!" Elizabeth, laughing, interrupted her father. "There were crumbs."

"—not even the barest crumbs left upon her plate, and she groaned piteously. The poor girl looked sick — and well she should be. An entire pudding. A fair-sized object. Lizzy clutched her stomach and she looked mournfully at me, and said" — Darcy watched Elizabeth blush prettily — "Papa, two horses draw the human soul, one full of reason, and the other which solely desires pudding. And I must strive to only give rein to that horse which will not give me such an awful tummy."

"Must you include 'tummy' every time you relate the story? It is a quite...childish word."

Mr. Bennet grinned. "No need to punish her; upon hearing such a statement, I knew the crime had become its own punishment."

Elizabeth rolled her eyes. "Mr. Darcy, I entreat you, do not build your *entire* impression of me upon such stories."

Mr. Lucas stood again. "The time for another dance."

"I am exhausted," Mr. Bennet said. "I shall retire and leave the floor to the younger blood. You do not want me and Mrs. Bennet to hover about the entire night — Elizabeth and Jane can host you admirably. Lizzy, do not light fires to the draperies to stave off boredom. The fire might spread to the books, and we would be left in the cold tomorrow."

"No promises, Papa. No promises. You ought to stay out if you wish to protect your drapes."

"Nonsense." Mrs. Bennet giggled, her color high and enthused from her dance. "You are quite old enough, the lot of you—"

"Even me, Mama? Unmarried as I am?"

Mrs. Bennet stopped and frowned. "Now, Lizzy, do not go on pointing it out to everyone. It does you no credit to refer to your age."

"I assure you, Mrs. Bennet, your daughter could pass with ease for a girl of twenty." Mr. Darcy bowed in her direction, wanting to do something to mollify the older woman.

Mrs. Bennet smiled in surprise at Darcy. "That is very kind of you to say."

"Goodness I hope 'tis a polite lie," Elizabeth replied. "Georgie, you are a pet, but I would not wish to be mistaken for so young as you."

"I am not so very young. And I have lived a great deal, and—"

"Youth, always believing itself to be maturity. I shudder to imagine how my aged self, when I am at *your* stage of life, dear Mama, will consider my current pretensions to wisdom. I quite despise, with just cause, myself at twenty."

"I," Mr. Darcy replied, "have a high opinion of *myself* at twenty."

"Heavens! That terrifies myself more than anything." Elizabeth grinned at him.

Mr. and Mrs. Bennet retired from the room. Mrs. Goulding returned to the piano, but Elizabeth pushed her away. "No, no, no!

Go. Dance. My pleasure this evening has been had." Elizabeth smiled brilliantly, and Darcy thought she looked at him as she said that "—Have your turn. I do not practice *so* much, but I can turn my way around a piano, a little. Mr. Darcy, I demand *you* to turn my pages for me — if the master of Pemberley can manage such a task."

"For a lady, I can manage anything."

"But what about me?" Georgiana bit her lip. "I must dance with Fitzwilliam to complete the set."

Elizabeth glanced at Mr. Lucas and then at Darcy. Both gentlemen gave small nods, and Elizabeth said, "You shall dance with Mr. Lucas for the next, and perhaps Mr. Goulding after."

"But..." Georgiana looked at Darcy, pleadingly.

"Do go on," he said. "I would like to watch you in a dance."

She looked at Mr. Lucas. "I never have... except Fitzwilliam, and... the instructors."

"It shall be my deep honor, and it shall also be my pleasure." He took her hand and charmingly brushed his lips over it.

The couples who were to dance lined up; Elizabeth looked at Darcy with her flashing eyes. "Pray, turn my pages. I need assistance."

"With alacrity, charming mademoiselle."

Elizabeth's lips twisted, and Darcy blushed.

He shook his head. "I greatly suspect that failed to be the prettiest speech you have ever heard."

Elizabeth sat down on the stool, and patted the seat next to him. "Do you intend to fish for a compliment?"

"Whatever vanity I possess — we established early that I *do* possess vanity — my dandyish or rakish banter are outside its wide scope."

He sat next to her, their legs brushing against each other. Darcy had *never* been so aware of anything as he experienced the closeness of her body. The smell of her rose perfume made his chest feel light.

She flipped through the notebook of copied music sheets, written in a neat hand. "You can follow the music well enough to tell when to change the page?"

"I can," Darcy replied, studiously not looking at where their legs touched. He was familiar with this sort of task from the days when Georgiana still played.

"Do you think all flirtations are rakish?" Elizabeth asked, shifting her weight in a way that pressed her knee slightly into the springy muscles of his leg. "Determinedly disapproving of the greatest feminine pleasure. A man who has *every* woman desperate for him, due to his *pile* can afford to disdain flirtation. Lesser men must — ah here it is."

Elizabeth looked up to make sure the couples were assembled in their positions, and she began to play. After she had played for long enough to have a feel for the tune, Elizabeth said cautiously, in a distracted voice, "You who have heard the finest of performers must disdain my petty efforts."

"Lovely. Entirely lovely."

Elizabeth's fingers stumbled, and she smiled widely. Unconsciously, Darcy thought, she pressed her thigh further into his. "I thought you disdained flirtation. And this is the easy part."

"You fill it with feeling."

"You must say that to all of the pretty girls playing music."

"I never say that."

Elizabeth flushed.

Darcy said with a smile, "Is it you who now searches for a compliment?"

"You *are* a charmer. Do you really never compliment a girl's playing?"

"Not with meaning. Except...Georgiana."

Elizabeth did not say anything at first, filled with the effort of a particularly fast part of the music. "Georgie can play? Jane said nothing of it."

"She does not anymore."

While Elizabeth's eyes did not leave the sheet of music, he thought there was sympathy in her manner.

Darcy swallowed. "She would, in the past, before Wickham. She had an extraordinary genius for music."

"What made her to stop?"

"I know not. She chose to not play. I always took great pleasure listening to her... She never played again."

"You wish she would begin to play again?"

"Only if she found joy in the performance. Not for the sake of acquiring impressive accomplishments."

"That...I approve. Papa always was much like that with what he expected us to learn. We might choose what we enjoyed instead of what society dictated."

Darcy shook his head with a smile. "I did not mean that as a suggestion to anarchy in studies. A child should both show application and be directed by her guardians."

Elizabeth laughed. "What accomplishments matter, if the impressive ones do not?"

"A sense of character. Firmness to do what is right. A care for children. The improvement of the mind through extensive reading." at Elizabeth's mischievous smile, Darcy immediately added, "Not Plato, I note."

"Of course not."

"But the piano... Music is not important, except as a fountain of pleasure for the player and the listener. A woman who performs exquisitely possesses no more *substance* than one who only plays ill."

"Do you refer to me?" Elizabeth giggled, making the tune flounder into missed notes.

Bingley called out, "Stop flirting with our pianist, Darcy. We need her to keep the rhythm."

"You can see," said she to Darcy, after Elizabeth had recovered the tune, "why *I* am relieved to hear your praise of women who play ill."

"You wish me to like you?" He meant to say it teasingly. But there was a desperate note to his voice, as though her answer mattered.

Her eyes glanced at him quickly, dark and bright and deep. They were aware of each other.

They sat close, and her leg pressed against his, and her silky dress rubbed against his wool coat. She would not have begged him to dance, she would not have ordered him to sit beside her, if she did not like him.

Darcy's heart pounded in his ears.

Neither said anything. Darcy watched Georgiana again. She brightly smiled as she was at last able to use her carefully trained knowledge of the art of dancing. She was happy, and he had not been the one to care for her.

"It is my fault. I realize that now."

Elizabeth cocked her head as she continued to play.

"Georgiana's isolation. I never made the effort to find people who would acknowledge her."

"You believed it impossible."

Darcy flipped the page for Elizabeth. "You and Jane prove the possibility."

"That is hardly *your* fault."

"You mean that you succeeded where I failed to try?"

"A failure of imagination is not a moral failing."

"My duty is to ensure her happiness."

"She is happy *now*."

"I cannot but think of how many years wasted — how her life would have been different, if I diligently looked for society that would accept her and Anne. I feel a dreadful guilt."

"One should strive to remember the past only as it gives one pleasure."

"My guilt is too grand for *that*. I do not enjoy social gatherings in general."

Elizabeth smiled at the piano as she played. "I know."

"After my inexcusable rudeness, you must — too many people pressing round about, who I have no or little acquaintance with. I far prefer solitude — or to be with my dearest companions at evenings."

"My favorite location in the whole of this world" — Elizabeth's hands slowed, and the music became sweeter — "is a bare twenty feet from where we sit. My father's library, when he occupies it. He and I need not talk, not at all. To sit next to him with a book, to look out the window, and drink from a steaming cup of chocolate or tea. I understand your yearning."

Darcy closed his eyes. Elizabeth's music interacted with his soul. She lacked technical perfection but there was a sensibility in her timing, a feel for the emotion, which made her playing beautiful. Darcy imagined her rhythm as a brilliant dawning of the sun, lighting the clouds reddish and causing a beam of light to burst through and illuminate a forested hill in the distance.

He sighed. "Georgiana's exclusion from society gave me an excuse to disdain the company of all except close friends, while making a pretense of a noble sacrifice for her sake. I was misanthropic and selfish — and I hurt my sister."

"Nonsense."

"She was denied all opportunity for society due to my selfishness."

"Would you have endured a thousand unpleasant evenings with strangers begging for your attention for her care?" Elizabeth paused for emphasis. "You would have. I know your character sufficiently to say *that*."

The dance ended, and Elizabeth stopped playing and bowed to the couples on the floor, who clapped for her. She looked to Darcy, her deep eyes touching his. "You need not feel poorly. Your failure, in so far as you failed, was a lack of imagination, a lack of a genius for understanding your fellow man — one ought never feel poorly for lacking any genius. We, none of us, choose the talents we are possessed by, merely what we shall do with them."

Georgiana ran up to them. "Lizzy, fine playing! Did you watch me, Fitzwilliam? You did."

"I did."

Mr. Lucas walked up. "I return Miss Darcy to you, Mr. Darcy. She has been a fine partner for the set."

"The evening is not over yet. I have another round of playing in me. And then," Elizabeth called to Mrs. Lucas, "it shall be your turn to display."

"Me?" The woman pressed her hands against her cheeks. "But I am not even the equal of *you*."

"Not even the equal? That seems more a hidden insult than a hidden request for a compliment."

"I liked your playing very much," Georgiana said.

"I am pleased to possess *one* defender." Elizabeth archly looked at Darcy. "Though my vanity lacks a musical turn."

This time Mr. Goulding partnered with Georgiana as the couples lined up.

"I have seldom heard any performer I enjoyed so much as you, Miss Bennet. That is truth."

"Lies! A sweet one, but I am not deceived by my talent."

"Talent is *not* the lone determinant of the enjoyment given by a performance. Pleasure in the performer can add pleasure to the performance."

Elizabeth's cheeks pinked. Darcy thought he was improving his skills at rakish banter.

"I am glad Georgie is coming out of her shell."

"I owe her present delight to you. It makes me feel...as though I am less than I should be."

"You care deeply for her."

"That is not enough. It is my duty, *mine* to make her happy. I was too suspicious of the people around. Motivations, I always questioned. Always doubting, always worried."

"Georgie's happiness is not your duty alone. She must live her own life."

Darcy enjoyed sitting next to Elizabeth and listening to her play. There was a peacefulness being with her that soothed him.

When Elizabeth finished her piece and shook out her hands, she pressed her hand onto Darcy's leg for a briefest second. "Your sister is happy. You have guarded her as you best you could, and that has been good. Do not despise yourself."

She stood.

Darcy missed the pressure of Elizabeth's body against his leg, as if something had been amputated from him.

Following this Mrs. Lucas took her turn at the piano, and Darcy danced with Jane while Elizabeth partnered with Mr. Lucas. Then the servants brought out ices to cool them down.

Darcy hoped to talk to Elizabeth, but she approached Georgiana and pulled her to the side. They stood in a corner, with little blue-veined porcelain bowls of ice cream balanced elegantly in their hands. Georgiana slowly took bites with her small silver spoon, as Elizabeth forgot the delicacy and spoke softly, but persistently to Georgiana.

His sister looked down and said something. Elizabeth exclaimed, "Nonsense!" in a voice that carried to Darcy.

He could not stop staring. Elizabeth was too absorbed with his sister to notice. The curve of her neck was lovely, and the dress she wore puffed around her breasts, making the hourglass of her waist stand out vividly.

Georgiana looked at him, and Elizabeth's gaze followed. Helplessly, Darcy walked towards them, and Elizabeth whispered something into Georgiana's ear. As he reached them, his sister nodded with a nervous smile.

"What matter do you two lovely creatures conspire about?"

Georgiana looked at him with shining eyes. Elizabeth said, "You shall discover our conspiracy in a few minutes — you *can* wait such length?"

"No."

Georgiana looked at him worriedly. "I hope you will be—"

Elizabeth put her hand over his sister's mouth. "Shush, Georgie. Even if he *cannot* wait, he must. I hope he shall survive."

"I shall not."

Georgiana laughed. She smiled and stood taller. "I hope you shall be happy."

What the deuce were they planning?

After everyone had finished their ices and recovered from the exertion of steady dancing, Elizabeth stepped to the middle of the drawing room and clapped her hands sharply, taking the place of the hostess now that her mother and father had retired for the night.

She commanded a room very well.

"We must have at least one more set of dancing. Miss Darcy agreed to play this time, so that everyone but our dear Jane, who never did learn" — the girl in question laughed tinklingly at her sister's teasing — "has a turn to display at the piano."

Darcy was only half sure he had heard right. His sister had agreed to play?

Georgiana flushed and looked down, but she nodded.

Elizabeth said to Darcy, "You need turn pages for her. I understand it has been some time since she played a proper dance."

Elizabeth had talked Georgiana into it. Most likely that had been easy. Elizabeth had not been scared to bring up the matter, and she had cut the Gordian knot of his terror of hurting his sister by suggesting she play.

Georgiana and Darcy sat next to each other on the hard mahogany bench in front of the piano. Darcy whispered, "Are you certain?"

Georgiana did not look at him, instead she hovered her fingers over the brilliant black and white of the keys. She brushed the tips of her fingers softly over the raised black keys, without making a noise. "Do you truly miss my playing? You never said."

"There is no player I ever prefer to hear."

Georgiana ran her fingers through the scales. At first her elegant thin fingers hesitated. She needed to remember. Then she ran her hands up and down lightly, her fingers a blur, almost confidently.

Nervously Darcy nearly asked if she was sure she could still play. It had been so many years. The couples lined up, the silk dresses of the women draping to the floors, while the gentlemen's breeches clung tightly to their thighs, and the white cravats gleamed in the candlelight. The speed and facility of Georgiana's scales grew, and she stared at the keys closely,

Perhaps she stared at them to avoid thoughts of the audience, rather than to help herself.

Then she switched from the end of a scale into a slow, light dance which had been popular years earlier. Georgiana practiced the delicate tune again and again. She had loved it.

Tears began at the edges of Darcy's eyes.

The couples walked through the steps, and Georgiana's facility with the music returned, and the pace of the keys sped up, and she inserted more difficult bits.

His sister closed her eyes, swaying slightly from side to side, with a soft smile on her face. She completely ignored the sheet of music he had brought out for her, instead using a distant memory that never failed.

There was water in his eyes, and the gentleman in Darcy needed to hide such evidence of emotion. He was not alone. The room was full of others. He wiped at his eyes quickly, surreptitiously, looking around to see if anyone noticed.

Elizabeth's eyes were on him, as she was in the far part of the figure. He felt so grateful to her.

She softly smiled at him, and then the dance continued and she stepped through the circle so that she was no longer looking at him. As he watched her form walk through the steps of the music something deep changed in Darcy.

Everything had been clouded before. The sky was now clear, and a brilliant sun shone down upon him, illuminating his soul in its brilliant glow. A voice, firm and confident, spoke from the innermost part of his heart, "You are going to marry that woman."

It was absurd, caught at his age, by a woman who, while beautiful, was not the most beautiful, with a modest dowry, and mixed connections.

Yet caught he was.

She was kind; she was lovely; she was brilliant; she accepted and helped his sister freely; she spoke her own mind; she was truly accomplished, in the ways which mattered most. He admired her entirely, despite her dissimilarity to what he had naively believed his female ideal to be. He never imagined himself falling in love with an unconventional, learned woman. But he had, and he was more completely happy than ever before in his life.

Elizabeth Bennet held Fitzwilliam Darcy's heart, and now he had to gain hers.

Chapter Twelve

The next morning was a brilliant, crisp day. Despite the season it seemed as if every cloud had been driven from the sky, and there was nothing but the glorious ability to see for miles. Elizabeth wrapped herself warmly in her favorite red jacket and shawl as she walked up to knock on the entrance to Netherfield. She had come to call on Georgiana and Jane.

Strange exaltation sat in her stomach. She did not understand her mood, even though last night had been a great success. Mr. Darcy was a fine dancer. She was now piercing through to his soul. He was so...vulnerable. He took so much upon himself, expected so much of himself, and he was miserable when he did not achieve it.

They liked each other greatly.

She could host his dinners and balls — he had *said* he was happy to do such things for those he loved. Nothing too grand, not too often. Darcy was not the sort who would like many grand entertainments, to impress the whole neighborhood, in the way of Bingley or Mrs. Bennet. But he had *liked* meeting new persons and beginning to become their friends last night.

He liked John Lucas and Felicia; surely that must be a sign.

Again. She was again imagining marrying Mr. Darcy. She'd told herself three times this morning to stop. She was losing control of herself. She could not stop thinking about him.

She *would* be rational.

When Mrs. Bennet had stood in the passageway, decked out in as much lace as a dressmaker's mannequin, to go out for the morning, Elizabeth had begged her to head in the direction of Netherfield so that she could call on Georgiana and Jane.

Elizabeth hoped Mr. Darcy would be gone, so that she could have a little bit of peace in which to question Georgiana about her brother. Georgiana would surely tell some story about him that would let Elizabeth put that *man* out of her head forever and return to the peaceful calm tenor of her life with her father.

Like she wanted to.

The carriage ride took its time. Three miles could not be traveled in a minute, even with a jangling chaise and a dry, cold day with neither ice nor mud. They called on two acquaintances on the way. Mrs. Bennet intended to use the day to crow like a cawing rooster to everyone about how well Georgiana had been received by John Lucas and his wife — the children of the knight — and the Gouldings, such an old and respected family.

Mrs. Bennet also bragged about the ball that Bingley planned to announce in a day or two for Georgiana. On account of Lady Lucas's interference with the assembly committee, Mrs. Bennet felt any success Georgiana achieved more keenly than the girl herself.

The second friend they called upon lived only a half mile from Netherfield. This was not more than a modest walk, so Elizabeth set off to the house alone. Mrs. Bennet exclaimed, as Elizabeth left, "Tell Jane greetings! And sweet Bennet too! But I shall not call today. I am far too busy, 'tis more important to finish the matter once started. After last night, everyone should hear from me. I warrant I *can* get Georgiana invited to every house without a young daughter. Except Lady Hampton — I do not like enthusiasts. They say she is low church."

Elizabeth left and started the walk along the hard dirt road shaded by bare oak trees with a smile. She rather doubted that her mother *knew* what the difference between high and low church was, but she certainly knew that being low church was not the *thing*.

Maybe Darcy would think her strange and forward to *walk* to the home, even though her sister was its mistress. At present Jane was overshadowed: Netherfield meant Darcy.

"All alone? I am disappointed in Jane. And your brother." Those were the first words Elizabeth spoke upon being led into the nursery where Georgiana supervised a game played between Bennet and Anne.

Both children leapt from their finely carved set of backgammon. "Lizzy!"

She laughed and picked each up with a giggling swoop to kiss them on the foreheads before placing them down. "Abandoned by all? Terrible."

"I am quite happy. Quite." She smiled. "Jane needed to make calls this morning, and my brother is quite used to how I sometimes prefer solitude."

"Goodness, a hint I ought keep this visit short?"

"No!"

Elizabeth laughed.

"I *am* happy to see you. You see, I had opportunity to think already — roll the dice, Bennet, it is your turn — *your* company is always welcome."

"Only mine?"

"Certainly not *only*."

"Does your brother often leave you alone? I imagined he would hover, to ensure you did not waste time on fruitless, overly learned pursuits. To ensure you do not read sentimental novels, or the like."

There. Subtle.

Georgiana could not possibly gather from that question that she was probing for a serious purpose. Which was to confirm it would be a terrible idea to marry him, if he should ask. Which he would not.

"I am so happy!" Georgiana bounced on the stuffed sofa, unfortunately ignoring the question. "I am exceedingly eager for Bingley's ball."

"It will be a little ball, do not expect one of those glittering parties in London with a thousand pair, all titled."

"Lizzy, the entire peerage is much less than a thousand persons."

Elizabeth blinked. "It is?"

"Yes. You can count the entries in Debrett's."

"Does that include the baronets? They are listed separately by Debrett in *The Baronetage*."

"Uhhh." Georgiana's face twisted in an odd expression. "I am not certain...no not the baronets. I did not count them."

"Gracious, Georgie, *when* did you count all the entries in *The Peerage*?"

The girl blushed and waved her hands side to side. "I liked Mr. Lucas and Mrs. Goulding so much. So kind! I admire them both. And thank you, thank you, thank you for encouraging me to play — Fitzwilliam was so happy — he cried a little. I swear. I'd never seen him do such a thing."

Elizabeth had seen him cry and wipe his eyes. It was...surprising. It filled her with something, strong and strange.

"I had so much *fun*..."

Elizabeth grinned at her sunnily beaming friend. Georgiana was really adorable, with her long neck and coltish pose. She looked so young, despite having a child and twenty years of age. Her eyes brimmed with enthusiasm.

The two children finished the round of backgammon, Anne winning. They begged permission to open the chests of toys across the room. The women smiled and shooed the children off.

"I felt odd, almost like I was in a dream, to be part of a dinner party. It is my fault Fitzwilliam never entertains."

"He told me directly yesterday that he does not enjoy parties."

"Did he? I...I can barely remember before...Wickham. He opened the house oftener. Last night was great fun, so he *must* wish to entertain more often."

He had enjoyed it last night. When she hosted entertainments for him at Pemberley, she would arrange matters so that he could have sufficient solitude to still enjoy his evening.

That deuced *ridiculous* notion again. Darcy and she would not marry.

Marry? Ha! No, she did not want to marry him. Him? She definitely did not. "Mr. Darcy chose not to entertain more. *His* failings are his own. Every one of us has failings enough to feel poorly about without addition."

"Not *you*."

Elizabeth laughed. "I have failings enough — I refuse to feel poorly about them."

"Why have you never married?"

Elizabeth blinked at the question. "Do not imply *that* is a fault!"

"Oops." Georgiana looked down and studied Anne and Bennet, who were engaged in some negotiation involving a wooden soldier Anne held, and a painted pink wooden pony, with a strand of real horsehair for the mane and tail that Bennet held. "I see where your joke came from — I am only curious."

"You speak as if it is *my* choice. A man must ask."

Georgiana had a superb skeptical look.

"I have, I confess, had suitors." Elizabeth smiled widely. She could convince him to ask. Elizabeth added in an airy voice, "A fair few, admirers ardent. Alas, none who I wished to wed."

Georgiana rolled her eyes. "*You* must have had rich and handsome men after your hand."

"Handsome men, I have had a few." Elizabeth winked. "And one or two with wealth. Alas, 'twas my misfortune that those with wealth had not looks."

"I do not believe you." Georgiana laughed. "There must have been *some* suitor both eligible *and* handsome. You have a sufficient dowry, and you are *so* pretty."

"Flatterer."

"Anyone can see it." Georgiana blushed. "My brother sees it."

Mr. Darcy thought her very pretty? She knew he did. But somehow Georgiana noticing that he noticed her… something twisted in Elizabeth's guts. Like a kitten chasing butterflies in her stomach.

Bennet and Anne ran up, with Bennet lifting his arms for Elizabeth to pick him up. "Look what Anne brought!" He held up a beautifully carved horse. "I want one like it too. Tell Mama for me."

Elizabeth laughed.

Anne said in an eager voice, "Uncle Will gave it! He can! He can get one for Bennet."

Elizabeth kissed her nephew seating on her lap. "Mr. Darcy would be happy to acquire such a toy for you."

Elizabeth looked at Georgiana. "The wrong man is worse than not marrying at all. I demand to be seen as an equal and never expected to act contrary to what I wish due to my husband's whim or will. A hopeless matter. I expect too much."

"No, no! — You shall find such love! I know! But, Lizzy, you are so clever, you dress so smartly; you are always *lovely*. Men always watch at you and stare as you speak."

Elizabeth thought of the girl's brother. Her heart pounded, her face flushed. She saw Darcy looking at her.

"You have! You have had a suitor you liked very much indeed!"

"Is *that* such a surprise? Men are handsome as a sex. Their best excuse for their ample failings."

Georgiana giggled. "My brother is not so bad."

"Nay, he is the worst."

"Tell me! Tell me about this man."

"I shall not."

"Please…as friends? What happened to him?"

"I do not know. Not every story is over. I doubt I could make this man happy."

"You should marry him! You deserve to be happy. You could make anyone happy." Was there something meaningful in Georgiana's look? As though she thought Elizabeth was thinking of her brother.

Elizabeth exclaimed. "Enough of *me*! 'Tis *your* turn to be teased. What suitors have you had?"

"Me! I could have none."

"Ridiculous."

"Lizzy! Everyone knows." Georgiana gestured at Anne, who was happily trotting the wooden horse while Bennet kept a soldier seated upon it.

"Fiddle. Most women with a child like yours marry sooner or later."

"What do you mean? I am a stain upon the family honor; I was probably switched at birth with a peasant girl who—"

Elizabeth laughed. "Switched at birth! How absurd. Who said that."

"My Aunt, Lady Catherine, said so, and she "

"Lady Catherine! Of course. You don't believe *her*."

"Well...no." Georgiana smiled at Elizabeth's amusement.

"I can hear that old monster saying that in my head. She has a way about her — a memorable voice."

"You know Lady Catherine?"

"My dearest friend married her parson — he is her ladyship's greatest admirer. Charlotte is content, nonetheless."

"Does...does Lady Catherine ever mention me?"

"In deep hushed tones filled with bottomless wells of eternal regret. But that is rare. She thinks the less said of the great scandal, the better — she knows you were not switched at birth — I understand she had a scheme to marry poor Anne—"

Little Anne piped up from where she played with Bennet, "Me! Marry who? Who? Who?"

Georgiana ruffled her daughter's hair. "We were talking about my cousin, Miss de Bourgh. You have not met her."

"She has *my* name? I want to meet her!"

"You both were named after my mother, who is in heaven now."

The seriousness of this observation quieted the little girl. She exclaimed to Bennet, "My turn to pick. Draw with crayons!"

"Yay! Crayons!"

The two children went to the box where such supplies were kept, and rather messily pulled out the supplies and thick paper given to the children.

"Lady Catherine demanded Fitzwilliam expel me, and she cut the relationship when he would not. The family was fractured, but Fitzwilliam will do anything for me."

An infatuated part of Elizabeth's mind swooned with Georgiana. How sweet of Fitzwilliam...errr Mr. Darcy...to give up so much for his dear sister!

Elizabeth voiced her *other* thought. "Ha. The entire matter was worth it because he *could* cut relations with Lady Catherine. Being forced to visit with her regularly is a matter of nightmares — I jest not, I had one about her once — 'tis alone sufficient reason for me to be happy I refused Mr. Collins."

"Mr. Collins?"

"Your aunt's parson. He is my father's heir also, so almost rich."

"Oh. He then married your dearest friend?"

"Rare poor judgement on her part. I have come to accept no *woman* is perfect. Even I err. Rarely."

"No! Not you!" Georgiana laughed.

"You are distracting the topic. Has anyone caught your eye since Wickham?"

"No one would *marry* me. It is a hopeless thing to wish for."

"Do you wish for it?"

Georgiana looked down. "I do not wish to marry a man who only wishes to have my fortune."

"You have an insultingly low opinion of yourself if you think that is the only reason a man would wish to marry you."

"I...perhaps. You are right so often."

Elizabeth laughed. "Do not think me wiser than I am. Even if you did not set your cap for him, some handsome creature must have caught your eye."

Georgiana blushed.

"Aha! There was."

"He could not have liked me..."

"Are you sure? Men like the look of you. You just do not notice."

"I cannot remember." Georgiana blushed, and she lowered her voice. "Near the time I had Anne, the steward's assistant. He was kind to me, and he explained everything about the workings of the estate that I was too frightened to ask Fitzwilliam — I had been so curious. We were friends. But then he left."

"Ah! The handsome steward's boy. You are still a gentlewoman — I would look elsewhere."

"I know — but...I liked him so much. If he had... Lady Catherine was right this far: I would never stand upon pretensions to being a gentlewoman. He was more than a servant, and extremely clever, and Fitzwilliam was unhappy when he left. Fitzwilliam and the steward had hoped to groom him to take over as the next steward or man of business."

"That makes this sound a little better." Elizabeth smiled. "But your brother would wish to see you marry higher than that."

"He did not make me marry, when I became with child."

"Mr. Darcy found you a husband?"

"Yes...well, Richard, my cousin, he was my guardian then, but he resigned it when Fitzwilliam refused to make me marry Mr. Carteret. Richard talked Carteret into it. But I...I didn't want to. I wanted..."

"What did you want?"

Georgiana looked at her hands.

"No matter of reputation is worth tying yourself to a man you do not love or cannot trust. Georgie, I admire you. Had I been fifteen I probably would have followed my guardian's orders."

"No, it would not have been — I have still felt guilty, because it would have been easiest for everyone if I married. He was forty and five, and...Fitzwilliam saw my tears. He only asked me if I was wholly sure I did not want to marry. Richard was furious. He had been Fitzwilliam's closest friend, and since they have barely spoken."

"Mr. Darcy did not try to make you marry?" Elizabeth asked with some surprise. "Not at all?"

"Not at all. All he needed was to know I wished to remain single."

"I may have misjudged him." Her emotion towards Darcy became warm and soft. She had always resisted the attraction she felt for him, because she believed Darcy had too great an expectation of obedience. But that tension in her was dissolving away if he simply listened to Georgiana when she begged him for her to be able to choose. "Most men," Elizabeth added, "would have done anything to hide the stain on the family name."

"He is the best brother in the world. I often wondered...if he would have been happier if he had made me to marry. He could have married then."

"Do not be ridiculous. He adores Anne, and he adores you. He has not married because he is a prickly man who only wants a prickly woman."

"You have made me realize *that*." Georgiana giggled at Elizabeth's description of her brother. "I am glad you are seeing my brother's worth."

"I as well." Elizabeth smiled freely.

Chapter Thirteen

One lazy morning, the Netherfield party sat around the breakfast table. The platter in the center was piled high with beef, ham and a half dozen delicious pheasant pies. One of those also sat half eaten in front of Darcy. Today Darcy planned to take a morning ride and then catch up on his reading.

He'd encountered Elizabeth once in the roads around Longbourn; maybe if he haunted them again he might run across her once more. The Netherfield party had no plans for the day, and while sunny and bright, the previous three days it had rained, curtailing the normal round of calls and connections. The road was steadily drying though, and with the strength of the sun it would be gone within a few hours. Besides, a true gentleman never let a little mud scare him from a good ride.

Bingley slapped his palm on the table. "Deuced boring day! I know what we must do."

Darcy winced internally. He would have to find *some* excuse if his friend was about to suggest another day of shooting. They'd killed enough birds.

At least Bingley's cook knew exactly what to do with them. Darcy took another bite of his meat pie. The flour of the pastry and the gamy flavor of the bird's meat mixed perfectly.

Soon fox hunting...

"Royston Cave!" Bingley exclaimed. "At last we will go. Tomorrow. Jane, you said it was worth visiting."

"Royston Cave? What is that?" Georgiana asked.

"A magnificent hidden chapel that was used by the survivors of the Templar order after the monarchs of Europe jealously murdered the defeated defenders of the Holy Land. It is said their treasure was hidden away there, and many men have sought to know the meaning of the carvings, but none have succeeded."

"I had heard," Darcy said, "that it is unlikely the caves were truly constructed by the Templar order."

Bingley rolled his eyes. "Of course they were built by Templars! A hidden cave, filled with mysterious carvings. Perhaps the treasure is still hidden in them beneath the excavations opened to the public."

"I do wish to go! Such a fine idea." Georgiana looked at Darcy. "Would Lizzy wish to go also?"

Jane said, "She was not greatly impressed when we visited as children, but I believe she would be interested in seeing the place once more."

That put matters in a decidedly more encouraging line: A trip with Elizabeth to explore dim caverns, carved with medieval piety, illuminated by a flickering lantern. Brushing against each other, entirely by accident, of course. They would joke about the unlikelihood of finding Templar treasure...

"Eh, Darcy?"

"Ahem, I did not hear the question."

"Growing distracted. We aren't so elderly you have excuse. Was *someone* on your mind?"

Darcy stared back, a little coldly. Then he grinned. His heart had bubbled the last few days, since he danced with Elizabeth, and she convinced Georgiana to play, and he realized he loved her. Bingley teasing him about his lovesickness for Elizabeth could not injure his buoyant mood.

"Maybe someone *was* on my mind. Tomorrow you say?"

"It is far enough out that we had best start in the morning. I'll send a message over to Longbourn to ask Lizzy what she thinks of the scheme."

"She will go along." Jane pursed her lips from right to left. "I hope Mama does not wish to come as well. She did not like the dark when we went a decade past."

"Send that in the message to Lizzy," Bingley said. "She will handle it all. But I have been here long enough; the time is past when I ought to make my effort to find the treasure. We will need more money with all these balls I'm throwing."

Bingley grinned at Jane, who swooned and kissed him on the mouth.

The next morning Elizabeth was brought early in the day by the Bennets' carriage to Netherfield. Her red clad form lightly hopped out of the low carriage, and she looked like a winter nymph. She wore a fur lined winter coat; a soft yellow bonnet had a pattern of flowers inlaid into it and a lace fringe around her face. Her cheeks were rosy and smiling.

There was a dusting of snow on the ground from the previous night, and the white created a contrast which made her form stand out. She wore blue kid gloves that he'd seen her wear the time he met her during a ride.

Elizabeth looked first towards him, and she smiled and curtsied, before she embraced her sister and then Georgiana. "Whose idea was a return to Royston?"

"I have not been," Bingley replied.

"I wish to see!" Georgiana's eyes glowed. "The Knights Templar are so fascinating."

Elizabeth laughed. She turned to Darcy and their eyes touched. Her smiling expression meant she must love him. But he could not be sure. She always smiled and laughed, even when he had angered her.

Elizabeth said, "Do give me your hand, Darcy. Let me shake it. There. We shall be the only sane ones on this fated excursion. You do not expect to find some vast Templar storehouse of the raided gold and gems of the Holy Lands. I depend upon you."

"You may always depend upon me." Through their gloves her small hand seemed to radiate a tingle which traveled up his arm, like magic. A strange witchcraft. She could not be ignorant of the effect of this simple touch.

Her color rose. He admired her clear skin, the few freckles visible on her nose, the pale English whiteness covered by a perpetual tan. She looked shy.

Darcy could not be precipitate. He must court Elizabeth properly. *This* was the one woman in the world who might refuse him.

Their eyes met again and held.

Bingley pushed Elizabeth towards the carriage by her shoulder. "Come you two. Faith, it is too cold to stand about like a pair of hobbled horses. I will freeze, though *you* two notice not."

It had been decided that putting the five adults in one carriage would make it more crowded than comfortable, so Bingley and Darcy were to ride alongside, providing a protective pair of outriders, and giving the horses and men a nice exercise. The three women comfortably bundled up with hot water bottles and heated bricks for the trip.

They set off. At first over the pathways near Netherfield, graded for a carriage, but not comfortable. Then they hit an improved section of a turnpike. After a half hour the carriage reached a tollpost, and Bingley rode direct to the booth where the gatekeeper sat and tossed him their fair. Quickly the barrier was raised, and they continued on, making a good pace.

The day looked warm and clear. It had snowed the previous day, and the further north they went the thicker the white powder stood on the sides of the ditches. No ice had formed on the road. Still Darcy kept his eyes open, especially when they went past shaded patches where difficult to see ice could form and stick.

Except for the evergreens the trees were entirely bare, and there were long grey vistas of brambles and grey hedges dusted with white. The fields had red brick farmhouses, with ascending columns of smoke going high into the air before they were dispersed by the soft winds.

The group passed several substantial estates and rode through a market town a little smaller than Meryton. The town was picturesque in the clear winter light, with timber framed buildings and white plaster walls and colorful signs proclaiming the business. Scissors and a thread for a tailor; a line of cloth for a haberdasher, a painting of a foaming mug of beer to advertise a pub, and one of a big four posted bed for the inn, a painting of a cabbage with apples and some other round fruit whose paint had faded too far for the color to be identified for a greengrocer.

Half an hour after they went through the town, they reached the village of Royston.

There was an inn yard they rolled into, and the grooms ran out to care for their horses and beg for tips. Elizabeth stepped out of the carriage. Darcy had eyes for no one else. She stretched her arms up, causing the fabric of her jacket to pull against her breasts, outlining their form. With her arms still held above her head she turned her neck from side to side several times.

Darcy's mouth went dry.

She lowered her arms and looked around and smiled at him. "I have been to Royston once before. When I denied the possibility of finding secret treasure, what I meant *in truth* was that I would be most put out with you if you should find its secret chamber when *I* could not."

"Perhaps, we ought hunt for it together, and then share equally upon the discovery."

She smiled back, and his stomach swooped. "I shall stick close to you, like a limpet, or as if we were nailed together."

"Yes, you should. I...I might cheat you of the treasure if you were not close."

Elizabeth nodded, her eyes aglow.

Their party was greeted by a white-haired smiling short man. "Greetings, greetings, Lords, Ladies! Greetings! Welcome to my abode!"

Bingley said, "You are the owner?"

"I am Mr. Watson. I built the tunnel that leads to the caves. Are you hoping to see?"

"I've heard a deuced lot about it."

"A fine sight, a fine, fine sight. Fabulous, beyond the carvings possible in our modern days — there is likely some treasure hidden within the caves. My family searched, and we've found nothing yet, but we do not give up hope." He waved them into the modest brick house. "Come. Come in! The entrance extends from under my house. I built the current entrance, many years ago now. When I was a boy visitors had to take a ladder down some twenty feet, and then we lowered a lamp by wire. Much improved now."

They were all brought into the front parlor of his house, a substantial two-story affair. The man clapped his hands, and when his maid came out of the kitchen, with a smudge of flour on her cheeks, he exclaimed, "The best! Bring it out. Mulled wine, pastries, some meat. You must be famished from your trip. Far better to eat here than get something from the inn." He lowered his voice and spoke half to Darcy and half to Bingley, "I fear me that the inn does not match the standard such grand personages as yourself expect."

"Also," Darcy ordered, "provide refreshment for our servants."

"Of course, of course. Six pence to visit the caves. Do you want them to see as well?"

"Deuced good idea." Bingley replied, "He would be a terror if Martin drove us all this way, and didn't have a chance to see the carvings."

"If you all go at once, the room would be crowded with too many people. After you gentlemen have visited, you might refresh yourselves a little longer while your men take their chance to look?"

After this was agreed, and Darcy handed the man a half crown for the refreshments and the fee to visit the cave, the five of them entered the thin tunnel. The stairs downwards were slippery with moisture, and almost warm, despite the season.

Each of the gentlemen was handed an oil lamp to carry, along with one held by Mr. Watson.

Elizabeth took Darcy's arm as they carefully stepped down. Her face was flushed from the wine and the cold. She grinned while looking at him, her face less than a foot from his. Darcy's stomach twisted. "I have not forgotten your promise to share the Templar wealth."

"We will share, together."

"I like that. Together."

"I would never cheat you."

Her sparkling eyes were barely visible in the light of the lamps.

"Ooops!" With a laugh Elizabeth's foot slipped under her, and Darcy caught her and held her arm until she was stable. His lamp swung wildly in his other hand, the iron bottom of it lightly bouncing against the rough stone wall of the tunnel.

Mr. Watson called back tensely, "Caution, sirs. Caution, the stones become slippery in winter."

"I am yet in perfect health." Elizabeth had a laugh in her voice, and she gripped Darcy's arm tightly. He gripped her wrist. "In all respects fine!"

When they reached the end of the tunnel, the cave was almost dispiritingly small after the long carriage ride. Crazy shadows from the shifting lanterns danced about, and the ceiling sloped upwards, to close off at a point at perhaps the height of a fashionable drawing room, a little more than twenty feet above them. That ceiling was barely visible in the dim light. The cave had a circular floor of about twenty feet around.

Mr. Watson pointed at the carvings, shining the light to make them more visible. "St. Christopher, the patron of the Templars. There — Mary, and the baby Christ." He held the lamp high, moving from image to image too quickly for Darcy to study and take in the carvings. "In those nooks, some statues."

Georgiana and Jane linked arms, and they laughed together and talked rapidly. Georgiana eagerly examined one carving after another, while Bingley and Mr. Watson held up their lamps for the women to examine the walls at their leisure.

Darcy and Elizabeth walked to the other side, with her hand resting softly on his free arm. Darcy held up the lamp. Many names and other pieces of writing had been carved into the soft limestone walls, around the carvings left by the medieval monks. "John & Rose, 1797"; "Tom Miller"; "Long Live myself!"

Darcy snorted. Elizabeth looked at him and he freed his arm to point. She then leaned down closer, holding his arm again to study it. Then she laughed, a tinkling good-humored sound. "A little disrespect to his Majesty, methinks."

"Pray tell: How do you know it was not left by the king when he visited?"

Elizabeth giggled, and she put her hand on his shoulder and leaned closer to Darcy. Her eyes glanced to where Mr. Watson stood, with Bingley and the other two women. "Upon my honor," she whispered into his ear, "*he* would have told us if ever a royal had visited."

Elizabeth stepped away.

Darcy looked at her, glowing and smiling, He leaned towards her. She obligingly tilted her head so that he could whisper his reply into her finely shaped ear. "But if he came in disguise? Like Henry studying the army before Agincourt."

Elizabeth dissolved into giggles, holding her mouth to keep them quiet.

"What amuses you two so much?" Bingley yelled out. "You are not flirting with my sister again, Darcy?"

"Charles!" Jane exclaimed, pushing his arm.

Darcy was in too good a mood to be annoyed. Elizabeth smiled. They walked in the other direction, moving along the curve of the wall a little further away from the rest of the party, keeping as much distance as the cramped cave allowed. They examined together the carving of St. Christopher.

Elizabeth jostled Darcy's arm. "I know you are despondent. Nowhere to hide the Templars' hoarded loot that would not have been seen when the cave was first excavated."

"I fear I must survive upon the rents from my pile."

"A most disappointing expedition," Elizabeth agreed, smiling at him, the dim light making the rounded skin of her cheeks glow softly.

"I am not disappointed."

"Neither I," she replied in a breathy voice.

He and Elizabeth felt alone and isolated from the others. The air was warm and humid and rich with possibility. Their eyes held each other, and Darcy felt with a terrified spasm in his stomach the idea that the moment was propitious and he should bring the matter to a head and ask for her hand. He couldn't look away from her face.

Darcy tried to open his mouth, but like a vise, nervousness grabbed him and clamped his teeth shut. The anxiety was like nothing he had ever felt before. He did not *know* she would reply in affirmative.

Elizabeth looked away from him, and then down. She talked at a quick pace, with an unexpected nervousness in her. She told a story that was unimportant, yet completely important, because it was from her childhood — the time she had seen the cave as a girl, with her father and mother and sisters.

The drone of noise from the opposite side of the cave continued. Mr. Watson kept trying to impress Georgiana and Jane with descriptions of the carvings and stories of the Templars being tortured. Bingley laughingly added nonsensical stories he made up about the matter.

Darcy felt so close to her, and so entirely certain that he would marry her and that he wished to marry her. He wanted to touch her cheek and pull her face closer so that he could kiss her.

Elizabeth looked at him, and desire was there in her eyes too.

In a snap the world and the existence of others came back. Bingley asked Darcy a question, and Darcy heard it and replied. Both he and Elizabeth looked at Bingley. They followed Bingley to the other side of the cave. Jane and Georgiana asked Elizabeth what she thought of a particular image.

Darcy's heart raced.

They discussed the artwork. One of the figures was a man in full plate armor, and Darcy said, "Such suits were contrived quite late. During the time of the Templars such a piece would be unlikely. I suspect the cave was made at least a century after the order was dispersed."

"What, no!" Bingley exclaimed. "He looks like a Templar knight."

"The dates are entirely wrong," Darcy replied. "Only in the fourteenth century did such armor become common."

"The Templars! I'll insist *that* to the end."

Elizabeth laughed. "I do not believe you! This is a scheme to make me lower my guard so you might steal the treasure by convincing me that it is not real."

Her eyes were so bright.

Darcy wobbled as they walked back up the steps to leave the cave and return to the modern world far away from this dimly lit remainder of the medieval. Their host immediately served them from a new heated pot of mulled wine. Their servants went down into the cave, while the party sat in the parlor and prepared themselves for the journey back to Netherfield.

There was a clatter outside, and when Mr. Watson looked out, he gained a deeply conflicted expression. Another group had arrived to tour the caves, but they were of lower status than Darcy and Bingley. It would not do to leave substantial gentry to their own devices to entertain a middling tradesman. But Mr. Watson obviously wanted the fees from the tradesmen.

To relieve him of the worry Darcy stood and shook Mr. Watson's hand. "A fine tour. A fascinating display. Are there any paths about town we might walk before we leave?"

"Yes, yes of course. You must have seen the ruined manor when you came in? On the hilltop? It was a palace of Henry VIII; you can take a pathway around to look at it, and to get to the hilltop. A fine view of the whole area."

"We will walk around then. Good day."

"Good day, sir! Good day!"

They walked back into the cold day. The winter sun had already passed its zenith and was beginning to lower, but it would still be many hours before it set. There was barely any wind stirring through the bare branches, bothering the blackbirds that perched upon them. The winter was a symbol of Darcy's feelings of his own life: Everything had seemed bleak and cold, and barren for so long, but beneath it there always had been flows of sap preparing for the coming of spring. Of Elizabeth.

Though the outer environment was in winter, Darcy's soul was in a full bloom and profusion of growing flowers and of trees pushing out endless green leaves.

Elizabeth exclaimed, "To the walk! I want to see the promontory. And I must walk some before I am imprisoned in a carriage once more!"

Chapter Fourteen

Bingley's ball was to be held four days before Christmas, and the day before that ball Elizabeth's favorite relations, Mr. and Mrs. Gardiner arrived at Longbourn. In tow with them was another friend, Mrs. Gardiner's cousin, Mr. Peake who had been in business with Mr. Gardiner for the past four years.

Mr. Gardiner strode confidently into Longbourn tossing his cap onto the rack, and allowing Mrs. Hill to help him out of his traveling coat. He gestured with his free elbow at the tall figure of Mr. Peake behind him, who bowed with more elegance than he showed a few years before when they had first met. "Do not mind an additional person?"

"Lord! No!" Mrs. Bennet happily shook his hands. "Be welcome, Mr. Peake, be welcome. Any partner of my brother's is welcome — you are now partner. You ought to consider marriage. We have many delightful girls in Hertfordshire you can meet."

"I am in no rush for such a connection."

Mr. Gardiner shook his coat off and put his arm around Mrs. Gardiner. "Marriage is a good thing once you can afford a wife. It settles you in the world, and other men of business take you more seriously."

"I am yet too much of a romantic to seek about with the intention of finding a fine wife." Mr. Peake half shrugged. He frowned a little and shook his head.

When they met Mr. Peake in Derbyshire, his manner of speaking while Mr. Gardiner sought to convince him to join his firm had made Elizabeth suspect that he had a strong admiration or attachment to a woman who he had no hope of winning in his modest position, and that escaping from the pain which a hopeless infatuation gave had been a source of willingness to leave. Perhaps he had never truly recovered from that first affection.

Elizabeth hoped, if her theory was true, that he would not allow such memories to control him for the entirety of his life.

Mrs. Bennet added, "Our dear children are married and gone — except of course Lizzy — so pleasant to host a friend. And ample room! I do wish Lydia would return for Christmas, but a friend in London, and gone off with her friend's family to Brighton for the season. I cannot understand why the memories of her poor Wickham would not drive her away from that city forever." Mrs. Bennet added in a stage whisper, "By the time Captain Wickham was lost at Waterloo, I fear that no great affection remained betwixt them."

"Captain Wickham's fate was quite too good for him." Mr. Peake replied, "I am not surprised Lydia learned to dislike him."

"I ought to defend my son in law, but I am possessed by *your* opinion." Mr. Bennet shook hands with Mr. Peake. "You are Lydia's superior in terms of conversation."

"Nonsense, dear." Mrs. Bennet pushed Mr. Bennet's shoulder. "More than ample room for him, and Lydia, and my brother, and Lizzy, and everyone else — only when all five girls lived here did the house become crowded during this season."

The Gardiner children then demanded attention, though the oldest girl was now fourteen and almost of an age she would enter society and become fascinated by gentlemen. While Mrs. Gardiner took the younger siblings up to the nursery, she was allowed to remain in the drawing room, and from her manners Elizabeth suspected Miss Gardiner had a girlish infatuation for poor Mr. Peake.

Elizabeth approached that gentleman. "Full partner. Decidedly impressive. And only twenty and five."

He laughed and flashed his white teeth, with his shoulders held back confidently. "Miss Lizzy, delightful to see *you* again."

"Don't be that way."

Mr. Peake was confident, lean, and still young. He had a genius for financial matters that Elizabeth could not begin to understand. The young man had matured enormously from the youth Mr. Gardiner had convinced to join his firm.

"I am now more impressed with you. I am now well acquainted with your old employer, Mr. Darcy. He is a man worthy of remark and giving up a position with him was a compliment to my uncle."

"Mr. Darcy? You are?" Mr. Peake cocked his head to the side. "When did you make his acquaintance? I had believed he was stuck permanently at Pemberley with...his sister."

"You must have known he is a friend of Bingley. Mr. Darcy and his sister have been present at Netherfield for a month now. This brings up a matter of importance. Tomorrow a ball at Netherfield, and both Mr. Darcy and Miss Darcy shall be there. The ball really is mostly for dear Georgie's sake—"

"Georgiana Darcy? Miss Darcy is present at Netherfield?"

The sharp tone of inquiry caught the edge of some memory of Elizabeth's. "She is. A sweet and shy girl. Jane made a pet of her when she and Bingley visited Pemberley, and *I* have met her now. We would fight endlessly over sweet Georgie if Jane was not such an angel."

"What has become of Miss Darcy? I hear from my friends about estate matters, but...we were...friends. Me and Miss Darcy. Does she do well? And her babe?"

"She does very well. I have been introducing her about this neighborhood — you may ask her yourself how she does within the hour. The Netherfield party is to call so Mr. Darcy and Miss Darcy can be introduced to the Gardiners."

Mr. Peake's eyes turned to the window outside, with a surprising intensity.

Was it her imagination? Georgiana mentioned a man who'd left Pemberley who she had liked. Who had been training to take the steward's place...

Mr. Peake had been the under steward. Elizabeth liked Mr. Peake, and he had made a success in a highly respectable line of trade. He was yet a little raw, but he imitated Mr. Gardiner's manners well enough that he could pass as a gentleman.

If there was mutual affection upon reconnecting, that Mr. Peake would do very well for Georgie, and Georgiana for him. An impossible attachment without Anne and Georgiana's scandal. But Georgiana could never make a *splendid* match. Such a marriage would connect the Gardiners in an additional way to her and Darcy — she should not assume that she and Darcy would marry. But...it *seemed* matters headed in such a direction. Georgiana's dowry would provide useful capital that would help the Gardiners expand and as conditions in the country improved.

The sound of the heavy coach and four pulling up brought everyone to the window to observe the large Darcy carriage pulled by four matched horses, with a splendidly dressed coachman in livery and a postillion and two footmen following on the sides. Darcy stepped out, ducking his head. A little too tall even for the oversized door of his huge carriage. He placed his top hat upon his head, making his lean, energetic figure even lengthier. How could a man be so tall, yet appear so solid?

Georgiana, bundled in a fur coat, followed him out, Anne jumped out after her, leaping into Darcy's arms. He caught her easily and swung the little girl around before placing her on the ground. Behind them the Bingley carriage trundled a little slower and less magnificently up the driveway.

Soon as they entered the house Darcy, Georgiana and Anne were brought to the drawing room.

Elizabeth watched Mr. Peake from the corner of her eye while Anne ran up to her and chattered about how sad she was that the snow from two days previous had melted.

Mr. Peake's eyes went straight to Georgiana as she entered through the drawing room. Elizabeth considered it clear that he wanted to continue looking. When Georgiana saw him, *her* eyes widened in recognition and with a smile she walked towards Mr. Peake.

"I of course recall *you*." Mr. Darcy extended his hand to Mr. Peake after the quick introductions between him and the Gardiners. "Mr. Peake, my word. You do exceedingly well for yourself. I am glad the position you took proved a profitable line of work."

"I as well." Mr. Peake bowed slightly, showing deference to Mr. Darcy, but also his pride in his present position.

Darcy smiled at Elizabeth, and looked at the Gardiners briefly as he said, "You told me you visited Pemberley with your aunt and uncle — I have been most eager to meet you both — but I had forgotten I held a grudge against you all."

Mr. Gardiner laughed. "Lizzy has told us that you are well worth liking, Mr. Darcy. But upon my honor, I do not repent the theft. Mr. Peake has been incalculably valuable to me. In truth, I *can* calculate his value, and the sum runs to many thousands."

Georgiana stood near them and said, "A shock. I am glad to see you also — again. Such a shock."

"You as well. As well. You are well?" Mr. Peake smiled a little anxiously. "I asked Miss Bennet, but—"

"Very well." Georgiana nodded rapidly, smiling. "Never so well. I do not think I have been so well as these last weeks. Lizzy and Jane have been such good friends. I—"

"Miss Bennet is an excellent woman." Mr. Peake smiled at her. "But you — no notion you were present in Hertfordshire."

"You had not? I had no notion either. *Lizzy's* uncle."

"I had. I had. Many years. I never forgot to think on you…and Pemberley. And Mr. Darcy — little Anne is well?"

Georgiana called the girl from Elizabeth's side, and self-consciously introduced her to Mr. Peake. Elizabeth decided that they *definitely* had a sensibility towards each other. She glanced towards Darcy to see if he noticed it, but when she turned to look at him, she found that Darcy had been staring at her. Their eyes met, and Darcy did not look away.

"You shall not despise me now that you know it was my dear uncle who stole Mr. Peake from you?"

"I admire a well-executed snatching — *you* too can charm and argue a valuable man into your service."

Elizabeth blushed at Darcy's sally. "A valuable man would not need to be *charmed* as well as argued by me."

"Deuced valuable man." Mr. Gardiner grinned. "Mr. Darcy, Lizzy has been writing all about *you* in her letters to us. You had quite an introduction."

Darcy blushed and waved it away. "Pray tell, how have you used my old employee? I must hear he is profitably employed — my loss should benefit another."

"He prevented my bankruptcy during the crisis. Mr. Peake has a genius for predicting prices."

Darcy tilted his head. "Forgive my asking, you did not suffer too much during the panic? Miss Bennet indicated your firm did well. But it is not always a matter that a woman who is a niece would be privy to. Was it not India fabrics that you work in? That has shown difficulties."

Darcy smiled at Elizabeth. "I apologize though for speaking of a matter of business. But I have always wondered how Mr. Peake got on — I thank you for your letters, you said you have been raised to a junior partner?"

"I ought not brag, but I am now full partner — the firm does very well."

"It's entirely his doing. Peake doesn't brag beyond his due." Mr. Gardiner clapped his wife's cousin on the shoulder, speaking in his typical clipped accent. "Making him a full partner, it was the thing to do. The man has some left to learn, but he inherited a little to make up the capital, and Peake is a true genius. I needed to keep him from being bid away. And a matter of gratitude, if nothing else."

"Gratitude?" Georgiana looked at Mr. Gardiner with shining eyes. "What is the story?"

"Before Waterloo I'd planned to buy a big shipment. Going to go in debt to purchase — the purchase looked like an excellent opportunity. There was risk, but no risk leads to no success. Peake convinced me — three weeks Newtoning numbers in the evenings instead of drinking with his companions, like a proper young man" — Mr. Gardiner delivered that line as a joke which brought everyone to laughter — "convinced *me* purchase would be a mistake. We sold as much of our stocks as we could and replaced them with *government* stock. I was terrified that day Waterloo was announced. You know the story of Rothschild — clever Jew. I respect the people. They are smarter than us — how he learned a few hours before how the battle went. Made a fortune—"

"The story is a myth," Mr. Peake said. "I have a friend who works in his counting house, he—"

Mr. Gardiner clapped Mr. Peake proudly on the shoulder again. "Such a fine fellow — friends with a Rothschild—"

"A clerk in the counting house."

Mr. Gardiner waved the difference away. "The story is too good to be false, even if it is not strictly true. Stories can be like that, while in real life we must stick to facts."

"I prefer my stories to be truth." Mr. Darcy glanced at Elizabeth and Georgiana. "And perhaps we should discuss stories. I would not wish to bore the women with tales of business."

"I quite prefer my stories to be entertaining," Elizabeth replied. "Too much truth, if boring, is unpardonable in a matter that relates to people who we shall never meet nor care about."

"I met Mr. Rothschild once and might well meet him again," Darcy responded. "*That* argument will not work upon me, Miss Bennet."

Elizabeth grinned back. "You claim you care deeply for Mr. Rothschild?"

"He was respectable enough, for one of his sort."

Georgiana said, "I wish to hear the story — what happened after Waterloo?"

"We held most of our capital in government paper at the time — not everything, but enough, and we made a tidy profit with Rothschild."

"I too held a great deal in mortgages and government stock," Darcy said. "My rents have fallen lower than since my grandfather's time, but the loss in income was been cushioned by that. I have purchased substantial acreage from less foresightful neighbors."

"True wealth comes from land," Mr. Gardiner said sagely.

"Nay." Mr. Peake shook his head. "Paper is just as much *income* as anything else. From the perspective of the *owner*, the difference is an illusion — Mr. Darcy, I have not forgotten *your* lessons. There is vast difference between a *landlord* and an absent owner. Supporting tenants is as much a matter of honor as it is income."

Despite speaking to Mr. Darcy, Elizabeth noted how Mr. Peake's eyes flashed to *Miss* Darcy as he made this speech. They flashed often to her, and in turn Georgiana glowed and forgot to look away shyly the way she did with most others.

Very promising. Of course it was not her place to arrange anything, but... "Mr. Peake, you will be present at our ball tomorrow?" Elizabeth said, "Would you mind attending Miss Darcy for the first dance — you are both friends."

Mr. Peake nodded. "I would be delighted, if you wish it, Miss Darcy..."

Georgiana bounced happily. "Very much."

Darcy frowned slightly, until Elizabeth turned her fullest, brightest smile upon him, with what she knew were bright sparkling eyes. "Mr. Darcy, I call upon the favor you owe me for your abominable failure to dance with me the first night we met, and I demand that you give me the first tomorrow."

Darcy blanched. "Pray, do not recall to me *that* story."

Mrs. Gardiner had returned from placing her younger children in the nursery and stood next to her husband. She grinned at the tall gentleman and tapped her forehead. "I fear, Mr. Darcy, it is committed to paper and the memories of many. Forgetfulness impossible."

"That shall *always* be that tale of how we met? Alas. But we will have an entertaining story." He smiled meaningfully at her and Elizabeth flushed at the intimacy of him suggesting that they would regularly recall it. "I shall offer an additional payment, as supplicant — would you desire me to also be your partner for the supper dance?"

"Such a charming partner could never be refused."

"Then," Darcy spoke with a happy, high tone to his voice, "I must give up having the first dance with you, Georgiana. But save the second and the last for me."

"I will! I will!" Georgiana replied blushingly with a color Elizabeth was sure was not primarily produced by her *brother's* request.

Chapter Fifteen

During the course of the afternoon prior to Bingley's ball, Elizabeth dressed with more than usual care. She had not been this giddy about the prospect of dancing since she had been a young miss in her first year or two within society.

Giddy, happy, irrational, hopeful, desirous, and frightened. She was like a carriage driver who had tangled the reins and could no longer control the horses. Perhaps she should neither encourage him, nor accept him if he offered. She was too independent, and despite her love of their conversation, sharp arguments and shared jokes were *not* sufficient foundation for a life together.

These doubts did not affect her preparations in the slightest. During the course of the afternoon, Elizabeth eagerly asked both her mother and Mrs. Gardiner for sartorial advice. Then she ignored their advice, after which she decided she looked terrible and changed her clothes precisely following her relations instructions. Then she removed half of *that* outfit to follow her own inclination again. She sent her poor maid down to Meryton twice to acquire ribbons and flowers not available at Longbourn.

Elizabeth settled upon lacing and Christmas blossoms woven into her hair. Her hair was fetching.

She went through every single one of her scarves and eight necklaces before settling upon the first shawl and the second necklace attempted. She however had grown tired of her absurd indecision when her hair was made, and for Georgiana's sake she wished their party to be present at Netherfield early, so she simply wore it without further adjustments past the first attempt.

Bingley's ball had turned into a large affair to which the entirety of the community was invited, and few chose to not attend.

It amused Elizabeth — no one in the community would have been the first to greet Georgiana Darcy. The Lucases and Gouldings met her due to their enduring friendship with Elizabeth and Jane. But once the society of the neighborhood collectively determined Georgiana Darcy was a sweet creature with no harm in her — and that she would not conveniently disappear — how to treat her became difficult question.

No one *wished* to miss a *Netherfield* ball, and Bingley would only invite a person willing to acknowledge his guest.

What a dilemma for the defender of morality and community standards!

Bingley's balls were the grandest affairs in the neighborhood, exceeding in splendor, not in size, the public assemblies. Everyone liked Bingley, and Jane was adored by every gentleman, and *still* liked by every lady.

This ball was to be particularly good — Bingley had hired musicians from London! Not the town players everyone hired and who performed the assemblies. And Bingley was using the last of the wines from the famed French vineyard in Margaux that had been placed in the cellars of Netherfield two decades past by the old baronet and sold with the house. Bingley's cook was the best in the neighborhood, and he always laid out a fine supper during the break.

Initially Bingley gave only a few invitations to people who were carefully selected to be willing to count a girl like Georgiana amongst their acquaintance. But once *they* agreed to come, the rest of the neighborhood did not wish to be left out of such a good party.

For almost all *that* was a greater consideration by far than any moral squeamishness or worry about what others would think if they acknowledged Georgiana Darcy.

But once all of the couples and matrons had begged and hinted their way into invitations, everyone agreed the young maidens should also be allowed to attend — what possible harm could occur in such a crowded venue?

In short, *everyone* was to attend the ball, everyone in the neighborhood was to be introduced to poor Georgie, and Elizabeth had strong fears for how the shy girl would support herself under the sudden exposure to near a hundred superficial well-wishers.

So with her hair pronounced beautiful by her father, her mother, her aunt and uncle, her enthusiastic maid and by Mr. Peake, Elizabeth set off in the carriage to Netherfield. She still thought a different style of flower would have been better.

Ridiculous. Why was she being ridiculous?

The carriage rolled over the cold road between Longbourn and Netherfield, with familiar fields and houses passing by Elizabeth's unseeing eyes.

The dark truth must be confessed: She loved Fitzwilliam Darcy. Her admiration was an animal passion; a spiritual connection; a bond in friendship betwixt their hearts. And she believed that he, with his elegantly trimmed head and beautiful long limbs, had formed a tolerably powerful attachment towards her.

She would agree to marry him, and he would ask. Always before she thought marriage meant loss of freedom and dependence upon the goodwill of a changeable man. She told herself and others that that was why she had never married.

A lie, Elizabeth now knew.

She had never married before because she had not yet met Mr. Fitzwilliam Darcy of Pemberley.

"Lizzy." Papa tapped her shoulder from where he sat opposite in the carriage. "You are distracted today. Thoughts of someone?"

There was both curiosity and worry in his eyes. What did *Papa* think?

Elizabeth suddenly had an urge to ask him for advice.

Mrs. Bennet exclaimed, "I believe Mr. Darcy admires you, Lizzy. Faith! He looked at you in a most particular manner yesterday. I cannot believe it! I do not understand it. But I saw *you* too. My dear daughter! Ten thousand a year! Even Bingley is nothing to Mr. Darcy."

"Mama." Elizabeth flushed and looked at the other occupants of the carriage.

Mr. Gardiner raised his eyebrows. "Mr. Darcy is an exceptional man from what I have heard, though he has a reputation for being a hermit and avoiding the company of women except his sister."

Papa shifted his legs to be more comfortable in the cramped family carriage. "No speculation on this topic. Unless Lizzy wishes to speak upon it herself."

Elizabeth shook her head. Matters had gone so far that even her mother expected an engagement, despite the initial meeting betwixt Elizabeth and Darcy having been comprised of Darcy insulting her and her laughing in his face.

Mrs. Gardiner had told her many years ago when they sat together in the Gardiners' yellow drawing room in London — in a speech Elizabeth had always kept deep in her mind — that in marriage disagreements would always arise. Couples always argued, and two persons, no matter how in love, never agreed on every matter. And Elizabeth and Jane — the occasion of this conversation was several months prior to Bingley's entering the neighborhood — must accept once they married that in the end their husband would choose when they disagreed. If a woman loved her husband, she could find joy in such submission.

That conversation was part of why Elizabeth had always kept her heart distant from every man who approached her and flattered her and made love to her — there *had* been many. She would *not* subordinate her judgement; she would not place herself under the control of another.

Perhaps the simple solution to the mystery of why she had fallen in love with Darcy. He *liked* when she argued and disagreed with him. She must make him understand that he must always allow her to disagree with him. He must allow her to maintain her own opinions and keep to her own judgement. He would not choose for her. He and she must be equal partners, if they were to be anything.

She could both be rational and in love. She thought through a list of questions she could ask Darcy about how he would behave once they married. She would demand he answer those questions in a way which satisfied her before she agreed to marry him. He would agree that he never expected her to *submit* to him, or they would not marry.

The carriage jolted to a halt. Mr. Darcy and Mr. Bingley stood in the carriageway to greet them. *He* helped her down from the carriage, smiling and complimenting her dress with his words and with his eyes.

Elizabeth's stomach leapt wildly. She was scared. There was something in his manner, there was something in her own. She imagined — not just fancy — that her fate would be sealed this night.

They entered the hall, and Elizabeth smiled to Georgiana. She felt lightheaded, but was still able to attend to her friend. Mr. Darcy watched their interaction with his happy eyes.

"Ready for the crush?" Elizabeth took Georgiana's long white ball glove in her wrist. "You look lovely — I did not know you had such a dress."

"It was delivered two days past. From London. Lizzy, I am scared. So many people."

"They all shall wish to shake your hand." Elizabeth thought light teasing would help her friend best. "You might hide from them. I know Netherfield well enough to sneak you away."

Darcy said, with a grave voice, "I as well have made the acquaintance of nooks and crannies where the guests will not light upon us."

Georgiana giggled and shook her head. She glanced briefly at Mr. Peake who stood with them, on the side of the conversation. "I am scared, but I shall do well."

Darcy put his arm around his sister's shoulders. "I am proud of you."

Georgiana nodded and smiled. "You have — it feels as though today is the beginning of something new, different. You have always been the kindest, and best, and most observant brother. I thank you, from the bottom of my heart, Fitzwilliam."

The first of the other guests arrived. Elizabeth, Darcy and Mr. Peake all stood next to Georgiana, as person after person was introduced to her, with a curtsy or a bow and a short conversation. For nearly an hour people passed through. Darcy shook everyone's hand as well, and he watched his sister like a hawk, but she stood up well, though Elizabeth detected signs of exhaustion in Georgiana by the end.

Then the time to dance was at hand. Darcy took Elizabeth's hand, and he led her out to the floor. His hand was warm. He smiled at her. She looked back, smiling widely.

"Miss Bennet." Darcy grinned at her. "Should you continue to look at me in that manner I shall grow concerned there is something about my appearance."

"There is something about your appearance," Elizabeth replied breathily. She wanted to hug and hold him and discover if he smelled as good as he looked. A faint whiff of his masculine scent touched her. The dance was surreal, like a dream. They talked no sense. How could they?

Everything felt right in his presence, and Elizabeth's being fluttered.

She never gained a very clear sense of the night. Dancing, food, wine, conversations with other people. Elizabeth's body whirled. She behaved almost rudely to others. The two of them talked more than half the time they did not dance — Elizabeth once forgot entirely a person on her card for a dance. The gentleman in question teased her about this for years.

After supper, the parties broke apart, and a confusion of people moved through the rooms and many guests left. A room with card tables was occupied, and other rooms for resting, and many of the women retired to the drawing room to rest and converse. More determined couples returned to ballroom once the supper table had been removed and the musicians brought out once more, though the hour was past midnight.

With a wordless agreement between them they decided to escape public scrutiny for a half hour. Elizabeth and Darcy found a small warm nook in the conservatory to sneak to, away from other eyes. The room was slightly warmed by a coal stove during the entirety of the year to protect the delicate plants.

The instant they sat next to each other, their knees brushing together, on the wicker chairs in the flowered room, Elizabeth and Darcy became awkward. They could no longer look at each other; though their bodies were only six inches apart, their eyes were against the opposite walls. Darcy sat still, while Elizabeth looked down and up and every way.

She decided to encourage him. Elizabeth could not allow his nerves to overcome his resolution. This waiting for him to speak was dreadful, and she feared something could go amiss and separate them, one from the other.

"Mr. Darcy." Elizabeth's voice cracked. Hardly a propitious beginning.

He looked at her, his eyes shadowed by the few candles they had carried with them.

"Your sister. She has become dear to me — to see her so happy."

"Yes...yes. Georgiana. I owe gratitude to you and to Mrs. Bingley. Without you—"

"It is you. You have ensured her happiness. I... You have been all that is good to her, all that is noble, and all that is kind."

Darcy smiled, a little weakly. "That differs highly from your usual description of my behavior. Over attending, controlling, without giving her sufficient scope for her own opinions — I value *your* opinions greatly."

"Mine!" Elizabeth convulsively placed her hand on Darcy's knee, and then drew it away self-consciously. They had touched each other before. They had been closer than this during the waltz, when he'd swung her down in his arms.

But now she could not bear to be near him without looking away and down.

The scent of the blooming flowers filled the air, rich and sweet. It mixed with the warm and toasty feel of the hot air radiating from the stove that Darcy had filled with coal and stirred fully to life when they'd entered the room.

The candle flickered.

"Elizabeth, I...you, that is—" Darcy's voice squeaked, and he fell silent.

The winter was quiet, and the stars shone high above them, glimmering along with the bare sliver of a new moon through the windows. A strain of violin and cello wafted through the door, only audible in the faintest way, drifting in and out of hearing. Darcy breathed next to her.

Elizabeth filled with confidence. He had called her by her Christian name. They knew both why they were here — because they passionately admired each other.

She put her hand upon his leg again and then her other upon his wrist cuff so that he looked at her. Elizabeth smiled at him. This moment required something other than too much of sweetness — she must tease him. "Fitzwilliam Darcy, are you well? You seem unaccountably silent. Now surely you can have little of import to say in a place like this, as we have already decided that I adore Georgie as a *sister*, and her dear daughter as an *aunt*. If only I were your *brother*..."

Darcy's mouth fell open. "You do not mean—" He smiled, seductively, slowly. "Is *that* what you wish? Because I would like you to be *Georgiana's* sister."

She shook her head, first yes, and then no, as she remembered what she had said. And then she frowned. She could not think. Not now with his eyes on her in this way. He took her hands, and he stood, sliding out of his chair, and then he knelt on one knee.

Her heart felt like to burst.

"Elizabeth Bennet..." He paused, not with hesitation but to savor the sound of her name on his voice. "Elizabeth, my dear

Elizabeth, you cannot be ignorant of my feelings. You must know that I ardently admire and love you."

She nodded, her face eager.

"Your goodness, your impertinence, your sweetness, and your cleverness. Your learning and your teaching. Your touch and your smile, your face and your spirit. Your heart and your soul — you call to me. Your spirit calls to me. I had never imagined I might, I had never hoped I might feel as I do with you. Your body glows in my eyes. When you speak I adore your voice, and when you make me listen I adore your mind. You are a woman — a woman perfect for me."

"Yes, yes. I am for *you*."

"I ask you for your hand, for you to let me hold your sweet hand for my entire future life. I beg you to travel my path with me, beside me always. I offer all of who I am, my estate, my name, my person, and my soul, to love and honor, as I shall love and honor you. We shall be happy, if you make me the happiest man in the world."

Elizabeth nodded eagerly. "Fitzwilliam, I..." Elizabeth could not speak through her smiling tears. "I am so..."

Darcy stroked her cheeks with one hand. Then he continued showing that he still did not always know when to stop. "I...I never imagined that my wife would be a woman such as you. I imagined my attachment would settle on a woman different...more traditional, lest forward, and with better connections, and a larger dowry, but you are nevertheless perfect for me, and—"

"Darcy — Fitzwilliam" — Elizabeth squeezed the hands he held her hands with, caressing them, feeling like a bird soaring above the clouds — "a proposal of marriage is no time for your celebrated frankness."

Darcy's mouth snapped shut. "It is not..." He said ruefully, "I just created another story that shall be told at length to posterity?"

"Only to my closest companions; the rest will hear only the first part."

He smiled to her.

"Fitzwilliam Darcy, I have come to ardently admire and love you. I will marry you. But repeat the earlier portion of your proposal again."

"Elizabeth Bennet," he brought his face close to hers, "I ardently admire and love you." He studied her lips, and then her eyes. She tingled with anticipation. He laid his lips upon her forehead. "Most ardently."

Elizabeth squirmed and moaned softly, her back pressing against the chair as she arched her chest and hips towards him.

He put his hand on her burning cheeks, and brought her mouth up to meet his. He kissed her softly.

Elizabeth's eyes closed, as she let his firm lips take the lead. He nibbled and sucked and she felt the pleasure of his touch pull at her loins.

It was entirely different, and better, to experience such a kiss than to hear or imagine what kisses were like. Elizabeth moaned, reaching up her hand to entangle the back of his hair. Darcy's abominable cravat kept her from reaching at his neck or skin.

He whimpered as her fingers pulled at his hair, and his arms went around her back, squeezing her tight. They slowly ceased to kiss, and he held her body against his, her head cradled against his chest, both breathing heavily.

"Elizabeth! At last I have the right to call you that."

"You still must ask my father." Elizabeth grinned at him. "After all women depend on the wisdom of their males to avoid mistakes in such matters."

He pulled her mouth to his and cradled her skull in his wide warm hand. "Imp."

Elizabeth's stomach was so light that it was a wonder she did not take off and float away like one of those hot air balloons.

Fitzwilliam — her Fitzwilliam — smiled as she did. The look of complete happiness became his face very well. He said, "Say we shall not wait long, a month for the banns to be read. Then you can come home to Pemberley with Georgiana, Anne and I. We will be a happy family."

"An entire month? You do not plan to drag me off immediately like a borderlander claiming his woman?"

Darcy kissed her again. He pulled her body tight against his; her ribs happily creaked. He declared, "My horse can manage both of us. In the noise of the ball they will not hear us gallop away."

"Mhmmm." He could carry her off tonight, with a blunderbuss to frighten off pursuers, the two of them on his horse, her clinging to his back. They would find some cave in the northern moors to hide in for the night, and there enjoy the fruits of love. Elizabeth's stomach spasmed with the image, and she pressed herself into his body, wrapping one arm around his back, and she dragged her fingers thru his hair.

He moaned into her mouth, making her quiver with delight.

"Drag me off, my frank barbarous lord."

Darcy laughed and picked her up, and held her in his arms, so that her mouth was level with his. Elizabeth kissed his face and cheeks, and kept her hands around his neck to help support her weight.

After a minute Darcy let her down with an *oof*. "You are heavier than you look."

Laughing, Elizabeth replied, "*That* smacks of insult."

They stood next to each other, their foreheads pressed tight. Their breathing calmed. It was impossible to stop smiling.

Darcy said exultantly, "Pemberley will be full of joy — you shall love the inside of my house — *our* house — as much as the outside. We shall be so happy."

"Ha — you expect my happiness to come from your pile."

"I know how ardently you admire my hair."

"Swear to never go bald or take up some strange fashion for close-cropped locks."

"Not only for us am I happy, Georgiana will be delighted to have you at Pemberley."

Elizabeth grinned. "She has hinted your case for weeks."

"Sly girl, I thought her too shy for such stratagems."

"'Oh, Lizzy, why have you never married? There must be *some* man who is both rich and handsome who likes you'."

Darcy leaned closer to her, his eyes moving between her eyes and lips. He whispered in a voice that suggested he paid little attention to Elizabeth's words, "Did she?"

"Those very words." Elizabeth placed her hand on her breast to swear the truth. Darcy's eyes followed the movement to linger on her female assets. She added roguishly, "Do you not like my eyes still?"

He kissed her once more and then buried his nose in her hair. Elizabeth nestled her cheeks against his coat. She had never felt so comfortable and safe in her life. Not even with her father.

Chapter Sixteen

Around noon the next morning Elizabeth paced in the breakfast room while Darcy asked her father for her hand. Her heart beat quickly. Despite the way Darcy and Papa seemed to like each other, Elizabeth was restless and anxious. Why she could not say.

Maybe Papa would speak some secret fear of Darcy's mind and convince him, while making a tease, that a woman slightly old and very bold was not to his taste. Elizabeth studied her dim reflection in a small mirror kept in one of the display cabinets Mrs. Bennet had littered around the rooms of Longbourn.

Ridiculous. She looked as fetching as ever. Her appearance had not changed in any great way in the last three hours.

Elizabeth picked up a book to make a pretense of reading. At last Darcy entered the room. Elizabeth saw his smile and the anxiety passed away, as though it had never been there. She was safe with him. She wanted to marry him.

"Your father wishes to see you."

Elizabeth briefly took and pressed Darcy's hand before she went to that most familiar room. Her father's bookroom.

The stove dimly burned red, and the light from the low winter sun illuminated her father. She had been struck once before that time was catching him. She saw it again. He had taken his spectacles off and Papa contemplatively studied the wall of books to the right of the desk. Two small cut-glass snifters and a dusty dark green bottle of fine cognac sat open on the desk. The glass in front of her father was mostly full, while the one in front of the chair where she usually sat had droplets of the golden liquid in its bottom.

Her chair had been moved to sit across from her father, instead of next to him. Evidently Darcy had used it. That gave a queer sensation, as though his moving her chair and sitting in it was a deeper intimacy than the kisses they had shared the night before. Almost a violation of some space around her sense of who she was.

Papa gestured towards the chair. "Lizzy, please sit down." He pulled out an additional glass, and filled it with a slender, carefully measured line of cognac. The fruity waft of the alcohol reached Elizabeth.

Elizabeth looked at her chair. She moved to move it back to its proper position, but then she paused. Her hand sat on the soft plush upholstery. Wouldn't sitting where Darcy had moved her chair be some sort of symbol of the way her relationship with her father must change now that she was to marry?

That thought was shrugged away.

Things between her and Papa would change in superficials, but in fundamentals they would be as they always had been. She moved the chair back to its proper place next to Papa.

He smiled to see her do it.

As she settled herself, Papa took a sip of his cognac and let it rest it in his mouth before swallowing. "Very good batch. Even Mr. Darcy praised me upon the flavor. Gift from Gardiner few years back; I hid it for a special occasion."

Elizabeth sipped, slightly surprised by her father's commentary. He was not a gourmand.

"I gave him my consent. Mr. Darcy is the sort of man I would never refuse anything if he condescended to ask. Besides, I don't have time for that nonsense about father's choosing. You have a mind of your own. My refusing my blessing would do nothing to change it, if you'd settled it."

Papa's dour manner frustrated Elizabeth. "You are capable of frankness. If you do not approve, say as much."

"I neither approve nor disapprove. I only worry — I did not marry well. Do not say anything, you know this. We live together tolerably, and I have been happy — I never really placed my expectations of happiness in my wife. A man can waste his time as he chooses, while women's time is wasted at her husband's choosing."

"Mr. Darcy would never mistreat me, or—"

"I know. I know. I know." Papa wearily held his hand out to stop her from speaking. "You are in love, and Darcy is *sans pareil*. The character of a perfect *gentleman*. He will never mistreat you, but you and he may differ in what you expect, and he is a man who will have his will done."

The perfect gentleman. Elizabeth threw that as an insult at Darcy once. She laughed. "Papa, I have not forgotten the *delightful* spats we had when we first met."

"He is a proud man, accustomed to having his own way."

"I am a proud woman, able to oppose him. I am who he needs. Mr. Darcy does not want a wife who would obey him in every way. He needs a prickly woman."

"What will he do with her once she is his wife? An extension of his family, name and self."

Elizabeth felt a cold and frightened. She thrust that emotion away. She loved Darcy; she trusted him. "I am no untried child. I know what I am about."

"There is time to change your mind — it soon shall be past such time. If you possess any uncertainty...Lizzy, I beg you to ask yourself rationally and be sure..."

"I have considered — you perhaps are jealous, Papa? You said I ought to marry, but this shall be a great change for us both. We have been so tightly connected, and...it will not change, not in the foundation."

"Dear Lizzy, I only worry for your happiness."

"And. Darcy *will* be my happiness — you shall always be welcome. Mr. Darcy will send his best carriage to fetch you if needed. Pemberley has a vast library; we will expect you to look at the rare books many times. You will come often, do promise."

"Lizzy, I will go anywhere you are, as often as I am wanted."

"That will be very much. Mr. Darcy agrees — he does not like too much company, but he will always welcome having you near."

"I hope so — since if he marries you I shall be there oft."

"If? Papa, I assure you, I have thought this through."

He sighed and patted her hand.

"I did not rush wildly into an attachment. My reason is as in control as it ever has been."

Mr. Bennet pulled his cap off his head and rubbed the bald patch on top. He then picked the cap up and put it back on. "I attempted to question him, subtly, but I have gained little sense of how Mr. Darcy shall act as a husband. I doubt he knows either."

"Oh, Papa." Elizabeth impulsively leaned over and kissed his forehead. "I do dearly adore that you care and put yourself out to such effort."

"I worry for you, sweet girl."

"I shall no longer be your burden."

"You shall *always,* no matter what, be my burden. You are my daughter — never a burden, always a joy."

"I will be happy. Papa, I will be completely happy."

"I hope so." Mr. Bennet swiped his hand over his forehead. "Please do not let me face the prospect of seeing my dearest child unhappy with her choice of partner in life."

Elizabeth was deeply moved, though she had always known of the depth of her father's care for her.

She embraced him.

He said, "My blessings you always carry with you. Be happy, my child."

But as she left, Elizabeth felt some odd presentiment of anxiety.

Darcy's tall lean form smiled at her. Anxiety, worry, and thought about other than him was passed away.

Chapter Seventeen

Christmas Day dawned bright, clear and cold. Thin snow whitened everything, and the crisp dry sun made the weather comfortable. A perfect day to celebrate the birth of the savior of all mankind.

Darcy stepped out as soon as he was dressed for a brisk morning walk. Next year he and Elizabeth would host everyone at Pemberley. He usually hated extended parties at home composed of anyone but his closest of friends. With *Elizabeth* he could tolerate any party.

The air pinched at his cheeks and the snowy ground crunched under his heavy boots. After a quick walk through the white blanketed woods and gardens, Darcy marched rapidly back to the house.

The past few years Bingley had held a big New Year's celebration including a fox hunt and a ball at Netherfield, while Bingley's mother-in-law — no one believed Mr. Bennet to be the one driving the Bennets to host — held a comparatively modest celebration feast on Christmas day.

Around noon Darcy and Bingley would ride with a group of local gentlemen around the neighborhood before they all headed to Longbourn. His fortunate sister and Jane were to travel to Longbourn and Elizabeth immediately following a Christmas breakfast.

When Darcy briskly stepped into the house, he saw that the Yule log still sat smoldering in the hearth. It had been dragged to the house from where it had been cut the previous day with all of the servants following and singing carols. Then the family members poured oil and salt over the wood and lit the log on fire using splinters from the previous year's Yule log that had been saved by the Bingleys. It was bad luck if the log went out too quickly, and Darcy took it as a pleasant omen, fitting with his high feeling this season, that the ashes had not died out yet.

Bingley came down the big stairs in an elegant dressing robe. "Darcy, old man. Darcy! Out already on Christmas morn! On such a day a man ought for once to sleep."

Jane — she would be his sister next year — stood behind her husband and smiled widely at him. "We saw you walk into the house — glorious day! Happy Christmas!"

"It is! Happy Christmas!"

Georgiana came from her room, wrapped in a thick woolen night robe. "Fitzwilliam, I am so glad!" She hopped happily. "Jane and I will be off to see Lizzy and Mrs. Bennet next."

"Happiness — I wish I were with you."

Everyone gathered in the breakfast room where rich Christmas cakes and hams awaited them. The staff of Netherfield adored Jane and Bingley and had produced a succulent spread. Darcy only half paid attention to the conversation. He had sent to London for a ring he could give her to symbolize their engagement and love, and he hoped to have a chance to give it to Elizabeth privately and to sneak a kiss from her.

Georgiana's exclamation caught his attention. "Oh! Mr. Peake is not to ride out with the other gentlemen?"

"The man is a good sport," Bingley replied. "Sprained his foot yesterday when we ran across the ice that had formed on Goulding's pond and—"

"Horrible." Georgiana clapped her hands together. "The weather is hardly cold enough for ice skating."

"This is why we did not invite the ladies." Bingley grinned. "No worry. Too small a pond to drown a man — not when his friends are there to crack him out if the ice cracks. Bare two ells deep."

"How does Mr. Peake do? Fitzwilliam, is he well?"

His sister's concern for their old employee showed well for her general concern for those beneath her. She had been raised well. "Mr. Peake took only a minor harm — he can even walk a little. The sprain is mild. But leaping on and off horses or dancing shall be beyond him for several days."

Georgiana nodded seriously.

When Darcy rode up to Longbourn early in the afternoon with the crowd of gentlemen come to be feasted for the evening, Elizabeth hurried out to greet him in the cold air, along with the other ladies coming out to welcome their men. Elizabeth smiled rosily at him. "Mr. Darcy — I have awaited you *desperately* this past hour and a half."

Darcy leapt down from the horse and kissed Elizabeth upon the cheek, as that was as much as could be appropriate, even betwixt an engaged couple, in public. "You? Did all Mr. Bennet's books burn up? I cannot smell smoke but—"

"I can talk rather than read," Elizabeth replied primly.

Darcy theatrically gasped. "Aha! You are bored on occasion by the society of ladies as well. I too suffer. Greatly."

"I am a lady; do you become bored by my company?" She raised her eyebrows and thinned her lips.

"I *know*. You are more a Lady than any other lady — Yet I am never bored by your society — I believe it to be a paradox philosophical." Her presence made Darcy euphoric, and he knew he talked nonsense.

She giggled.

"You should have occupied yourself giving French opinions to other women."

"French opinions?" Elizabeth grinned. "The novelty of being *engaged* still managed to distract me from every word spoken by my friends. Did *I* distract *you* from your ride at all?"

"I survived without being thrown, so I must have paid some attention to where I went."

"I *am* glad you did not get thrown — even though it shows a startling lack of feeling for me."

"Do not worry, Lizzy," Bingley laughed, holding Jane around the waist. "He has been the most horrid company since the evening he met you. Calflike and loverlike. You need not worry how obsessed our Darcy has been."

"Calflike?" Elizabeth spiritedly smiled. "Mr. Darcy, you ought to be made of sterner stuff than *that*."

"How can I protest? If I claim that Bingley exaggerates, then I will downplay the depth of my affection for you. Yet I hardly *enjoy* being compared to a yearling."

"What a difficulty. Poor Darcy — but you must choose whether to disappoint me by admitting a similarity to a bovine juvenile, or by confessing you do not love me enough to act like one."

"Inside, inside. Move the dispute inside." Bingley waved them in from the cold, half pushing Elizabeth by the shoulder. "Lizzy, *I* can tell you! The day after you met, he *insisted* he did not desire to court you. Very loud. Never heard a clearer expression of intent."

They entered the warm house, with its blazing hearths and crowd of guests. The portraits of Bennet ancestors greeted them along with the housekeeper helping to pull off the gentlemen's heavy overcoats.

Elizabeth put her hand on Darcy's arm. "I *am* glad to hear your affection for me went so deep as to disclaim any interest for me so quick. 'Twas well done."

"You are fortunate, madame." Darcy pulled her hand up and kissed it. "Not every Miss has a lover who will make such a declaration so quickly."

"You do not mean to tell me that you only disclaimed a desire for my hand to hide the intensity of your affectionate love, which developed on the first eyeballing—"

"It was the first tongue lashing."

"Did you attach such import to hiding your deepest heart from Bingley?"

"Nay! You misunderstand us. I declared my honorable intentions to your defending brother immediately. You *heard* him. That was his example of a *calf-like* behavior."

Bingley held up his hands. "I only report upon Darcy's behavior. I do not wish myself to be examined. Lizzy, can't you be satisfied with teasing Darcy? I am not the one who must be teased mercilessly. Darcy must be teased — punctuating his eternal smugness is the greatest advantage of the match."

Darcy looked down upon Bingley, peering over his nose. "You used to be intimidated by my height."

"Ha! Jane gives me confidence to face *even that*."

When they entered the drawing room Darcy immediately looked around for Georgiana, as she had not come out to greet him when the group of gentlemen arrived.

Georgiana sat in the corner of the drawing room, kindly keeping poor Mr. Peake company. Mr. Peake sat with his leg elevated on a footrest with drinks and chocolates near him. He looked comfortable adjacent to the blazing fire, and he sat in what must be the most comfortable stuffed chair in the house, except the one that Mr. Bennet occupied. Elizabeth's young cat sat on his lap allowing the gentleman to slowly scratch his ears. Darcy no longer pitied him.

Everyone spoke loudly and happily.

Darcy found the buzzing friendly instead of oppressing. He would face *anything* to stay in the same room Elizabeth smiled in. However rather than sticking *calf-like* to his love, Darcy had a duty he must attend to. While he thought Mr. Peake was safe for his sister to speak to, Darcy thought he should speak with him and Georgiana for a while to ensure there was nothing of concern in the man's manner towards Georgiana.

Mr. Peake tilted forward as he spoke, his wrists wide and open. Georgiana sat on the edge of her chair, cupping a glass filled with the mulled wine whose scent mixed with the mistletoe and holly hung around the room. Cut evergreen branches decorated the mantelpiece and window sills.

"I — or Mr. Jones, our clerk — takes the cheque to our own bank." Mr. Peake gestured animatedly. "That evening each bank sends a clerk to a tavern on Lombard Street to exchange the cheques received during the day and they settle any residual balances owed in cash. Quite an efficient system."

"But how do they prevent mistakes?" Georgiana leaned forward with rounded, unblinking eyes and every pretense of eagerly listening to Mr. Peake describe the minutia of London banking. "You must tell me more — oh, Fitzwilliam, Mr. Peake is telling me how banks worked. I always wondered how you can pay a dressmaker who banks with Barings with a cheque drawn against our bank at Lloyds—"

"Good god, Peake. You entertain a lady with tales of banking."

"I find it interesting!" Georgiana replied almost indignantly.

The man in question smiled and spread his hands wide. "She asks detailed questions."

Darcy tilted his head and shook it. He sometimes did not understand Georgiana. "It is kind you indulge her. I am glad you have not found the enforced inactivity a cause for unhappiness."

"Quite the opposite. My Christmas Day has been precisely what I wished it to be."

"Yes." Darcy nodded. "You monopolized female attention whilst we were gone. But alas for you, the other gentlemen are arrived, and your immobility will prevent you from pursuit of your favorite."

Peake laughed uncomfortably. "I expect to be content."

"A girl with you upon her mind would be drawn to you — I begin to speak like Bingley." Darcy shook his head. "I am in an ebullient mood, like none I have known."

"I already presented you my sincerest congratulations, but your good fortune is great. Miss Bennet is an extraordinary woman — I never have met her like."

"Nor I, and I am the fortunate one who has captured her."

"Capturing women?" As if called Elizabeth stepped up next to his shoulder. "You are not overattending your sister again?"

"I merely describe my heartbreak when she did not come outside to greet *me*." Darcy winked at Georgiana.

"*I* was not enough?" Elizabeth replied brightly.

"Your presence was beyond ample to ensure my happiness. But yet my sister ought to have rushed to my side the first instant I arrived — in past times she would do so."

Georgiana laughed. "Lizzy is *quite* enough greeting for you — you did *not* wish a substitution."

Soon others joined their conversation, and everyone had a happy time. An hour later the mixing of the party led Darcy and Elizabeth to be alone together speaking in the hallway. Too many people were chattering around for him to kiss his Lizzy, despite the bright green mistletoe with its small white berries which hung from the roof above. However, he at last had her alone.

He pulled the box for the ring he had chosen as a Christmas giving and a symbol of his love. "Would you..." Darcy flicked the box open. "Would you wear this for me? I shall put a ring upon you when we marry, but I want you to wear something more *specific* than a wedding band. And I want you to *now* wear my ring."

"It is lovely." She took the gold band from him and held it up to the pale light from the window. "A poesy ring? Aha! The marriage of true minds — from the sonnet?"

"We both admire Shakespeare greatly and...we are such a marriage."

"Let me not to the marriage of true minds admit impediment."

"Love is not love," Darcy replied, "Which alters when it alteration finds, or bends with the remover to remove. O, no! It is an ever-fixed mark."

She slipped the ring upon her finger. "Perfect. Fitzwilliam, perfect."

He nearly bent forward to kiss her, but there were several other persons conversing in the hall, with steaming mugs held in their hands.

Darcy leaned close to Elizabeth's pertly shaped ear. "Lizzy," he whispered happily. "Do you not *hate* the presence of other people?"

She pushed his chest, in a manner intended to pull him closer. "Abominable statement. On *Christmas*."

He leaned again to her ear, and breathed softly over the delicate ivory skin. Elizabeth shivered. "I cannot kiss you the way I crave amongst so many."

"Are you capable only of thinking about kisses?"

"I have the capacity to keep my mind upon many objects at one time — a necessary accomplishment: I am incapable of *not* thinking about kissing you."

She laughed and darting, kissed his lips when hopefully no one looked. "Darling man! But now I have given you your Christmas kiss, and you can expect no more."

"No?"

"No!" She laughed. "Now I *must* have some act of grand arrogance from you, to remind me of the man I marry, since we shall grow cloying if we continue along so well."

"We must *argue* to be a satisfactory couple?"

"No, no. We must argue to avoid being cloying. *You* despise an excess of sweet as well."

"Is there no *other* way to avoid such excess?"

"Kisses will *not* rescue us."

They leaned their heads, one towards the other, captured by the kissing of their gazes.

A loud clap startled both to straighten. "Darcy, Lizzy! Here you are." Bingley grinned boyishly. "Were you occupied?"

Elizabeth rolled her eyes, while Darcy replied, "If we *were* engaged in a private confidence, you could hardly expect us to admit it."

"A private confidence? Is *that* your preferred term?" Binley puckered his lips as though he were kissing. "But carols! You must join; both of you. Carols!"

With a laugh Elizabeth dragged Darcy by the arm into the drawing room. Everyone assembled around the hearth, holding glasses of mulled wine or hot punch. Georgiana stood close to Mr.

Peake who balanced himself with his hand on the back of a big wing chair to keep from placing unneeded weight upon his ankle.

Georgiana turned and smiled at Mr. Peake, holding open one of the song books to share between them. Darcy frowned. Perhaps he should not be so sanguine about giving Georgiana leave to spend time with Mr. Peake, even if *he* filled the time boringly with conversation about matters of business.

Despite his dearth of rakish skills, Darcy knew quite well such conversation could not lead to a woman's heart. Darcy shook his worry away. Even if attraction existed betwixt them, Mr. Peake had been employed at Pemberley and been reared within five miles of the estate. Peake understood that a tradesman could never aspire to the hand of the sister of the Master of Pemberley.

The singing began, led by Bingley and Mrs. Lucas. Darcy had a well-trained baritone which mixed perfectly with Elizabeth's voice, their voices rose in melody with the other singers:

> *While shepherds watched their flocks by night,*
> *All seated on the ground,*
> *The angel of the Lord came down,*
> *And glory shone around,*
> *And glory shone around.*

The merrymakers sang nearly an hour, and when the singing ended, Darcy and Elizabeth went to the punch bowl smiling together. Singing gave an extra glow to Elizabeth's cheeks and brighter light to her eyes. She had never looked so alluring as at present, with his ring upon her finger. They had not more than half finished their punch when the bell was rung for dinner.

The mid-sized dining room was crowded by the horde invited to the holiday celebration. They all sat packed so that they only had a few inches to move their arms about around the thick oaken table.

The guests were scattered every which way by Mrs. Bennet's seating arrangements, and Darcy found himself seated on the opposite side of the table from Elizabeth, and between Mrs. Lucas and Mrs. Goulding. Darcy was relieved, as he had been favorably impressed by both persons. Often he found a crowded dinner party a bore.

The social custom was to keep couples from sitting too closely to each other in a dinner party to make conversations more interesting. This never seemed unreasonable before. But now, Darcy wanted Elizabeth.

Roast goose, joints of beef, thick white soups, long strips of savory venison, pheasants and ducks. And squash, potatoes, carrots, all cooked to a fatty deliciousness. The presentation in the crowded dining room lacked the spectacle of high society dinners in town, but Darcy liked how the food had been prepared to be eaten, instead of looked at.

The time he dined in the Prince Regent's pavilion in Bath, there had been puddings in the shape of castles, roast pigs dressed up as soldiers, and living centerpieces with food was served off the bodies of nude women.

The Bennets' meal tasted savory and sugary in turn. The wines were excellent and the din of conversation made it almost impossible to hear anyone beyond his neighbors. The entire evening was infused with a convivial spirit of goodwill and the genius of the season.

The platters of food were half emptied and then carried away from the overfull diners, with the remainders to be given to the servants and then the cottagers. Then heavy black Christmas puddings were ceremonially carried into the dining room on silver platters and placed down on the table. The puddings had been aged for the past month and were now delectably ready to be eaten. Celebratory brandy was poured over each pudding then they were all lit at the same time. Blue and yellow flames leaped up, dancing in the air.

The footmen dished out onto the gentry's plates the burning plum pudding, full of raisins, cinnamon, and nutmeg and bits of dried apple and held together with suet and egg. The smell of the brandy that made the thickest part of the mixture wafted with the fruit to their noses.

Darcy smiled at Elizabeth sitting across from him and lifted a forkful to his mouth, as though saluting her. She winked back at him. He really detested the rule which kept them on opposite sides of the table.

The sweet rich taste of the pudding melted in his mouth. Darcy closed his eyes to concentrate on it. He now understood Mr.

Bennet's story about Elizabeth stealing one a few days before Christmas to eat alone. He hoped Elizabeth would bring the Bennets' recipe to Pemberley with her.

The alcohol in the pudding burned pleasantly in his mouth. Darcy swallowed the tasty bite. Then too quickly for elegance, he shoveled another into his mouth.

Mrs. Lucas, seated at his side, amiably said, "The Bennets have an old tradition of using a recipe that goes back to the time of Eliza's great grandmother, I believe. The rest of the meal is exceptional for them. Mr. Bennet usually does not allow Mrs. Bennet to splurge so high on food."

"An excellent meal."

"With your marriage to Miss Bennet, perhaps her *mother* now contrives to convince Mr. Bennet to relax the tight purse strings far enough to allow her to spend closer to the grandeur she wants. Ever since I arrived in Hertfordshire, it was clear Mrs. Bennet had a jealousy of how her daughter and Bingley live in a much wider style than she."

Darcy shook away a vague surprised unease. He knew Mr. Bennet always set aside money for the support and dowries of his daughters. His marriage to Elizabeth would end the need. Mrs. Bennet had fortune enough for personal needs, and with five daughters married — though one *was* widowed — and two having married wealthy, she would have no need to fear or worry for a place to live.

His connection with Elizabeth was, in major part, a spiritual thing, untainted by money. But she, and by extension her family, were wealthier now. It was rational for them to spend more freely. Darcy slowly enjoyed the flavor of another bite of the Christmas pudding.

He liked being richer than Elizabeth. He liked being able to bring her into a higher life. It somehow filled the grand name and old dignity of Darcy with new life. The point of such status and consequence was that he could share it with Elizabeth. His grandeur, his pride, his place would become hers.

Darcy ate the pudding carefully and slowly, savoring the taste. But by the time he'd finished his seemingly ample portion all of the leftovers from the first round had been claimed by the other diners. Darcy stared in surprised dismay at the empty platter, with a charred spot from where some of the brandy had incompletely burned and congealed into a thick syrup. He thought about scraping it off and picking at the crumbs of bread and the few raisins left on the platter, but that would be beneath his dignity.

Elizabeth's laughter rang across the table. Her cheeks were red and there was an additional light in her eyes. She leaned across the table and pointed at the platter. "We have others set aside — I shall ensure a pudding is brought to Netherfield for the New Year especial for you to eat alone."

Feeling slightly embarrassed by shouting across a table, Darcy replied, "I expect *you* to join me in the repast. I would not want an injured tummy."

Elizabeth blushed and laughed, flapping her hand as though she wished to drive it away. "Do not remember *that*."

"You recall my embarrassing moments."

"I would claim it is different, but alas, your point is valid."

Soon the female dinner guests withdrew to the drawing room, leaving the gentlemen alone in the dining room. Everyone continued to enjoy mulled wine, punch, eggnog and some ale. The crowd was loud and happy, though the presence of many older gentlemen kept the high spirits of the younger generation contained. Darcy continued to talk, laughing with Mr. Peake and Mr. Lucas.

After a little less than an hour the gentlemen rejoined the ladies in the dining room. When they entered the drawing room, Darcy's eyes immediately searched for Elizabeth. A bowl of hot punch was set upon one table and upon a stove in the corner near it a pot of mulled wine. Elizabeth and her mother and sisters were happily talking and pouring and preparing hot chocolate and coffee for everyone. Sprigs of mistletoe decorated the ceiling.

He approached Elizabeth and she liltingly laughed. "Not so soon! You shall not grab me again for your own purposes. Not *yet*. Go talk to someone elsewhere. Now what is your preference?" She gestured at the coffee, chocolate, tea and the wine and punch.

"You."

Mrs. Bennet stood behind his love, and she tittered and winked. If Darcy had not been slightly foxed he would have been slightly offended by the vulgarity, both his own and Mrs. Bennet's. As it was he bowed to Mrs. Bennet, who without waiting for his choice, poured Darcy a full glass of the punch. "Very good, made with the best Jamaica rum. My brother purchased for us. You'll not find better, not even on your fine estate."

Darcy sipped the punch. He had drunk too much already to be able to tell whether the rum was good or not, but he thought that the punch tasted like alcohol. Elizabeth laughed and pushed him again, her hand lingering on his chest. "Go talk to someone. A little separation is good for the soul — Mr. Smith, chocolate or punch?"

Darcy had already talked too much today. His head buzzed, and he knew the sensation of a crowding of his thoughts that happened after overlong house parties. He amiably spent a minute talking to two or three people, but when one of the guests with a more distant house left the sofa to prepare his carriage and family for the journey home, Darcy seized his chance to sit and hopefully be allowed peace until Elizabeth joined him.

It had been a fine Christmas, but...even if he had Elizabeth near him, he disliked too much social intercourse. Elizabeth laughed and happied where she stood handing out chocolate and punch to her guests. His Elizabeth thrived under such attention. If he could be allowed to spend a mere two or three hours conversing, and then simply watch Elizabeth laugh and smile and throw those piercing glances of understanding towards him.

She winked and waved at him from across the room, before supplying a rotund woman with large bustles and a feather in her hair a steaming mug and a biscuit.

Darcy was so happy. This was what happiness was.

Music began. It was a familiar air from Handel's Messiah. The sound was rich and complex. Georgiana sat at the piano with Mr. Peake next to her, his leg propped up on a small footrest. He sat in a position where he could serve to turn the pages of music.

Georgiana had been separate from male company for so long — as soon as he and Elizabeth were married he must contrive, though it may be easy with Elizabeth's help, to introduce her to appropriate men. Good God, one day his sister might marry. Such would have been a tragedy for him before he had Elizabeth to fill his house. He would have made himself to think happily upon the event no matter what.

A matter for the future. Darcy's mind wandered. He had woken fairly early, and the alcohol left his head spinning. He closed his eyes and drifted.

"You *did* avoid the company."

Darcy blinked open and grinned at Lizzy.

"I am proud of you. You attended to the company and talked happily for quite a while. The neighborhood has quite forgiven you your *first* night." Elizabeth plopped down on the sofa next to him, with a mug of hot cocoa spiced with rum cradled in her hand. There was a lilt in her voice from the punch and wine. "I must ask you a question, Fitzwilliam—" She laughed. "I still delight to name you that. Though I feel a little like Georgiana."

Darcy blanched. "Do not say *that*. I will then think of Georgiana each time you call me *Fitzwilliam*."

"Noooo!" Elizabeth giggled. "Terror and confusion."

Helplessly Darcy imagined himself engaged in marital activities, Elizabeth moaning his name, *Fitzwilliam*. And then a thought of his sister involuntarily coming to him.

"Pray tell." Elizabeth giggled and her cup shook, though she didn't slosh any of her chocolate onto the saucer. "Which thought gives your manly face that disgusted expression?"

She giggled far more when she had drunk a bit more than one glass. He felt fondness and tenderness. Elizabeth was so perfect, so beautiful, so completely his. She loved him, and she would depend upon him in the future. Till death do us part. It made him more of a man. "I adore you."

"What thought! I demand satisfaction. No distractions!" Elizabeth grinned happily at him. From the way her eyes dropped to his lips, he thought she was imagining their long kisses.

Darcy self-consciously looked around the room. There were too many other people. Maybe they could find later tonight *somewhere* to hide for a little while. "I cannot recall what I was thinking."

Elizabeth huffed with a wry turned up expression of disappointment.

Darcy poked her. "Don't be disappointed, thinking about you made me forget."

"Flattery will not give you 'scape from *my* inquisition!"

"I do not *want* to escape from you." Darcy caught her eyes and looked into them as he replied in a low voice.

"Oh my." Elizabeth's face flushed. She leaned towards him as though to kiss him, and he saw that disappointed realization in her eyes when she recalled the presence of other people in the room. She looked at them, frowned, and sipped her milky, alcohol infused cocoa. "I recall: I was to ask you. A serious question indeed. You must make an account for me. *When* did you first come to love me?"

"I hardly know, I was in the middle before I realized my true danger. It crept up upon me, our every encounter adding to my appreciation of your charms."

"No, no!" Elizabeth punched her free hand in the air and sat higher, pushing up one of her most charming features in a way that added to Darcy's appreciation of *its* charm. "That does not satisfy. There must have been some moment when you first had an inkling."

"I believe it was that first night we met, when you walked away — you were wearing a neatly cut yellow dress, and you had given me a righteous set down which I entirely deserved, and then as I admired your backside..." Darcy paused dramatically as he looked for some reaction from Elizabeth.

"You expect me to be *shocked*? I admire your backside quite often."

"Nay." Darcy grinned at her pearly smile. "I did not expect to be shocked — I was seeking to be complimented by you."

Elizabeth laughed.

"As I watched your finely clad backside walk away from me that night, with a slight sway to your hips which I could not look away from, and I knew I had suffered defeat during our argument, I thought to myself, *that is a damned fine woman*."

"Swearing in front of a lady?" Elizabeth giggled, and her free hand leapt forward to touch his hand. "I *knew* you admired me from the first. It was why you were so insistent on telling me that I couldn't trap you. You were frightened of the bait my neat backside offered. You needed to be careful to avoid the parson's mousetrap."

"I never have been happier to be disappointed in my plans."

"I am a *particularly* fine disappointment."

"And, my darling, when did you come to realize *you* loved me?"

"You called me my darling! You haven't said that before." Elizabeth looked at him with shining eyes and a brilliant smile.

"I haven't? You are *my* darling. My dearest darling."

She settled the cocoa and its saucer on the sofa next to her cautiously, and then leaned up to give Darcy a brief kiss, ignoring the other people in the room. Fortunately they had decided to ignore the lovebirds cooing at each other.

"You must yet answer my question." Darcy paused, and leaned forward to give Elizabeth a quick kiss of his own. "My darling."

Elizabeth sighed. "I shall become a puddle of melted butter if you continue to speak to me in that manner." She picked up the saucer and took a sip of her cocoa. "Let me consider? — it *certainly* was not the first night." Elizabeth grinned, with a mouth that begged to be kissed. "I hope you do not mind, but even if you do, I shall be laughing about that story for many, many years."

"So long as you are laughing *with* me, I shall be satisfied."

"Always."

Darcy looked at her eyes. She looked back. His heart started to beat. She smiled.

He knew they could not be too intimate in this group. Self-consciously Darcy broke their gaze. Mr. Bennet sat on the opposite side of the room talking to Lucas and Bingley. Elizabeth's *father* was in the room.

When Darcy broke their eye contact, Elizabeth looked down with a small seductive smile. "I think it was that day you escaped hunting with Bingley to pester your sister at Longbourn—"

"My care for my sister *did* move you."

Elizabeth grimaced. "Nothing of the sort — it is cloying. You are too present with Georgiana. You did something *else*. You picked up Anne in your arms as she squealed and ran to you, and you swung her about. You *never* look so handsome as you do with that little child." Elizabeth pressed her hands on her suddenly flaming cheeks. "It is an image that will be with me till the day I die."

"Oh." Darcy's voice lowered. "I had realized she was an attractive prop — she is exceedingly attached to you also, we were *partners* in seducing you."

"My, my." Elizabeth flapped her hand in front of her face and then drank the rest of her cocoa, putting the cup to the side. "Have you any notion what you do to me when you look like that."

"Yes." He deepened his voice further. "Do you have any notion what you do to me when you smile in that way?"

"What way?" She smiled at him, in that way, making Darcy's stomach leap. He felt a complete happiness come over him, and he just needed to smile.

"You ought to know," Darcy said, "I remember that day clear. The way you picked up Anne and held her enhanced *your* attraction. You shall be a fine mother."

Elizabeth looked down, with something like shame. "I was trying to look maternal."

Darcy laughed. "We both wanted the other to like us. Even before we really understood."

"I dearly love you." She smiled at him.

"I love you as well and deeply."

They both still glowed when the carriages took them apart. A few weeks more and he would be united forever with Elizabeth Bennet.

Chapter Eighteen

Elizabeth shivered as she lighted from the Bennets' carriage in front of Netherfield on the last day of the year. The sun had not yet risen, but rays of light over the horizon glinted off a few white fluffy clouds high in the air. The crisp air was filled with the baying of hounds, the stamping and braying of horses, and a cold wind penetrated through her heavy winter coat and made her nose redden.

Bracing.

Most of the gentlemen were already gathered and mounted on the lawn in front of Netherfield. They sat on their horses, with gloved hands clinging to leather reins, as the horses stamped and stomped against the cold. Footmen circled about delivering crystal glasses of whiskey and porcelain cups of cocoa or coffee for warmth against the cold.

Almost two dozen men on horses waiting for a few stragglers. Tomorrow was the New Year, and Bingley was hosting a great hunt for the gentlemen of the neighborhood and a grand dinner afterwards for the ladies. Elizabeth had not needed to come so early, but she wanted to see Darcy off, before spending the day in conversation with the ladies who were descending upon the house.

As Elizabeth glanced around she saw that Georgiana was out as well, smilingly talking to Mr. Peake who sat on a grey gelding he had borrowed from Bingley's stables. It surprised her how well he took to managing the horse. He could not have much opportunity to ride in London. Mr. Gardiner loved to fish and enjoyed shooting, but the fox hunt was too much of a young man's game for him. But Mr. Peake had grown up in Derbyshire and worked on Darcy's massive estate for five years before he took his position with her uncle.

Elizabeth's eyes surveyed the lawn, seeking her prey.

There he was.

Darcy sat tall and splendid in his red hunting jacket with large gleaming buttons and knee-high boots. The white tights that clung to his muscular thighs gleamed like snow. His horse was a massive stallion who frightened Elizabeth at first, but she'd been introduced to the beast, and now she knew that he had a sweet temperament and enjoyed apples and bits of sugar. Darcy looked proud, stern, like the great gentleman and master he was. His eyes looked calmly over the men.

Then he looked at her.

His smile took her breath away. With the smallest motion of his legs he directed his horse towards her. The smile destroyed the impression of noble severity. It made her stomach flip in little fluttering circles. He only looked at her this way.

She hurried to meet him, her boots crunching on the hard ground.

Darcy took her hand and leaned low on his horse so that he could kiss her, the warm breath heating her through her thick gloves.

"Off to kill some poor fox?" Elizabeth smiled gaily at him. "What has he ever done to you?"

"One hopes it shall be a dame, so that we can reduce the horde of pests destroying the livestock of this country that much more."

"Nay, nay — horrid notion. To plan to kill a *woman*."

"A Lady Fox. But then she would be a whig."

Elizabeth giggled and then groaned at the pun on the name of the famous politician. If he had not been sitting on his black snorting beast, she would have shoved him. "Not such a joke. No. No. Whiggishness is no excuse to kill foxes."

"It is my pleasure to entertain you with such word play."

"No! I do not give encouragement to such jokes."

"Of course not, my dearest."

Elizabeth flushed with happiness, though she could see from his eyes that he fully intended to use any other puns which crossed his mind. "Not *that* easily. You cannot call me my dearest and expect me to accede to everything—"

"Our life would become a dreadful bore if I could."

"The pun is a vulgar form of humor, far beneath you."

"It is poetry, rhyme. Rhythm — you admire the Bard. He uses puns oft. We have before discussed the farce in Midsummer Night's Dream. You referred once to the character by the name of *Bottom*."

"Horrid, shocking man — if I loved you not, I would be obliged to slap you."

"Only for *your* benefit do I make such jests."

"You are a strange benefactor—but I throw my hands in the air" — Elizabeth dramatically threw her hands into the air — "And I wash my hands of the matter. If *the Bard* uses puns, I cannot expect a mere mortal such as *you* to resist."

"Nor will I expect a mere, mortal female such as you to resist the addition to my allure such humor gives."

"Arrogant man."

"You admire me for it."

"Take care. I would be made miserable if you hurt yourself leaping some gate you ought not attempt."

"Do not worry — you can ask Bingley — I am the soul of caution during the chase."

Elizabeth raised her eyebrows skeptically.

"Perhaps not the *soul* of caution. I show some moderation." He openly ogled her person. "I have too much eagerness for our wedding to let it be put off by a bad fall."

"*That* thought I shall depend upon."

The gamekeeper sounded his brass horn, and the hunt gathered into its formation, Darcy near the front. Everyone laughed and chattered. They all were splendid and handsome in their jackets upon the healthy horses. The hounds were released and they leapt around the kennelmaster. The horn was blown again in a tight *taroo* familiar even to Elizabeth. The hunt set off.

Georgiana walked near Elizabeth and they stood together, watching the clump of horsemen, with Darcy's head sticking up above them all, descend down the carriageway to Netherfield, and then around a bend in the road which took them behind a tall hedge and hid them from the sight of the half dozen ladies who had come out so early. The top of Darcy's cap bubbled up, barely above the line of the hedge as they rode along, and then the group turned down the road again, and even that disappeared.

Elizabeth looked at Georgiana. "Inside, Georgie. Too cold for *us*, the wiser sex, to stand round whilst the men hunt and freeze."

"Oh no! It gets far colder in Derbyshire. You shall become used to *that*! I am almost comfortable at present."

She looked at Elizabeth, as though she wished to say something, but then Georgiana bit her lip and shook her head and walked inside. They greeted and talked to the other women. Mrs. Goulding was there, and she had a kind word for Georgiana.

The women clumped themselves in the breakfast room to get rolls and coffee before retiring to the drawing room to wait out the exciting day of dangerous leaps that the men would enjoy. Elizabeth believed in Darcy's caution and skill with a horse, but in the course of her girlhood, in just the narrow confines of her part of Hertfordshire, a half dozen men had killed themselves or been permanently injured during the hunt.

In London she had once listened to a strange philanthropist who railed against the barbarism of how the hunt cruelly hounded the poor foxes. He had been a ridiculous man who believed all ailments could be cured if men adopted a diet with no animal matter, not even milk or cheese. He had learned of such ideas when he met mystics who lived hundreds of years in India. Or so he claimed.

Elizabeth strongly doubted both the salutary effects of removing meat — everyone knew *that* led to weakness and a loss of strength as sure as too much meat led to fatness and gout — and she even more doubted that the mystics lived longer than the normal course allotted to a man.

Perhaps it was not *nice* to hunt foxes. Foxes were not nice animals. Elizabeth had seen what happened when one of the sly creatures gained entry to a henhouse. The true barbarism of the hunt was how it led foolhardy young men to take foolish risks to impress each other. Darcy was past thirty though, too old and too proud to play such games.

The conversation of the women moved to the drawing room and became excruciatingly dull. More women arrived, and Georgiana was kept in conversation by Jane and Mrs. Lucas, so Elizabeth had no need to keep an eye on her soon sister's pleasure.

Every gathering of women turned into people obsessed with servant troubles, the incomes of their husbands, fashion and fripperies. Only smallish doses of such discussion could be enjoyed! Today Elizabeth could not entertain herself with them. Darcy was everywhere in her mind. His lips. Everywhere. His touch on her forearm, the way he stroked his hand softly over the little hairs of her forearm, bare from where the gloves bunched up fashionably around her wrists. Their hands fit perfectly. Him sitting high and proud on his great horse — the tallest man in the group. Picking up his niece and holding her aloft, swinging around the giggling happy little girl.

Elizabeth imagined him holding his son, her son, *their son.* A little boy with his eyes.

She was going distracted.

With a laugh Elizabeth realized she'd sat for the past fifteen minutes without saying a word, and a doubtless absurd lovesick face. She made an excuse to leave the room and wander to the library. With her mind so full of Darcy, it would be impossible to actually *read* a book, but Elizabeth was confident she could read *at least* two whole paragraphs before her mind drifted off to obsess in peace.

Bingley's library had scanty pickings, though not nearly so bad as it had been in the months when he and Jane courted. Elizabeth had still read everything in the library, except Debrett's *Baronetage.* A wedding gift from the baronet Bingley had purchased Netherfield from, with his own entry bookmarked. Not even boredom would drive Elizabeth to *that* level of desperation.

Elizabeth studied the gold embossed leather backs of the books. The editions were expensive and fresh. A proper library had books with a beaten, read, appearance. Jane was no great reader either. Once Bennet grew a little older, it would fall to Elizabeth to make a determined effort to entice him to emulate his *grandfather.* Else Bennet would grow to be one of those hail and well met country squires who only had hunts and entertainments on his mind.

If Bennet combined the good looks and good manners of his parents, he would do far better as such a country squire than as a scholar. Some men were called to great deeds of the intellect, while others preferred feasting their fellows. Bingley had *not* missed his calling. Though her brother-in-law held a clever mind beneath his easy charm.

Aha!

Elizabeth's hand darted forth to grab a slightly used copy of *Midsummer's Night Dream.* She had read it in part several times while at Netherfield. Along with *Othello*, it was the only Shakespeare in Bingley's possession. The jealous Moor and Iago did not fit Elizabeth's current mood at all. But *he* had referred to *Midsummer's Night*, which made it precious.

With a laugh at that conceit, Elizabeth settled next to the frosty window. Despite no one being in the library at present the stove glowed to keep the room warm so that it would be comfortable later in the day when larger crowds of guests arrived. Before Elizabeth began to read, Georgiana entered the room. She hung near the door, not quite looking at Elizabeth.

"Enter, enter, dear. Bored as well?"

"No! Everyone is so easy and so kind."

"They are Jane's friends."

"Unkind" — Georgiana looked at Elizabeth and gave her a little adorable smirk that Georgiana wore when she decided to be brave and tease Elizabeth back — "to say they were boring."

"I claimed to be bored — which is a fault of mine, not the conversation."

"You are so like Fitzwilliam. He would not *say* such a thing to me, but he thinks it often" — Georgiana walked across the room and brushed her fingers over the spines of the books — "he said as much to me as you did about his behavior; *my* loss of reputation was an excuse to spend less time amongst others."

"He only needs a person to push him to join, and then keep an eye on him so that he can be sent to bed when he gets tetchy. Bingley only managed half the task, but I am quite prepared to order him to his room."

"I am yet astonished you can easily say such a thing about Fitzwilliam — or to him direct. He is so grand."

"Do *not* tease him in quite my manner. There is a great deal of difference between how such a liberty will be perceived from a wife and how taken from a girl twelve years his junior — but you ought tease Fitzwilliam a *little*."

"I will!" Georgiana replied with a smile.

The girl frowned and looked around. She had perched lightly on a floral pattern armchair next to Elizabeth's. But Georgiana didn't relax into the cushions, as though she half planned to leap up and flee the room. Without looking at Elizabeth, Georgiana said, "*Midsummer's Night Dream?*"

"My dear *sister*, you sought me for a reason. It was *not* to comment upon my choice of reading."

With a blush Georgiana laughed. "You are so wise. That is why I wanted to come to you to ask. You will know. I do find it difficult to speak of. You know."

"Not *yet*. Your manner happily suggests you do not have a dire criticism of *me*, or some worse secret about Darcy to reveal before I innocently and helplessly am drawn into his Gothic web set at Pemberley."

"No!"

"No?"

Georgiana smiled and relaxed into the joke. "Pemberley is bright and sunny. And even in the winter everything is crisp and cold. Entirely unlike a musty Gothic mansion. Also we have no *curtains*."

"I need not fear what makes the door to shudder at night when all are abed?" Elizabeth laughed. "Nor a headless monk."

"Well...the headless monk is really sweet. You should not *fear* him."

Elizabeth laughed and clapped. "Bravo, bravo. A fine return."

Georgiana shyly ducked her head.

"I have a suspicion of what you came to talk about. Might I venture a guess?"

Her friend's wide eyes shot up to her. Georgiana nodded with her lips parted.

"You have a strong attachment for your old friend, the handsome and capable Mr. Peake, and you are confused and wish some advice from me."

"How do you know!"

"You have been *quite* obvious. It is adorable. Anyone who pays attention to you must be aware of your preference."

She blanched. "Even Mr. Peake?"

"*That* is a less certain matter. He is as fond of you as you of him. In such matters lovers oft have the *least* ability to see."

"No! He cannot be. He *likes* me, a little, at least. He always was kind, even before...Wickham. And after... But he is too... He is kind by letting me talk to him, and letting me listen to him about everything. And he adores Anne."

"I despise repeating myself, but" — Elizabeth patted Georgiana's hand, and the girl's wide eyes looked at her, searching for reassurance — "in such matters lovers oft have the least ability to see."

"Do you really think so?"

"I am certain. The instant your name was mentioned he stood to attention and *begged* to know how you did. And after a separation of so many years."

"He did?"

"Your real presence can *only* increase his affection. A man does not stand near a woman as much as he does you, if he does not care."

Georgiana's eyes were wide as she considered this.

Elizabeth grinned at her soon-to-be sister. Elizabeth was so happy that any affection between others simply enhanced her joy.

"But...I am not so attractive as many. Do you know how I could maybe...be a little prettier?" Georgiana sweetly looked at her hands. "Like you and Jane? I am too shamed to ask Jane, even though I know she would be helpful. Everything looks perfect upon her."

"Not on me? My sweet dear, you need no advice of *that* sort. He likes you quite well as you appear today."

"But..."

"I am only glad he found a woman who *likes* to listen to him. I assure you most women would not be interested in the details of import regulations, while I saw you nodding along quite intently and encouraging him the day past. *That* is art enough."

"No! I was entirely unaffected! I swear. You should listen too. His work is so interesting! I *adore* listening to stories about it."

Elizabeth bit her lip to keep from teasing Georgiana further. Nothing could be a clearer sign of true affection than happily listening to stories about keeping warehouses stocked and selling materials at the best prices, and how easiest to manage His Majesty's custom agents.

"Don't you listen to Mr. Gardiner talk about his business?"

"Beyond a general way, not often. *He* knows better than to flirt with women in such a manner."

"Oh. But Mr. Peake is not flirting with me."

It was time to offer some sage advice. "*You* will need to encourage him."

"What?" Georgiana squeaked.

"Mr. Peake is not Wickham. He is a little shy himself, you know. Good with his profession, but not such a great social creature. And he is a tradesman. It would seem to him presumptuous to ask for your hand."

"Ridiculous, there is no difference of that sort. Not any longer. I lowered my name such that *he* is above me. All of the advantage would be on my side."

Elizabeth pursed her lips and looked at Georgiana.

"You don't think — I know I have a great fortune. But... He is doing very well. Right? I do not understand business, but the stories he tells me makes me think his firm must show a good deal of profit."

"I am *certain* his attachment is not of that sort. Though — let us be honest — the presence of a fortune never *lessens* the charms of a girl."

"I am scared of making a mistake, after Wickham...I always depend upon Fitzwilliam for such decisions."

"No — no." Elizabeth frowned, a strange anxiety and terror of possessing an opinion entirely different from Darcy in her guts. It was strange after they argued so much that she now would be frightened of disagreeing with him. "Even if you do not think much of your just claims, any longer, your brother has a high opinion of them. He is likely to dislike such a match, simply because Mr. Peake is in trade, and educated for it, rather than educated to be a gentleman."

"No! He would not oppose my happiness on such grounds. You know how sweet Fitzwilliam is — I am beneath any tradesman. I *have* repented. But I sinned. That sinning, and Anne, will always be with me."

Elizabeth pursed her lips. She *knew* Darcy would not consider it in that manner.

"You must be mistaken. Mr. Peake could not like me so much."

"He does not take time to talk to *every* pretty girl in his path."

Georgiana frowned thoughtfully. And sweetly. She really was a pet, so worried about this.

"No thinking of this sort. You are well matched in temperament and mind, and there is a strong mutual affection which survived a separation of many years. That is what matters."

Her friend bunched her hand up in a fist and resting her chin on it looked out the window at the clear, crisp morning. "You really think he admires me? A little, at least."

"He does."

They sat quietly. Elizabeth's eye studied the familiar vista. The woods denuded of leaves. The wagon track leading around the house. The fields bare, waiting the sprouts of winter wheat to poke their heads above the ground. Half of the tall stone barn was visible from this window.

"But I want to *know*!" Georgiana exclaimed plaintively.

Elizabeth raised her eyebrows and Georgiana blushed.

"I sound rather childish, do I not?"

"Very sweet" — Elizabeth poked her friend — "Pay attention, and you will see — you must pursue your own path in this. Follow your heart and your head."

"You still think Fitzwilliam would oppose such a match." Georgiana shook her head. "He only hopes for me to be happy and he likes Mr. Peake."

Elizabeth loved Darcy, and she believed he *would* accept his sister's choice in the end. But such a match would make him unhappy. *He* knew the value of Pemberley too well, and he thought much too highly of his sister to think she had been lowered to the level where a man in trade — a man who had once been employed upon his estate — could be an equitable match.

"If..." Elizabeth swallowed. There was a strange feeling in her gut. Darcy would disapprove of what she planned to say. Elizabeth shoved that emotion away. Darcy loved her. He did not expect them to share all opinions, and he was no controlling ogre. "If he opposes the match, do not let *him* do more than make you hesitate."

"I could never go against Fitzwilliam's wishes!"

"It is your life, not your brother's. You have the final guardianship of your own happiness. And, Georgiana, happiness is what you deserve."

"You believe in me. It makes me braver. But I could never ignore Fitzwilliam's wishes, not after what happened the last time."

"You told me Wickham convinced you Darcy would be pleased if you married him."

"I remember." Georgiana flushed. "I could not have been *really* so foolish. I must have known."

"You were fifteen. Do *not* underestimate your potential for foolishness at such an age."

Georgiana rubbed her cheek. "No *wonder* you do not blame me for what I did then. A girl capable of believing *that*..." Georgiana shook her head and whistled in awed disgust.

"You are different today. Wise and sensible."

"Never against Fitzwilliam's wishes. Perhaps he will oppose... I am *not* who I was."

"If he argues *listen*. But when you have better knowledge from your own reasoning, act on what *you* know. Your brother is only a man, he makes mistakes."

"How could you marry him if you think that?"

"I love him — I expect him to listen to me." Elizabeth smiled. "Mr. Peake listens to you?"

"Oh, yes! I can tell him anything. But he *is* wiser than me."

"You do not think he is wiser in *everything*? If so, I fear you will be disappointed."

Georgiana giggled. "Not *everything*."

"I am glad you know. An unequal marriage is never a good thing."

Georgiana bit her lips and grinned. Then she looked down. "But what if he is not fond of me in such a manner?"

"Then you will depend on my advice to make you prettier, and more forward. A man likes to know he is liked before he ventures on such a venture. Show him that. Bring him to ask you — ask him first if it comes to *that* necessity."

"Surely not!"

"Would you not like to be so brave?"

"It would be ridiculous — you did not! Not with my brother?"

"No — I *was* a little forward to encourage him. A lady ought never simply *wait*. Your brother had made up his mind — well before I had determined my own. You shall find this a difficult matter to believe, but he was nervous. I gave him a little reassurance."

"Lizzy, I am so glad you are to marry Fitzwilliam."

"I am *even* happier."

Georgiana grinned.

"Especially since you are to marry Mr. Peake so soon." Elizabeth added smilingly, "It would not do to leave Fitzwilliam alone in Pemberley."

Chapter Nineteen

The morning after Bingley's fine fox hunt — a day as good as he'd been promised — Darcy whistled and grabbed an apple tart from the piled plate on the wide table in the breakfast room. It was freshly baked so that the family and guests could enjoy whenever they woke. He savored the sugary richness of the apple combined with the flakey tenderness of the crust. Even food tasted better now that he was to marry Elizabeth. Darcy put the tart down and poured himself a strong mug of coffee from the carafe set out and mixed in the cream and a lump of sugar.

He tasted it, and the coffee tasted better than it ever had before. Taste. Her lips. The velvety taste of her tongue. The friction of lips rubbing against each other.

The house still slept, despite the hour being past nine. The dissipation of the past night had not ended until many hours after they toasted the bell tolling midnight. Bingley yet lacked thirty; *he* had excuse for not sleeping, but the bed had called too strongly to Darcy for him to resist, or even try to resist, after Elizabeth and the Longbourn party left.

Why would he *wish* to resist and spend hours with Bingley's other guests when he could dream of Elizabeth?

Darcy's entire being glowed at the memory of their dances last night. Her hand. Touching her hand. Her trusting smile. Her laughter. Her flashing eyes. The sweet curve of her bosom.

He loved her. He loved her and he had her. A man in such a fine situation had an excuse for whistling as he breakfasted with coffee.

Darcy whistled the tune from the final dance of the previous night's ball.

After he put away the roll, Darcy rang the bell to call a servant. The uniformed footman immediately responded, looking fresh and ready when he entered the breakfast room. Impressive. Darcy had noted this same man awake, partying the birth of eighteen hundred and seventeen late the past night. The footman had been dancing a spinning reel on the lawn outside with a pretty maid. Darcy said, "A sheaf of paper and quill and ink."

When the supplies were brought, Darcy seated himself at a small writing desk kept in the room next to one of the windows for the purpose of people being able to do such work while still remaining part of the party. His partial break with his cousin had lasted long enough. He still cared for Colonel Richard Fitzwilliam dearly, and if Richard would stand in a room with Georgiana, he dearly wished the man to be present at his wedding, and as more than simply a distant guest. They had been distant the times they had met for family matters since he had not made Georgiana marry Mr. Carteret.

Elizabeth had mentioned meeting Richard at Rosings Park when she visited her friend, the wife of the parson. It caused him to have a longing to see his cousin again.

Richard,

I know not what salutation to use. You were angry with me, and I refused to argue with you. I withdrew from everyone following the events with Georgiana and the birth of Anne. I ought to apologize to you, and I think you ought to me. Neither of us were happy, neither of us provided the friend the other needed. I do not repent of allowing Georgiana her choice to not marry. However, I heartily repent of allowing you to retire from me, and of not making an energetic and close effort to return our friendship to what it had been.

I am to marry in a few weeks. A woman who you met once at Rosings, she tells me, Miss Elizabeth Bennet of Longbourn in Hertfordshire. I am entirely in love with her. It changes a man, when he makes the choice to marry. Love for her fills his dreams and his breakfasts and travels and evenings with a glow. And Miss Bennet is wise; when I think how my relations with you appear to her, I appear petty in my own eyes. I realize how I have missed our friendship and companionship.

If you attend my wedding, it would be an added joy to a happiest day. You are my friend and my cousin. Once we were as close as brothers. I wish that again.

Please attend and come a few days early, if you can, so we might reminisce. You remember Mr. Bingley, I am resident at his manor, Netherfield in Hertfordshire near the town of Meryton. Please come.

Yours sincerely,

F Darcy

Darcy closed the letter, and he held the wax up to a candle. It had been thoughtful of the servant to bring a stick of wax along with the writing materials. He sealed the letter, pressing his ring into the gooey wax that dripped onto the stiff paper, and he called for the servant once more. After the footman took the folded letter, Darcy let out a long breath.

That was done. He felt powerful and happy. It was strangely difficult to make such a move of reconciliation. Before he always had hesitated at sending a letter of this sort to Richard, afraid admitting his own wrongness would make him seem weak, or afraid he would be misinterpreted by his cousin.

Elizabeth made him better.

Darcy poured himself a fresh mug of coffee. He put his nose close to the cup so he could enjoy the strong aroma and then cradled the saucer in his hand and walked to the window to smile at the icy day. Colder than the previous day when they were hunting. It had been a fine game. Along with Darcy, Mr. Peake had managed to outride many of the local gentlemen, showing off a certain Derbyshire pride.

Georgiana had danced the last dance with Mr. Peake. She had looked too...happy. His sister looked like she was in the grip of something more serious than a mild infatuation that could pass without any consequence.

Damnation. And everything was going so well with his sister. He at last had begun to feel as if she was well and happy. And now an unsuitable infatuation.

Darcy looked back out the window. A farmer walked along a distant road, bowed under with a big table he carried awkwardly. A woman in a patched dress walked up to him from the other direction, and the farmer put down his burden and kissed the woman. Then they both picked the heavy table up, and walked forward easily carrying it between them.

Elizabeth would help him with his sister. Everything was better now that they could carry his burdens between them like the happy farm couple on the road.

She might disagree. Elizabeth's beloved uncle was Mr. Peake's partner, and his business would benefit if Mr. Peake gained a large sum of capital. Mr. Peake himself was the cousin of Elizabeth's equally loved aunt.

Darcy paced back and forth along the wooden floor of the breakfast room. He put his coffee and saucer down on the brown window sill so he did not spill it. Elizabeth was not mercenary. She understood the importance of the distinction between a gentlewoman and a tradesman.

Also, Mr. Peake was a good man.

Darcy understood his character: he was solid and honorable. He would not abuse Georgiana's infatuation. There needed to be separation between them, so Georgiana's fondness could cool.

Elizabeth could give a discreet message to Mr. Peake, asking him to be more distant with Georgiana, for Georgiana's sake. In a few days he and the Gardiners would return to London, and Georgiana would not see any of them.

A few more weeks. The banns needed to be read. Then the marriage. He would possess his Elizabeth. The right to hold her body. To press her breasts and stomach against him. To flatten her body tight against his as they embraced. To undress her slowly, undoing her dress, one pearl button at a time. And then letting it fall away leaving her chemise exposed and—

A cough behind him startled Darcy.

"Fitzwilliam. I...I have a matter..." Georgiana trailed off.

Darcy looked at his sister, caught off guard by her entrance into the breakfast room.

"That is — well, about Mr. Peake. I...I have formed..."

Anxiety blended with Darcy's frustration with having his thoughts about Elizabeth interrupted. She must be confessing her attraction to Mr. Peake, and he needed to discourage her carefully, so that she would not be torn apart by the end of the fantasy. "What," Darcy spoke softly, kindly, "have you formed?"

Georgiana looked at him through her long girlish eyelashes. The breakfast chairs had two carved wooden posts with the curved back between them, and Georgiana's hand curled around the top of one of those posts.

"You...you always approved of Mr. Peake. Approved. Clever. Honest, hardworking. And happy, I mean unhappy. You were unhappy when he left."

"Mr. Peake is an exemplary *worker*. Clever and indefatigable in his duty. We know his people. I was unhappy *then* to lose him, but always happy to see him gain the opportunity to display his talents in the way most remunerative for one in *his position in life*. He has furthered himself far better than he could have in my employ. Mr. Peake is remarkably capable in *trade*."

"Oh." Georgiana smiled and relaxed. "I became nervous. Elizabeth thought you disliked him."

"Elizabeth did?" Darcy was confused. Of course he didn't dislike Mr. Peake, and he had shown him proper condescension. Oh, Georgiana must have found it easier to ask a woman for advice first, and Elizabeth had counseled his sister against her interest in Mr. Peake. A woman in the grip of an infatuation, Georgiana had not wanted to listen to the counsel of others.

"She thought you...well, he is in trade. So you would not approve...well that is—"

"He belongs to an inferior rung of society than us. I do not judge a man poorly for the position he is born into, so long as he does not strive to rise higher than himself. But, in spite of his virtues, his station means we must always keep a distance betwixt us and him."

"Oh." Georgiana deflated, and her smile fell. She sat at the table for support. Her eyes resolutely studied the Chinese tracery inlaid into the porcelain surface. "Is that...important?"

"Yes."

"I mean...so significant to you? The only matter you hold against him?"

"Hold against him? He is in his place and we, the Darcys of Pemberley, are in ours."

"Elizabeth is beneath us in consequence."

"Dear, dear, sweet sister." Darcy sat next to her and placed his hand comfortingly on Georgiana's arm. He soon would embrace her while she cried, he thought, as he had several times after her pregnancy was discovered. "Mine and Elizabeth's case is different. She is entirely a gentlewoman, even if she has connections to trade. Her father's family has owned this estate for generations. Her dowry, despite being less than customary for a man in my position, is sufficient. A few will think I married beneath myself, but once they meet Elizabeth... Enough equality exists betwixt *us* for happiness in a relationship. However..."

Georgiana shivered and pulled the fabric of her sleeves down in a self-soothing gesture. She wouldn't meet his eyes, still studying the pattern painted onto the table.

Darcy was stuck, as he looked for the comforting words that did not come to him. He wished Elizabeth was here.

"But...my daughter. Anne. Fitzwilliam, it isn't like before. I am not...there is no reason for me to worry about social standing and, and — I am surely *worse* than Mr. Peake. He is the one doing a favor to me, with Anne..."

"No! You are my sister yet! You are yet Darcy! Not less than before. Nothing less than before."

"I want to marry him. I love him."

"Did he speak that rot — that idea that you are now lower than him?"

"You do not doubt his character, or his good nature, or..."

"A Darcy. Not for a tradesman. My sister will not marry a man in business. She will not marry a man forced by his position in life to oversee his warehouses every day — and more, you will not marry a man who quits his business to live off the income of his wife's fortune."

"No! Allen would never do that! He adores his work far too much to retire from it. I love hearing him tell me about it."

Darcy stared in worried frustration at his sister.

"He becomes bored by the end of a day of dissipation and party, like yesterday, and—"

"Allen?"

"Oh." She worried her hands terribly, and lifted and put back down her cup of coffee three times. Georgiana started to pant. Darcy became quite anxious. He wished Elizabeth was here to comfort her. "You do not understand."

"Dear Georgie. I spoke harshly. You like him very much to be imagining such things—"

"We agreed to marry. Last night."

Darcy was quite sure he had misheard.

"We did. I love him and—"

"You yet seek for a man to take advantage of you for your fortune. You learned nothing."

"No! Not like that."

"Then what is it like? Another impoverished fortune hunter is—"

"Oh, all wrong. This is gone wrong. Allen — Mr. Peake — he didn't. You must not think *that*. He is wholly different. I love him; he loves me. We—"

"Like Wickham approached you for love?"

Georgiana looked pale and stricken as though slapped.

"I...I ought not have said that." Darcy put his hand over his face. "Your news is a surprise. I incorrectly possessed a high opinion of Mr. Peake. I had considered him to be man enough that he would refrain from taking advantage of your obvious affection. But, it surprises me not that you lacked the wisdom to see through the rake's pretense of love, since—"

"A woman!" Georgiana stood and glared. "Since I am a woman? Do not insult my fiancé so. Mr. Peake took no advantage of me. He is principled and good." Her voice and eyes dropped to their normal shy manner. "You misunderstand. Oh," she wrung her hands, "if I can only make you understand."

"Oh, Georgie, I must save you from this mistake. You will not have my permission. Not to throw yourself away on a tradesman."

"Please, his profession cannot be *all* you have to say against him."

"His position in society is enough."

The door to the breakfast room opened. Darcy expected to see Bingley or his wife. He hated that such an important conversation would be interrupted.

Elizabeth and Mr. Peake stood in the entrance to the breakfast room being shown in by the Bingley's housekeeper. She looked beautiful, but nervous.

Mr. Peake looked at Georgiana who cried.

Darcy said sharply to him, "I have no audience with you, Peake. No business. I answer every answer you seek: *no*. I am shocked by your presumption in staring so high. But like Icarus your high flight shall be burnt from the sky. I once held high opinion of you, no longer. Any faith any man put in your character was bestowed ill. You took advantage of a girl who has been secluded from society for the past years, and you manipulated her affections so that you could have an opportunity to gain thirty thousand pounds. You disgust me. You ought have known I would not allow my sister to marry my former under steward."

The man stood tall and proud. He had a firm control of himself. Mr. Peake bowed slightly. "I see you are immovable. I believed such likely. I only wish you to know that my interest in your sister was driven solely by a deep and abiding affection for her spirit and her mind, and that the pecuniary considerations you think were so central to me had no influence."

Darcy stared at him. He studied Mr. Peake. The righteous anger crumpled into pity.

It had been upon Darcy's mind earlier this morning. Love could drive a man to mad acts. Darcy knew that now. Mr. Peake's face was stiff, yet pained deep. Darcy ached with sympathy. If he lost Elizabeth, he would look much the same. It was a pity Peake was not of an appropriate station and family. Darcy said, firmly, but kindly, "I spoke in anger and my assumption was fallacious—forgive me for impugning your character. But my decision cannot be changed. You are no fit match for my sister."

"Fitzwilliam." Elizabeth walked towards him, a worried face. "Do not be precipitous."

Darcy looked at her. "Nothing exists to consider. He is no gentleman."

"Do not be hasty, you already realize you misjudged Peake's motives." Elizabeth's eyes flashed, like when she was angry.

"He is no gentleman. There is nothing else to be said."

"My uncle is as much a gentleman as Peake."

Darcy clamped his jaw tight. No matter what her opinion, Elizabeth should not argue with him in front of others. Perhaps Georgiana, but Peake was not part of the family, and the housekeeper still stuck her head in through the open door, watching the drama curiously.

Georgiana looked between Elizabeth and Mr. Peake, Mr. Peake walked towards her. Darcy said sharply, "Peake, if you are a man of honor, I beg you have no further intercourse with my sister. Mrs. Nicholls, show him to the door."

Mr. Peake looked at Georgiana, with some silent appeal in his eyes. Georgiana looked at him, sobbing and shook her head. He retired from the room.

Georgiana stood and rushed from the room, without ceasing to cry.

It was like a blow in Darcy's guts. In his chest. How could he help his sister? "Elizabeth, talk to Georgiana. Explain how this is for the best. She listens to me, but if both of us—"

"No. Not for the best. The best is for you to offer your permission and blessings. Mr. Peake is a fine man, I know few better. Do you intend for us to avoid my uncle and aunt as well?"

"Your uncle is better educated and from a more respectable family. Peake is the first of his line to make anything of worth of himself. I would not allow your uncle to marry my sister either."

Elizabeth ground her teeth together.

A gust of icy wind outside rattled the windows. The sky was turned grey. Darcy's coffee sat on the window sill, gone cold.

"You should not argue with me on such a matter," Darcy added.

"Not *argue* with you? Heavens! Not argue? What next will you demand?"

"You — not in front of others. You *know* I do not mean every argument. But on a serious matter, when we are married, I expect all respect to be shown in public."

"Appearances? *That*." Elizabeth spat. "Georgiana is miserable. Your sister. For no reason. Your sister made miserable by your obsession with appearances."

"Mr. Peake and Mrs. Hood watched. And Georgiana. We should present a unified front to them all."

"She will never achieve a splendid match."

"Elizabeth..."

"Peake is her choice."

"Her marriage is not *her* choice. I am her guardian. Her brother. It is my place to determine her happiness."

"Why do you not wish to see Georgiana happy?"

"*Elizabeth*."

"I should not have said that." She covered her eyes and pulled out the chair she had gripped and she sat heavily on it. Elizabeth looked at him with her deep soulful eyes. "I am made so angry. But, pray, let us talk rationally."

Darcy nodded, but then he said, "I fear we have nothing to speak of. Georgiana is my responsibility. I will not sell her to a tradesman, no matter what."

"*Sell*? Where is this obsession with money? Besides, Peake does not have enough to buy her."

"Then he is a fortune hunter."

"They love each other. You *said* you saw that."

"Beneath. Under. He is under her."

"Breeding creates inferiority, in addition to sex? Georgiana and I cannot make our own choices because we are women, and Mr. Peake is not worthy of happiness because he wasn't born with a giant pile."

"A Darcy woman, a granddaughter of an Earl of Matlock, will not marry a tradesman. The shades of Pemberley would rebel at such pollution."

Darcy took a firm pose. He stood before the breakfast table with one hand behind his back. He needed to make Elizabeth *understand*. He felt an uncanny anxiety. Why did she need him to explain? She should just know. His wife should feel in her guts the consequence of the Darcy family. She should *feel* the grandeur.

"The *shades* of your estate? You intend to ruin the happiness of your sister and of a decent, respectable man, to protect the tender sensibilities of your *ghosts*. I had joked with Georgiana about your estate having gothic tendencies. And now you tell me it 'twas no joke. Have you other secrets I should know before we embark on matrimony?"

"This is not a-a matter of humor. Work with me to keep Georgiana from suffering—"

"I am working upon *you* to spare her unnecessary suffering. Permit her to marry Mr. Peake."

"*You* ought to see that it speaks ill of his character that he sought to persuade Georgiana. The difference in status. You must understand. Why can't you understand? Georgiana has been isolated, and she is brimfull of affection. If he had been a good man, he would have made no offer of marriage. It speaks ill of his character. Lizzy, just understand."

"*Georgiana* made the offer. Mr. Peake demurred at first for the reason you suggested. I had the entire story from him."

"He sought to cast himself in the best light."

"You are not listening to me."

"I do listen to you, but *you* do not speak sense."

"Isolation? That is your excuse? *You* kept your sister locked alone because you hated company and parties. That is *your* failing."

Darcy clenched his teeth together. Elizabeth was right. He failed his sister in that way, and he ought not resent Elizabeth for reminding him so explicitly. Yet, a little, he did resent her for it. He had told her he felt that way in confidence, and she had comforted him, and told him he had done the best he could for Georgiana.

The color drained from Elizabeth's face. She looked down and opened her mouth several times. "Forgive me I—"

"The thought had crossed my mind," Darcy spoke loudly, ignoring her words, "that you might be motivated by a concern for your uncle, rather than a concern for my sister. The hopes for expansion he possesses — you must have thought that Georgiana's fortune would help him greatly."

"You accuse *me* of base motives? When *you* judge a man solely by his position in society?" Elizabeth's face turned red. "Do you not wonder about my own agreement to marry you? Perhaps I solely accepted for your fortune?"

"I do not expect your affection to be entirely disinterested. I know you care for me deeply — have you *never* thought with pleasure on my estate and what you might buy with the pin money that will be settled upon you? You like money as much as every other girl. No lies, Elizabeth. You think it would be a good thing for your uncle's partner to marry a woman with Georgiana's fortune."

"You. You." Elizabeth growled, standing up and throwing the chair she'd been seated in backwards. It tipped over to clatter against the floor. Elizabeth said icily, "To think of the presence of money as a good, is entirely different from being driven by base motives. I am *insulted*."

"Then what motive for supporting the match between a man of no consequence in trade and my *sister*."

"You great, vain, careless *gentleman*. You so choose that all connected to you shall be well connected themselves."

"I do. My pride demands a better match for my *sister*. My pride ought to be *your* pride as well. You will be a Darcy too. What motive, base or foolish, drives you to argue for diminution of *our* house?"

"Her happiness — Georgiana and I talked about her fond memories of Peake several weeks ago. She has not forgotten him, despite being apart for many years."

"I must hold an even worse opinion of Peake, if he made love to her at her most vulnerable time those years ago."

"That is *absurd*. They talked."

"He should have never *spoken* to *my sister* with such a thought in his head. He should never have permitted himself to feel anything. Especially then. A servant. I feel a creeping disgust beneath my skin at the simple thought of such a man and my sister. It is more polluting than Wickham."

"And *this* is what you think of me and my family."

"Enough. No more. My decision is made. On any other topic, I would respect and wish to hear your opinion. But Georgiana has always been in my charge, and the sacred duty was entrusted to me by our father to watch over her and ensure her happiness."

"No more? You say no more? I am not allowed to speak anymore? You silence me."

"You would silence yourself if you felt as you *ought*."

Elizabeth stood and paced the room. She chopped her hands through the air rapidly, speaking in a clipped angry tone. "*Her* choice. A right to disapprove — you have *that*. But who. Who she marries is. Her choice. Her life. Her choice. *Hers*. Delay, but not deny. A substantial delay. That is wise, as they have not seen each other for years. But to prevent—"

"I have spoken. Elizabeth. Nothing further. Speak nothing further towards me upon this matter."

She furiously turned towards him. Her eyes flashed. The fabric of her dress swooshed around her legs and hips. There was a flash of lightning in the far distance as a storm approached, the light made the red in Elizabeth's cheeks stand out vividly. Rolling thunder sounded, pounding through the bare fields of Hertfordshire like the cannonade from a Man of War.

"You cannot end this matter. You cannot stop me. I will speak. I will be heard. You cannot end Georgiana's hope for happiness. It is *her* life."

"*My* choice. My right. It is my right, and it ought be my right. I will not never, ever —- I will never let her marry someone so distant below her, myself and *you* once you have married me. Georgiana deserves better. She deserves the best."

"Lord! Such a fool."

"I am not a fool."

"I. Me. I am the fool!" Elizabeth threw her hands up in the air and paced. She refused to meet his eye. Every line of her person was tense and radiated unhappiness.

A nervous squealing feeling entered him. It was in his stomach. His chest felt like it was being squeezed, and his throat was caught by a vase. Something was dreadfully amiss. He could not read Elizabeth. She was angry. A voice in his soul said he needed to do something to mend matters. She was a proud woman, independent, and fiercely committed to her ideals.

He would not be moved in such a matter. She needed to understand that in their marriage, he would be the final maker of decision.

The storm hit the estate. It fell down, pouring rain in a heavy pattering on the roof, and the wind drove splatters against the window, making it impossible to see outside, except when lightning strikes illuminated the whole grey sky.

Elizabeth paced.

He must say something. He could not allow Elizabeth to *think*. She was thinking the wrong thing. "Lizzy, please, come here."

"That is all I am? *Mr. Darcy*. A pretty creature at your control? You think my *passions* can drive me to irrationality. You think you have right to dictate to me."

Darcy bit his tongue. "I will always respect your wishes."

"Add not *lies* to thine faults. Your very manner of standing shows you do not respect me. You plan to allow me what freedom your whim gives me, so long as that whim remains your whim. But no respect."

"The philosophies of Wollstonecraft will move me no more than Georgiana's tears or your earlier arguments."

"You do not desire a marriage of equals. You plan to make me your object."

"If I desired a pretty thing to play with, I would have chosen a very different woman. Your mind is your chief attraction."

"No. Not now! I'll not listen to your flattery. Your low voice will not enslave me once more."

"It is not flattery it is—"

She pulled her ring off her finger. The gift from him, to symbolize their engagement, and she threw the gold band on the breakfast table. It bounced harshly and leaped off and rolled against the wall with a clang.

"Theatrics will not lead me to relent. My position is final: Georgiana shall not be permitted to marry Mr. Peake."

"You think this is theater? That I jest?"

Everything froze in his stomach.

"The irony is you were right: My head said I could not trust you. But my heart" — she tapped her bosom, above that organ — "demanded you. My passions overrode my reason — and my father's advice."

"Elizabeth, stop this."

"Yes, my father — he was cautious in how he said it, but he believed I made a mistake. But he *respected* me far enough to do no more than to advise me to think carefully upon a match with you. Ha! If I'd been guided by my reason and my male relatives, I never would have even considered your offer. How does that make you feel? To be the poor lusty choice of husband."

"That is nonsense."

"You are so vain. I am not going to marry you. I am jilting you, abandoning you, think however ill of me as you wish. I will not marry you."

"No...no, Elizabeth — you love me. I — no! You cannot. I love you. I adore you. After how we kissed. You feel it too. You still feel it."

He grabbed her shoulders and tried to kiss her. She wrenched herself away. "No."

"You are too serious of a woman to do this. To break an established engagement. Please — I...I always will keep you and protect you. Georgiana's position has nothing to do with it. You—"

His guts were frozen. Elizabeth began sobbing.

"I do not wish to hurt you. But...Mr. Darcy, my reason tells me I cannot be happy with you. You have behaved in...in *too* gentlemanlike of a manner. I will not be happy with you, and in the end my unhappiness would become your unhappiness. Good bye, and...and God bless you."

"No. Lizzy." Darcy grabbed her arm to keep her from leaving. "You cannot — you will be happy. You will!"

"Not if I am under your control. Not with a man who does not respect me. Not with you." She ripped her arm away, and fled through the door before he could catch it again.

Chapter Twenty

When Elizabeth stormed out of the breakfast room, Mr. Peake stood with his shoulder leaning against a door post in Netherfield's entry hall. He had a defeated expression.

Bingley stood there awkwardly making desultory conversation with Peake.

She shambled past them to the coat rack, and she jerked her heavy blue winter coat from the wooden hook. Elizabeth forced her arms into the coat, and then she yanked away from the housekeeper when Mrs. Nicholls approached Elizabeth to help smooth the coat on. Elizabeth ordered the woman, "The carriage. Bring it. No delay."

Bingley waved to Mrs. Nicholls to not go yet and raised his eyebrows. "Awful weather — not yet. By no means, not yet. Jane will be down presently, I am surprised she is not yet down. Pray, do not leave so soon. Anne and Bennet will be brought down and—"

"Faith! Bingley, you ramble on too deuced much. Call my deuced coach! Give my deuced apologies to Jane, and...and...and...she can visit me."

"You and Darcy argued."

Mr. Peake asked, with a helpless manner, "He does not relent — there is no change in what he says?"

Elizabeth opened her mouth to reply with the mix of anger and hurt she felt. Instead she shook her head no. Her stomach hurt. Tears were interfering with speech.

"Peake, you asked to marry Georgiana? That—" Bingley whistled, and shook his head with impressed disbelief. "Darcy has grand family pride. He ought to — *you've* seen Pemberley. Nowhere it's equal...nowhere. Lizzy, you argued about Georgiana with Darcy?"

"The carriage." Elizabeth said sharply to the housekeeper, who had not moved to follow her earlier orders.

The older woman looked at Bingley for confirmation. Elizabeth growled. It was her own damned carriage, not Bingley's. Or rather Papa's carriage, which came to the same point.

"Not in a fortnight, Mrs. Nicholls. *Now.* Bring the carriage round."

At the tone in the Elizabeth's voice, the housekeeper skittered off, shaking her head. Elizabeth pressed her hand against her face. Was this how she dealt with pain? By rudeness to everyone else?

"Lizzy, what is the matter? Tell me how you and Darcy fought...perhaps I might help."

Bingley placed an arm around her shoulder as he spoke in a soothing tone. Elizabeth shrugged her brother-in-law off and walked to the corner next to the door.

Alone. She wanted no one, certainly not Jane's eternally cheerful husband. She had just jilted Bingley's friend and *thrown* his ring upon the ground. She shouldn't have, no matter how much Darcy annoyed her. The sky hurled down a freezing sleet, and often lighting flashed and thunder rumbled.

Bingley hemmed and said, "Bad weather, eh wot?" No reply. "Unpleasant for the poor coachmen and horses."

"I'll order James to take the road slow. No hurry to get back."

Bingley raised his eyebrows. The obvious question was, if there was no hurry to get back, why was she in such a hurry to leave his house. Bingley was kind enough not to ask.

Mr. Peake pressed his hand over his face and rubbed his fingers over his cheeks again and again. He looked ill. Bingley shuffled his feet as they waited. He clapped his hands and grunted. The air in the hallway was chilled.

Looking out the window, Bingley remarked, without meeting either of their eyes, "Don't think it'll last more than two hours."

Bursting upon them, like the body at the end of a ghost story told round a campfire on a summer night, Darcy walked into the hallway, tall and masculine. Elizabeth felt the pained shock. Elizabeth saw the tightness of his eyes. He said to Bingley before he saw her, "I leave with Georgiana this afternoon. I will—"

Darcy saw her. He pulled up short, his eyes widening. His mouth hardening. They stared together, cold eyes meeting.

Elizabeth already wore her coat. She opened the door without ceremony and walked out into the freezing rain to wait for the carriage.

The piercing wind blew the cold rain into her coat and the cold cut through the heavy wool and into her skin. Grey, cloudy, foreboding. The carriage pulled round, and Mr. Peake walked out of the door to join Elizabeth while their disgruntled footman helped them in.

"Where to, ma'am?" The coachman frowned from where he perched on his seat, the water streaming off his cap and oiled coat. "So abrupt? The weather will let up in two, three hours, or I'm not Hertfordshire born."

"Longbourn. The deuce to Longbourn."

"Righty, righty, ma'am. Not a pleased mood, eh, Miss Bennet?"

It was near certain James had looked forward to a normal stay of three or four hours, like had been usual of late when Elizabeth called at Netherfield, and being called suddenly to rehitch the carriage after barely twenty minutes did not please him.

Good. Darcy's deuced stubborn, gentlemanly, high-handed — damned man. She liked that someone else was given a poor day by the man.

Elizabeth entered the carriage and tried to let her body relax into the pale velvet covered cushions. She shut her eyes and let out a long breath. Her nerves were too tight. She kept seeing their argument again and again. No thoughts. She did not want *thoughts*. Elizabeth's face felt numb and queer. As though she was not quite real.

Oh, God, God, God. Her chest was bruised, and she ached with a lacerated feeling of loss and wrongness.

To distract herself, Elizabeth wondered why she treated the coachman that way. She was not a petty person who abused her moment of pain as an excuse to aggrieve and annoy those around her. Or was she? She would not be such a person.

Elizabeth sat vibrating in her place as the carriage set off, with the bells of the horses ringing slowly, Mr. Peake listlessly sat on the other side of the vehicle. The huge wooden carriage wheels squished through a giant puddle, splashing mud as high as the bottom of the carriage window. There had been no time for new hot water bottles to be prepared, or the brazier to be lit. The air froze inside as well as outside. Their breath clouded with each exhale.

The ride to home was several miles length, and the carriage's muddy bouncing endless.

"Do you think..." Mr. Peake's voice cracked as they neared Longbourn. "Is there hope Mr. Darcy might... I did not expect him to immediately accept such a connection but—"

"No hope."

The sharpness of Elizabeth's tone cut the man off, and he sat back into the carriage without speaking for the remainder of their trip. After so much time in the cold, Elizabeth shivered.

When the carriage pulled to a stop Elizabeth stared at the soggy driveway and the big double paneled front door. Candles and fires flared from the windows, due to the dark of the storm. The light made Elizabeth unbearably sad.

Why did light and life make her so sad?

Mr. Peake climbed out of the chaise quickly, and nimbly. He went around to Elizabeth's door and politely opened it for her.

The wind and rain lashed her and the upholstery, and she stared blankly at his face. Oh, yes. She needed to exit the carriage. It took another aching pause before she could impel her muscles to move. Without taking his hand Elizabeth slowly stumbled down the step, as though she were aged and infirm.

Mr. Peake looked at her with a worried frown. Realizing her rudeness, Elizabeth said quietly to Mr. Peake, barely audible over the slashing rain, "I apologize — that was incivil, but I am in a poor mood."

"I as well."

Elizabeth nodded, aching in her heart. They were together in this, broken hearted. Perhaps Georgiana would one day decide to rebel against her brother's orders, maybe after she reached her majority in a few months.

Mr. Darcy would never be a man different than he was.

The coachman and footmen worked the carriage into its housing so they could unhitch the horses and wash the mud off the carriage. The coachman turned to Elizabeth, "Are you going *elsewhere* of sudden, Miss Lizzy?"

"I..." Elizabeth took a deep breath. James had been with them long enough that informality was natural. The Bennets never treated their servants with the conventional stiffness of much greater houses. Would Darcy have expected her to act in such a manner with *his* servants? Idle question now. "My apologies for the suddenness." Elizabeth pretended to smile. "If I have a desperate need to leave Longbourn in the next half of an hour, I shall run into the wind and rain unaided."

James tipped his hat and smiled. "Not on *our* account. We'll take you anyhow. Spite of weather."

Elizabeth and Mr. Peake went into the house. Mrs. Hill took Elizabeth's coat and scarf from her while exclaiming loudly her surprise that Elizabeth could bear to part herself from her Mr. Darcy so quickly.

Everyone. She needed to tell *everyone*. More *embarrassing* than even Lydia. Mama would be difficult, and she had not the stomach to deal with her mother's shrieked demands that she reconcile with Darcy because he was so rich that he was as good as a Lord.

Elizabeth took several deep breaths. Delay would not ease the shame of jilting a man of ten thousand a year and admitting all her impetuous mistakes. "The entire family is in the drawing room?"

"Yes, Miss Lizzy, Mr. Bennet and Mr. Gardiner moved their backgammon to the room as the Gardiners leave tomorrow."

Elizabeth walked to the door, her hair damp from the wet blown by the wind under her bonnet. She stared at the handle. Despite his unhappiness Mr. Peake felt no such anxiousness. He walked past her, opening the door and holding it for her with a half-hearted smile.

All were assembled there. Mr. and Mrs. Gardiner returned to London the next day, and they knew the nature of Mr. Peake's trip to Netherfield to ask for Georgiana's hand. It was clear in their anxious expressions that they knew from the manner and time of the two's return that Mr. Peake had been refused permission by Darcy.

Mr. Bennet sat next to Mr. Gardiner his hand caught in an excited gesture as he turned to see who had entered. The backgammon board had been pushed to the side, with the position of the pieces showing that black had won. Unsurprisingly the two continued good naturedly chatting without setting up a second game.

"Back so fast?" Mrs. Bennet frowned at Elizabeth. "Mr. Darcy should have kept you longer. You have pleased him best you could? Men can be fickle — I understand neither you, nor him. When me and Mr. Bennet went courting, I never missed an opportunity to spend an hour's time with him — is that not true, dear?"

"That is very true," Mr. Bennet replied frowningly towards Elizabeth. "Lizzy—"

"And Jane and Kitty and Mary, none of them would have missed such an opportunity with their betrothed. However, I should speak not. I never understood you, nor Mr. Darcy. To first declare you too old to look upon and then to become your dearest friend, through *arguing*, and then to marry you. He makes no sense unto *me*. But it is only two weeks until the wedding, and—"

"There will be no wedding."

Mrs. Bennet blinked cowishly at Elizabeth. Then she gasped and shook her head. "No — no! I will not allow it."

Elizabeth tilted her head, curiously waiting to see how Mrs. Bennet would attack her for ending the engagement.

"You must marry! You can't live together without marrying — I am not so French as to accept that from my daughter — not even from *you*."

"No. We are over, finished. We are not to marry at all. No marriage. No connection between us." Elizabeth's voice was like a tolling church bell declaring the end. "I am not to marry Mr. Darcy. Not at all. Our engagement has been ended. Our friendship, our relationship. Over. Everything over. *Finis*. Terminated. *Done*."

Mrs. Bennet peered at Elizabeth with concern.

Mr. Peake exclaimed, "Not on my count! I pray he did not break your engagement because you pushed my cause."

"I do not understand." Mrs. Bennet touched Elizabeth on the shoulder. "You do not look any older than you did yesterday — though your eyes are pained and you are unhappy — but that is because — Oh my poor, poor girl." She embraced Elizabeth. "That perfidious man! After the engagement was even announced in the papers! To throw you over then. He knew your opinions and manners, and he had *no* cause to complain after the engagement when he discovered you would behave the same way you always did — was that it? That you would not cease to run about as you always have? I have told you, Lizzy — but now is not the time. My poor girl! Upon my honor, he should not have treated you in this infamous manner."

The tight hug was comforting. And surprising. She expected to be accused. Yet...somehow the assumption that Darcy had been the one to end matters due to Elizabeth's behavior still irked.

Mr. Gardiner frowned. He gestured widely with his hands. "No. I believe it not! Not a man like I thought Darcy was. He broke with you over your support for Peake's suit? — too far on his part. Too far. He is deserving of thorough disrepute and opprobrium. You ought to sue for breach of contract. But you would not wish to. The scandal. Such a man. Such a man! I am shocked."

"No." Elizabeth stepped away from Mrs. Bennet. "It...he did not."

Mrs. Gardiner had come next to Elizabeth. She embraced her niece. "What happened, Lizzy?"

"I..."

"Lizzy, my dear daughter." Papa came close and touched her. Elizabeth threw herself into his arms and sobbed.

The numbness was gone, and though kindly meant, each word spoken by her family was a claw scratching and scraping raw flesh. This morning, she had known this morn what happiness was.

She had ended her engagement: And the fire burned in the grate; and the rain, its drops splashed against the window; and the others in the room, they breathed easily, though she barely could draw breath.

"What is this, Peake?" Mrs. Bennet asked in a confused voice, as Elizabeth cried. "*Your* cause?"

"I hoped to marry Miss Darcy, but Mr. Darcy refused my suit, and Miss Bennet argued my case."

"Mr. Darcy jilted her for *that*? And he cared nothing for his sister! Sweet Georgie, so sweet! She deserves happiness — anyone could see you are intended for each other. And thirty thousand! My dear brother's firm could use such money very well."

"I swear, that was no motivation for me," Mr. Peake replied quietly.

"Heavens! Perfidious man! Lord! Such a creature. To think I liked him — to think I forgave him — to think what a dishonor it shall be. What infamy! Everyone will know he dishonored you. I'll speak. I'll not be silent. I'll ensure the entire world knows how Mr. Darcy betrayed you. I swear, Lizzy, I'll make the whole shame stick unto him, and I'll—"

"You'll tell no one nothing." Elizabeth pushed herself away from Papa. She brushed her tears roughly away with the sleeve of her woolen dress, which scratched the skin around her eyeballs.

"He jilted you. Lord!" Mrs. Bennet looked to the plaster of the ceiling as she called upon deity. "And to treat his sweet, sweet sister so. He deserves to be *despised!*"

"I! Me! I did it. I jilted him. I ended that damned engagement."

Elizabeth looked around the room. Papa frowned. Elizabeth said to him, "Pardon — I ought not use the damned word damn. Ladies cannot speak as gentlemen are suffered to. But I'll not be controlled. I'll not be silent. I'll not let a *damned* man dictate me. I'll speak as I wish. I'll be listened to or I'll leave. Darcy would not suffer me to run on as Papa suffers me. *I* ended our connection. Scream at me as you will."

Elizabeth stared fiercely at Mrs. Bennet. Her mother had shrieked, shouted, and sworn never to speak to her again when she refused Mr. Collins's suit years before.

Mrs. Bennet's eyes nearly popped from her face. Her mouth went into a big O, but she said nothing.

Mrs. Gardiner put her arms around Elizabeth again, "My dear girl, are you entirely sure? At present you are in a passion. This...this is sudden — you had been so happy."

"Damned fool womanliness. He was *right* that I could not control my passions. If I must be angry to be sane, so shall it be."

"But how — what did he say?" Mrs. Gardiner tapped her hand against her cheek. "Is no compromise possible? Is there a chance yet to speak with him and reconcile? Such a decision should not be taken suddenly or lightly. Never in anger. And such a man, with such grand consequence. He should not be lightly spurned. Though we could *wish* he would choose otherwise, you could not *expect* him to give permission for his sister to marry Mr. Peake."

"If I'm a fool in a rage, then I am a fool in a rage. I have no expectation for others to understand."

"Lizzy, you should reconsider. You..." Mrs. Gardiner cleared her throat. "I see you are angry. But be *wise* also. I beg you: *Think* while you yet have opportunity. I hope you have not offended him too greatly. A couple must learn to manage through difficulties, and not to abandon each other the first time that they differ on an important matter. And a wife must learn to submit herself to her husband's will. You will not be happy if you cannot learn to accept that gentlemen are not as you wish, and—"

"Fanny!" Mrs. Bennet cut her sister-in-law off. "Lizzy is different from you and me. Lord! You give excellent advice, but Lizzy has chosen well enough for her own happiness in time past. We have security enough that she need not marry except if she wishes to. Lizzy, I do not understand you but you are my daughter. You shall never hear a word of reproach or advice from me."

"You were so happy that I was marrying." Elizabeth studied her mother's face. "You will bear the shame of my action amongst our neighbors, and—"

"Fah, it would bore me to crow over Lady Lucas if my daughter was married to a man of ten thousand a year. I do not need *you* to work for my happiness. The proper course of matters is quite the opposite."

"Are you really so untroubled...when I refused Mr. Collins..."

"Pah. Heavens! To expect me to act the same as I did five years past, when none of my girls were married. I know *you* better now." She embraced Elizabeth. "Do not weep overmuch. Men are not worth such grief."

"I...I thank you, Mama."

"Mr. Bennet — you will not berate Lizzy either."

Mr. Bennet smiled at his wife, also clearly surprised by what she said. "I had not the slightest intention of doing so."

Pain stabbed Elizabeth in the gut once more.

She had jilted Mr. Darcy. She would never banter with him happily, or kiss him, or let him again hold her. Elizabeth pressed her hand against her chest. "God, God, God." She pressed her hand over her beating throat. "I — I must...be alone. Pardon."

Elizabeth retreated to the safety of the library. Papa's place, where no one else was. The fire crackled in the stove and warmed the air for Papa, despite the lashing storm outside. Elizabeth clumped herself onto the chair. The weather made the day sound like a ruined castle. No — like a ruined hut whose owner had believed it to be a castle.

That damn, damn, damned man. Georgiana sobbing. *No, you may not speak; I shall not listen to you.* He thought she was beneath him. Beneath *him*. He thought she only agreed to marry him for his money — did Darcy think so *little* of his every other attribute? And so little of her?

She didn't need his deuced money.

She'd proven that.

Ha! Elizabeth growled and rose. She paced forth and back, sweating despite the chill on the air that the smoky smelling fire did not drive away. Too much smoke curled into the room — the chimney needed to be cleaned again.

The ring, his ring had pulled smoothly off her finger, as though the band did not belong upon her hand and wished to be gone. The glint of gold in the air. The clank, in a moment of silence between rolls of thunder as the ring bounced against the table and then the wall. Where had her ring rolled?

So angry. How had she become so angry?

God — the look on his face. Never should she have ended their engagement like *that*.

He lacked respect for her, her position in life. If he despised her uncle and his partner so grandly, surely some despite must fall upon her also.

That was unfair to Darcy. The abominable standards of society claimed it reasonable for a gentleman to marry the daughter of a gentleman whose brother-in-law was in trade, but not allow his sister to marry a man who was in trade himself.

This was not hypocrisy, because Elizabeth's station in life was higher than Mr. Peake's.

A sick pain bled into her stomach. She doubled up and pressed her hand against her guts. He would never look at her like *that* again. With that light in his eyes and that low seductive voice. The smell of his coat. She missed the smell of his coat.

Never, ever, ever. She would never find anyone whose conversation she enjoyed so much as Darcy's. It was ten years since she had entered society, and she had never before met anyone she liked like Darcy.

Couldn't he have *listened*? This was his fault. Everything — the pain she felt now. Her pain; his *damned* fault.

She had been cruel when they argued — he had been *trying* to care for his sister. He was merely bad at it. But that was not right either. She could not think lucidly.

Damn, damn, damn.

So sure when she pulled the ring off her finger. She had been so sure. She had raged. Now she was beset round about by doubts.

Elizabeth leaned her forehead against the cold window as the rain lashed against her forehead. She cried again.

Pain was another passion. She could not marry a man who would not listen to her, and who dictated to the women under his control.

Elizabeth plopped again into her stuffed leather chair, and squeezed herself back into it with her arms around her legs. She stared at the gruesome grey day. A taste like the bitter dregs of a cold cup of tea sat in her mouth.

The door softly opened. Elizabeth did not look away from the window. She felt disgust at being interrupted in her misery. A silver tray stamped with a floral pattern was softly placed on the desk next to her arm.

Elizabeth looked at Papa, and he softly smiled at her and moved quietly to sit in his own chair. He picked up the newspaper, and shook it out with a posture that indicated that he would happily be ignored by her, but that he would be present for her to talk when she wished.

On the tray was a steaming mug of cocoa, a bottle of rum and a small tumbler glass, and a teapot and cup. Not knowing *which* form of liquid comfort she would desire, Papa provided three options. And rather than speaking, he quietly sat down to give her silent comfort from his presence, letting her choose when to come to him.

She felt less alone. Papa, at least she had Papa!

He sat, his eyes softly running over the newsprint, but Elizabeth knew his manners, and knew his mind was not on the paper, though he showed her the kindness to *not* subtly pay attention to Elizabeth. How could she have ever considered leaving home?

Elizabeth picked up the spiced cocoa Papa had brought to her and sipped cautiously. A perfect temperature, hot, yet it did not burn her mouth. There was rum in the thick liquid. Elizabeth breathed in the scent of the ground cocoa through her nose, and she sipped again luxuriating in the taste. She closed her eyes, to keep herself from thinking and relaxed into her soft chair. The warm comforting weight of the cup wrapped around her hands.

The sense of peace lasted less than a minute. The phrases Darcy had used, his demand that she always agree with him in public on anything which *mattered*. The scornful sneer, holding his head ridiculously high, as he insulted Wollstonecraft's philosophy. She had already *told* him that she considered Wollstonecraft's approach flawed. Did he *never* listen except when he spoke himself?

He did. He remembered so much of their little conversations. *I will not be changed by theatrics.*

Ha! She'd been serious in ending their engagement. Ha!

Elizabeth put her mug down harshly on the tray. "You had the right of it." Papa looked up at Elizabeth's bitter words. "I near fashioned a terrible mistake."

Papa shrugged. He did not smile, but he put down his newspaper to the side, folding it carefully down the middle, forming a thick paper cover for the desk. Sharply defined lines of newsprint on the white paper. He directed his full attention towards her, the way he always did when she needed him.

"You did — you were kindly about it" — Elizabeth smiled sadly — "Darcy would blame you for not refusing your blessing and consent entirely."

"Whatever effect it may have had upon Mr. Darcy, I knew you far too well to believe my refusal would stop *you*."

Unexpectedly Elizabeth laughed at Papa's statement. She would not have taken such a demand well.

Papa smiled at her amusement, but it did not reach his eyes.

"So strange — to laugh when I am entirely miserable. I am miserable, though *I* ended it. I should be relieved that I evade a mistake. How can I laugh at anything? I suffer as though I can never be happy again. I must be made for laughter if I can *laugh* whilst I am despondent."

"I laughed at a jest of my godfather the day my father died, though we both were heartbroken."

"*That* shall not do! This is the end of a relationship. Nothing so serious as a parent's death." Elizabeth shivered at the idea. "It is a small thing—"

"You intended to spend the entirety of your life with Mr. Darcy — if you consider that a *small* thing, you were far more mistaken in *that* matter than you could have been in accepting his engagement."

"I was...precipitate. I see now. But...I *felt* I was sober and rational at the time, but like Wollstonecraft, or dear Georgiana, or all the women Darcy despises—"

"Many men as well."

"Like all the persons despised by my once gentleman suitor, I was driven by passion and, blockheadedness. Until now I thought I knew myself! I thought myself too wise, too strong, too...I have escaped the mistake you saw I was making—"

"I only suspected your connection to Mr. Darcy to be a mistake. I possess no conviction, even now."

"No! Not that. I need you to be confident, for I doubt myself."

"Of course you do."

"Papa! You thought I mistook a mistake."

"It *scared* me."

"I was a fool. A fool. A twice... *you* would not be happy I know the word which comes to mind. But verily I was a foolish fool fooling her way into foolish disaster."

"What happened?"

"What happened! He would not listen. He destroys his sister's life. He denies her every hope of happiness, he chooses for her the choice that is above all others *her* choosing."

"I gather there was a matter between our friend Mr. Peake and your and Jane's sweet friend."

"They had agreed to marry and Darcy absolutely refused because he is a man in trade. A man in trade! That is his *excuse* when he ruins, perhaps forever, his sister's happiness."

Mr. Bennet tilted his head to the side and pursed his lips.

"Gentlemen! Fah! Surely you do not agree with Mr. Darcy."

"He does not wish my agreement — I *understand*. For a man of such pride to allow his sister to marry a tradesman — I *understand* why his first reaction was revulsion."

Elizabeth snarled. "I do not. Except...I *do*. He cares so much for Georgiana. He does wish the best for her. But he is *wrong*. He is hurting her. And Mr. Peake is my uncle's partner — it means he despises my uncle. If he despises Mr. Gardiner, by extension he despises *me*."

"That is a reason for concern. Do you think that is what he thinks?"

"Mr. Darcy does not *despise* Gardiner." Elizabeth slumped, some of her anger oozing away again. "But he said he would not allow Georgiana to marry a man like my uncle either. And I love Mr. Gardiner dearly."

Papa leaned forward and placed his hand on Elizabeth's arm. "My dear, dear daughter. What really struck you so hard that you ended matters with Mr. Darcy?"

Elizabeth deflated. She had been so angry, for an instant she could only remember the tightness in her chest, the passion and certainty of her rightness, and Darcy's noble mouth. "He ordered me to be silent. First in front of others, and then together. He absolutely would not *listen* to me. I expect that at least. I expect to be heard and to be respected."

"Ah."

"He would act the same in our private life. He is sweet, charming, and always happy to talk so long as that is his noble whim. But the instant I wish something unbecoming the wife of Mr. Darcy, the oppressor of ten thousand a year, *then*, *then* the truth will out. He will not listen; he will use a gentleman's will to determine for me without even *listening*. Heavens! Such a fool to think I could ever marry."

Mr. Bennet took the tumbler from the tray and poured a thick helping of rum into it and pushed it towards Elizabeth. She gratefully took the glass and drank the whole in one quick swallow, realizing she wanted alcohol in her innards to burn away the pain in her guts.

Elizabeth wiped her mouth, inelegantly. "The night we became engaged — I had decided a list of questions to ask him before accepting his offer — do not look at me so, I was to frame them politely — questions to ensure that he understood what I wished from a husband, and that he agreed to allow his wife such liberties. And I did not ask."

Papa took out a tumbler of his own, and poured the spirit into it, and sipped from it. "Why not, Lizzy?"

"I think — it would have been awkward in a way, but mostly, I think I was frightened of the answers, and I loved him so much then. I do yet. I love him, despite my anger, I love him right now. Did I make a mistake, Papa?"

"How can *I* know? But if you feel any uncertainty about a matter as solemn and irreversible as marriage, you ought not to carry through — in *that* you made no mistake."

"We were impassioned. There must have been a position betwixt our demands, a way for us to speak about it. But *he,* he wouldn't *listen* to me. I tried — perhaps I might have tried more, but I begged him, repeatedly, to listen and speak rationally with me."

"I am proud of you, for making the attempt."

"He would not. That is the end of it. I will not marry a man who does not listen to me."

Mr. Bennet smiled. "A wise resolution."

"I will never marry anyone."

Papa smiled. "We know you can fall in love."

"Such hurtful things I said things to him. Why? Why did I say *that*? I accused him — no I'll not say what I accused him of, but...you see, Mr. Darcy confessed a terrible fear, that he had failed Georgiana in a particular way. And when we argued, I accused him of failing her in that way, knowing it would hurt him. Only because I lost my temper."

"Oh, Lizzy."

"If — I wish I had kept my calm. I was driven *again* by my passions in place of reason. If I were calm, he would have calmed and then eventually been brought to *listen*. I just needed — the refusal to Georgiana was within the bounds of *reason*. But we do not live by reason, nor by bread, alone. Love — Oh, I feel so unsure. To end a solemn engagement in such a passion. I should have waited till we were calm — but the engagement was a mistake — it was. *Reason* inform me of *that*. He did not listen to me, he did not respect me, and he feels the right to control and manipulate the lives of those around him without their consultation."

"If you see Darcy in that way, you would be wrong to marry him."

"If only I had not been so angry. We could have talked once we calmed. I was not angry at first. He said he would not listen to me, and that I should already agree with him. His wide eyes and open mouth; I shall always remember them — he accused me at first of theatrics when I threw my ring away. If I was calm, I do not think I could have ended the engagement. When he realized I was in earnest..." Elizabeth pressed her hand to her stomach again.

Papa looked at her with a queer expression. Half horror and half amusement. "You threw your ring back at him?"

"It is horrible! How could I do that? I am a terrible person."

"Poor Mr. Darcy." Papa laughed.

"No matter how...how enraging I find him, he deserved better from me."

"You two had not learned yet to speak to each other as equals. It is natural that such disagreements would arise between two proud and obstinate persons."

"And now we will never learn to communicate. It is over. The account is settled and closed. I should have given him more of an opportunity, I should have explained *why* I cared so much. I always believed he would *listen* to me when we argued. I do not think he *understands* why I ended it."

Papa embraced her. He smelled warm and of tea and books and the newsprint on his hands. "Lizzy, my dear Lizzy. I always adored you more than my other children. I could not help myself — ever since you were able to talk and toddled about in my wake. You mimicked my gestures with the serious face of a tiny angel. Jane stayed where Mrs. Bennet put her, but you..." Papa smiled at the reminiscence. Elizabeth knew these stories. "You loved to learn; you listened to me talk for hours without boredom, and I loved company if it was yours, and teaching if you were my pupil. Once it became clear we would never have a son... What I have done to improve the fortunes of our house, to ensure dowries for you each, I did it because I needed to be sure *you* were cared for, even if I would have rathered to sit in the study every day reading my books, and not attend to estate matters and argue with Mrs. Bennet each time she spent a pound or two too much."

"You have told me, Papa."

"Lizzy — I know you and your mind. You may be foolish at times, but never a fool."

She did not understand why his saying that made her feel incomparably better, but it did. Even though she *had* been a fool. Elizabeth embraced Papa tighter, pressing her face against the scratchy wool front of his winter coat.

He smiled at her tearily. "I also know you will be happy soon enough again."

"I have too much passion in me."

"Ridiculous. You are perfect as you are, mistakes and successes."

"Papa, I am not perfect, but but...oh, I hurt so much. Why does ending an engagement hurt so much? I never knew anything could hurt like this."

Papa embraced her and held her close. His arms were the arms of the one fixed star in her life, the man who had always cared for her, who had always been her favorite person. Elizabeth cried again, and Papa's coat became so wet from her tears that it took on the faint wet wool smell of a soaked dog. But her tears restored her this time. She felt whole once again, even though the next weeks and days would hurt.

Behind her the rain had stopped and a single sunbeam broke through the clouds.

Chapter Twenty-One

Bingley stood next to Darcy in Darcy's rooms as his valet packed fine woolen trousers, embroidered silk vests, and linen shirtsleeves into the heavy iron-banded trunk.

"Bingley, I thank you," Darcy spoke with a repressed anger towards Bingley, irrationally blaming his friend for part of the pain which he felt, "for your hospitality. However, you must admit it is natural for me and Georgiana to leave and leave immediately."

"I...I can only imagine — is it entirely ended?"

"Over. She threw my love back at me. She threw my ring back at me. She prefers...pray tell, what am I to do? I am a man. A proud man. I responded to her dramatics and to her arguments with calmness and presence of mind. I will not chase at her like a sniffing *dog*. Matters are at an end between us."

"Oh." Bingley looked unsurprised and almost relieved. He should show a sympathetic expression instead of a thoughtful one.

"Damn you, man. You introduced her to me. *Your* sister. What sort of woman jilts a man because he will not manage *his* ward in the manner she wishes? Elizabeth is not so good a woman. Not so good as I believed."

Bingley twisted his hand in his pocket and grimaced. "That is how you see her at present?"

Darcy felt sick. The storm whipped against the windows, renewing its strength. She had gone out into the rain, in her safe carriage. Gone. Falling water separated them.

"Elizabeth, she..." Bingley sighed. "Elizabeth expects to be listened to. For her opinion to be respected. If you cannot...it was for the best that you both discovered this before your marriage was solemnized."

"Georgiana is *my* responsibility. *Mine*. I failed her once. I won't fail her again. Not for Elizabeth's sake. If Elizabeth willfully denies that it is *my* decision who Georgiana marries, then...then...then this was for..." Despite his anger, the horrid feeling in Darcy's chest meant he could not agree, ever, that losing Elizabeth was for the best.

"You are used to having your way in all matters. I am not surprised a conflict arose between you two. A mismatched pair in *my* eyes, but I never deeply understood either of you, and I did not consider it my place to say anything."

"*Et tu, Brute*? Elizabeth said Mr. Bennet disliked the match."

Bingley put his hand on Darcy's shoulder. "There, man, there. Don't keep the pain in. It hurts."

"Why do you all disapprove? I am the richest man she could possibly marry. I have a grand estate; I am a responsible master — I *am* a perfect gentleman. She said I was *too* gentlemanlike."

Bingley looked like he was beginning to cry.

"How can a man be too gentlemanlike? Too concerned for the care of others. Too honest and upright in his bearing. Too noble in his antecedents. She is immature and unwilling to subordinate herself to anyone. She is another example of how radicals destroy the minds and morals of women who take them seriously. She should not be permitted to marry at all."

"Don't be like the fox with the grapes. Do not try to pretend you are not desperately unhappy."

"You tell me it is for the best."

"Elizabeth expects a great deal from her husband. If you cannot offer her what she wishes, you should not seek her hand. Life...it is not some game. Marriage is compromise. If you cannot accept that—"

"She couldn't accept it!"

"You and she would not have been happy together. I am glad Elizabeth saw that before it was too late. But I hope...I hope I shall not lose your friendship forever."

"We would have been happy. If only she wasn't so...so... Damn, man! I will not cry. You will not make me. Order my damned carriage to be prepared."

Darcy left Bingley. He went to the hallway. He hid in a servant's closet with a wooden bucket, three dirty mops, and a fat spider, so that no one could see him cry.

The cave at Royston, her hands brushing against his arm. They had planned to walk every day the whole way around the park, so that Elizabeth could see Pemberley come alive in Spring, and detail every bit of the growth of green. He would never walk around the park with her.

Bingley was right. For the best.

He'd been eager to walk the park with her. What was the point of having a park if he could never walk around it with Elizabeth?

He would not bend, bow or change. Not in *this* matter. Elizabeth was not a fit woman to marry a man such as he.

He needed to mail to everyone the news of the end of the engagement. After it had been posted in the newspapers. Another scandal.

They would all think, when they heard about the engagement ending, that *he* had come to his senses and abandoned the woman who had a modest dowry and poor connections. He would look dishonorable. And he was honor bound to keep from explaining to his friends that it was *her* fault. That she was a cruel woman who casually and callously stomped upon the soul and spirit of a man who ardently adored her.

He still wished to walk the circuit of the park with her.

===

During the day following *that* day, the one during which his fiancée threw the ring he had given her to symbolize their connection and happiness in his rough direction, Fitzwilliam Darcy had the awareness thrust upon him that his sister, Georgiana Darcy, was not merely unhappy, but that she was in fact unhappy with *him*. It was no great surprise.

Women were inconstant in their temperament and prone to spiting those who cared most for their welfare.

"Pray, Georgie, would you wish," Darcy said, hoping for a reply, but knowing it was unlikely, "to speak upon matters from yesterday?"

His sister stared at the hot coffee and the porridge she had ordered for herself after Darcy had, in hopes of raising her spirits, asked the inn to bring out all of its finest pastries. Anne, satisfied by her consumption of the sugary concoctions, stickily tore the excess strawberry and lemon tarts and chocolate cornets apart and strewed little threads of breading around the edges of the tablecloth in a complicated pattern which only a child's brain could properly appreciate.

Neither of her guardians stopped her. Darcy had not eaten a great deal either, lacking the stomach for food as well.

Never marry. Never.

That was his new decision. The softness of mind and manner required to deal kindly with the mutability of females eluded him. Fortunately the need to brick off his heart had been stabbed into him before he took vows, before church and man, burdening himself with the unending care and management of one Elizabeth Bennet.

Lizzy, why?

Darcy looked at the crisscrossing brown beams of the ceiling. She would not have appreciated being told that marriage would have placed her under his management — he never thought of it in such a way. When he imagined their married life, he'd seen fascinating disputes, happy celebrations, light and laughter and friends brought to Pemberley, a sensual sequence of Elizabeth-scented nights. What they would do if they disagreed deeply had not crossed his mind.

Georgiana was the child — girl — not a woman adult, under his management.

Anne was distracted by her guardians' distraction, and she started throwing crumbs at the fireplace. They blew up into little bright flames before blackening and giving the room a smell of burnt bread. Georgiana did keep half an eye on her daughter to ensure she did not wave her hands too close to the fire, but otherwise allowed her to do as she wished.

The three of them were trapped in this inn, at least until noon, along with their servants and the rest of their accoutrements. Ice had formed on the road thirty miles to the north of London. Perhaps they might have proceeded at a very slow pace, but now that he was a sufficient distance from *there* — when one wrote *there* one also wrote *her* — Darcy had no hasteful hope to reach his vast empty estate. A comfortable inn — Anne liked the way she could make a toy out of the pastries; the room was as warm as home; and Darcy had stayed here several times before while traveling between Pemberley and London.

Too much of a gentleman? What did that even mean? If he was too gentle a gentleman, Elizabeth was too laddish a lady.

"Uncle Will, Uncle Will." Anne pulled at Darcy's sleeve. Darcy looked in concern at the wool fabric, but his niece had cleaned the jam off her tiny fingers with a bit of water and a napkin before demanding Darcy's attention.

He turned his attention to the girl, glad for the distraction from his thoughts, and he smiled at her.

"Pick me up! Pick me up! *You* aren't doing anything."

Mr. Darcy stood and bent to follow the girl's orders, as he after all was *not* doing anything. However before he could Georgiana rushed from her seat where she had sat poking the congealed porridge and lifted Anne herself, carrying her away from Darcy. "Not now, Annie, Uncle *Fitz* does not wish to be bothered." Georgiana opened the bag with Anne's toys that she always had with her, and pulled out a big doll in a pink tulle dress. "Play with Charlotte."

Anne pouted. "I want to be carried around the room. Around the room!"

"I'll give you a cookie and...and we'll make a new dress for Charlotte."

"A silk dress?"

Georgiana nodded eagerly in agreement. "But do not try to play with Uncle Will today."

The girl turned towards Darcy for confirmation of these orders. Darcy smiled at her and waved. Anne ran to the corner of the room and made Charlotte to march around and beat her wooden hands against the wall with tiny taps.

"Georgie." Darcy spoke in a mild tone.

She glared at him.

Yes, his suspicion was confirmed. Georgiana was not merely displeased by the end of her engagement. She resented him for protecting her future well-being.

Darcy added, without changing his tone, "That was remarkably petty of you."

Georgiana's glare broke and she blushed embarrassedly, looking down and rubbing her fingers over the tablecloth.

"Anne should not be used to punish me."

Georgiana stared at her fingers and the green and orange floral pattern of the tablecloth. Darcy maintained his stiff expression, waiting to see how she would respond. The silence sat pregnant upon the table. Darcy felt an unaccustomed nervousness. He did not know how to help Georgiana regain her happiness and accept that he had made the right decision for her.

She coughed out, without looking up, "I apologize. I should not have."

He did not like to see Georgiana unhappy with him.

Darcy absently grabbed the half of a lemon tart which Anne had left untortured and stuffed the sugary concoction into his mouth. His mouth was dry, and the cloying flavor stuck as he chewed and chewed until he could swallow and force the bread and sugar like a rock into his stomach.

This wasn't supposed to be like this.

"How?" Georgiana formed her hands into small fists; she sat upright like a marble column; she clenched her jaw so tight that it pulsated. "*How* could you do it?"

"Our father placed you under my protection. Even if it gives you transient pain, I must do as best I can to—"

"Not *that*." Georgiana's lips twisted angrily, and she jabbed the air. "*Elizabeth*. How could you end matters with Elizabeth because she supported me?"

It lashed him again. She had thrown him away, like a bauble, like a ring tossed against the ground. Why did he long for her — she felt so little for him.

Like a flash he saw the look in her eyes as he proposed to her. The way she bent her lips forward to kiss him, and the simple enthusiasm his Lizzy had for everything in life.

"Oh." Georgiana's voice was soft and soothing. She stood and went round the table and placed her hand on his arm, and then her arms around him. Darcy at first was stiff. He comforted his sister, and he would not cry in front of her.

He couldn't stop. He tried, but he couldn't stop the images of their weeks together and her smiles and happiness and the pain of that aching *why*.

He hugged Georgiana back, hoping she would not see his tears as he did hold himself back from sobbing. She saw.

Anne stopped playing and came to them and realizing something was amiss with her adults, she wrapped her arms around their legs. "Is this because we are going back to Pemberley house, and leaving Aunt Lizzy and Aunt Jane and Bennet and everyone behind?"

"Yes, sweetling," Both Georgiana and Darcy replied to Anne at the same time.

Darcy wiped his eyes and picked up Anne to sit on his lap. This time Georgiana did not stop him as he hugged her head against his chest, able to smell her hair, and the little girl hugged him back. He would hate it when Anne was too old to hold like this.

Georgiana sat close. "Fitzwilliam," she asked softly, "what happened?"

"She, she... I cannot understand. *Why?*" Darcy felt too sad to be righteously angry, and he knew that insulting Elizabeth to his sister would not win her to his cause. "She ended our engagement. She chose it — I would not have. Never."

His sister placed her hand on his arm, and Darcy's eyes clouded over with tears again.

"I did not deserve it. I did not. She encouraged you in your infatuation — but I would not have thrown our love away for that. She threw mine away the first time I did not follow her demands."

"Fitzwilliam..."

"She took my ring from her finger and threw it to the ground so that it bounced and bounced."

Georgiana's eyes widened and she gasped.

"Ha! You are surprised your friend treated me in such a brutal fashion."

His sister clapped her hand over her mouth. "What did you say to her to place her in such a rage?"

"You accuse me?"

Georgiana mutely shook her head, with her hand still over her mouth.

Darcy slumped into the chair, still holding Anne against him.

"But she... not normally, Lizzy would not have done that."

"Aunt Lizzy!" Anne clapped and squirmed so she could sit up in Darcy's lap. "When will Aunt Lizzy visit us in Pemberley? She told me she was coming with us."

"Never."

Anne stared into his eyes with her big wet blue eyes.

He kissed her on the forehead.

"When Lizzy come?" Anne repeated the question.

Darcy kissed her on the forehead again. She quieted down but squirmed out of Darcy's arms and went to play with her doll again.

"Georgie, I apologize." Darcy smiled with a skull's grimace. "I am overwrought, and I should not speak insultingly of your friend — you can only sympathize with me to a limit, she grew enraged in pursuit of *your* cause."

Georgiana covered her eyes with her fingers. "I had no idea — none. Oh, if I had known my hopes would destroy you and Lizzy, I..." Georgiana halted a frown over her face.

"Blame not yourself. Her affection for me was not great, not if it could be changed by... No means could have been driven *me* from her, except, alas, her orders. *They* drove me away, for I *am* a gentleman. I will not force myself upon a woman when my presence is unwished. I will not push *my* longings upon a girl who spurns my name. I will not pine for her. I am complete in myself as a Darcy, an island standing high above the sea, alone amongst the crashing surf while the seabirds whirl in circles and caw lonely cries above, with only you, my sister, and your daughter, growing as sweet trees upon my windswept shore. So it has been, and so it will always be. For *she* threw my ring on the ground."

"Oh, Fitzwilliam. I...I grieve for you. As much as for myself."

Darcy had a duty. Georgiana's words reminded him of it. "How...what do you feel — Mr. Peake. I again exposed you to an unsuitable attachment. I am glad that the damage has been less this time, but..."

"I love him — it is different. Not like when — not like Mr. Wickham. Not at all."

Darcy opened his mouth to argue, but he knew that would not work. Georgiana needed to believe he listened to her, or else she would never be able to accept the rightness of his choice. Not if she was doubting. He pulled his chair closer to her and softly asked, "How is this different?"

"Oh! In every way. Mr. Peake never attempted to seduce me. He is my friend, like Jane and Bingley or you and Lizzy... Oh! Lord, I... Fitzwilliam, I am so sorry."

Darcy nodded.

"My friend. I can talk to him about anything, and he speaks to me about the matters that are deepest to him, his work, and his life in London, and his family back home, in Derbyshire. His hopes for the future. And he is so sweet about everything."

Darcy smiled a little. "I thought he talked to you about bills of exchange, and when to buy and sell government stock. That sort of nonsense."

"Oh, yes!" Georgiana enthusiastically exclaimed. "I adore it. He speaks to me like no one else does, treating me as interested in his business, and worthy of hearing about it. He always did."

"How *did* he treat you when he was in my employ?" Darcy leaned forward with a hard gaze.

"Oh! No, no, no. Surely you don't think — Mr. Peake is a good man. Honórable. Not while he was in your employ, besides," Georgiana giggled, "he thought himself much too far beneath me to look at the daughter of the house with serious intent. He told me that he *did* love me then, and I had an admiration for him, but we were too young. We only talked; I asked him everything about the estate business and collecting rents, and the sorts of things you don't like to be bothered by a woman with. But he enjoyed explaining."

"He did? You say he loved you then? He told you that now?"

"You are terrible suspicious. Though Wickham...suspicion is not unjustified."

"Did he make love to you then?"

"You are not listening. Even though he knew all about my disgrace, he still thought I was above him."

"You *are* above him."

Georgiana waved her hand. "Nonsense. I am outside of normal society — even in Hertfordshire, they all see me differently because of Anne. Even if they are courteous, I am not treated the same as other girls. So you see, you really have no reason to oppose us. I should not be treated as before, I sinned, and even after repentance—"

"You are a Darcy. You were born a Darcy. You cannot cease to be a Darcy."

"I could marry. Then I would quit the name." Georgiana smiled at him. "Please listen, Fitzwilliam. I am not being irrational — I know what I am about when I wish to marry Mr. Peake. I can explain—"

"No you cannot."

"You can hardly know whether I can explain or not if you do not listen to me." She spoke in a reasonable tone, but Darcy could see in the eagerness in her eyes, that she still hoped he could be convinced.

Darcy sighed and pulled at his hair. "When did you become so combative and forward?"

"Lizzy taught me—" Her face shined as she grabbed Darcy's wrist. "Matters are not ruined irretrievably. If you only listen, you will understand that I am not *really* above Mr. Peake, and there is no reason to stop us from marrying, and we can return straight away, and you and Lizzy can reconcile, and we will all be happy the way I thought we were yesterday and—"

"She threw my ring away because *I was too gentlemanly*."

"You are crying for her, and—"

"Do not speak of *that*."

Georgiana pursed her lips, and tilted her head to look at him as if he were a strange insect trapped in amber in an eccentric gentleman's curio cabinet. "Why ever not?"

"It is not done. Not done. Bad form."

"Crying?"

Darcy felt full of shame now at remembering how he had sobbed. His eyes were still red. A gentleman such as him should be able to hide his tears.

"That is the most ridiculous thing I have ever heard from you. Tears relieve pain, it is natural."

"A gentleman should not be weak enough to need such relief."

"Lizzy called you too gentlemanly?" Georgiana rolled her eyes and shook her head. "She was right — stop being too gentlemanly. Apologize, she still loves you, and—"

"I have *nothing* to apologize for."

Georgiana's eager motions halted. And her face fell. Darcy hated to see it. "I do not desire us to be unhappy," she said.

Darcy was unhappy. Georgiana was unhappy, even if her brief moment of hope that she could change his mind made her forget it. Darcy softly tapped his foot against the leg of the table and looked at Anne peacefully playing with her doll. One of them was happy at least.

"I lost my right to the family name."

"You did not."

"Our aunt, Lady Catherine said—"

"She is a fool who no wise person listens to."

"Fitzwilliam, why is it important I don't marry a tradesman? Surely *you* would not be hurt more by such a connection than you are by the presence of me and Anne in your house."

"I do not care how it affects *me*. You will not marry a man in trade."

She looked down and bit her lips. Then Georgiana quietly whispered something to herself. Darcy could almost swear she whispered, "What would Lizzy do?" Georgiana placed her palms on the table. "You are not being rational. Pride is a passion as much as anything else. You are not being reasonable."

"How is it possibly *reasonable* to marry a tradesman?"

Georgiana sat straighter. She tilted her head and crossed her legs. She was consciously adopting Elizabeth's posture when she argued with her father or Darcy. "We disagree on this; I think I am being reasonable by wishing to marry Mr. Peake. You must say something more than simply repeating that it *is* unreasonable. What makes it so?"

"This is not a matter of logic. This is not a matter of argument. You are my sister, and I am your guardian, and I expect you to obey me in this matter."

"Did you tell Lizzy that?"

"If your graven figurine cannot bear to be opposed, it does not matter to me."

"I shall not leave you alone until you give me a satisfactory explanation — I shall not make a brilliant marriage, no matter what. You know that. And I have no interest in participation in grand society. And I have money sufficient to live well, and Mr. Peake has excellent character—"

"He *works* for a living — you certainly have not enough to live as you have at Pemberley. Costs in London are so high, and once he has sucked the capital of your dowry dry, and wasted it in a business venture that ends in bankruptcy — many ventures do, even if the tradesman is of the greatest skill and diligence, temperamental luck often plays a decisive role when one depends upon the vagaries of prices and customers rather than land for income."

"You cannot possibly fear that you would need to support us again, enough would be set aside in settlement to support us decently, besides *you* have no need for money."

"You are the daughter of one of the grandest families of Derbyshire. Hundreds of years of history exist behind our name. We have dwelt in the hills of Derbyshire, master of all we could see, since the time of the Stuarts. Our family name goes back to the men who supported Bolingbroke against the hunchback. We are the Darcys. And not in solitude is the line of your father grand. By your mother's name, you are a Fitzwilliam. A newer creation than the Darcys but with a higher title, created to ennoble the blood of a descendent of Charles II. Illegitimacy did not rob *that* blood of its great status. The blood which flows through your limbs flowed also through the veins of a king, and that a king of England, a hundred and fifty years past. Such lines — they shall not be commingled with the blood of a man who makes his living by moving goods about and convincing fools to pay a higher price for them than what he paid in the first place."

Georgiana clutched her arms around her body. Her cheeks burned and she studied the weave of the tablecloth. Tonelessly she said, "Merchants provide a valuable service by allowing the flow of trade to function — the merchants add as much benefit to society as growing corn and delving for coal or lead—"

"The deuce! Georgiana Darcy, I care not in the slightest what Mr. Peake quoted from Ricardo, or Smith, or whichever economist is popular amongst the Cits to justify his profession unto you. He is not worthy to be husband for a woman of your blood."

"You cannot be reasoned with. Your pride demands that your sister should not marry outside of the ranks of the gentry."

"My pride? *Your* pride — what *ought* to be your pride. This *ought* to have been Elizabeth's pride also. I care not for myself. The world can despise me, or it can adore me. I am indifferent. I act for *your* sake. For *your* own sake, you shall not marry him. You will perceive one day your rank again as you ought, one day you will wake to what you owe the name, the grand name: Darcy. You will thank me, on that day. For your own sake you will thank me. You will thank me for protecting you from such a blunder."

Georgiana rubbed at her eyes and did not look up. She appeared to be on the verge of tears. Darcy reached forward to touch her arm in comfort, but she pulled her wrist away from him.

It had not rained at all for the past hour, and through the window it appeared the sky had less grey than before. When Georgiana made no further motion, Darcy rose and looked out the window. "I shall ask whether there is news about the state of the road. I believe we shall be able to set off soon."

Chapter Twenty-Two

Upon his return to Pemberley, Darcy had to accomplish the unpleasant chore of following his engagement letters with his jilting letters.

Darcy found it a task of some difficulty. The first draft he produced was written in a fit of anger against Elizabeth. It described in detail the scene — her petulant demands that he throw his *sister* to the clutches of her relations; the way that she threw a gunpowder tantrum when he did not meet her demands; how her reason had been enfeebled by female learning and philosophers; and finally how she had taken his ring and hurled it against the ground. Where *ever* did the ring fly? He had been too... angry to look for it or ask for it before he left. Darcy had an image of one of Bingley's servants leaving his service possessed of a substantial windfall when the maid who found the ring managed to sell it off to a gypsy camp.

Upon rereading what he had written, Darcy crumpled it up, placed it in the stove in his office, lit the close written page, and stirred the ashes to ensure none of it could be reconstructed.

Holding his hands against his burning anger to keep them warm, Darcy hardened his face. He was a gentleman with a gentleman's pride. He would not descend to Elizabeth's — Miss Bennet's — low station. He was too gentlemanly to hold an unmanly grudge, to engage in petty revenges. As a man of honor he had no right to in any way tarnish Elizabeth's reputation.

He did the right thing. He wrote the letters to his family and friends which simply announced that the engagement betwixt him and Elizabeth Bennet had been terminated by mutual agreement, and that she had done nothing which could smudge her reputation or give him just cause to end matters between them. He knew that few people would imagine that a woman would voluntarily end an engagement with a man of his consequence, so they would assume that he had ended it.

Some shame would settle on Elizabeth, as men suspected he had discovered a proper cause to end matters between them, which he did not choose to share with the world out of a gentlemanly discretion. Others though would believe *he* had been the dishonorable one, deciding in the end, once he had come to his senses, that her modest dowry and connections to trade were not worthy of the Darcy name.

Such was the response Darcy received at the earliest possible moment from his aunt Lady Catherine de Bourgh:

To my estranged nephew,

Your scheme to lead me to change my mind and allow the marriage planned by your mother and me to proceed shall not succeed. Not so long as that stain upon the names of Fitzwilliam and Darcy and her low born spawn still resides with you. The very shades of Pemberley are polluted by the presence of G. The ancestral shades. Such pollution I will not allow. My Anne is of a delicate constitution, and the diseases that creature received from your father's pet would sicken her and be the death of my Anne. The moral pollution would destroy the fiber of her children — your children.

So long as she is present at Pemberley, Anne will never live there. Never!

I see through your scheme! Through your pretended engagement. You were clever. I did think much upon what might have been after receiving the news of your engagement to this Miss Bennet. I have met the girl, and I knew that she was too low, too impertinent, and too scheming to be fit to take Anne's place as the mistress of Pemberley. I had feared that your good sense had been rotted by the disease that led you to keep HER and her spawn with you. But your scheme is now unfolded to me. It was an art to induce me change my mind and seek you out desperately once you were "free" once more.

You have failed. So long as your estate is despised by the world entire due to the presence of that false claimant to the Fitzwilliam blood. That girl who was no doubt substituted at birth with an impressionable peasant creature instead of my true niece. So long as this state continues, you shall never marry my Anne. Eject G, remove her from your presence, remove her from your life, then I shall allow your true bride to join you. Not until then.

Your Loving Aunt,

Lady C de B

Darcy wanted to show the letter to Elizabeth. This was outrageous and bizarre. *She* would appreciate the laughability of his aunt.

But by God, was he grateful Georgiana remained with him. He did *not* wish to be descended upon by Lady Catherine and her sickly spawn — daughter. Her sickly daughter. The deuce, why had she needed to stick that word in his head?

Shaking his head, Darcy looked at the letter again with an amused chuckle. His eyes caught the line: *The very shades of Pemberley are polluted by the presence of G.*

The phrasing was familiar, and distinctive. Who could possibly have used those particular words recently? Darcy frowned and paced around his room, looking out the large windows that oversaw his noble domain and massive park. Who would someone speak about polluting Pemberley? Maybe when Mr. Peake asked after the tenants and estate matters he worked upon when he was employed at Pemberley. They had spoken about lead mining works set up in a hill owned by a neighbor which released substantial dirt and unhealthful fragments of lead into a stream which flowed through Darcy's fields.

Darcy remembered. Elizabeth's harsh face, filled with anger. *"You will make your sister miserable to avoid offending your ghosts?"*

It felt sick, like something wasn't right, as though he'd made a mistake. It was the first time he'd felt anything of the sort since she had thrown his ring at him.

He'd said the shades of Pemberley would rebel against Georgiana's marriage to a tradesman. He'd used Lady Catherine's words to explain why Georgiana could not possibly be allowed to marry Mr. Peake.

A knock sounded on Darcy's study door. He stood and called out for the door to be open. It was opened, and before his butler could announce the guest, Brigadier General Richard Fitzwilliam stepped lightly into the room.

The two men stared at each other while Darcy's butler withdrew and closed the door.

"The deuce, Darcy. Upon my word! Tall as ever."

"Richard!" Darcy grabbed his cousin and embraced him, and Richard embraced him back. The two men then separated, with wide grins.

"You laughing fool — what happened with Miss Bennet? But not *now*. Not at all. Zounds, I am glad to see you happy to see me."

"And you a general. I haven't even seen you since the promotion."

"Mainly means more salary, and I can't sell my commission any longer."

"No extra responsibility?"

"Eh, I have that. You'd think they could hardly find work for me to do with the army shrinking since the end of the war but I impressed *him*" — Richard pointed to the ceiling — "at Waterloo, so he keeps me busy."

"Do you mean God or Wellington? I heard from your father that your regiment had been involved in the worst part of the fighting."

"Damned close run thing. Damned close run. And now I'm punished for holding firm by being kept busy, even though the army has nothing to do. Darcy, you look both hale and hell burnt. And Georgie? I must apologize to *her*. Deuced, damned fool. What sort of man would throw a fit to force a crying child of fifteen to marry a cold, dead stick like Carteret — worse, I had no reason beyond spite. But zounds, I am glad to see you again."

"I too...I am..." Darcy nearly teared over, he was smiling so hard. "It is *good* to see you."

The two men grinned at each other.

Georgiana was delighted to see RIchard. She accepted his apology, and she broke out of the sullenness she'd shown, even after their conversation. She had been quiet, though no longer resentful in the way that she had been the first day.

The three talked and laughed, and little Anne slowly warmed up to Richard, and in turn he was charmed by the little girl. In the afternoon they went outside and fought an epic snowball war in the park which lasted nearly till dark.

Shrieking and laughing, they returned to the house, warmed up with chocolate and hot punch, and talked for hours, while Georgiana played for them several times.

Darcy could see Richard's curiosity about Georgiana's manner towards Darcy. That there was a tension between Georgiana and Darcy was clear, and he must want to know what had happened between him and Elizabeth.

After Georgiana retired for the night, the two gentlemen made their own shift to the billiards room for a game of snooker and a decanter of fine cognac.

Darcy told Richard how he met Elizabeth — somehow his ill mood and incivility when introduced to her had been transformed by the passage of time from an embarrassment to an unbearably touching and tender memory, and he could not speak the story without tears.

Then he became engaged, and then Georgiana developed her infatuation with Mr. Peake, and then Elizabeth had ended their engagement when he did not follow her orders to allow Georgiana to marry Mr. Peake.

Darcy sought to keep resentment and reproach from his voice when he spoke of their argument which led to the final rift. His success was mixed.

After the story was done, Darcy leaned against the wall, with his glass in his hand. Richard was quiet for a while. The officer pulled back his cue stick to strike his ball. It hit the red ball that was placed in the center of the table. The red ball then shot into the right pocket with a crack. Richard's cue ball bounced off the red ball and hit Darcy's cue ball, knocking it into the left pocket, and then Richard's ball rolled slowly towards the right pocket. It was on the line towards the pocket, but as the friction slowed its motion, Darcy thought the ball would not reach the edge.

Both men tensed watching. The ball stopped on the lip of the pocket. Darcy let out a sigh of relief while Richard sagged. Then prompted by some untimely gust of wind, the red ball tipped over into the pocket.

Richard pounded his hand. "Canon, losing hazard, and winning hazard! Ten points in one shot. Fifteen ahead."

"Bravo!" Darcy clapped at the other gentleman's performance. He felt rather mellow and better than he had since Elizabeth had jilted him. Talking made him feel as though a surgeon had lanced the boil that her treatment of him caused to grow and allowed the poison to drain out. Friendship and closeness restored with a fellow gentleman could create such pleasant and happy feelings.

He needed no woman to be happy.

Darcy swallowed half of the cognac remaining in his snifter. He placed the glass on the wooden edge of the billiards table, and stared at the felt table with purpose. He would likely lose the current game, but that was no excuse for not making an earnest effort.

Richard picked the red ball out of the pocket and handed Darcy his cue ball. Darcy placed, and then he picked up his cue stick. Despite the dark outside, the table was lit enough for Darcy to easily discern the marble balls. Six lamps with wide white shades were suspended from the ceiling, lighting the twelve-foot-long table.

"You made a deuced good shot." Darcy shook his head. "You'll not match it."

"Nor you, often. A good bit of luck for you I missed the last shot." Darcy struck his ball on the center and it hit the red ball, knocking it against the green felt of the table's border. Then Darcy's cue ball spun backwards and fell into one of the middle pockets. Darcy made a face and shrugged. "Still three points."

Richard shrugged and picked out his cue ball, marked with yellow as he was the second player in turn. He set it down in place and swallowed the rest of his cognac before setting up for the shot. He hit the ball with a hard, ringing strike, and swore as it bounced over the green surface, before missing the red ball and then hitting the back wall of the table and bouncing over it.

Darcy laughed good naturedly and grabbed the square bottle of alcohol from where it sat on a side shelf. He poured Richard more and then refilled his own snifter. "Foul. Two points to me."

Richard laughed. "Overconfident — I am still well ahead of you."

"If you continue to play like *that* I'll catch you, we have another hundred points left in the game."

The two shot another round.

Richard said, "This, talking to you...seeing an old friend is a great source of happiness—"

"There is little that can match true companionship."

"This is more than simply friendship. We were half brothers at one time."

"Only in the past?" Darcy smiled.

"Ha! In the future as well. It was my fault in the main. The separation. I should not have been so... My treatment of you was not prompted primarily by Georgiana. The war. You had not been there. I needed to finish fighting our battles before I could come here and...apologize or be your family once more. I should have said something before."

"I should have as well."

"I would not have replied with any friendship before, oh, the middle of the year eighteen hundred and sixteen. I was a wreck by the end. The war ended, but it took a great time for me to stop fighting it in my mind."

"I worried greatly when you were at Waterloo. Even though it had been years."

Richard struck the cue ball, which bounced the red ball into a pocket before following it into a different pocket. "Ha! Further ahead."

Darcy hummed. Richard had just been present for him. He wanted to be present for Richard.

"All soldiers have ghosts." Richard looked him in the eye. "I mean those who fight real battles. Maybe not every soldier. But many. I had ghosts, but they left me after a while. I mean after several years. For years, not only you — everyone who had not fought. I was angry at everyone. Matters with my brother and father..." Richard laughed. "It is an excessive good fortune for me that I gained so much in spoils in Spain. After the things I said to them... Father would have cut me cold if he thought I would be hurt."

"I am sorry."

"A tradesman. Ha. My father would have hated that."

"What right do any of them have to care on the subject? They have not visited since Georgiana's pregnancy was unhideable."

"Miss Bennet. A charming girl. I would never have expected *you* with a woman such as her."

Darcy grimaced and nodded in agreement. He drank more, the smooth alcohol burning a line down his throat and into his gut. One of the lamps guttered as its oil ran out. He rang for the servant, and silently pointed.

"You are torn up over it," Richard said once the man had left to fetch oil to refill all of the lamps. "You made a mistake, letting her go so easily, since you feel so strongly yet. I remember Miss Bennet. I'd not have lost a woman like that on any account. A fine, fine lady."

"She ended our engagement."

"Really?" Richard's eyes were a little skeptical. "You mean to say you had no part in it."

"She went so far as to take the ring from her finger and throw it upon the table. I don't even know where it bounced to. She *threw* my ring upon the table. On the *table*." Darcy angrily shot, missing both Richard's ball and the newly placed red ball. That was two points to Richard for the miss. Not that Darcy cared who won their damned game.

Richard made another shot. It was a cannon, bouncing off Darcy's completely white cue ball, with only Richard's cue ball ending up in the pocket. "It sounds to me," Richard stepped back from the table, and leaned against his cue stick, "as though you are trying to convince yourself of something. Ha! I'd *wondered* what you'd say if I could get you to admit where that simmering anger towards the miss came from. Threw your ring to ground! I can picture her pretty face, angry and hurling. What a woman!" Richard whistled.

"Damnation, what do you mean to say?"

"I want to help you. You were always a fool about women."

"I should be angry. I am *right* to be angry."

"If your happiness is constituted in anger."

"Why? I cannot understand *why*. How could I have been so mistaken by her character? No respectable woman would have treated me in that way. I don't understand."

Richard rolled his eyes. But he didn't say anything. Darcy got the decided impression that his cousin did not take his side in his dispute with Elizabeth. The two of them traded rounds, and Darcy's play had deteriorated substantially. He missed both shots. Perhaps that had been Richard's goal when he brought her up: To ensure Darcy could not catch his lead. The servant returned with oil and filled up all of the lamps, and then filled the half emptied decanter of cognac.

"Georgiana isn't excessively unhappy," Darcy said once the man left. "She never talks about Mr. Peake."

Richard skeptically stared at Darcy from over his nose. He took a sip from his glass. "I was glad to see her. She does not seem cut up. Women can hide things. She's hiding something."

"Georgiana? She knows to obey me. I'd know if she hid anything."

"Darcy, do you want my advice, or my agreement? We do not see matters face to face in this." Richard grinned. "I'll not yell at you when you ignore me this time. You do not even need to hear my thoughts if you do not ask."

"A false pretense of my being allowed to hold back. After you have said so much, I would be quite incurious not to ask more." Darcy sighed. "What would you have me do with Georgiana?"

"Let her marry that tradesman."

"She is half Fitzwilliam blood. I did not expect that from you."

"If you gave a damn about her *respectability,* you would have made her marry Carteret. You were right not to. I have a perfect picture of that day. Georgiana sobbing, and me angry. But I cannot recall what possibly made me think we should force her to marry him. I said earlier, it was spite, because neither of you needed to return to Spain."

Darcy grunted.

"Women are...damnation, you don't try to control women. They do as they will. Pull together, life is well. Pull apart, life turns to hell."

"Women need protection. I protected her. I told you, she understands."

"Has Georgiana said that to you? That she thinks you were right?"

Darcy grimaced. He knew she did not.

"Just what *did* you do to make Miss Bennet so angry?"

"Are you purposely trying to annoy me? So that I realize I had nothing to miss during those years?"

Richard laughed and made another high scoring shot. "Little chance of you catching me *now.*"

"I cannot *care* if I catch you."

"You said you do not understand. Try to remember. Try to think of matters how they would appear to your woman. Can you think as clearly as you used to? Make the attempt."

The argument had been too painful to dwell on. He'd remember fragments and snatches of it, and thrice Darcy woke in a cold sweat from a nightmare about the argument. He'd never really thought upon what had been said. Elizabeth treated him wrongly, and she ought to have accepted his authority over Georgiana, and she should have felt Darcy pride. That was all there was to it.

"Too much learning made her irrational, and a woman's emotions are intrinsically fickle."

Richard laughed as though Darcy had made a joke. "Did you tell your lady *that*?"

"Of course not — I..." What *had* he told Elizabeth? The scene rose before his eyes in a jumbled heap. He'd told her she was mercenary. She apologized for her anger and passion when she said unkind words, but every time she asked for compromise, or demanded he listen to her, he said there was no reason to talk. He was decided.

She had *tried* to talk to him.

Darcy had a sour frown. As he thought, they played through the final few rounds of the game, and Richard won by twenty-nine points.

He still loved her.

Darcy had absolutely refused to let her speak her piece, or to consider seriously what she said. He of course would have rejected everything she could say about Georgiana and Mr. Peake (but would he have? Elizabeth could be persuasive), he owed his wife the honor of not being immovably convinced of his decision before he had heard her out.

The two gentlemen leaned against the window sill, looking out at the darkness, and their own flickering reflections. Darcy said, "She trusted me far enough to agree to a marriage because when we argued, I argued with her as an equal. Whatever I *said* about distrusting female learning, I took her mind and her words as seriously as I would any other combatant — I had no choice. Miss Bennet's mind is dazzling, radiant. She is as clever as I am."

"Too clever for a simple soldier like me."

Darcy looked at Richard from the side of his eyes. "Had you been attracted to her?"

Richard laughed. "How could any man not be? I am not insensible. But no serious thoughts. I had not sufficient money *then* to please myself, and Papa would have been angry. Besides she *is* much too clever for a simple soldier."

"I told her I would not listen to her about any *serious matter* — that is how she interpreted what I said — I proved such by not allowing her to speak to me about Georgiana. My sister's well-being is mine to care for. I choose, in the end. But..."

"You could hardly expect Miss Bennet to be satisfied when you refused to even *listen* to her opinions the first time you had a serious disagreement."

Darcy stared out into space. Had he made his own mistake? But Elizabeth had thrown his ring to the ground. She had been full of passion and anger as well.

Richard poured Darcy another thumb of the cognac. "Drink up. I have fulfilled my duty tonight."

Chapter Twenty-Three

Life continued at Pemberley.

As Brigadier General Fitzwilliam *had* become a favorite of the military command, he only could stay at Pemberley for a week. But it was a good week. Darcy felt calmer and happier when he farewelled his cousin.

Their days were much as they had always been. Georgiana walked and rode more, visiting different parts of the estate, and often taking Anne with her to show his niece parts of the estate she belonged to by her Darcy birth. When he could, Darcy went with them.

Georgiana did not cease playing piano. Darcy had feared she would. His life would be entirely empty without her and Anne. Before, he expected it to be filled by Elizabeth, and her society, and her laughter, and her interests.

He had been mistaken in how he treated Elizabeth. And this gave him an ache, a sense that if he could repeat that horrible day once more, if he could simply speak that conversation with Elizabeth again, and keep his temper in good regulation, he would yet be happy. He just had needed to convince her he would listen to her, and never rule over her in a manner which principally affected her.

Darcy had not been mistaken to deny Georgiana's wishes. There was sadness in his sister, but much less than Darcy had expected.

Darcy spent a great deal of effort planning Georgiana's birthday party. It was to be her twenty first, an auspicious age, and one which Darcy thought marked the beginning of an even better life for his sister. But still just the two of them. Darcy had not come to understand how to engage her more deeply in Derbyshire society, the way Elizabeth had in Hertfordshire. He did not understand how to make people feel sympathy with him, not in the way Elizabeth could.

For her birthday Darcy hired a famed pianist to perform and to offer Georgiana several weeks of focused lessons. She'd told him once, years ago, that she wished to take lessons from Mr. Maier.

They had planned to employ him when they spent time in London after the summer that Georgiana would spend in Ramsgate. Now at last Georgiana would fulfill that dream from before.

The morning of her birthday, Darcy looked over the daily business and then went out to examine the preparations for her party.

Boxes and boxes of fireworks had been purchased and stored in the garden sheds — safely distant from the main house. They had arrived two days ago, and Darcy inspected them with the servants. Georgiana and Anne would shout in delight when they watched the rockets fly up and explode with colors filling the cold night sky. Darcy beamed at the boxes and he opened one up to examine the fuse and the frame of a rocket. "Excellent collection. Excellent — be careful in handling them."

The chief gardener who thoroughly enjoyed the chance to handle fireworks bowed with a barely concealed grin.

Darcy returned to the house and sighed in relief when he reentered the warm air from the freezing outdoors. Such a good day. Such a day for his sister's happiness. He handed his gloves and heavy scarf to the servant who greeted him at the entrance and went to the breakfast room to see if Georgiana had come down yet.

She entered the breakfast room with Anne as Darcy arrived.

Georgiana had dressed prettily, in a day dress suitable for travel. Did she plan to go to the nearby town for some purchases after breakfast? He had planned out festivities for much of the day, but while Darcy disliked upending such plans, it was *Georgiana's* birthday, not his own. He could call in the pianist, Mr. Maier, during the course of breakfast, and they would be returned no matter what in time for music, fireworks and cakes in the evening.

Georgiana smiled at him, but something strange was in her expression. Darcy's chest squeezed.

He ignored the anxiety and hugged his sister and kissed her cheek before picking up Anne. "Happy birthday! Happy birthday, Georgie! Congratulations on your twenty first!"

"Thank you, Fitzwilliam." She was quiet and she looked down.

Darcy let Anne down, and she ran around the room crying, "Happy birthday, Mama! Happy birthday!"

Georgiana smiled weakly.

Darcy said, "Please don't look melancholy — I have fine gifts. Fireworks have been prepared! A magnificent time today. Did you wish to go out for a while after breakfast?"

"You do?"

"Of course I do. I have done little but plan for your birthday this past week."

"Oh, Fitzwilliam." She patted his hand.

Darcy's stomach did not feel right, as though it was warning him of something. Georgiana said nothing further.

"You...you cannot still be very unhappy," Darcy rambled. "You have been resilient and avoided the maudlin, or playing the ill-used girl. We have not spoken of the match you wished to make. Not often. But you have been dignified and calm. I expected you to be far unhappier. It is proof I was right."

Georgiana looked at her hands.

"It has been a painful time for us both. Elizabeth... both our mistakes."

Anne said, "I miss Aunt Lizzy."

"Go play with Uncle Will." Georgiana pushed her daughter who grabbed Darcy's leg and pulled on his pants, grinning.

"Don't do that." Darcy smiled at her, feeling still worried but happy.

Anne giggled. "Mama told me to."

Darcy picked her up and swung her around in a wide circle, before he placed her on his lap.

"You and her — it has always warmed my heart to see how happy you are with Anne." Georgiana smiled softly. "You are a wonderful uncle. You will be a wonderful father one day."

Darcy harrumphed. "Too much a bachelor. I am too much a bachelor. I have no interest in most women. It shall not happen."

"Oh, Fitzwilliam. You have not sent any letter to Bingley, have you?"

"Jane sent you letters. I gave them to you. You know as much of them as I do."

"Lizzy — she is still — you could yet try. I would dearly like to see you happy."

"She would not accept me, and...I am a proud man. She chose to end matters with me, and I will not beg or return to where I have been pushed away."

"Your pride is not a virtue."

"My pride is part of who I am."

Georgiana looked at the ground again. Awkward silence enveloped them. Something scared whispered in his stomach again, like fear.

She said in a low-toned, pitying voice, "I know."

Darcy said, "Let us breakfast. Your favorites are cooked and prepared — I have a surprise gift for you."

"Fitzwilliam, you — I wish you would allow me to marry Mr. Peake. I wish you could give us your blessing, that you could...accept that I choose not to have your pride, our family pride. I am happy being humble, not living up to our legacy."

"What are you talking of? We have settled matters."

She cried.

"Oh, Georgie. I am sorry that I have hurt you. That you still hurt. Oh oh, my poor sister. But you will eventually learn to like him less, and forget him and—"

"I will not forget Mr. Peake."

"You will, you forgot Mr. Wickham, and you—"

"Do *not* compare them." Georgiana rose up, and wiped off her eyes. "I shall not *argue* with you. But the men are entirely different. And you... Fitzwilliam, you are too certain of yourself."

"You had accepted that your engagement to Mr. Peake had been a mistake, like you know Wickham had been a mistake."

Georgiana looked at her hands again.

This was not what Darcy had expected today. He wanted to see her happy. "You are not — you have...you have not been unhappy. Not very."

"I stopped blaming you," Georgiana replied. Her voice was tinny. "I do not blame you in any way. You are who you are."

"He is a tradesman, and he brings nothing to the family, and he was not educated in the way you were."

"I know."

"We will have a wonderful time today. Let me call in your chief birthday present. He arrived yesterday morning."

Georgiana smiled softly. "I heard horses and coming and going yesterday. But I was good, and did not attempt to discover."

The famed concert pianist, Mr. Maier was brought in, and Georgiana smiled when the man bowed to her.

"Mr. Maier," Georgiana smiled and said sweetly, "I am delighted to meet you."

"I as well to make acquaintance of such a talented girl. I care nothing for the silliness of those others. It is your love for the art — I heard you five years past play. Remarkable skill for a woman of your age, with the natural deficit of your position in society."

"For a time I abandoned the craft. I believed... It is not important. I was younger and more foolish."

"You have the basis. If you had not played until you were fifteen nothing could be done. Without steady application as a child you cannot become truly great. But damage from an extended break once full grown is remediable. Mr. Darcy said you wish to regain your past facility."

"I do."

"I am yours for the next two months, to learn from."

"Oh." Georgiana closed her eyes, as though in pain. "This is your present? It is so thoughtful. It is so—"

"I only wish you to be happy." Darcy looked at her. "I perhaps have too much eagerness to see you play again; you had planned to take lessons from Mr. Maier after the summer that year."

"I remember..."

"Then you are happy?"

Georgiana bit her lips. "Mr. Maier, forgive me, but I must have a conversation with my brother. I look forward to speaking with you at greater length."

"Yes, Miss Darcy." He bowed and after quickly looking between the two retired from the room.

Georgiana was white faced. "Anne, come back. I want to hold you."

"Yes, Mama."

Darcy set her on the ground and watched the little girl run to her mother.

"Enough. Enough. I must tell you." Georgiana took Anne into her arms and gripped the child so tightly that she squirmed. Then Darcy's sister exhaled. She looked him in the eyes directly. "We are leaving."

The fire crackled in the hearth.

Georgiana studied Darcy. She evidently expected him to say something.

He was confused. "What are you talking of? Where? Into Lambton?"

"London. If…if Mr. Peake still cares for me, we shall marry. If not I shall live with Jane, or perhaps at Longbourn with Lizzy."

"You cannot leave."

"I am one and twenty. I know the terms of Father's will. I now have control of my fortune. I now have control over my person. I now can marry as I choose."

"You cannot leave."

"Fitzwilliam…I hate that I shall leave you alone."

"You — no. No."

"I am leaving. Anne is coming with me. I…I am sorry that I shall leave you alone. But this is…you chose this."

"You cannot leave."

"I can. I have already sent out letters to the family's lawyer to have control of my money turned over directly to me. The arrangements for a post carriage to come to pick me up a little after noon have been made. My clothes, those which I wish to take, have been packed. I am leaving."

"No…you…no." It was as if he was moving sluggishly. More shock than when Elizabeth jilted him. Not Georgiana. She never rebelled. "Elizabeth wrote you. Those letters. In Jane's."

"You will not listen to me. I know it. But I still care for you. I…*why* must you be so much yourself? So proud. Beg Elizabeth for forgiveness—"

"Threw the ring in my face. She *threw* it."

"You are not happy this way. I want you to be happy. But even more, I want to be happy. I want Anne to be happy."

"You…" Why hadn't Papa done like many other families and required that the money remain under the control of the guardians until she had reached twenty and five? That would not have helped. She *still* could have married Mr. Peake. He no longer was her guardian. She was of age. "Must I lose you too?"

"You — don't need to, don't — come with me. Fitzwilliam…"

"Be gone." The shock was now pain. Darcy stood and swallowed. "If you intend to throw yourself away, to throw away the pride of the Darcy name. Do it. I only curse the day we met the Bennets."

Georgiana Darcy left with her daughter.

Fitzwilliam Darcy stared at the flickering flames of the fire, eating away the substance of a tree that had grown for decades before being chopped up to be burnt in a petty conflagration.

Chapter Twenty-Four

The noise from the crowds of pedestrians and carriages along Gracechurch Street woke Elizabeth shortly after dawn. She looked out the window of Mr. Gardiner's townhouse. What cause could possibly wake *so* many people at barely six o'clock in the morning?

London, the greatest city in the world, was alive.

Mr. Darcy had not returned south with his sister.

When Jane first exclaimed the news that Georgiana was to marry Mr. Peake, Elizabeth's heart had leapt in hope. Strange that she hoped for something from him. For several minutes she was too crushed by sadness to rejoice in her friend's fortune. Georgiana at one time was to become her sister. Now she had chosen to defy her brother, and he had chosen to sit brooding upon his dark estate, keeping company with its ghosts, whose sensibilities could not be defied, even at the cost of all happiness for himself and those he loved most.

Georgiana had traveled in haste to London, arriving two days after her birthday. In a dramatic gesture she had her carriage driven to the warehouses of Gardiner and Peake, and then while the coachman protected its position on a crowded London street from the screaming cab drivers and cartmen, she entered the offices. She found Mr. Peake with Mr. Gardiner in the middle of an interview with a crusty East Indiaman ship captain with a pegleg and a pirate's earring.

The natural result was that Peake and Georgiana were to be married as soon as the papers were signed and Peake's business settled — money was no object, so a special license had been procured — both Peake and Georgiana had particular ideas on how to protect Anne and Georgiana in the marriage settlement, and it took several days for the lawyers to legalize the documents. Also Peake needed a period of time to set his affairs in order such that he could have a holiday of two weeks from his business. He and Georgiana would honeymoon along the seashore — *not* in Ramsgate.

When Mr. Gardiner told the story, the crusty sea captain leered at Georgiana as she and Peake kissed upon seeing each other, until he was charmed by Anne asking about his earring, and the carriage in the street caused a traffic snarl at least a mile and a half long — Elizabeth suspected her uncle to exaggerate, but the ward of Cheap was a prosperous and busy section of London — and his warehousemen stopped dragging carpets and bolts of fabric from one side of the building to another to stare. Which meant the entire business of the day was set back by several hours, and they missed a delivery to an important customer, who forgave them upon being invited to the impromptu engagement celebration at the Gardiner's fine establishment on Gracechurch Street a few blocks away from the warehouse.

A very romantic story.

Georgiana would be resident in the Gardiners' spare guest room for the time before the papers were written and signed, and the business was settled, and she was married to Mr. Peake at the nearby parish church at Gracechurch. The church was a big pretty building with the look of a Romanesque steepled church in the middle of crowded London.

An express had been sent that evening to Mr. Bingley and Jane to inform Georgiana's friends in Hertfordshire of her marriage, and to beg Jane and Elizabeth to attend the wedding.

The trip took two days to arrange, as Elizabeth was to go with Mr. Bingley in his carriage, and Jane of course needed a period of time to have everything placed in preparation to take Bennet to the big city. London always was cloudy, drizzly, and a thick quilt of smoky fog from the hundreds of thousands of chimneys suffocated the city during the winter. At least there was less pestilence during the course of the winter.

Two hours past noon Bingley's carriage entered the city. London. A million people — an entire million — rushing about. Tall buildings crowded and smashed together. Manicured lawns and well-watered trees. Poorly cleaned plaster blackened by soot. The crowded center, with handsome façades of marble and red brick, and crazily angled streets. Statues of men on horses, and men with guns. Parks with tall wrought iron fences to prevent the entry of those without permission. They entered the city from the east and drove along the Thames, past the white Tower of London, with the flag of Britain flapping proudly in the wind.

Then along Lower Thames Street. They passed the massive column of the two-hundred-foot-tall monument to the Great Fire of London, white and gleaming, with inscriptions in Latin around one side and bas relief scenes carved into another. One clear summer day when visiting, Elizabeth had paid the few pence to climb the stairs all the way to the top and been rewarded with the most astonishing view, which still did not allow her to see the entirety of London.

The carriage turned onto Gracechurch Street, and bankers in fancy suits ran in front of carriages as though they had no fear of being run over; aristocrats with long leggings calmly walked the streets, entering establishments they had business with; and tourists stood, gazing each way in anxiety, before cautiously crossing the roads and being nearly run over by screaming drivers for their slowness.

They trundled halfway down the street and pulled up to the handsome home Mr. Gardiner owned, and Elizabeth allowed her brother-in-law to help her down, while the footman knocked upon the door. He'd barely touched the knocker before it was opened, and Mrs. Gardiner and Georgiana spilled out of the house, and encouraged their servants to have the trunks quickly carried in.

Anne enthusiastically joined them, with several of Mrs. Gardiner's children, all of whom jumped around happily, clinging to Aunt Lizzy and Aunt Jane and Uncle Bingley and then eagerly incorporating Bennet into their games. The young boy was quite social and happily followed along in their play. They were all pushed into the house by Mrs. Gardiner, to keep the young from catching their death of cold in the grey weather — not that Mrs. Gardiner worried; it would only be a frustration to nurse the children through a harmless illness when everyone *ought* to be full of celebration.

Jane and Bingley planned to go on to the fashionable outer borough two miles away where they had rented a house for the month, but the two were persuaded to send their carriage round to a nearby stables and yard to wait for them. They entered the house with Bennet. Everyone sat in the drawing room, and crackers and tea were provided. Georgiana glowed. Elizabeth wanted to talk to her in private, to ask about Mr. Darcy — she cared even though she had given up the right to concern herself with his well-being. But in this crowd it was only a chance for everyone to speak at once about joint topics.

Georgiana was made to repeat the story Mrs. Gardiner had given in her letter of how she had found Mr. Peake and told him she still wished to marry him, and Jane begged every detail, and they spent an hour in rapid conversation, by which time Mr. Gardiner was to arrive in just another hour or two from the offices with Mr. Peake — one of the servants had been sent to the office to tell them that they had arrived, and of course Jane and Bingley were convinced to stay for dinner, and then for the evening. It was decided they would go to a play a mile away at Haymarket Theatre.

A messenger was sent to the stables where the carriage had been sent, telling it to go without Jane and Bingley to the house they had taken so the carriage could be unpacked, and then the vehicle would return to wait for them to call later tonight. Mr. Gardiner arrived, and Mr. Peake and Georgiana snuck a kiss in the entry room, but Elizabeth saw them. They were like she and Darcy had been. Everyone laughed and they all were happy, and after dinner they watched *As You Like It* from a box with red velvet seats.

No opportunity to speak in private to Georgiana occurred.

Waking up now, Elizabeth decided to convince Georgiana to take a morning walk with her. She always enjoyed seeing the sights of the city during the first day or two in Town. Elizabeth went down to the breakfast room to wait for her friend, and she tried to read a book.

Georgiana entered the breakfast room in a simple day dress that made her bloom. She smiled upon seeing Elizabeth. "My dear Lizzy, I so desired to speak with you last night."

"And *I* had the same desire. But we *now* can before the others breakfast. Will you walk with me? I wish to reacquaint myself with the city."

"Of course. Of course. Towards St. Paul's? I have spent most of my mornings walking in other directions, or taking the carriage to Hyde Park when the weather is kind."

Elizabeth laughed. "That is not today."

They both looked out the window. "It is not promising," Georgiana said. "The more need to set out promptly, in case of rains."

The two walked out arm in arm, bundled up in their winter coats so they could survive a mild drizzle and followed by the Gardiner's footman.

"At last! At last!" Elizabeth clapped. "Alone with you!"

Georgiana grinned at Elizabeth's enthusiasm. "I as well looked particularly forward to *your* conversation."

"Yesterday was a good evening, still that endless talk, and then the theater, and then the children."

"Do not forget that excellent late-night meal of melted cheese and toast." Georgiana shuddered with pleasure. "Your aunt and uncle have *such* a baker. That bread—"

"It was an excellent night *except* we could not speak. And that gave it a lack. I rail not against fine company, excellent food and good entertainment *often* — though we shall never be sisters in church law, you are my sister in heart."

"I...I feel that way as well."

"Jane feels equally close — see how quick your call brought her to London. And so early in the year! We in general avoid Town at the beginning or end of the season when *everyone* descends upon the capital."

Georgiana giggled as their footman blocked the street, stopping a carriage so they could safely cross the crowded street. There always was a special energy about London. Elizabeth would not wish to *live* here, but she loved to visit.

"I am so happy you shall be happy. And Mr. Peake, he glowed with delight! Such a happy end to a...to a situation that was not full of happiness. Last night, my pet, he and you were adorable to watch."

"We were?" Georgiana clapped her hands together and bounced happily on her toes.

Elizabeth winked and tilted her head.

Georgiana grinned. She suddenly looked down and pressed her fingers together. "Did you...feel jealous? You looked hurt at times."

Heavens! It *still* hurt. Why? She had ended it with Darcy, and he yet lived. And their marriage never could have been happy and calm.

"Oh! Forgive me — I should not have said anything."

"I have, in the most, put my melancholy feelings away. I *did*, I must confess, blacken my windows, eat nothing but bread and water — not a great deal of either, I assure you — and lie somnolent in bed at first, composing sodden poetry." Elizabeth laughed. "But such did not last long. I have too great a requirement for exercise and activity to be a proper heroine."

"Lizzy — you... I do not want to see you—"

"I assure you, I am well. I am in the main as happy as I was before I had ever known such a man as your brother existed. Maudlin, depression, playing the tragic, sighing heroine. *Not* my nature — I confess a *little* jealousy, but—"

"My dear friend..." Georgiana unconsciously pulled and straightened a curled lock of hair. "If you blame me, I understand. I blame myself, and—"

"Heavens! The only person I blame in any manner is myself. Not even your brother — though he has faults sufficient to earn blame. A fool unknowing of herself. That was my case before I met your brother. I had entire confidence in my wisdom, in my control over my emotions, in myself. I could not know, in that untouched state that I would *feel* and such *feeling* would chase *thought* into a distant land far away and unreachable. I am, I hope, wiser."

"You and Fitzwilliam would be happy still, if not for me and Mr. Peake. My happiness is the cause of your unhappiness, it eats at me, and..."

"Stop that." Elizabeth pulled Georgiana to a halt next to the entrance of a shop whose sign proclaimed the presence of the finest silk and cotton stockings. The entire wall of the building across them was painted as a proclamation that the finest ales and wines could be consumed within. "*Our* differences were not your fault. There was a fissure betwixt us, such that we should never have entered our engagement. You did both Fitzwilliam and I a great favor by being the subject of a disagreement before we made oaths before God."

Georgiana's manner showed she did not agree. They continued forward until they reached the garden around St. Paul's cathedral. The large square was surrounded with tightly packed three-story buildings, with the bottom floors of each given over to crowded shops and busy businesses. Elizabeth studied the bell towers of the cathedral. A drizzly rain had begun.

Elizabeth said, "I understand we are to have a large dinner with Peake tomorrow evening, at hired rooms in Guildhall? You are to be contaminated by mingling with your future husband's — and my uncle's — many acquaintances in trade."

"Yes!" Georgiana nodded eagerly. "I am so eager to meet them all, and learn about what they do, and to see Mr. Peake amongst his friends and...and everything!"

"A good sort, most of them. I have met them. But you do not fear the contamination because they must work assiduously to earn a living by selling and buying?"

Georgiana tilted her head. She stuck her tongue out at Elizabeth.

The two walked into the cathedral for protection from the rain which had begun to quicken. The building was quiet and solemn, though a few other worshippers prayed before the altar, and several other pleasure lookers looked about as well. They admired the pristine white and gold decoration of the massive pillars supporting the structure. The pews and balustrades were made with fine woodwork. They walked to the small monument that had been erected where Christopher Wren, the famous architect who had rebuilt the cathedral after the fire, was interred.

"One day after our dinner, we intend to marry — Peake has nearly settled his business. It was done more quickly than we expected. And the settlement has been written up and signed." Georgiana giggled. "Both our lawyers have been kept up quite late to earn their fees the past week."

"You have protected your interests? Even with the best intentions, a man can gallop over the interests of a woman and—"

"Not at all! Mr. Peake is the kindest in this way."

"Georgie, I know something of financial matters. Papa has talked my ear off about *his* boredom with them, so I might be bored as well — I understand you are putting some money into the partnership."

"Half of my fortune will be invested into the company, with an associated ownership share attached to me by the settlement. But the other half is more than ample for us to live off should something go amiss with your uncle and Peake's business. More than fifteen thousand, and the interest from that—"

"A sufficiency — that will not support the life you are used to. Not its scale, or all the little pleasures."

"I am tired of that life!"

Georgiana's shout echoed in the large space, and several of the other people around looked at them frowningly, including a stern middle-aged man in heavy embroidered clerical robes. Elizabeth thought he might be a bishop.

She giggled, a little self-consciously, and took blushing Georgiana's hand. "I am glad to hear your passion. You should feel that way about your marriage."

They wandered about the massive open space, admiring the artwork and the columns. They craned their heads up to look into the three-hundred-and-fifty-foot-high dome.

"Very big," said Georgiana.

"Too large for my comfort," replied Elizabeth. "I would not desire to live in London — though I enjoy visits."

"I love the city. Though the country is calm and pleasant, I have always spent part of each year in London, and I shall happily be here the entirety of the year. Mr. Peake has engaged tidy lodgings two blocks from your uncle's along East Cheap Street, we shall be snug — not taking more space than we must; we hope for more children, of course, and shall need to launch them creditably. A *little* frugality early shall establish habits which ensure *that* will be easy. But space enough for us both, and my maid, *and* an extra room we can squeeze you into when you visit. Promise you shall visit, though you normally stay with Mr. and Mrs. Gardiner in Town. And beg your mother to visit as well."

"You *want* Mama to visit?" Elizabeth laughed. "She has risen in my estimation as well of late."

"I always adored her. She was so kind to me from the first."

"She has always been kind to *you*. I shall relay your invitation, and she will be delighted to make such a visit. And proud that you requested her."

The two strolled along the nave towards the massive banded wooden doors, past the rows of intricately carved pews made from dark woods. "We have talked around the subject sufficiently." Elizabeth smiled weakly. "What of your brother? How does he do?"

"He...he..." Georgiana shook her head. "I hardly know what to say."

They stepped outside. The rain had stopped, but the sky was still overcast, and the rain had washed the thick London fog. Their footman joined them again. Elizabeth took Georgiana's arm to lead her towards the Thames to walk along a footpath that looked out over the river between the docksides.

The two were quiet; the streets were not.

After a short walk the road took them to a leafy prospect with a wrought iron railing they could lean upon and watch the Thames flow below. The London Bridge, piled high with houses, stood east of them, and the mighty sluggish river flowed its slow way, with skiffs and canoes and ships sailing in each direction, and crowds of people, and the beauty of the packed buildings along the waterline.

"Fitzwilliam was foolish. He pushed you — I know! He told me the story. How could he be so *stupid* as to make you that angry!" Georgiana hopped with anger. Then she deflated, and stared sadly at the ships. "I wish..."

A bird hopped from branch to branch on the bare tree above them. Elizabeth sighed. The bird looked at them and cocked its red head and chirped.

"I keep hoping he will come." Georgiana did not look up. "When carriages unexpectedly stop outside, I imagine it is him following me to admit he cares for me more than family pride. I will sob if he is not present at the wedding."

"Oh dear girl! I counseled you to act according to your own best lights. Will you be happy without Fitzwilliam's blessing? There is no hurry. Hurry is something I never would encourage in matters matrimonial."

"So long. We waited, and then another month. I delay no longer."

The lark flew away and the two walked back through wet crowded streets to the Gardiner's ample townhouse. A stiff breeze blew, knocking their curls astray, blowing their bonnets askew and chilling them through their coats.

"If he comes back, promise to listen to him, and let him apologize." Georgiana looked pleadingly at Elizabeth with wide eager eyes. She seized Elizabeth's hands and squeezed them. "You two were perfect for each other."

"We were not. Not at all. We argued at every turn; we shared neither values nor philosophy. A dreadful match."

"You were. Perfect together."

"Georgie..."

"You were. You *are*. I want you for my sister and I want you to be Fitzwilliam's wife. I still hope for it."

Give up hope.

Instead of a harsh reply, Elizabeth shrugged. Georgiana wanted what Georgiana wanted. It was not likely to happen.

"Promise you will listen to him when he returns."

"I promise, that, in the utterly unlikely case your haughty brother condescends to speak to me about our past connection, I promise that I will sincerely listen to any apology he makes, and that I will then ask my reason if an intimate connection betwixt us would have any likelihood of success. But my reason will speak nay once again."

They reentered the house, and after their coats were hung up and their walking shoes removed, the housekeeper left the two alone again. Georgiana looked at Elizabeth with hurt soulful eyes.

"I do not desire reconciliation. I ended matters between us for excellent reasons. Fitzwilliam cannot wish a reconciliation either. Not now that he has had chance for his passions to cool — and further now that he has *further* example of my pernicious influence—"

"He loves you. He *cried...*"

Elizabeth closed her eyes. She did not wish to recall their happiness.

"Lizzy, love is the most important thing in the world. You love each other still."

"Love is not the only important matter."

"It is, when it is true love, and when—"

"You and Mr. Peake are in a different situation than me and Fitzwilliam. And I would kindly ask you to leave off discussing this matter."

Georgiana cried. She smiled through her tears. "There *is* hope. If you do not wish to talk about your *love*, you must still feel much. You must love him still, as he loves you still."

Elizabeth rolled her eyes. Why did she think that Georgiana was qualified to make her own decisions about marriage?

"I...Lizzy..."

"Georgie, if you only intend to marry because you think Fitzwilliam shall join us, and then marry me — I consider you my sister already."

"That is not it."

"Darcy is a proud man; one who will not support a woman in her foolishness. We are best off without him."

"Are you very angry at him? You *should* be. He can be infuriating — you feel that worse than I. But anger is not...your love matters more."

"I shouldn't have had to do it."

"What?"

Elizabeth slumped. She would not have been able to throw off the ring in a calm manner.

The poesy ring was stored safely in the bottom of her trunk awaiting the proper time to return it to Fitzwilliam. One of Bingley's housemaids had found it the day after, rolled in a corner under the tiled stove. Some part of her hoped what Georgiana had hoped, and like a *fool* she had brought the ring with her to London, instead of leaving it stagnant in the bottom her jewelry case in Longbourn.

Stuffing the love ring into an envelope and mailing his *ring* by post — too cold.

Georgiana shook her head. "You both will realize the mistake you are making."

"It would be irrational. I have determined to never let my passions misguide me again." They stood next to the drawing room door, but Elizabeth stopped Georgiana from opening it. "I am happy for you, Georgie. I am happy that you shall marry. You shall be happy. But I...I confess the truth you have guessed: though I pretend otherwise, I am not wholly happy at present."

Elizabeth left Georgiana by the drawing room door and walked to her own room. She felt Fitzwilliam's memory, like a physical presence. He could kiss her so well. They had been happy.

Elizabeth stared out her window. Carriages rushed past. Men wore top hats and workmen's caps. Women wore bonnets and fashionable small hats. The clouds had begun to weep once more, and a hawk circled high in the mournful sky.

Damned old maid.

We can discuss nothing. You have no voice.

She had not made a mistake.

Chapter Twenty-Five

A substantial crowd of well-dressed men in respectable lines of trade gathered in a rented dining hall at Guildhall to well wish Mr. Peake before his wedding. Elizabeth stood near the shy Georgiana, who smiled and blushed and nodded each time an acquaintance of Peake bowed to kiss her hand; usually their business acquaintances displayed polished manners, but sometimes they greeted her with the crudity of manner the high gentry such as the Darcys expected from Cits.

There was convivial chattering, discussions of business, and a great many wives and daughters of the guests were also present, having dressed to their best to match what they imagined was the splendor of the aristocratic woman who had captured the heart and grand business prospects of Mr. Peake. Within the closed circles of the London merchants in his line of trade, he had been seen as a promising catch, especially since he had been made a full partner of Gardiner.

Thus the *women* gathered there often felt an inkling (at least!) of jealousy towards Georgiana Darcy. There certainly was conversation of the scandal, and some of the women were determined to be a little rude only on that account. But the soon-to-be-former Miss Darcy was too sweet, too shy, and too much the elegant blushing bride to let people disdain her for long. She talked at length to several of the vicars of local parishes, and they all could speak for her *speaking* morality, and that she was repentant.

The tradesmen present all wished to remain on the good side of Peake, especially as it was expected that the money his marriage would bring to Peake would lead his firm to make substantial purchases, and that he would either become a more formidable competitor, a more valuable customer, or supplier of greater importance. The women studied Georgiana, but her dress was elegant simplicity itself: modest, unassuming, lacking flash, yet made of the finest materials, and with the best lines. She neither outshone those who must shine, nor did she sink beneath the notice of those who looked with critical eyes.

In sum Georgiana was a success amongst this group of London merchants, just as she had been in the rural society of Hertfordshire.

Two hours after the crowd gathered, and a little before the large dinner was to be served and everyone was to sit down, Mr. Darcy's cousin who Elizabeth had met at Rosings Park was ushered into the building to give his greetings to Georgiana.

"Good day, and congratulations, Georgiana — if your cousin might give you such." Colonel Fitzwilliam — no Elizabeth had heard from Darcy that he had been made a brigadier — stood grinning and pleased.

Georgiana allowed General Fitzwilliam to embrace her. Then she studied him. "Did Fitzwilliam send you? What does he want me to know? Why could he not come himself?"

"Fitzwilliam? No, no. Not him. I am present to deliver my *father's* message that you ought abandon your plan to debase the noble Fitzwilliam blood. We — you and I — descend from royalty on the wrong side of the sheets, and to debase this royal blood of sceptered kings with that of a bottom dwelling tradesman, who is not even ridiculously rich, is a stain upon our families, a blot. Your marriage is the inky darkness which will be used to obscure your name in the family tree. Your choice, he ordered me to inform you, will bring you nothing but deepest unhappiness and the universal despite. And so on and so on, and so on for a deuced long time — Aunt Catty was present, and the two topped one another for a *great* length in this vein. I took no notes, so I cannot do their rant justice, but if you should visit the old earl, he might repeat the choicest bits before having you thrown out upon your ear."

Georgiana laughed. "I thought they finished with me long ago."

General Fitzwilliam grinned and exchanged a knowing look with Georgiana. "Congratulations, Georgie. Congratulations. Deuced glad to see you show some spirit. You were too nice to Darcy for my taste when I visited Pemberley. But you had this sly plan in your mind already, did you not?"

Georgiana blushed. "I did."

"Sly girl! I hope the man is worthwhile, but if Miss Bennet jilted my cousin over the matter, he cannot be a bad sort." General Fitzwilliam bowed and took Elizabeth's hand and kissed it easily.

"Lovelier than ever. Pity my cousin's pride and your temper ended matters. *I* would have delighted to call you cousin."

"I thank you," Elizabeth replied with a little stiffness. "Did he tell you the manner I ended it with? I would not have thought he would speak of it."

"We are close. Again close. I am glad for that. Damned fool, Darcy. But he is my close cousin, and we care deeply. I owe you a deuced great deal, Miss Bennet. Darcy sent me a letter asking for a reconciliation — we had not been close since Georgie's youthful indiscretion. I am very glad."

"I hope for him to have friends."

"He will not be alone — though he has lost you." General Fitzwilliam lowered his voice so those around them could not hear, and he said with a sly smirk of approval, "Throwing the ring!"

"Not on this matter. I pray, laugh upon another subject. No laughter here. This still hurts."

"I apologize." Colonel Fitzwilliam bowed his head. "I might say I am a crude military man, unused to the society of proper women after so many years. But you would know that to be a lie. I sympathize too much with Darcy having seen his pain."

"My uncle and your brother? How do they do?" Georgiana touched General Fitzwilliam's arm to gain his full attention. "They of course are angry, but do they actually care that I am marrying Mr. Peake enough to be unhappy?"

"Unhappy? Delighted rather. It takes you away from Pemberley and Darcy. Aunt Catty is happier with your *brother* than she has been for many years."

"Aunt Catty! Such a good name." Georgiana snorted.

"She came to London upon receipt of the news — and she traveled to Pemberley with Anne to push *her* upon Darcy again. I will travel to Pemberley as well, tomorrow. I do worry for your brother." He glanced between the two women and cleared his throat. "I...well I hope to achieve a reconciliation. Darcy needs you. Both of you."

"I hope so! I hope so!" Georgiana clutched her hands together and bounced in her adorable manner. "I desperately want to have him yet be my brother."

"Do not count upon my success. Darcy is a proud and stubborn man."

"If only he would still marry Lizzy."

"Georgie, I have asked you," Elizabeth said, "to give up any such hope. I will not marry him."

"Are you a proud and stubborn woman as well?" Colonel Fitzwilliam smiled at Elizabeth.

"I am determined. In the future I will be *rational*. I shall not be driven by passions into making a mistake."

Colonel Fitzwilliam held his hands wide. "To ignore your deepest heart's feelings. To ignore what chance you have for human happiness. To live in fear of what might go wrong, when you could be killed upon any happening. That is not rational."

Elizabeth ground her teeth together, but before she replied the dinner bell rang.

Georgiana and Mr. Peake sat next to each other — the dinner was to celebrate their matrimony, so they must be seated together — and darted glances to each other. Elizabeth chatted with the gentlemen and ladies around her. She could not help feeling some jealousy and unhappiness at seeing Georgiana's happiness. It was irrational, wrong to feel, but she still ached in that way.

It was late when the dinner finished. As the dining hall was less than a half mile from the Gardiners' house on Gracechurch Street, and as the weather this evening was unseasonably mild, they bundled up and walked the short distance rather than waiting for a carriage to be brought round. Mr. Peake held Georgiana's arm, while Elizabeth walked to the side and behind them. Mr. and Mrs. Gardiner hurried together ahead of the slowly strolling couple, who admired the façades of the houses, the occasional street with trees along the road, and the light traffic as a few late carriages ran back and forth, with lamps hanging from every side.

Even though it was past midnight, neither Mr. Peake nor Georgiana were ready to sleep; it was just two days until they planned to marry. They settled into the drawing room to talk and enjoy a light late supper, while Elizabeth provided a chaperone. Mr. and Mrs. Gardiner, being older and wiser, went direct to sleep. Elizabeth yawned, and looked at a book while the couple cooed at each other. She did not mind staying up later, as her novel had reached its most interesting point.

Elizabeth smiled when the door was quietly snuck open.

Little Anne had apparently been woken by the noise. Georgiana picked her up and embraced her on seeing the girl, but after a few minutes Georgiana's attention had returned to Mr. Peake, and Anne went to Elizabeth. She squeezed Elizabeth's thigh and said happily, "Aunt Lizzy!"

"Yes!" Elizabeth picked the girl and sat her on her lap.

"Will you stay with *me* in London? Mama spends *all* the time with Daddy Peake — I shouldn't call him that until Mama *marries* him. But I can to you!"

"Yes." Elizabeth kissed the girl's forehead. "You can say anything to me."

"I miss Uncle Will! Why did Mama come without him? Uncle Will must be lonely, lonely without me."

There was a low outside rumble, like a carriage arriving, but it was too late in the evening for any late guest to arrive. There was constant traffic along the street at all hours. Only a wagon passing along, delivering its load.

Elizabeth kissed Anne on the forehead. "I miss him too."

"*You* keep him company! Mama won't let *me*. You don't do anything but walk, and Uncle Will can walk with you." The heartbreak was returning. She would probably never have a child — and was her independence worth that loss?

Elizabeth gave Anne a biscuit she had gotten from the kitchen but not finished. "Eat this, sweetling."

"Oooh!" Anne pointed. "It's so pretty. Looks like a dragon! I want to keep it."

"Yes, sweet — we can get you a carved dragon, just like this. We will paint it green, if you wish, for your birthday."

Anne thought carefully and pushed her little fist against her mouth. "But I want a pony."

Elizabeth laughed.

There was a loud knocking upon the outside door. Elizabeth looked up frowning and walked to the window. At *this* hour?

The butler had been awake, so he opened the door for them. They all stood and looked out, but no carriage was visible on the street. Mr. Peake said, "I hope nothing is amiss with the business — I was once awoken at this hour due to a shipwreck."

"Uncle Will! Uncle Will!"

Anne leapt from beside Elizabeth and ran towards the drawing room door. Mr. Darcy stood there, with intense bloodshot baggy eyes. He looked at her. Elizabeth's stomach seized with some emotion that mixed terror, longing and happiness.

He bent and picked up his niece when she grabbed his leg and he kissed her. The girl squealed about how she had missed him.

Everyone looked at Darcy. Mr. Peake hovered next to Georgiana almost defensively.

Darcy looked wonderful. He looked terrible.

He wore a dirty overcoat, getting dust over Anne's pretty dress. His hair was wild and a mess, with part of it flattened against the side of his head in an odd shape, where Elizabeth suspected he had slept on it in his carriage. His eyes were drooping and he had the beginnings of a stubbled beard around his chin that made him somehow look more male.

Georgiana cautiously approached her brother. Mr. Peake followed his betrothed, eyeballing Mr. Darcy. Elizabeth remained by the window.

Darcy put down his niece and in a flash he embraced Georgiana. "I — I am so sorry. I was wrong...your happiness is not worth my pride. You were not happy, and...only promise you shall be happy. Peake" — Darcy shook the man's hand, still holding his sister — "I know your character. Your basic decency. I judged wrongly."

Peake hesitated and then asked, "Mr. Darcy, have we your blessing?"

"You do not need it — but for what worth it has, you do. Am I too late, have you yet married?"

"Your blessing matters to me. So very much." Georgie spoke with an upturned, smiling face. "I am so happy. So happy. You can give me away still. It is as I always wanted — you will?"

"Yes."

"And Lizzy is here. Lizzy, come here."

Elizabeth stumbled slowly forward. She was terrified. His magnetic eyes held her. He looked so handsome. But she was too scared. Too scared.

"Elizabeth... I..." He pressed his hand over his mouth. "I had not expected to see you so soon."

"I had not expected to see you. Not ever."

"I can imagine well you did not."

"Why are you here? What changed? *Why*?"

Darcy blinked. He smiled. "You are like always — *my* frankness is not alone."

"*Why*?"

"I no longer hold such a high value upon the pride of the Darcy family." He yawned and rubbed his eyes. "It is also quite useless to pretend I can control my sister, when I cannot."

"Really?" Elizabeth's voice sounded thin in her ears. "Does this not reduce you as a gentleman?"

"Lizzy, you promised!" Georgiana exclaimed, pushing Elizabeth's arm.

"What did she promise?" Darcy tilted his head and yawned again, and shook himself and rubbed his eyes. "I apologize, I have been on the road for many hours. I am in no fit state for an important conversation, though I wish I were."

"She promised," Georgiana said, "to listen to what you said, if you were to apologize."

"Ah." Darcy looked at Elizabeth with his candlelit eyes. He had a serious expression. But he softened as she looked at him. Elizabeth felt a terror in her stomach — what if he *wasn't* going to offer for her again.

Elizabeth said with a squeak, "Are you really here only to bless Georgiana's marriage...at last."

Darcy tilted his head. He looked at her as though he'd not heard the question. Then he shook his head. "I ought to return to Darcy house soon — you had been vague on when the wedding would occur. 'When business was settled?' That is not a date, Georgie. Not at all."

"I apologize." The young woman blushed. "But we did not know for sure. We discovered yesterday that we can have it be the day after tomorrow, even sooner than planned."

"I am glad I shall be there. Lizzy, I *did* have a burning extra motive. One of greatest import, which drove me from Pemberley as fast as I could order my carriage prepared."

She looked at him. Both annoyed and with her heart fluttering.

"I had a desperate hope to avoid my aunt, who has encamped herself at Pemberley. I think at worst it will be at least another day before she can catch me in London."

"Aunt Catty! — Richard told me that she was to attend you."

"He did not warn me." Darcy grinned. "Georgie — might you come to stay at Darcy house, one last time as only my sister and under my roof? Our Aunt Catty cannot cross the threshold when you are present."

After a laugh. Georgiana scrutinized Darcy. "You do not — are you really accommodated to the marriage?"

"Give credit to Aunt Catty." Darcy chuckled. "Was it you or Richard who gave her *that* name?"

"Richard."

"She repeated to me, almost down to the very words, the argument I made to explain why you ought not marry Mr. Peake. The question of honor, and the family history and — oh all that nonsense about the blood of kings and everything else. Hearing my own words in her voice..." Darcy shrugged. "I was uncertain inside from the first. But her words had a salutary effect. I only hoped I might reach here before the wedding."

"Heavens!" Georgiana whistled after her uncharacteristic outburst. "To think I must be grateful to Lady Catherine."

Darcy laughed, and then yawned again. And with one more searching look at Elizabeth he and Georgiana woke her maid to have a change of clothes packed. They called for a hackney cab — Darcy had sent his exhausted carriage driver home immediately — to convey them to the Darcy's residence in a fashionable square in the aristocratic section of London near St. James Palace.

Chapter Twenty-Six

The morning Georgiana was to wed dawned with a fog that, as they said in London, was thick as pea soup. Darcy's cousin, Bingley and Mrs. Bingley had all joined him at Darcy's townhouse along with Georgiana, and during the day yesterday the house buzzed and boomed with comings and goings.

Since Georgiana was to marry a Cit, the omen of the weather was good: London was welcoming her without changing its habits.

Darcy was still thrown by his long carriage journey, and rather than waking before everyone else, he entered the baths at the same time Bingley did, while Richard had already lounged in a large tub, with the hot water being periodically refilled by the attending servant for some time. The three men, old friends now, splashed water at each other, made a mess of the floor, their valets, two of the three dressing robes brought out, and everyone's dignity.

With their hair toweled off and combed by their valets, and stuffed into fine coats, the gentlemen descended in a dignified manner from the bath to the breakfast room for coffee and light food before the wedding.

Georgiana was still dressing with Jane attending her, so the three men stood around, holding their cups of coffee. Darcy smelled the scent from his. The scent was divine, and he knew fine coffee, though he drank tea more often.

Richard asked, "Where the deuce did you get this coffee? In my regimental mess we would have killed — I joke not — to gain a supply such as this."

Darcy laughed and tapped his forehead. "Secrets — horridly expensive, I warn."

Richard shook his head. "Only time I've had the equal was Spain after we drove off Napoleon's brother and gained his kitchen and silver chamber pot. Promptly mixed a good punch in the bowl after giving the silver a good cleaning."

"Chamber pot!" Bingley coughed and spewed the coffee from his mouth. "You drank out of *that*!"

Darcy had heard the story several times before, and *this* time kept his composure. The tale still sounded...unhygienic.

"We cleaned it well."

"I still would not."

"Pusillanimous creature."

"What?"

"I mean lily livered — true men drink from some receptacle of their conquered foes."

"I had thought the typical practice of soldiers," Bingley replied, "was to drink ale from their enemies' skulls."

"We did not capture 'King' Joseph, only his toiletries, so the opportunity to remove his skull did not come. Besides, a large punch bowl is required for an entire regiment. The Bonapartes have small heads."

"Did the men know they were drinking from what the King of Spain had relieved himself in?"

Richard laughed gaily. "My boys? Zounds, they did."

Darcy grinned at the interplay. He took another swallow of the hot coffee. A perfect brew.

"Hello." Georgiana and Jane entered the breakfast room, both dressed for the wedding. His sister wore a lovely pale yellow dress with pearls around her neck that Darcy recognized had once belonged to his mother. There was an old sapphire-encrusted hairpin which had always been a favorite of Georgie's because their father had given it to her.

The earl's daughter would have disapproved; her husband too.

Georgiana smiled but when her eyes met his there was uncertainty. The previous day had been busy, and Darcy had talked for more than two hours with Mr. Peake. But he and Georgiana had little chance to speak, and she was to marry before noon.

Bingley coughed and said to Richard and Jane. "Well. Well — we all have matters to attend to. Out! Out! There will be food enough to feed us later."

The two were left alone in the room. There was an awkwardness between them. Darcy did not know what to say, but he knew it was his duty to say something. He looked between Georgiana and the oaken door frame. "Very different."

She tilted her head at his cryptic statement. "You wanted me to marry a different sort of man. But I have loved Peake for years and—"

"Not that." Then Darcy shook his head. "Though I should not interrupt a lady in the midst of her speech."

"You do not despise me secretly? I hoped you would come. I desperately hoped it — but you made it clear that Mr. Peake is beneath you, and that you cannot respect him, and even though you said... I am afraid you don't *really* accept my choice and..."

"I respect him a great deal. Georgie, I had it wrong — my pride is not worth your happiness."

"Do you mean that? Truly?"

Darcy nodded. She embraced him again.

"I shall miss you and Anne," said Darcy.

"You shall always be my brother."

"But we will be so different."

"I hope — it is something Lizzy said — friends must be equals. Perhaps now that you no longer must guard and care for me, we can be truer friends."

"I would like that."

"You must ask Lizzy again! She still loves you. She does — she does not like to admit it, and she says that love is not enough, but you can convince her that you will not dictate her behavior, and that you respect her, and...everything. That you love her."

"Georgie, I will try."

"You must! I expect you to try *very* hard. I shall help you! Let me tell you everything Elizabeth said about you."

"What did she say?" Darcy flushed.

Georgiana laughed. "You will need to ask her — but remember, she loves you, and even if she pretends she does not, she does."

"Did she say that she still loves me? When?"

"Begging for information told to me in confidence — you have changed! That is ungentlemanlike."

Darcy rolled his eyes.

"Uhhh." Georgiana frowned. "Never mind what she said. She just needs to be convinced you love and...respect her."

This was not entirely encouraging. "Georgie, confessing your friend's secrets to a gentleman admirer — if you are to do so, at least do a creditable job of betraying her trust."

Georgie snickered. "If Lizzy didn't want me to tell you, she had asked me not to...she claimed to be quite convinced you would never relent in your opposition, and we would never see your form again. *I* always believed in you — why *did* Lady Catherine visit?"

"Now that the pollution provided by you has been thrown from Pemberley, time has arrived for Anne and I to contract our long foreseen nuptials."

"Gah!" Georgiana jumped back with a disgusted expression. "You couldn't ever."

"On the contrary, nothing would have proven easier: Lady Catherine had acquired a special license before she set off from London."

"How did you disclose that you shall never marry her to Lady Catherine?"

"My other inducement to London. I left in secret by my carriage and gave orders to my servants and the locals to tell her I had gone north to Scotland."

Georgiana's mouth fell open. She clapped her hand over her mouth. "Not you! You did not!"

Darcy tilted his head. He tried to channel how Elizabeth would tease Georgiana.

Clearly the effort was a failure, as Georgiana giggled. "I near believed you."

"I am trying to be less...less proud."

"Do not change too greatly." Georgiana embraced him. "I would have cried! I was so scared you would not come."

"Time is here for *you* to marry." Darcy embraced her tightly. "Since Papa died, I have always, always...tried."

"Fitzwilliam! You have been the best, the kindest, the sweetest brother in the whole of the land. You have cared for both me and Anne, and you... I always depended upon you, and your judgement, and your affection."

"I made mistakes. You know I have. And I allowed you to leave without following you. I have not—"

"You followed me!"

"I have not always been the best guardian — but I always tried. And I am so...so proud of you. And so happy that...that you have done so well for yourself despite my failings. Georgie, I am...proud. Deeply and completely proud you are my sister."

"And *I* am proud you are my brother."

"Then let us see you married to Peake. I will be happy *now* to meet *him* as a brother."

Two hours later the ceremony was done, the vows said, the rings exchanged, the register signed. Georgiana and Peake shook hands with the vicar while Bingley and Elizabeth talked quietly next to a statue of the virgin that dated to before the reformation, and which apparently had survived Cromwell and the fire by hiding.

Darcy's eyes met Elizabeth's. Elizabeth stared at him, she frowned consideringly. Then she walked towards him, pulling something small out of her reticule. Darcy's stomach leaped as she came close, but her expression did not encourage him.

She stared at his face with her fist gripping some small object. Bingley followed behind Elizabeth, walking up to the two, which Darcy rather thought was unkind of his friend.

The silence hung, and even though Elizabeth had approached him for a purpose, she opened and closed her mouth. She said nothing. Elizabeth's gaze looked everywhere but Darcy's eyes.

Darcy felt scared in his gut, like when she paced during their argument, before she threw his ring away. She needed to give him an opportunity to speak and explain. He had never loved her so much as he did in this church, as she nervously stared at her fist.

"Miss Bennet, no opportunity—" Darcy's voice cracked, and he squeaked. Why did Bingley need to watch? He loved Elizabeth, and he would tell her. Darcy began, now confidently, "Until *now* no opportunity has presented to us for you and I to speak at length since my arrival in Town. I have yearned to speak with you."

"I must...I must apologize to you." She did not look up from her closed fist. Her voice was quiet, and sad. The collar of her dress was lilac. Elizabeth held out her hand, and he expected her to open it to display what she held, but the fist remained firmly closed. "Mr. Darcy, I should not have ended matters between us in a fit of anger. I was unkind; I was wrong."

"I as well. I was mistaken to tell you not to speak to me. I was mistaken to believe we never could disagree, and I was mistaken when I did not...respect you enough. I was mistaken when I did not...did not seek to speak to you again, before I left."

"Do you mean that?" She pushed her hand up towards him. "I could not mail it. But it is yours."

"What?" Darcy looked curiously at Elizabeth's fist which she still had not opened.

She stared at her hand. Was that a tear on the edge of her eyes? She opened her hand so he could see. The ring he gave to Elizabeth, she was returning it to him.

Darcy's stomach seized. No. No. Not yet. She must let him apologize. He could explain why they would be happy. He *needed* her. He could not go back to Pemberley without her. And... "Please, *Lizzy*. No."

"I cannot...I must not keep it."

"Do you wish to return the ring?"

"I..."

"I do not wish it back. I do not wish matters to be ended betwixt us — Elizabeth Bennet I yet...I yet ardently admire and love you. I yet wish you for my companion, my partner in life." He closed her fingers over the ring. "Give me the chance to convince you that we might yet be happy, give me a chance, I beg you. Just give me a chance — if...if you yet believe you must return the ring, once I have spoken, I will accept it, but not until you listen."

She brushed away tears from her eyes. "You *now* demand *I* listen to you! You would not let me speak a word. What will you do if I refuse to let you speak a word now?"

"I was *wrong* to not listen to you. Wrong, and I have learned. I beg you to not repeat *my* failing."

Her eyes were wide, and staring into his.

"Please, believe, Lizzy. We can be happy. I cannot depart, not until I have made every effort to convince you to accept me once more. I ought have done this before. I ought have never allowed you to leave."

"You never allowed me to leave, Mr. Darcy. I chose to leave."

"You are right. You are right. It was your choice. It *always* will be your choice. I allowed my anger and my pride, my abominable pride in my family, in my character, and in my rights to make me ignore that which was most important to me, to my happiness, and to *our* happiness. I will not again."

Bingley cleared his throat. From how Elizabeth started, Darcy thought she too had forgotten he was there. "None of this. None of it. You both came to your senses — think of the arguments you two had with each other. And to make love to each other in a *church*. I never did the like."

Both Darcy and Elizabeth stared at Bingley.

"What?" He flushed.

"Really, Bingley?" Elizabeth replied crossly. "This is no time to interrupt us."

Darcy extended his arm to Elizabeth. "We perhaps should leave; it has been brought to my attention that this is such a conversation as is not appropriate for a house of God."

"I..." She hesitated and looked at Darcy. He wanted his eyes to convey everything he felt and thought. She returned the ring to her reticule and took his arm, saying, "A house of God is a perfectly appropriate place for such a conversation — it adds solemnity. This is not a matter of flirtation, but of reason."

Bingley threw his hands in the air. "*I* counsel you both against such a match, but it is not *my* permission you must seek, Lizzy."

"I seek no one's permission."

"Upon my word. A house of God is no place for a proposal of marriage," Bingley replied stoutly.

"Why," Elizabeth asked sharply, "is it proper to *marry* in a church, but not to decide whether to marry in one?"

Bingley stomped away, shaking his head and muttering. Georgiana, Mr. Peake, the Gardiners and the vicar all watched them talk.

"Perhaps, whatever our opinions," Darcy said, aware of the audience, "we should respect Bingley's tender sensibilities, and there is a fine drizzle outside that has mostly cleared the fog."

"Do you intend to offer marriage to me again?"

"Yes." Darcy found himself oddly filled with confidence. This was right. This was entirely different from the awkwardness attendant upon his first declaration. "Do you intend accept me?"

"I do now know yet — how can I? How can I trust myself? Or you. I will not, not unless I am convinced my reason supports such a match."

"You shall be convinced. For we are a *reasonable* pair."

"Even if the drizzle has ceased," Elizabeth replied with something like happiness, "I am quite certain that we will not be oppressed by any sun."

"In London! Heaven help us if we are."

"I am too passionate. I trust myself with you no longer."

"Then trust me with you. I can care for you when you cannot, and you shall care for me when I cannot."

The two stepped out into the fine drizzle. Perhaps the best drizzle Darcy had ever stepped out into. He waved for his footman who was waiting with his carriage to hand him an umbrella, and he opened it and held it so that Elizabeth was sheltered from the rain.

The line of Gracechurch Street stretched to the north and south, shadowed by long blocks of buildings with dozens of windows facing out to the street. The two set off south along the street towards the Thames. Elizabeth's arm nestled against his.

"Why?"

"That," Darcy replied, "is an enigmatic question."

"You know what I mean — why do you think we can choose to marry without expecting disaster — you are a gentleman, you are proud, and you always believe you know best. You care so deeply for those within your scope; you cannot bear to see us make mistakes; and when you are certain, entirely certain, you cease to listen."

Darcy contemplated with what words to reply.

Elizabeth pulled her arm away from him and looked through her reticule. "Take it. Take the ring, we are not meant for one another."

"Elizabeth, you are frightened."

"Of myself, of my feelings. Of...you."

"Me?"

"I ended matters between us. You'll not seduce me again."

"I, seduce you? I had believed my attempts at rakish behavior to be failures. You, madam, seduced *me*."

"Again! Cease it."

"Cease what?"

"You are here to convince me you've changed, and that you...you mean to tell me I can entrust myself to you, because you were willing to shake Mr. Peake's hand as a brother. Cease looking at me like that! That smirk!"

"Do you admire this smirk? A quite fetching smirk."

"You are as much a gentleman as ever, you still have the same belief that all should bend to your will."

"*Too gentlemanly.* Lizzy, I confess that has rattled round my brain the past month. What manner of insult is that? A striking expression. Originality, I give you. Your objection was made clear, and it was a *gentlemanly* way to express your displeasure."

"Mr. Darcy, I beg you to cease trying to seduce me; if you have an argument to present my reason, give it. I will not be a slave to my passions."

"Good god, Lizzy, your hand is trembling."

She looked up to him soulfully.

Darcy needed to say something, but all eloquence abandoned him. He must say something. Something true. "I often make mistakes."

Elizabeth tilted her head when Darcy did not continue.

He smiled at her.

She took his arm again. "*That* should give me confidence in marriage to you?"

"Yes."

"You would have ruined your sister's life! Look how happy she is!"

"I know! I would have!"

Elizabeth, she smiled at him. "Quite emphatic agreement."

"I can admit my failings." Darcy could not stop smiling. Elizabeth's face had softened. "We both are fortunate Georgiana reached the age where I can only counsel her."

"If I marry you, then I would be under your power, like Georgiana before she came of age. It is easy...easy for you to say you shall treat me as an equal when I am not under your power. But *will* you?"

"I am a stubborn and determined man, and I strive to better myself. I do not often make the *same* mistake once I have been taught my error."

"I will not depend upon your whim."

"Do not depend upon my whim. Depend upon my promise, my oath, my word of honor — one need not only make the promises in the marriage vows. I swear, solemnly, as a gentleman, as a Darcy, as a man ardently in love. I will never demand your silence. I will never treat you as my object, a possession. My wife; my helpmeet; my dearest partner. That is who I wish you to be."

Her face. She was melting for him.

Darcy smiled. "You can trust my oath because I am *too* gentlemanly."

Elizabeth giggled. "I told you to cease seducing me."

"I want to make you laugh. I adore that sound above all others. If *you* find that seductive, it is your matter."

"*When* we disagree…" Elizabeth swallowed. She paused for a long time. She knew the significance of that *when we* which had slipped from her pink lips. "You will not force me to act as you wish."

"I will never force you to act in any way you do not wish. That is my word, my oath."

"I am terrified." She placed her hand on her stomach.

"Fear is a passion as much as love — perhaps your passion and not your head is what makes you hesitate."

Elizabeth smiled softly. "My philosophy is that the passions and the reason must be united, not opposed."

"Do not fear. We will be happy."

She shook her head, inclining her body closer to his. "Have you certainty?"

A magnetism existed between him and Elizabeth. Darcy smiled into her eyes.

"I shall despise you forever if you are lying to me — I expect equality."

"In our marriage, in our lives — when we raise our children — always. Except when we argue philosophy. Then I shall crush you with my excellent reason."

"Ha! You have lost often enough to know that is an empty boast." She laughed.

Their eyes held.

She kissed him, full on the lips on the open city street.

When they separated, as other pedestrians passed them with disapproving looks, Elizabeth said, "I trust your word, and I will marry you."

"Trust a rake's word?"

Elizabeth laughed. "You *still* hope to be seen as rakish?"

Darcy kissed her again. There was an exaltation and a release of tension, as though he'd nearly been run over by a careening carriage. "*You* enjoyed being called dangerous."

"My rakish lover. I am incapable of resisting your charm. But I insist we start the banns anew and are married by a clergyman whose character *I* know — I have heard too many stories of fictitious clergymen used by rakes to seduce honorable maidens into mortal sin."

"Ahhh! I am so rakish that you cannot trust that I will not give a false license and clergyman?" Darcy grinned at her happily.

"Is your name *truly* Darcy?" She frowned, but her eyes smiled. "Several persons of undoubted reputation must attest to it."

"Bingley and my cousin are present."

"No! No! I must hear from your aunt, Lady Catherine — she is not one of your male cronies."

Darcy's expression was aghast.

"Will she attend our wedding?"

"Faith, I hope not."

Their walk had carried them through the center of London and out to the river. They stood next to the famed white-walled Tower of London and looked out at the river which flowed through the greatest city in the world.

"I am not the only one." Elizabeth smirked at him. "You must gain my father's blessing again."

Darcy's stomach swooped with a new anxiety. But he then shook his head and laughed. "I can convince him that we shall be happy — you shall see."

Chapter Twenty-Seven

Mr. Bennet considered it passing odd when the wheels of a heavy carriage rolled up to Longbourn several hours before noon the day after Georgiana Darcy's wedding in London. The hour was too early for social calls.

The window of Mr. Bennet's study faced the garden, not the carriageway. Mr. Bennet preferred it this way, because he liked seeing the hedges and trees, especially when they bloomed in spring. Today his view consisted of the brown bare branches of winter, as his plants waited the end of the frosts and that message of warmth telling them to burst into beautiful vibrant bloom. The old oak tree in the center of the window had lived here for as long as Bennets had been at Longbourn.

Mr. Bennet shrugged. He returned his attention to a large volume detailing the excavations of the Roman site at Pompeii, with many finely done engravings and descriptions of the location. He had subscribed several pounds, he had forgotten how many in the interval, to the project which produced this volume seventeen years before. This was a better outcome than many such subscriptions, where the money disappeared, but the scholar died or absconded to foreign climes, and the promised production of science never emerged.

If this early visitor required his attention rather than Mrs. Bennet's, such need would be revealed soon enough.

So it was while Mr. Bennet studied the fascinating paintings found on the walls of houses in Pompeii that his daughter Elizabeth burst into the room.

Mr. Bennet blinked at her and stood, smiling. "I am surprised to see you. I had believed I would not see you for several days more. Why so early? Nothing ill happened to Gardiner or Jane?"

"No nothing. Nothing of *that* sort." Lizzy chewed her lip, nervously.

"Well what brought you so early? Sit; let me show you this book. We have waited for this volume since before the year eighteen hundred. The parcel arrived yesterday."

"Papa, I—" Lizzy swallowed, glanced around the room, and ran her hand through her hair.

"My dear daughter." Mr. Bennet stepped up to Lizzy and took her hand. "Whatever is the matter?"

"I do not know how you shall take it — this must surprise you — but I am to marry Mr. Darcy."

"Again?" Mr. Bennet tilted his head and widened his eyes, as though surprised, though he was not. "You gave me to understand you mistook a mistake when you entered your *previous* engagement to that young gentleman."

"I *did*. We did not speak sufficiently about our hopes and demands. But now we have made all clear."

"*All* clear? That is a speedy working upon your part."

Lizzy nodded, eagerly, her cheeks shining.

"I cannot approve of repeatedly breaking and entering engagements. What shall the neighbors think? You do gain the advantage of them offering congratulations a second time, but that imposition upon their good nature is—"

"Papa!" Elizabeth sat down in a huff. "I am not in jest."

"I know." Mr. Bennet smiled widely at her. "Pray tell, how did such a *remarkable* event come about? Darcy brought himself to London? Or was this arranged via letter?"

"Of course he brought himself to London — are you being difficult purposefully?"

"Pray tell further, have you studied this matter with your reason this time? Are you satisfied there is no chance of a mistake?"

Lizzy glared at him. Then she softened. "I am more... We have spoken, he understands why I became so angry. He will always listen to me — and he swore an oath as a gentleman to never make a choice for me, and since he is *too* gentlemanly, I can trust him to keep such an oath. Besides he can learn."

"A gentleman who can learn?"

"Yes!" Lizzy grinned. "Am I not excessively blessed by fortune? I have caught in my clutching woman's claws the *only* one."

"As a gentleman, I claim also the ability to learn."

"Oh, you aren't a gentleman, you are *Papa*." Lizzy kissed him on the cheek. "If you are teasing me so, you are not so dissatisfied as last time."

"Nor am I uncommonly surprised. He attended his sister's wedding?" At Lizzy's nod, Mr. Bennet added, "It speaks well for his family feeling that he did not let pride stand betwixt them, and that he could accept such a choice as she made. And I imagine he engaged in pretty speechmaking to *you*."

"Very pretty — do you wish to hear the particulars?"

"Do you yearn to share such with your father?"

"We—" Lizzy blushed and shook her head. "I am supremely and completely happy this time. A happy marriage shall require effort, work, and compromise — though to Mr. Darcy, I will not need to submit myself to him, as we are agreed in all matters to be equals. And—"

"Such an extraordinary young man!"

Lizzy stuck her tongue out at Mr. Bennet. "You shall not annoy me today. My Mr. Darcy is perfect, and tall, and he *does* listen to me, and he will argue matters philosophical and absurdical with me whenever I choose."

"Then I am entirely happy for you."

"I shall now bring Mr. Darcy in." Lizzy clapped. "You shall not tease him excessively — but pray, question him at however great length you wish."

"That is hardly necessary," Mr. Bennet replied, as Lizzy went to door. "I already had *one* interview on this subject with Mr. Darcy, and I despise *deja vu*."

Upon the door being opened, Mr. Bennet was presented with the odd spectacle of his wife berating a tall and immaculately dressed man, who made a small bow of submission each time Mrs. Bennet stabbed her finger towards his chest.

"You *will* let my Lizzy run on, just as much as Mr. Bennet does! *Nothing* like how you treated darling Georgiana."

"Of course not, madam," Mr. Darcy replied with a bow.

"Heavens, I am most seriously displeased with you, and it shall take at *least* a week of the most loverlike behavior from you towards my daughter for you to exit my black books."

Another elegant bow. "I deserve nothing else."

"And you will return to my blackest books if you annoy Lizzy ever again."

"Mama!" Lizzy exclaimed. "Do not berate Mr. Darcy."

Mrs. Bennet raised her nose and sniffed. "Someone must. He has quite too high an opinion of himself. Even if he does have ten thousand a year and likely more."

Mr. Darcy bowed again, and Mr. Bennet ascertained a wry smile. "I do, Mrs. Bennet. Much too high."

"Mama, you snatch my task. My chief burden *and* consolation is to berate Mr. Darcy until he considers himself as only a little more august than an ordinary man." Lizzy laughed happily.

Darcy now bowed to Lizzy, in exactly the same manner he had been bowed to Mrs. Bennet. "Exactly so, madam."

"Enough dilly-dallying! Mr. Darcy, I understand you have business to conduct with me, a *second* time on the same matter. In my day, we didn't bother a father every time *we* had a falling out with our diamond jewel." As the bows seemed to work so well for Mr. Darcy, Mr. Bennet imitated him by bowing to Mrs. Bennet. "Not that *I* ever fell out with you, my dear."

Mrs. Bennet in reply flutteringly pressed a hand against her cheeks, and from her wink Mr. Bennet suspected her bedroom door would be open to him this night.

With a furious scowl Mr. Bennet glared at Darcy. "Fashions change. Fashions change."

So saying, Mr. Bennet waved Darcy into the room, and waved Lizzy and Mrs. Bennet away. "You both may order the gentleman around at your leisure once *I* have done with him."

They entered the book-lined study, and Mr. Bennet closed and locked his door behind Mr. Darcy.

"That is an ominous sound," the gentleman said, walking to the desk. He put his hand on Lizzy's chair to move it around.

"Not that chair. It is Lizzy's."

Darcy studied the brown gentleman's leather chair levelly. "The chair is much like her."

"At the least you see that. Draw that one by the window up. You ought have seen Lizzy's face when she entered the room on the *previous* occasion and she saw that you'd moved her chair. I think she had not quite realized *her* chair could leave *her* spot next to me. She promptly picked up and placed the chair back where it belonged."

"You ought to have told me this was *her* chair, so I could have known to leave it in place." Rather than settling the chair he had picked up across the desk from Mr. Bennet, Darcy placed it next to Lizzy's. "The symbolism is now appropriate."

"You next to her, and she between you and me?"

Darcy scratched his cheek and shrugged. "Should I expect this interview to be more involved than the previous one?"

Mr. Bennet pulled out the fine cognac and two crystal glasses he kept hidden in his desk for such occasions. He did not drink a great deal. This was the same bottle he'd opened when Mr. Darcy requested Elizabeth's hand the first time, still half filled. He poured modest helpings into the pair of snifters. "*Elizabeth* has my permission to marry whomever she chooses, and she has my blessings no matter what she does in life."

"*I* wish your blessing as well."

"You wish me to be happy you are marrying my Lizzy."

"Yes."

Mr. Bennet gestured for Darcy to pick up the snifter, and they did together and clinked the glasses and sipped. Mr. Bennet paused to savor the aroma, as he knew he was supposed to with fine brandy. "She said you swore an oath as a gentleman to listen to her in the future when you argue, and to let her make her own decisions."

Darcy inclined his head.

"Not enough."

"What do you wish me to do?"

"Put it in the marriage articles, that your promise will be confirmed by an annual interview where Elizabeth must testify to two of her male relations, while you are not present, that you have listened to her when she disagrees with you, and not made any decisions for her."

Darcy looked the picture of confused curiosity. He tilted his head and placed his glass down; he scratched his forehead and furrowed his eyebrows. "I cannot tell if you are in jest. Such is a safeguard to Miss Bennet — though what threat can be placed to ensure I follow this condition? Or that Elizabeth answers honestly if I am a brute? It strikes my pride as a gentleman to have it suggested such an expedient is *necessary* once I have given my word. *Her* objection was that I was too gentlemanly."

"Would you prefer me to jest or be in earnest?"

"I accept such a condition, if *you* consider it a necessary safeguard for Elizabeth."

"Nonsense. Settlements can only enforce financial matters, and we both know you are not a brute. I wonder instead at your intention to let Elizabeth disagree and choose for herself. What about your children? If you and she disagree about a matter of education, or of who a child might marry, or how they may be entertained, who will decide? Your son shall either gain permission to marry the dairy maid who has caught his fancy at sixteen, or he shall not."

"I consider it unlikely *Elizabeth* would approve of such a match either."

"Her? She would never approve of a boy rushing off to marriage at such a tender age — *you* would argue for that match."

Darcy slowly smiled and he picked up the brandy again and sipped it. "Mr. Bennet, you ought to submit a list of such conundrums, for me and Elizabeth to debate together ahead of time. Then we might be prepared for such occasions."

"But who *would* choose?" Mr. Bennet lifted his glass and sipped.

"The child, in the end."

Mr. Bennet laughed. "Well answered. Well answered. No matter what you and Lizzy choose. Children are like that."

Darcy continued to sip from the cognac, and when he finished savoring the glass Mr. Bennet poured more for him. From his manner Mr. Bennet thought Darcy had the sophistication to enjoy such a fine spirit properly. Mr. Bennet did not.

Darcy said, "I have been informed you disapproved of my match to Elizabeth before — you ought to have said so — I do not wish to marry Elizabeth until I have assuaged your worries, not until *you* can give me your blessing whole heartedly."

"If I never could? Would you delay marriage until my death, like many young couples faced with the determined opposition of their relatives?"

"Your permission I possess already — I only *wish* your happiness. Elizabeth adores you, but we do not need it. My sister. She was right to choose the future she wished over following my desires in her choice. And I was wrong to make her choose."

"Elizabeth had the wrong of it. I was not unhappy. I was concerned. The two of you were precipitate. You had not tested yourselves well enough, and I worried greatly how you would act together when you disagreed. I never *disapproved*, I was anxious."

"You mean to say that the manner of my return and what I have said of my intentions removes your anxiety."

"I do not cease to worry. I shall always worry for my girl. Always. She will not cease to be *mine* solely because she becomes yours as well. And I care not the slightest what the law says on that matter — you recall that day I threatened you with a rifle."

"If I hurt Elizabeth, the next time your weapon will not be unloaded?"

"That approximately is what I mean."

"I worry for Georgiana, though she is happy, and I am happy for her. But not for the reasons I opposed the match, simply because..."

"Life is long, full of uncertainty, and marriage is an irrevocable step."

Darcy agreed and finished his glass, and Mr. Bennet finished his own glass of cognac, unforgivably simply swallowing the end of the burning liquid without sloshing it to each part of his mouth to taste all of the shades of the flavor, as he'd been told to when Gardiner gave him the bottle. He refilled both their glasses.

Mr. Bennet said after he took another sip, "I worry in the fashion I worry when she goes to London that I might hear of a carriage accident. You both are of age, and well matured. You both have experience with each other's sharp edges and despite that experience you desire to marry. I *expect* Lizzy to be happy with you. I cannot ask for more. Wait, I *can*! I have one condition before you might have my permission!"

"What *decisive* consideration must I meet?" Darcy replied dryly.

"A standing invitation to your library."

"I thought you wished that. You may live among the shelves, if you so choose."

"That is unkind, to not offer your father-in-law a *bed* to sleep in."

"One would be dragged to the library from one of the bedrooms — I shall keep the guest bedroom nearest the library always open for you." Darcy dragged his chair closer to Mr. Bennet with his feet. "Not in jest. That room henceforth is yours."

"I shall use that liberty more often than you might like. Lizzy has been...she has been a great deal to me. Hertfordshire is hollow in her absence. She shall be two days journey to the north."

"Bennet, I *expect* to see you often — else it would be a waste to set aside a room permanently for your use."

"Often. Most often." To hide his tears Mr. Bennet lifted his glass, and Darcy did as well. They clinked together, and with tears starting on his eyes Mr. Bennet said, "To you and Elizabeth and your happiness."

Chapter Twenty-Eight

One day in the Longbourn drawing room, Elizabeth and Darcy sat chaperoned by Mrs. Bennet. Mama rocked back and forth in her chair next to the fire with all her attention upon the blue and white threads of her embroidery.

Elizabeth was in a mischievous mood, and she asked her soon husband, "What philosophers have you taken advice from upon the nature of marriage — I have been searching of late in the most learned and ancient sources for wisdom, and I have learned to better despise the ancients."

"That surprises me not. *You* would despise the ancients, simply because everyone else gives them such high praise."

"That makes me sound terribly predictable — which I hope I have not been. I am possessed of excellent reasons to be offended. They are quite worse than *you* ever were."

"*Ought* I be jealous of Plato and Plutarch? Will they steal your heart away from me through an excess of gentlemanly offense?"

Elizabeth giggled and patted his hand. "I am attached to *you*."

"What did the ancients say which offended you so? I can only rest easy once I know the particulars."

"Plutarch is my favorite, I confess. For sheer...effrontery he exceeds all. He wrote, in an essay to advise young brides and grooms, that should you engage in a 'peccadillo' with a maidservant, I ought to feel respected, as respect for me leads you to share your wantonness and licentiousness with other women."

Darcy drew his lips into a sour expression.

"Mr. Darcy, this is to be a marriage of equals." As Mrs. Bennet was studiously not paying the slightest intention to them, Elizabeth dared to place her hand upon Darcy's thigh and squeeze it. "When you engage in drunk, wanton, and licentious behavior, I am entirely prepared to be wanton and licentious *with* you."

Elizabeth delightedly enjoyed the way Darcy coughed and blushed.

"Ought we," Darcy replied when he recovered, "add this to the settlement documents?"

An image popped into Elizabeth's mind: Her dressed in a light billowy dress explaining to their barrister, dressed in a dark, heavy wool coat, how Darcy must *absolutely* include her in *all* his licentious activities.

"I can see from your smile," Darcy said, "that we ought."

"If only I could rewrite the Church of England services, I would have you to swear it as part of the marriage vows."

"Along with my promise to always listen to you, and to give you reign to make the final decision in any matter which principally affects you?"

"Every occasion and situation specified! In sickness and in health, for richer for poorer, etcetera, not exhaustive."

"I believe that 'till death do us part' is intended to cover your *etcetera.*"

"Had I written the marriage service, it would include: And these vows shall be understood to hold all conceivable situations, including those not specified elsewhere."

"The darkest misfortune of England is that the book of common prayer was written by theologians with a bent for poetry, rather than lawyers lacking one."

Elizabeth pinched Darcy's side. He imperturbably continued to smile. "Fitzwilliam, but should we someday feel we are only possessed of a sufficiency, and that we both are in indifferent health? Then the vows would no longer hold, as written by the church."

"I," Darcy replied in a gallant manner, "would continue to hold you close to me as my wife in such a case, motivated solely by the deep affection I hold for you."

"And, I," Elizabeth replied, "would still honor and love you, but would entirely cease to *obey.* I quite would prefer if men also were required to obey in the marriage vows, and then we might order conflicting things, and order the orders to be revoked, and fall into an unending regress."

"Aha! And we return to philosophy." Darcy dared a kiss upon Elizabeth's cheek, in spite of her unattending mother. "Might I answer your question about how I have been counseled by philosophy upon marriage?"

"You might," Elizabeth replied primly, sitting up stiffer.

"You, Lizzy, are not the only one of us who has been thinking upon this subject of late. How to avoid dangerous errors, and how to ensure that we remain happy and that our bond remains intact through the storms, vicissitudes, and quarrels which shall erupt betwixt us."

She grinned at him. "You as well? We think alike!"

"Plutarch's advice comes from the great gentlemanly mistake that you rebel against, that a gentleman knows better than his wife what will constitute her happiness — amongst my peers I know some who hold to Plutarch's philosophy without irony. You have lived enough to know that solely because a man swears vows before God that does not mean he ceases to seek pleasures elsewhere — many such men consider they do no disrespect to their wife by such. *She* is the one they 'love', and have married, and her children shall inherit."

"I will not take the part of my sex to be horribly offended by such persons. It is not a form of marriage I would enjoy, but for a woman whose principal goal *was* to gain a respectable establishment, so long as he does not compromise *that* she receives the respect she demanded."

"Hmmm." Darcy smirked adorably at her. "I understand what you mean to say — I can compromise the name of the Darcy family ever so much as I want, so long as *you* are my partner in offending the shades of Pemberley."

"I expect these shades to raise mighty rebellion against the pollution we bring."

They looked at each other with close kissing eyes.

"My dearest," Darcy replied, "simply because the best interest of the beloved motivates a man, that is insufficient. A man will twist what he sees according to his beliefs and prejudices. I cannot be trusted with your happiness or Georgiana's and barely even my own. You know more about yourself and your own happiness than I ever could."

"*Quite* a different tune to which you dance now."

"When the music changes, only the worst dullard continues to step to the old rhythm."

Elizabeth laughed. "You *are* a fine dancer." She sat up and raised a finger. "Another person can often see us more clearly than we can ourselves. A single overheard conversation might grant more knowledge of the self than the greatest exertion to examine one's own soul. Perhaps a wise person would allow someone who can see better than they themselves to choose in such a case for them."

Darcy rolled his eyes. "You delight in being contrary."

"You adore me for such."

"The solution to your conundrum is what *you* preached to me. We must have the liberty between us to converse upon any subject. But the person principally involved makes their own decision *after* due consideration of their mate's opinions. The danger of the opposite is greater."

"Conversation prior to decision? That is a plan to reduce the deleterious effects of passion upon the reason which I wholly approve of."

Mrs. Bennet stood, the multicolored threads from her embroidery dangling down. "You make love in such a roundabout manner. Both of you. Not nearly loverlike enough for my taste. Passion. Lord! I showed more passion as a *girl*," she added, in a sly voice, with a wink at the two of them. "I must look in on the cook. An important matter I just recalled, and which cannot wait, and which will keep me away for *at least* half of an hour."

Mrs. Bennet left the drawing room, securely shutting the door behind her.

The two looked at each other, bright shining eyes flickering between each other's eyes and lips. In a moment Elizabeth was on Darcy's lap, passionately kissing him. They clearly had her *mother's* support for these liberties, though Elizabeth had no intention allowing matters to progress so far as *her* parents had before their marriage. Darcy's hand gripped her hips, holding her body against him, and she played her fingers over his neck, his cheeks, and stroked them through his thick hair. He moaned in appreciation.

"I had thought," Elizabeth murmured into Darcy's vest once they slowed their impassioned kisses, "that *I* was a lax chaperone before Jane and Bingley married. I would quite happily look the other direction."

Darcy squeezed her head against his chest. He smelled warm and tasty.

"I am delighted I need never worry about being principally responsible for *your* welfare. You are my equal in sense and my superior in wisdom."

Elizabeth kissed Darcy for such a speech.

"Only a little my superior in wisdom," he added once her lips pulled away. He grinned. "You have an ample reserve of foolishness as well."

"Horrible to say!"

"It is a good thing, if you would always be the wise one, you would grow frustrated with my fallibility in time, and I would not enjoy always being the foolish one. This way we both have ample opportunities to tease the other."

"*That* reasoning *is* much to my own liking."

Darcy inclined his head to hers, and they pressed their lips together again.

Darcy said, "I was too arrogant — I did not even consider that Georgiana might choose for herself soon as she reached her majority."

Elizabeth pushed Darcy's shoulder. "Arrogant nitwit," she said fondly.

"I am your arrogant nitwit."

"Mine."

They kissed softly.

Darcy squeezed an arm around Elizabeth and pulled her close. "Maybe Peake is right that I should focus on investments in businesses and paper instead of additional land—"

"That was what was on your mind as we kissed?" Elizabeth giggled, as Darcy protested. "Has he been seeking to convince you to also invest in Gardiner and Peake? Naughty boy."

Darcy shook his head laughingly. "Quite the opposite in fact. He thinks I ought to make investments in companies that have nothing to do with him, and in government paper. He argues that there is less risk involved when your wealth is spread among a wider set of sources of income. Land prices and rents can rise shockingly and then fall with suddenness, but so long as the government can be trusted, income from Consols will remain."

"You plan for us to have perpetual bonds?"

"A pun! From you!"

Elizabeth blushed.

"I shall enjoy *consol*ations of married life."

"*Noooo.*" Elizabeth pushed away from him, and still grinning widely, sat on the opposite side of their plump stuffed sofa.

Darcy waggled his eyebrows. "In our happiness and connection I put much *stock. Mark it.*"

"Fie! Fie! That reminds me. You are not an adherent, I hope, to St. Augustine's philosophy?"

"I do not believe so. I read something of him... the Confessions, I—"

Elizabeth interrupted him giggling. "He wrote a book titled *The Excellence of Marriage.* In a marriage minded mindset I picked it from the bookstore shelf and brought it home — I had not yet given up my study of ancient wisdom."

"You do not intend to follow St. Augustine's advice *either?*"

"Abstinence," Elizabeth said, her voice taking on a lilt, "from all sexual union is better even than marital intercourse performed for the sake of procreating. However, marital intercourse *solely* to satisfy lust is a venial sin, but pardonable. And it has value as a fence against temptation to fornication—"

"The marriage service says that as well," Darcy added, as Elizabeth took a breath. "You simply enjoy being able to say 'sexual union,' without being more than markedly crude as you quote an ancient saint."

Elizabeth giggled. "As an unmarried old maid, *I* lived in the most superior manner. You should be shamed, Mr. Darcy, tempting a celibate such as myself into the lustfulness I feel towards you."

"I should?" Darcy replied dazedly. He smiled seductively. "I told you I am dangerous, rakish and naughty. It *was* shameful to seduce you wickedly into Holy Matrimony. *And*, while I look forward to children, marital intercourse solely to satisfy — how did you put it? My lusts. I would convince you into such."

"Ooooh. Your lusts." Elizabeth shivered and grinned happily. "This is what female learning does — it brings us to discuss our lust, one for the other."

The two kissed, passionately. Mrs. Bennet *was* a convenient chaperone.

The two separated, pressing their hot bodies against each other, breathing heavily.

"My beloved Elizabeth, you have convinced me to value female learning."

Alas, before she could kiss him for saying so, the *at least* a half hour Mrs. Bennet had promised ended, and with great rattling of the door knob, and muttering to herself outside, and other forms of warning them of her presence, Mrs. Bennet entered the room.

Grinning at each other, Elizabeth and Darcy began to discuss learned topics once more, in the dullest manner they could manage, with the intention of giving Mrs. Bennet an entirely incorrect notion of what the past half hour had involved.

However, Darcy's cravat had been thoroughly disordered in a manner quite distinctive, and which Elizabeth trusted the eye of *Mama* to understand the meaning of.

Chapter Twenty-Nine

And in conclusion, Elizabeth wrote, *I must beg you to send Mr. Darcy and I every amusing detail of Lady Catherine's behavior. Though it shames him to admit such a relation, she has been valuable to us, and we hope, by providing amusement, she will continue to be such.*

I now sign, my dear Charlotte, my name one last time as,
Yours affectionately,
E Bennet

Elizabeth put her quill down beside her ceramic ink pot and dried off the end on her blotting paper. She closed the little lid to her inkwell. Elizabeth then put the inkwell and quill in a box that sat in the corner of the room, waiting to be packed up to go to Pemberley with her. She'd written so many letters with this small pot over the years that the pot felt almost like a friend.

She loved Darcy. She wanted to see Pemberley, explore the halls, the parks, the rooms and attics, and offend the sensibilities of the ghosts.

Everything would be different tomorrow.

Elizabeth sat on the chair nearest the window, surrounded on both sides by tall, familiar bookshelves. Every book on those shelves was a friend.

Papa watched her with an unfocused gaze. He said slowly, "Letters complete?"

Elizabeth returned to the desk. But before she could sit, Papa stood and gave her an embrace, and she embraced Papa tightly as well.

They smiled together, and Elizabeth tried to memorize the feeling of her father's dressing coat, and the smell of his sideburns, and the flickering candlelight, and the happiness she had known with him in this room.

"I shall miss you. Terribly."

"I know, Papa. I know." Tears clouded Elizabeth's eyes. "I shall miss you more."

"*That* I doubt."

"I will miss you very, very much. Write many letters to me — no matter how you hate the practice. Dictate to a servant if you must — I will write many letters to you."

"You must care for yourself. And keep your young man's high ears pinned down. What is the purpose of a grand estate and a clever mind if not to be confounded often?"

Elizabeth squeezed Papa again. She closed her eyes as they stood embraced. She remembered Papa two decades ago in this room, his hair completely dark, and with the smile in his eyes as he asked her to sit on his lap and recite what she'd learned from the book she'd just perused. She remembered him reminiscing about university. Their enthusiasm when he purchased a particularly fine rare book.

Growing older. She sat in the chair as a vivacious young woman in a fine dress. His hair partly grey. How they talked before she left on trips to London, or to Charlotte, or to visit one of her married sisters. Every time, every single time Papa told her he would miss her until she returned.

She wouldn't be returning. Not like before.

"How can I ever leave? So happy here."

Papa patted her head. "I shall keep your chair exactly as you ordered it — do you recall? You were most insistent — and you shall discover in a few years how insistent a child of five can be — that your chair be *exactly* like mine."

Elizabeth giggled wetly.

"I had no choice except to obey, even though you could not fit in the chair. You curled up in it, with your feet on the seat. During winter you disappeared under a fuzzy blanket, only a pert nose sticking out."

"Oh, Papa."

"Those were my favorite days. I..."

Elizabeth laughed. "I thought your days at the university arguing with other young scholars were your favorite."

"No...it was certainly after your birth. I loved those years, when you were old enough to cease crying to get your way — you had me wrapped round your finger. I fulfilled your every *reasonable* demand; at a certain age, you could be talked round to agree unreasonable ones need not be filled."

"I was a good daughter?"

"Do not expect your *own* children to be like that. I expect them to have something of the Darcy spirit and manners. I cannot imagine *him* being talked out of a tantrum."

"I know how, now."

"And he knows how to put you *into* a tantrum. High strung girl. I have loved you so."

They sat together as they had for many years. Papa looked distant, sad. Elizabeth did not like to see it. "I wish *he* moved to live with us, rather than I leaving to live with him. Another unfairness women must endure."

"Have you asked Mr. Darcy if *he* would take up residence in Hertfordshire? Ideally in the guest room, but another building in the neighborhood might do almost as nicely. I hear High Court is vacant."

"*You* have not seen Pemberley, if you can suggest such an exchange."

Papa smiled and then he tapped his fingers on the desk and mumbled something to himself.

"*What*, dearest father, are you thinking?"

"I merely calculate the earliest date I might visit this vast estate and its remarkable library — I wrote letters, when it first became clear in what direction matters were headed, asking what my acquaintance knew about Mr. Darcy. I believe many believed I desired to learn about his library."

"You did! Of course you did. You have always done what you must to care for me."

"I have tried."

"If you wish to live with us, you have *my* permission. And so long as you do not bother us overmuch, I am quite sure I can convince Darcy not to object."

"He has already invited me to have a bed dragged into the library so I might sleep in it."

"The best man! Except you, for you are both *my* best men."

Papa laughed. "I shall only visit. Someone must keep your mother company now that she is bereft of children to worry over."

The two smiled at each other.

"You are happy this time. I can see." Elizabeth smiled.

"I am, this time."

Elizabeth crumpled up and flicked a piece of blotting paper that sat on the desk from when she had been writing at his nose. "You did not stop me from entering the engagement *last* time."

He flicked the ball of paper back. "I did the closest I could with such a daughter as you."

"Mr. Darcy and I will be the happiest couple in the world. You see how I laugh."

"I do. But I still worry."

"You need not worry. You have raised me well." Elizabeth embraced her father. "I hope Darcy and I raise our children as well as you raised me."

"*Better* than I raised some of my children. But, Lizzy, children choose for themselves much of who they are. A parent can only help or harm so far."

"You mean Lydia chose for herself, even if you were negligent in sending her to Brighton."

"My word itself." Papa took out a pair of glasses and a decanter from their desk. "A celebratory toast. I *do* worry — any marriage *might* progress poorly."

Elizabeth groaned. "A useless statement. It neither reassures, nor worries me."

"When you are a parent, even when you expect the best...you will always worry for your child. Lizzy, I will always worry for you."

"I... Papa, I shall miss your presence so much."

Papa poured the cognac into the glasses. "You already travel from home on occasion. You and Darcy shall come south with frequency, and I shall make the expedition north oftener. We shall spend ample time together. Though, *this* room will no longer be our special place."

Elizabeth nodded, teary eyed. "I am so entirely happy, but I could not be happy without *your* happiness."

Papa handed her a glass and he raised his. "To my Elizabeth and her Mr. Darcy; to your future and to your happiness."

Chapter-Thirty

Dear reader, you shall be unshocked and unsurprised to learn Elizabeth and Darcy married.

Though Bingley adored both Elizabeth and Fitzwilliam Darcy, he never grew to enjoy the combination of the two in one location. For that reason he and Jane saw less of them than *Jane* would have preferred, for despite their endless arguments, Elizabeth and Darcy were inseparable and always laughing. They were very much a pair, with those around them, except *her* father, unable to follow their darting minds, and even Mr. Bennet could not understand their indecent pyramid of private jokes.

Georgiana and Mr. Peake made an elated couple, and they had five children, besides Anne. The firm of Gardiner and Peake prospered. They were involved in many profitable ventures, early railroads, Bessemer's steel mills, a steamer line, and many others. By the time both he and Darcy reached their seventies — all our favorite characters lived a long course of life, well beyond the three score and ten allotted to man — Mr. Peake was the wealthier man by a substantial margin.

Darcy had long since forgotten that he ever opposed the match between his sister and Mr. Peake.

Mr. Bennet visited Elizabeth and Darcy for almost six months out of the year. Longbourn would have gone to ruin had Darcy and Bingley not convinced him to hire a steward to take over the duties. He was rather at lost ends once all of his daughters were well married.

Mrs. Bennet always was an adoring grandmother, who delighted in providing the children with an excess of sweets and then returning them to their parents to energetically run about from the sugar. To the day Mrs. Bennet died she retained an iron grip over the community, leading the assembly committee, the committee for the relief of the African orphans, and the committee for the promotion of crinoline hoops in lady's dresses.

Never again did any foolish Lady whose husband gained a knighthood on the account of a speech made to the king upon his visit to Meryton question who the *true* leader of Hertfordshire society was.

Mr. Bennet loosened the drawstrings round his money box, thus mixing a metaphor and allowing his wife to spend close to her delight. Now that his beloved Elizabeth was married to a man with a vast pile, and none of his other children needed support, he began to spend most of his income. A grand part went to the books, but Mr. Bennet had free and full access to the Pemberley library. That superb specimen of the family library was a work of generations; generations of vastly wealthy bibliophiles.

Even if had he dedicated his entire income to the pursuit, Mr. Bennet could not hope to compete. He instead contented himself with finding opportunities to acquire particular rare and odd editions which Darcy did not possess. He planned in his will for all such books to be given to Elizabeth, and thus placed into the Darcy library, continuing the grand work of generations, and also showing by what means the rich might become richer.

Besides many years of moderate self-denial had blunted Mr. Bennet's desire to spend.

Not his wife! Not her for whose usual nagging met with more than usual success! During that part of the year when Mr. Bennet was present at Pemberley, he granted her a large budget and liberty to use this budget as she wished to entertain. Mrs. Bennet had never been happier in her life.

Everyone in the entirety of Hertfordshire — and even parts of Kent and Sussex as well — agreed that God had been very good to her.

Fewer thought such of Lady Catherine. She now was left with no hope at all of marrying Anne to Mr. Darcy. This did not bother her for a full year, believing as she did that Darcy had simply chosen to live in sin with his mistress as a way of taunting her, while pretending to the rest of the world that he had married.

However, upon the birth of Elizabeth's first child, a son, Lady Catherine learned from her solicitor that the young boy was in fact the true heir to the estate, and that the marriage between Elizabeth and Darcy had been witnessed, solemnized and registered, and then consummated frequently and thoroughly, and was not a gesture to taunt her.

Loud and long did Lady Catherine shout when she visited Pemberley to bitterly complain about the fate of the now aging Anne. Short and silent were Darcy's sympathetic replies. Elizabeth showed much more kindness. She promised that they would exchange visits, and she discovered from Anne that she was happily unmarried, and matters were patched up between the family so they stayed on the barely passable terms until the death of Lady Catherine. Anne and Elizabeth carried on a correspondence, which lasted for many decades, and crisscrossed with her correspondence with Charlotte Collins.

Some decades later Elizabeth's second son inherited Rosings Park upon Anne's death, after he added the last name of de Bourgh.

As for the question you have read this entire epilogue to discover the answer to: Jane's son Bennet and Georgiana's daughter Anne married as adults. They too lived a happy and prosperous life, and they owned many cats, many ponies, many rocking horses, and many of all the things they loved most as children. Neither, alas, were great readers, despite the best efforts of their Uncle Will and Aunt Lizzy.

The End

Afterward

I always wanted to one day be an author who sticks a section at the end of my books to talk about how I wrote the book, the research I did, and like matters.

Today is the day.

Those who have read my *other* books (some are really good!) already know that I tell my readers to donate to Doctors Without Borders. You should. That organization does good and important work, and one of the best things about being a writer is that I can ask my audience to join me in making a better world by helping them with money. So donate, because you want the world to be a better place too.

But I also want to write things that are more *fun*.

The genesis of this book was a combination of two ideas: a more mature Elizabeth and a good Mr. Bennet. I'd been looking for a good Mr. Bennet idea for some time, since despite the way he often is viewed as a bad father in fanfiction, when I first read *Pride and Prejudice* as a teenager he was my favorite character because of his jokes.

As it happened, it was surprisingly hard to write this novel. I wrote the first chapters, up through the scene where Elizabeth returns home after the assembly, two years ago. Each time I reread that section, I thought Darcy and Elizabeth meeting in this story was one of the funniest things I have written — you may disagree, of course — but I had no enthusiasm for what I planned to write in the rest of the story. So I switched to a different project. It was either the first collection of notes on *Colonel Darcy* or the first draft of *A Dishonorable Offer*.

The first chapters of this book charmed me so much that I, on three separate occasions, planned out different ways of finishing the story, before giving up in dissatisfaction. It in fact reached the point where I promised myself I would not waste time again trying to finish it, since I'd decided the book was a time black hole.

However, as you already know, I eventually found an idea I liked. I was able to produce the remainder of the first draft for this book during June and July of 2017. One final thing about the writing of the book is while doing the drafting of the new scenes, I often would do a round of editing the new material the day after I wrote it, and before trying to write new scenes. Before my usual policy had been to wait to look at my first draft until I started work on the second draft. The immediate editing helped me capture the character's voices better.

Royston Cave is a real place which was discovered in the middle of the eighteenth century while someone was doing some digging for some purpose, which I do not recall, but which either the Wikipedia page or the Cave's webpage will tell you. I discovered its existence when I googled "date ideas in Hertfordshire" as part of my highly sophisticated research strategy. I *did* shift the geography somewhat. The location of the caves is in the far north of Hertfordshire, fifty miles from the center of London, while we are told that Longbourn is twenty-four miles from Gracechurch Street. This means there are at least twenty-five miles between Netherfield and Royston Cave, which would likely take three hours to travel, making the caves rather distant for an easy day trip.

Something else you can discover with a simple Google search is the stages of the moon in the early 19th century. It really was right after the new moon on the night of Bingley's ball for Georgiana.

Speaking of Gracechurch Street: My American readership shall be vastly more impressed by the following announcement than my British readership, especially that portion of my British readers resident in the great city of London.

Dear reader, I have visited London.

This not particularly momentous, but a fun event occurred between writing the first and second draft of this novel, and I have a picture of myself standing next to a sign for the ward of Cheap, and I have walked down a substantial portion of Gracechurch Street. I also have a picture of the street sign.

This visit to the center of *modern* London had a substantial influence on the scenes at the end of the novel when Georgiana marries Peake. Most notably, when I initially wrote that section the action occurred for some reason at Netherfield.

I would recommend to my American readers they visit London and other parts of the United Kingdom if they have the opportunity — I have an unfortunate tendency to want to tell people about useful things I've discovered. So if you purchase in advance, airfares between the US and London can be surprisingly cheap. I am planning to fly back to the States for a few weeks in January, and if I purchased the tickets right now, I could get between London and LAX for around $200 each way.

A further point I should mention, for the sake of not continuing misconceptions if I can end them, teething did *not* in fact lead to the negative consequences Elizabeth, and others in early nineteenth century, attributed to the process. However, it is completely accurate that doctors and parents *believed* teething was dangerous. I had read, some years ago, in a *Pride and Prejudice* novel — I am not sure, but I think it was in *Memory* by the excellent, if long winded, Linda Wells (booknut) — that several percent of children during this period of time died of infections during teething. That seemed plausible, true, and horrible. It stuck in my mind.

There often is some ambiguity about historical evidence, but while teething is unpleasant, unfun, and often treated with antibiotics today, there seems to be relatively few deaths directly caused by it without treatment. However during the regency period people *believed* teething to cause almost anything bad which happened to a child during its course.

Having said that, antibiotics are really, really good. And together we can help people who don't have access to antibiotics get them. You really should donate to Doctors Without Borders.

Now that I've made *that* appeal a second time, here is a self-interested one: Review the book if you liked it, or even if you didn't. And then go buy some of my other books.

One final addendum, which actually is a little self-interested, in a weird way: I'd like to give a few book recommendations: *Goodly Creatures* by Beth Massy was one of the first big P&P variations I read, and it kept me up all night until I finished it. Angst, a fantastic strong Elizabeth, and a blundering Darcy. *Haunting Mr. Darcy* by KaraLynn Mackrory has a very entertaining and fun plot twist, and I particularly liked the romantic resolution at the end. Finally, you probably are aware of Abigail Reynolds books, and while her books are not actually perfect, there is a reason she is so popular. *Alone with Mr. Darcy* is a personal favorite.

Budapest, October 2017

About the Author

I am from California, but currently I am living in Budapest with my girlfriend. I first discovered Pride and Prejudice on a long day of travel out of Mexico as a teenager. I recall being very impressed with myself for getting the jokes. I read a lot of nineteenth century literature that year, of which Austen and Charlotte Bronte, of course, were my favorites. It was years later that I discovered and repeatedly binge read Pride and Prejudice fanfiction.

Now I get to add to the pile of fanfiction able to binge – and I love it when I get messages from people telling me that they are binging on my books.

If you liked this book, leave a review. It is a way of helping other people find books they liked.

I can be reached at timothyunderwood.author@gmail.com.

My Other Books

Colonel Darcy: My most popular book! Fitzwilliam Darcy never forgot his promise to write Elizabeth, but when he is released from prison after the war, it might be too late, because Elizabeth's family is forcing her to marry a baronet.

Mr. Darcy and Mr. Collins's Widow: My first book, and probably my most popular. Will Elizabeth's memories of her horrible first marriage to the man who inherited the estate from her father when she was fifteen keep her from finding happiness with Darcy?

A Dishonorable Offer: Elizabeth is very poor and socially disgraced after Lydia married a muscular blacksmith. Darcy likes her very much and wants to help and have her, but there is only one sort of offer he can make a girl whose status has fallen so low

The Return is another romantic comedy: What if Mr. Bingley ignored Darcy and married Jane immediately? Obviously, Elizabeth and Darcy would argue at the wedding once Jane and Bingley were safely away for the honeymoon.

The Trials: After Mr. Bennet dies, Elizabeth becomes the governess of Lady Catherine's unwanted ward. One day she collides with Mr. Darcy in the halls of Rosings. But it is too late for her: Mr. Darcy is engaged to his cousin, Anne...

Mr. Darcy's Vow: Darcy's spendthrift father left Pemberley deeply in debt, so Darcy swore to never indulge himself. He could not marry a penniless girl.

Made in the USA
Middletown, DE
27 October 2022

13600572R00172